Mr Darcy's
Noble
Connections

Abigail Reynolds

To Sophie,
I'm so glad you discovered Jane Austen!
Best,
Abigail Reynolds

WHITE SOUP PRESS

MR. DARCY'S NOBLE CONNECTIONS

www.pemberleyvariations.com
www.austenauthors.com

Mr. Darcy drew his chair a little towards her, and said, "You cannot have a right to such very strong local attachment. You cannot have been always at Longbourn."

Elizabeth looked surprised. The gentleman experienced some change of feeling; he drew back his chair, took a newspaper from the table, and, glancing over it, said, in a colder voice, "Are you pleased with Kent?"

- Jane Austen, *Pride & Prejudice*

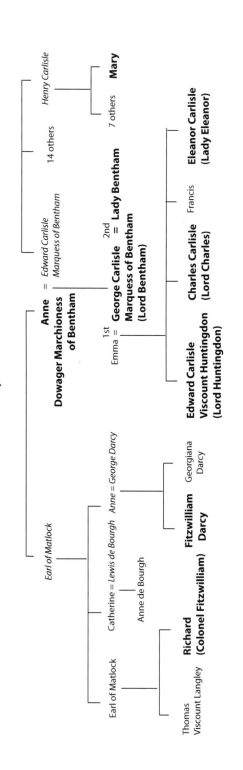

The Fitzwilliam Family

The Carlisle Family

Earl of Matlock

Earl of Matlock

Thomas
Viscount Langley

**Richard
(Colonel Fitzwilliam)**

Catherine = *Lewis de Bourgh*

Anne de Bourgh

Anne = *George Darcy*

**Fitzwilliam
Darcy**

Georgiana
Darcy

**Anne
Dowager Marchioness
of Bentham**

= *Edward Carlisle
Marquess of Bentham*

Henry Carlisle

14 others

Mary

1st
Emma = **George Carlisle
Marquess of Bentham
(Lord Bentham)**

2nd
= **Lady Bentham**

7 others

**Edward Carlisle
Viscount Huntingdon
(Lord Huntingdon)**

**Charles Carlisle
(Lord Charles)**

Francis

**Eleanor Carlisle
(Lady Eleanor)**

Characters appearing in this book are **in bold**
Deceased family members are *in italics*
Forms of address for characters appear (in parentheses)

Chapter 1

AS THE CARRIAGE made its way down the elm-lined lane, Elizabeth removed a spot of lint from her white kidskin gloves. The widow who had chaperoned her on the stagecoach had worn a dark brown wool cloak with a tendency to shed. By the time Elizabeth had finally left the coach, she had been dotted with bits of brown fluff. Not wishing to arrive looking like a refugee from a kennel, she had spent the last half hour painstakingly picking off lint. It was an improvement, but no matter how careful she was, she would still look like a poor relation when she reached Bentham Park. Not that she ranked as high as a poor relation; she was only a poor connection of one of Lord Bentham's poor relations.

It hardly mattered, though. Whatever faults her appearance or breeding might present, she would once more be at Bentham Park. For years it had been like home to her, but she had thought she would never see it again. What did it matter if her dress showed a little lint? Lord and Lady Bentham might not be in residence, and even if they were, she would likely see them only at dinner. Lord Bentham tended to be off in his own world and never paid much attention to her, and the new Lady Bentham had standards Elizabeth could not possibly meet, so there was no point in fretting over them. She was only coming to Bentham Park at Eleanor's request, and she would not care if Elizabeth appeared in rags. A lack of interest in the latest fashions was one of the traits they shared.

Elizabeth's spirits lifted as the lane opened onto the familiar imposing vista of Bentham Park. The butler at the door was less imposing but more supercilious, making clear with one sniff his opinion of young women who travelled accompanied by no more than a maidservant. "I will see if Lady Eleanor is at home," he intoned.

Given that Elizabeth had just arrived in Eleanor's carriage which Eleanor had sent to meet the stagecoach less than an hour before, it seemed unlikely that Eleanor would not be at home, but Elizabeth managed to suppress the urge to point this out to the butler. She would laugh about it later with her friend. Instead, she ran her hand down one of the marble columns supporting the magnificent dome over the Great Hall. It was good to be back.

In a few minutes, the butler, with a pained look engraved on his gaunt features, led her to the sitting room where Eleanor sat in an exquisitely ladylike pose, each blonde curl precisely in place, and greeted her with the languor so fashionable among the *ton* — a manner quite different from the desperate letter she had sent only a few days earlier. Elizabeth had expected no less, since Lady Bentham's hawk-like eyes were upon her stepdaughter.

After a few pleasantries, Eleanor suggested that Elizabeth might wish to rest after her journey. Setting a sedate pace, she led Elizabeth upstairs to a small but elegantly furnished bedroom, making idle pleasant conversation all the way.

As soon as she closed the door behind her, Eleanor's smile faded. "Thank you for coming, Lizzy! I have been desperate for your good sense and friendship."

"So I gathered from your letter." Elizabeth took Eleanor's hands in her own. "I came as quickly as I could, but not as soon as I would have liked. Your letter worried me so! It is not like you to send out a call for help! What has happened?"

"So much – I hardly know where to begin! It is such a muddle. Papa has taken it into his head that it is time for me to marry, and I simply cannot bear it! He has opened discussions with the gentleman he has chosen for me." Eleanor shuddered. "Papa plans to announce the engagement in September, and we are to marry at the beginning of the Season."

Elizabeth was well aware of her friend's propensity for dramatics, but her voice held a tinge of desperation this time. "Is he so very bad?

Eleanor twisted her fingers in the embroidered rose silk of her skirt. "No," she half-whispered. "It could be much worse. He is not ill-tempered and has no disgusting habits, but he is such a dandy! If he cares about anything beyond the latest fashion in waistcoats or the perfection of the knot in his cravat, I cannot ascertain it, and he assumes that everyone else is as fascinated by his wardrobe as he is. At our last meeting, he unbent so far as to tell me that he had some ideas as to which milliner I should use for my wedding clothes, since it is crucial to his reputation that I meet the same standards of sartorial elegance that he himself does. And, of course, he is one of my stepmother's friends."

"Oh, I am so sorry. Is your father absolutely set on it?"

"Irrevocably. But I have not told you the worst part yet."

"There is more?"

Eleanor nodded miserably. "I am in love with another man."

A knock at the door announced the arrival of tea, and Eleanor raised a warning finger to her lips. The two young ladies sat in perfect silence until the tea tray was arranged and the maid had departed.

"Oh, dearest Eleanor! Is he unsuitable?"

She shook her head. "Not to me, but to my father he is – utterly unsuitable, merely because his father was in trade. It does not matter that Geoffrey is a perfect gentleman, as well educated as my father or any of my brothers, and master of a fine estate. He is hopelessly tainted in my father's eyes." Eleanor squeezed her eyes shut to force back tears.

Elizabeth stroked her friend's arm. "How did you meet him? Was it in London?"

"No. I first met him when I was six, though I did not see him again until last summer. He is one of our nearest neighbors, and he is the only man in the world who does not expect me to be someone I am not. I cannot bear losing him, Lizzy."

"Does he know of your feelings?"

"He knows everything. Sometimes we manage to steal a few minutes together, but it is not often. My stepmother is too attentive a chaperone, and my parents do not approve of the connection, even as a friend. It is only in the last two years, since Geoffrey's father died, that they have acknowledged his existence at all, and even now they will not invite him to the house. He has a gentleman's education and appears no different from any of our friends, but his father was a weaver before making a fortune in the mills." Her expression fell a little. "I liked his father, though, the one time I met him."

Elizabeth frowned. "If your parents did not acknowledge him, how did you come to know him or his son?"

Eleanor stood and went to the window, her fingers tracing the frame as she looked out. "Without permission, of course." Her voice was colorless. "It was during the summers, back when I ran wild, you see. Before my father remarried... even before I met *you*."

"That makes more sense." Elizabeth wondered if Eleanor realized how much her own life still resembled what Eleanor called "running wild," which had included everything from walking alone in the countryside to squabbling with her brothers. All that had ended for Eleanor five years ago when her stepmother, a noted beauty only eight years Eleanor's senior, decided it was time to begin the process of transforming Eleanor into a young lady. Eleanor's high spirits dimmed over the years under her stepmother's strict tutelage, which had been so successful that sometimes Elizabeth had wondered if the lively girl she had played with was gone forever, leaving only the perfect debutante. Elizabeth had never warmed to the new Lady Bentham, but the worst was watching the change in her friend. It was good to see the old Eleanor again, even if it was because she was suffering.

"I know, I was fortunate to have any time when I could fly free, but I hate it so much – being a proper young lady, that is, and a credit to the family." Eleanor's eyes filled with tears. "At the time, I did not realize how fortunate I was. That summer I was too busy pitying myself because my brothers refused to play with a mere girl. They thought themselves too good for Geoffrey as well, so he and I became friends, even though he was older than I was. He taught me to catch tadpoles." She moved restlessly around the small room as if it were too small for her.

"How did you come to meet him again?"

"At a ball in London, if you can believe that. He has friends enough in the *ton* that he can attend some of the lesser occasions. I did not recognize him at first, not until I passed him in a dance and he said that he hoped I had no tadpoles in my reticule. And then I knew him, but I also knew something had changed between us. The way he looked at me – it made me hot and cold at the same time. I danced the next set with him, and then the dinner dance. He made me laugh, and I spoke more to him than I had to any gentleman all Season. It was heaven. I was so sorry to leave him, and as soon as I entered my carriage after the ball, my stepmother began to scold me for my hoydenish behavior. Proper young ladies do not laugh at balls; they must feign ennui. Nor do they talk to men beyond what words are necessary to entice their interest, always assuming the man in question is an appropriate prospect." She paused, then collapsed on the bed as if the weight of her elegant dress were too much for her. "That was almost a year ago."

"Are you certain that your father would not permit a marriage between you?"

"Certain beyond a doubt. At my urging, my brother Charles raised the question to him, saying that financially it would be a good match. My father said he would rather see me dead than married to one of the Paxtons."

Elizabeth tried to imagine how that might feel, but it was too foreign to her own experience. It was impossible to conceive of anything she might do that would lead her father to prefer her to die, but she did not doubt Eleanor's story. Lord Bentham was nothing like her father.

"Geoffrey wanted to ask his permission anyway, arguing that the worst he could do would be to refuse, but he is wrong. That is not the worst. If my parents had any inkling of my interest in Geoffrey, they would make it impossible for me to see him again. We are together little enough as it is, but to be denied even that – it would be intolerable. I would run mad."

Feeling helpless in the face of her friend's misery, Elizabeth said, "I am so sorry. I wish there were something I could do to help."

Eleanor pushed herself up on her elbows, her eyes now alight. "But there is! That is why I asked you to come."

That look of Eleanor's usually meant trouble. What could anyone possibly do to help? Surely she would not expect Elizabeth to serve as a go-between, or, worse, to cover up an elopement! With some trepidation, she said, "I hope you are not thinking of running off with him."

Her friend's shoulders slumped. "I wish I could. Geoffrey is willing, but I cannot. It would mean leaving everything I know and love. My family would disown me. No, I have given up any possibility of marrying Geoffrey. All I can hope for now is the chance to spend a little time with him before it is too late."

"I understand your desire to be with him, but will that not make it all the more bitter when you must part?"

"You would not have asked that question if you had ever been in love. Yes, seeing him is worth any pain."

So she must be desiring help in setting up an assignation. Elizabeth felt the pit of her stomach clench. "And if you are caught with him?"

Eleanor beamed. "It will not matter if you are with me as my chaperone."

"Could not your maid do as much?"

"She would immediately report the meeting to my stepmother, who would prevent it from ever occurring again. But it is different with you. As long as I do nothing improper, you would not need to tell anyone, would you?"

Uneasy, Elizabeth said, "If your parents discover it, they would be furious, and with good reason."

"I have a plan for that as well. If we are discovered, I will tell them that Geoffrey is interested in you, and that I am encouraging it. He has invited a friend as well, an earl's grandson of impeccable reputation, and nothing could be more natural than for us to make a foursome."

Elizabeth shook her head in disbelief. "A counterfeit courtship between me and your Geoffrey?"

"Yes. It would delight my stepmother, since they would no longer need to exclude him if he married a gentleman's daughter. She has wished for such a match for him. She could not condone having him marry someone of *our* class, since that would be getting above himself. Little does she know! You would be the perfect solution, a gentleman's daughter, but poor enough that you could overlook the source of his fortune; and your manners are good, so you would be an acceptable neighbor."

"Whereas an earl's grandson would be suitable company for you, I suppose!"

"Well, perhaps not to marry, but for social interactions, yes." Seeing the look on her friend's face, Eleanor added hurriedly, "I hope you are not offended, Elizabeth. I did not mean to imply that you are desperate for a husband or that there is anything wrong with your family. Just that it is different for you."

Elizabeth laughed. "I am not offended. I have heard far worse about my family, and I know we are not your equals in society. As for a husband, I have never been less desperate for one in my life. Sometimes I feel as if I do nothing but refuse proposals of marriage!"

"Someone made you an offer, and you did not *tell* me?" demanded Eleanor.

"Dearest Eleanor, I will happily share anything else with you, but I will not humiliate the gentlemen in question by telling you or anyone else their names. Suffice to say that two eligible gentlemen of property offered for me in recent months. One was a fool and the other ill-tempered and resentful, and I never gave a moment's consideration to accepting either of them."

"Oh, but I wish to hear all the details! You know I shall tease until you tell me."

"I am not even to be allowed the opportunity to wash my face and change out of my dusty clothing?" Elizabeth asked with a smile.

"Oh, of course you may, you silly girl!" Laughing, Eleanor reached for the bell.

"I do not need a maid if you are here to unbutton my dress," Elizabeth objected.

Eleanor waggled a finger at her. "You are at Bentham Park now," she intoned. "If Lady Bentham were to hear that you were not attended by a maid, she would scold us both until we wept."

"*You* might weep, my dear. *I* would laugh."

It was not until later that Elizabeth realized she had never actually stated her objections to Eleanor's plans.

Paxton was usually a temperate fellow, which is why Darcy watched with concern as he poured his third glass of port in half an hour. He debated asking straight out what was troubling him, but decided against it. A few months before he would have presumed on their old friendship to do so, but that was before Elizabeth Bennet had the audacity to accuse him of behaving in an ungentlemanly manner. He would never forgive her for that, but it had made him more cautious, even with friends as close as Paxton. Instead, he said, "This port is potent stuff."

His friend raised his glass and examined it. "Potent stuff for an impotent fool." He swirled the port as if it were brandy. "Darcy, have you ever been in love?"

Could he never escape from it? Love was the last subject he wished to discuss.

"Never mind," said Paxton. "Forget that I asked. It is none of my business." He took a long swallow of port.

Abruptly, Darcy said, "Yes. I have been in love. It did not end well."

That made Paxton look up in surprise. "I always thought that sort of thing would come easily to you. You have it all – birth, fortune, youth."

"As do you." Darcy finished his glass and poured another. Perhaps Paxton had the right idea.

"Fortune and youth, yes. Not birth."

"That has never mattered to you before."

"I never cared what the gentlemen's sons thought of me. I thought little enough of *them* – present company excepted – that their opinions did not matter to me. Until now."

"A lady of quality, then? And she will not have you?" Darcy only wished he had as good a reason to explain Elizabeth's disdain of him.

"*She* would have me happily. Her father will not. I am not good enough for the daughter of a marquess."

If her father was a marquess, it was hardly surprising. Many fathers in the nobility would not allow their daughters to marry outside their ranks, although there were also those whose financial straits were dire enough that they would overlook the source of a man's fortune. Still, it must sting. "Is there no hope of changing his mind, then?"

"None. He has already picked out her future husband, and plans to announce the betrothal soon." Paxton set down his glass with a sigh. "And that will be the end of it. Most likely I will never see her again."

"I am sorry to hear it. If there is anything I can do to assist you, if it might help for me to speak to her father on your behalf, you need only ask." How foolish it sounded! Of course there was nothing he could do. He could not even manage to make a proposal that did not insult the woman he loved.

"You have always been kind in offering to use your connections on my behalf, and my pride has always led me to refuse. In this case, I have lost my pride, and in fact I invited you here to ask for your assistance."

Darcy had never seen his friend in such despair. "I would be happy to do whatever I can."

"I need an entrée into Bentham Park. You have connections to Lord Bentham, do you not?"

"Yes. It is his daughter, then?" That was indeed hopeless. Perhaps more port was in order.

"Yes. Lady Eleanor Carlisle." He spoke her name with a certain reverence.

Darcy had a vague recollection of a thin, somewhat disheveled little girl. Presumably she had improved since then. "I was already planning to call on Lord Bentham. You can accompany me if you like, but I imagine you could do as much on your own."

"Unfortunately not. They have never invited me there or called on me here. I fare better than my father, though – at least they will greet me in public."

Darcy winced. "I am sorry."

"I am not asking you to advocate for me. I only want a chance to have a conversation with Lord Bentham, to prove to him that I can behave properly and that there is no dirt under my fingernails. And if he condescends so far as to treat me as a gentleman, I intend to ask him for his daughter's hand. He will refuse, of course, but at least I will have tried."

"Does Lady Eleanor know of your plan?"

"No. She has also invited a friend to visit in the hope that we can steal a few moments together, but I have not told her that I plan to try a frontal assault. She would attempt to dissuade me, fearing it would anger her father." Paxton's mouth was set in a firm line.

"I have no objection to noting your finer points to Lord Bentham, but perhaps this should be taken in stages. If we call on them, they will have to either return the call or at least invite us to dinner. It would be difficult for them to ignore my presence nearby. Although I have seen little of Lord Bentham in the last few years, my father was his closest friend, and the Dowager Marchioness is my great-aunt and used to be quite fond of me. She is a practical woman and might be willing to take your side."

"The Dowager Marchioness? In her day, she ignored my parents, but it hardly matters. She no longer lives at Bentham Park. The current Lady Bentham does not care for her company, and even the dower house is too close for comfort. The dowager has her own establishment some twenty miles from here."

Darcy raised his eyebrows. "I cannot imagine she took that well! She was always a lady who spoke her mind."

"I do not know what happened, but my Eleanor is fond of her. Do you think Lord Bentham will heed your opinion of me?"

Darcy stretched out his legs in front of him. "He will listen to what I say, for my father's sake, if nothing else. My parents introduced him to his first wife, though there is no love lost between his current wife and me. His eldest son was my particular friend, but he is in exile and out of favor, so that is of little use. Still, Lord Bentham has tried to stay in contact with me these last few years, so perhaps he will be pleased to see me." It was true; Darcy had been the one to refuse all the overtures Lord Bentham had made to him.

"If I can catch even a glimpse of Eleanor, it is worth a try. Although Bentham Park is but three miles from here, it has been difficult for us to meet because she is chaperoned so closely. Nothing can come of it, of course, but it is some comfort to be in her presence."

Darcy wondered if it would be comfort or torture for him to be in Elizabeth's presence. It was unlikely he would ever find out. Still, if a sympathetic ear would help Paxton through his despair, Darcy was willing to listen, especially if another glass of port might chase away that light and pleasing figure that insisted on haunting him.

After downing three more glasses, Darcy had given up hope of forgetting Elizabeth's fine eyes even for an hour. All in all, Paxton was more fortunate than he was. "At least you can console yourself with the knowledge that Lady Eleanor cares for you." It was more than he had. If Elizabeth had cared for him, but been unable to marry him, it would have been enough. Or was it the other way around – that if she had married him, but not cared for him, *that* would have been enough? His thoughts were no longer clear enough to tell for certain.

"I take it the lady you loved did not?"

"No." The port burned in his throat. "She detests me."

"*Detests* you? That is ridiculous. Is she such a fool as that?"

"No, I am the fool, for not realizing how she felt before I was mad enough to propose to her."

"Come now, Darcy; it may be true that you offend people from time to time, but no one detests you."

George Wickham's face swam before Darcy's blurred vision, followed by an echo of Elizabeth's voice. *You are the last man in the world I could be prevailed upon to marry.* "She found me arrogant and self-centered. I met her in a little country town where I was visiting my friend Bingley. Do you know Bingley?"

"Darcy, you are drunk. I introduced you to Bingley."

Darcy tried to recall it, but could only bring up a fuzzy vision of a dinner party – or was it a shooting party? "I was bewitched by her, though she was nothing more than the daughter of a poor country gentleman with low connections. She had one sister who was presentable, but the rest of the family behaved disgracefully. Marrying her would have been a degradation, and I feared raising expectations I could not meet, so I said nothing. I left the neighborhood as soon as I could and determined to forget her."

"Beneath you," said Paxton bitterly. "How well I know it. Love is of no importance, not when compared to your parentage."

"None of it mattered. She did not want me." Darcy heaved a sigh, then repeated the words more slowly. "She did not want me."

"How can you say that, when you left without a word?"

"I met her again later. I offered her my hand, and she refused me in the harshest terms. I had spent months admiring her, showing her attention, but it turned out she had no idea of it. That is how much she disliked me – she could not even conceive of me as a potential suitor. I had thought she was flirting with me, but I must have been blind. I did not know her at all. I believed her to be sweet and caring, and if it had occurred to me that she might reject me, I would have thought she would do so in a gentle and kindly manner. Instead, she berated me, made accusations, told me my behavior was not that of a gentleman. I had paid her the highest compliment I could give a woman, and in return, she attacked my character." Elizabeth had proved she was not the insightful, intelligent, caring woman of his dreams. So why could he not forget her?

Paxton shook his head, then placed his hand to his forehead as if he needed to steady it. "She sounds like a shrew! You had a narrow escape, my friend."

Darcy hunched his shoulders, lacking an answer. He had never seen signs of cruelty or vindictiveness in Elizabeth before that night. She had hidden it well, or perhaps she was only a shrew when it involved him. Still, his sense of justice would not let the explanation end there. "She had some slight excuse in that she was under a misapprehension about me. Do you remember George Wickham? He had plied her with his lies about how I mistreated him. But she *believed* him."

"George Wickham could charm the birds out of the trees if he set his mind to it."

Darcy's mouth twisted. "That is true enough."

"But why did she think you ungentlemanly? Had you made advances she might have deemed improper?"

"No. She simply did not like the way I spoke of my honest scruples about her family and her connections. It was all true, though. She *is* my inferior, and I thought my frankness would show her the strength of my love."

"You said she was inferior to you during your proposal?"

"It is not as if she were not already perfectly aware of it!"

"Still..." Paxton, his face stony, drained his glass so quickly that it made him cough. "Suppose a Duke... no, a Royal Duke, asked you for your sister's hand, and told you in the process how inferior you are to him, how degrading it was for him to even consider marriage to a woman without a title, and that your relatives were an embarrassment. Would you feel honored by his frankness?"

"As if there were a Royal Duke alive whom I would permit Georgiana to marry," grumbled Darcy. The picture Paxton had painted was an unpleasant one.

Paxton sighed. "Never mind. Even so, I would have thought no woman would refuse a man with as much to offer as you do. Was there another man she preferred? A better match, perhaps?"

"There was no other man, at least not that I was aware of." The idea made his stomach roil. "She could never find a better match than me. She has no fortune. I was probably the most eligible man she had ever met."

His friend gave a soft whistle. "She must be mad."

It was precisely what Darcy had told himself time and again, but hearing the words aloud somehow broke the spell. "No, she was not mad, just not mercenary. She simply thought me unworthy of her notice. I loved her. God, what I would not have done for her!"

But he knew what he had not done for her. He had never tried to earn her respect, only to buy her, and she could not be bought. With a trembling hand, he sloshed more port into his glass.

Chapter 2

"NOW, LIZZY, I insist that you tell me about the gentlemen who proposed to you." Eleanor led the way down a path into the wooded area of the park.

"There is very little to tell."

"I do not believe it! Which one came first, the fool or the ill-tempered one?"

"The fool. He was a cousin of mine whom I had never met, a clergyman who will someday inherit my home. He came to visit us with the express plan of choosing a wife from among my sisters. Oh, if only his interest had lighted on Mary! But we had no such good fortune. I cannot tell you how obsequious and foolish he was. Everyone was laughing behind their hands at his pompous manners and lack of understanding. He could not even dance without making himself look silly! I had the most mortifying dance with him at a ball. The next day he proposed to me on bended knee, expressing his most ardent love, although he had known me less than a fortnight. It could have been a scene in a farce. He did not believe me when I refused him, even when I became downright rude! Then, when he was finally convinced that I meant it, he proposed to one of my friends three days later, claiming ardent love for *her*."

Eleanor covered her mouth with her hands to stifle her laughter. "He did? What did she say?"

"She accepted him, believe it or not, because it was a prudential match for her. I was horrified, but she seems content enough with him, or at least able to ignore his idiocy."

"And what of the other one, the ill-tempered gentleman?"

Elizabeth looked away, pretending an interest in a stand of beeches beside the path. "That was much worse. I had taken a decided dislike to him when we first met because of his insufferable pride, and then because of some stories I heard about him, stories that later proved to be untrue. I had a horrible dance with him as well, at that very same ball. I should have taken greater care around gentlemen who were in attendance that night since they had such an odd tendency to propose to me!"

"Was he eligible?"

"Oh, very – quite beyond my reach, in fact, both in wealth and birth. Your father might even consider him an appropriate suitor for *you*. That was part of the problem. It never seems to have occurred to him that a woman in my position might not wish to marry him. I did not even realize he admired me until the night he shocked me by proposing. It was a nightmare of a proposal, all about my low connections and what a degradation it was for him to marry me. He was stunned when I refused him, and we quarreled bitterly. It is an embarrassment to recall that episode. I behaved no better than he did."

"I cannot believe that. You are always so kind to everyone."

"I was very *un*kind to him, not to mention vain and nonsensical. I made a fool of myself by accusing him of horrible things, which were later proved to be untrue. I am still vexed with myself for how I treated him. You have no idea how often I have wished since then that I could go back in time and give him a calmer answer."

"Would you accept him now that you know the stories are untrue?"

"No, for I still have no wish to marry him, or even to see him again. I am complimented by his attachment and I respect him, but I cannot approve of his proud behavior. Besides, can you imagine how humiliating it would be to encounter him again? I would be mortified. He knows what a blind fool I was."

Eleanor's brows drew together. "It sounds as if you still have strong feelings about him."

Elizabeth inspected her hands. "I am sorry for his disappointment and that I made matters worse by condemning and upbraiding him. But I imagine he must hate me now, and I doubt he has any respect left for me. Until that day, I had always prided myself on my perspicacity, but he showed me how foolish and gullible I am. It was not a lesson I enjoyed."

"You are far from gullible, and there are plenty of other men in the world. The guests for my stepmother's house party will be here in a few days. Perhaps one of the gentlemen will fall in love with you and make you a proposal you can accept," said Eleanor with a smile.

"It is hardly likely, given the guests your parents receive. How many of them are titled?" Then again, it was no more unlikely than Mr. Darcy admiring her. She still could hardly believe it.

"Most of them, no doubt."

"Is your foppish almost-intended one of the guests?"

"Lord Deyncourt? You must be joking. He would never travel here; Yorkshire is much too far from his tailor. Hyde Park is almost too rustic for his tastes; and he would consider even a jaunt into Kent or Sussex as a venture into savage lands. No, we are perfectly safe from him here." Eleanor halted in front of an old oak. Standing on tiptoe, she reached past the lowest branch where it met the trunk and pushed her hand into a crevice in the rough bark. When she withdrew her hand, she displayed an envelope sealed with red wax, then pressed it against her lips.

"From your Geoffrey?"

Eleanor took another letter from her pocket and placed it in the crevice, then leaned back against the oak. "This is our post. We discovered it when we were children and hid our treasures there. Now we use it to communicate. He writes me every day. Occasionally we manage to meet here, but I never know when my stepmother will permit me to walk out. It will be so much easier now that you are here."

Looking around at the secluded area, Elizabeth wondered what would happen if Eleanor were ever discovered there with him. It would be quite compromising. Would that make her father more or less likely to approve of a marriage between them?

By mutual agreement, the two gentlemen decided to postpone their ride the following morning. The hammers pounding inside Darcy's head did not predispose him for any activity beyond sitting in the library and pretending to read a book. It had been years since he had indulged to the extent he had the previous night, and he fervently hoped it would be many more years before it happened again. Since he was not yet certain he would survive the aftermath of this event, it seemed pointless to worry about repeating his mistake.

Still, he would not have any regrets, except one. Keeping Paxton company as he drowned his sorrows had been the right thing to do for his friend. Darcy's recollections of the previous night were hazy, but it was engraved on his memory that at some point he had poured forth the bitter saga of his failed efforts with Elizabeth Bennet. His only comfort was that he had not named her, and he had given the impression it had taken place years before, not less than two months past. Even so, he regretted letting the port loosen his tongue. The entire affair was an embarrassment he preferred to forget.

Paxton strode into the library with a paper in his hand, looking more cheerful than anyone had a right to be after a night of imbibing heavily. "Darcy, are you still willing to call at Bentham Park today?"

Darcy winced, both at the very idea and at the sound of Paxton's voice. "Of course." He hoped the hammers in his head would have stopped by then.

"Excellent! Eleanor writes that they are expecting guests in the next few days, so it would be best if we called before the house party begins."

"She writes to you?"

Paxton fiddled with the cuffs of his coat. "There is a hidden place where we leave letters for each other. Since I cannot see her, it is our only connection. But perhaps now that will change."

Darcy's pleasure in seeing his friend more in his usual spirits almost made up for the throbbing in his head.

"Darcy!" Lord Bentham, somewhat more rotund than the last time they had met, bounced to his feet with surprising alacrity and shook Darcy's hand heartily. "By God, if you are not the very image of your father as a young man! I cannot tell you how pleased I am to see you. What brings you to Yorkshire?" He then seemed to notice his companion for the first time. "Paxton," he said civilly but without enthusiasm, and there was a moment's hesitation before he offered to shake his hand. At least he *had* shaken it, but clearly Paxton had not exaggerated Lord Bentham's sentiments.

Paxton made a very correct bow. "My lord." His perfectly tied cravat stayed precisely in place.

"I am visiting Paxton, who is an old friend from my Cambridge days. When I discovered how nearby Bentham Park is, I decided I must call at the first possible opportunity. It has been too many years since we last met."

Lord Bentham's face sobered. "Yes, at your father's funeral. It was a great loss to us all when he passed away."

"It was indeed. He valued you highly. Do you recall those days when our families were so often in company together? I remember someone saying that if there was a Fitzwilliam in the room, you could depend on finding a Carlisle and a Darcy nearby."

"Oh, yes, those were fine days! Did you know that your mother introduced me to my first wife? They were the best of friends, those two!"

Darcy had heard the story retold more times than he cared to remember, but his goal was to remind Lord Bentham of the ties between them for Paxton's sake. "Is that so? I am not surprised; I remember how devoted my mother was to Lady Bentham, and vice versa."

Lord Bentham chuckled. "Always up to mischief, those two! My late wife was devastated when we lost your mother, and nothing would do except that she would take Lady Anne's children home for the summer to distract them. You were far less of a hellion than my sons, though! How old were you then? Twelve? Thirteen?"

"I was eleven. I must say, usually when I return to a place I have not been since I was a child, I discover it is smaller than I remember it, but Bentham Park seems larger than ever." Flattery was not among Darcy's skills, but he was determined to do his best.

"No one will ever call it small!"

Taking a deep breath, Darcy decided it was time to introduce the other topic on his agenda. "It is a pleasure to be back again among old friends. I always wished to keep up the ties between our families. Back when I was at Cambridge, it seemed that we would always be together. In those days, it was Richard Fitzwilliam – Lord Matlock's son, that is -- your Edward, and I who were always together, along with Paxton and one or two others. We were considered a force to be reckoned with! Richard was the college champion with pistols, and I with swords, while Edward and Paxton were constantly vying for the top academic honors and to win every horse race. Those were good days."

Abruptly, Lord Bentham said, "Do you hear anything from Edward?"

Darcy inclined his head, grateful for the opening. "He writes to me regularly now that he is in Portugal. When he was fighting as part of the Spanish resistance, he rarely had the opportunity to post a letter. Now that he is fighting alongside Wellington's troops, it is easier for him."

"He is well, then?"

So Edward's father had not found his own sources of information. That did not bode well for Darcy's mission. "He was badly wounded at Alba de Torres in 1809, but recovered enough to return to the front some months later. Of course, he said nothing of it to me. I only know because he asked another soldier to send me word when he was not expected to recover. Then he nearly lost a leg back in January at Ciudad

Rodrigo, and his recovery has been slow. The surgeon expects him to walk again, although there may be some impairment of function in that leg."

Lord Bentham's ruddy complexion turned pale, making him appear older than his years. "What will he do now?"

Darcy shrugged. "You would have to ask him." At least that was true enough.

"Well, he made his decision four years ago, and now he must live with it," Lord Bentham said heavily. It sounded like something he repeated to himself often.

Darcy's hands tightened on the armrests of his chair. "We must all live with our decisions," he said icily. He did not trust himself to say anything more.

Lord Bentham turned to Paxton. "You knew Edward as well?" he asked sharply.

Darcy held his breath as Paxton said, "I did. He won our last race by a head after cutting me off with that high-seated curricle of his, and I have yet to forgive him for it."

Lord Bentham gave a bark of laughter. "You take your racing seriously, do you?"

"I race to win," said Paxton coolly. "But I am not dedicated enough to travel to Portugal to demand a rematch."

Darcy thought that had gone as well as it could, given that in truth Paxton had barely known Edward.

"Charles is due here soon," said Lord Bentham. "He will be pleased to find that you are here as well."

"I hope I will have the opportunity to see him," Darcy said in his warmest manner. He cordially detested Lord Charles Carlisle, Lord Bentham's second son.

"We will be celebrating his return the day after tomorrow, and you must join us. Nothing as formal as a ball, just a small gathering -- a few guests, some neighbors, and there will be cards and dancing." Lord Bentham hesitated. "And Mr. Paxton as well, of course."

"We would be delighted." Darcy hoped this would help Paxton; if not, he would be tolerating both a large party and Charles Carlisle for nothing.

Lady Bentham rose to her feet. "Eleanor, you may choose a list of dances for the musicians," she said as if granting a great favor. "No more than two hours' worth, I think. We do not want to over-tire our guests so soon after their arrival." She swept out of the room.

"Oh, yes," said Elizabeth dryly. "It would be a shame to allow the guests to choose how much they wish to dance when we can decide it for them."

Eleanor gave a look of mock horror before starting to giggle. "You need not worry. After two hours, my stepmother will explain to them that they are tired, regardless of what they believe, and immediately they will start drifting off to sleep like characters from a fairy tale. What is your favorite dance?"

"Mine? You had best choose. I would no doubt pick something that would betray my low origins and make a terrible impression on poor Mr. Paxton." Elizabeth imitated Lady Bentham's refined accent. She had heard far more of it than she wished. In the old days, she and Eleanor had taken their meals in the schoolroom rather than a formal dining room presided over by Lord and Lady Bentham. The change was not an improvement.

Eleanor heaved a dramatic sigh. "Very well. A few country dances, a reel or two, and of course a waltz since we must be modern – and because I have a specific person in mind with whom I wish to waltz. Do you waltz?"

Elizabeth laughed. "Of course not. I have never even *seen* a waltz. In Meryton, it would be shocking even to speak about it!"

"Oh, you must waltz here, though! I will teach you."

"If I am not mistaken, unmarried ladies must have permission from the patronesses at Almack's before dancing the waltz, and I have not received that. Of course, I have never *met* any of them, either, so it would be quite surprising if I did!"

"Nonsense. In town, yes, we would have to pay attention to that; but this is a private party, so we may do as we like. No one will be in the least surprised."

With a smile, Elizabeth shook her head. "I will be perfectly content merely to watch."

The butler materialized at the door to the sitting room. "Lord Charles Carlisle, your ladyship," he announced.

A tall young man with tousled, windblown hair strolled past him, his shirt points fashionably high. "Eleanor, my dear!" he exclaimed as he bent to kiss her cheek.

Eleanor said warmly, "This is a surprise. We were not expecting you until tomorrow."

He grinned. "You know that it is a point of honor with me to always do the unexpected."

"In this case, it makes me wonder what or whom you may be fleeing! But will you allow me to introduce to your acquaintance my dear friend Miss Bennet? Lizzy, this is my brother Charles."

Lord Charles turned his gaze to Elizabeth, raising an appreciative eyebrow before bending over her hand to bestow a completely unnecessary kiss on it. Elizabeth's cheeks grew hot at this unexpected forwardness, which seemed to please him, as he made a point of holding onto her hand for a good half-minute after he should have released it. "I would have driven faster had I realized there would be such beauty at the end of my journey."

Elizabeth rallied at this. "Do tell me, Lord Charles, how often you have employed those exact words in the past? They have an air of long practice."

He threw back his head and laughed. "Shall I say instead that your eyes would teach the torches to burn bright? Those words are even more practiced. If only we had some torches for your eyes to teach! Eleanor, you must arrange for torches at the next opportunity."

At least he had a sense of humor and could tolerate being laughed at. "Torches are too smoky for my taste, my lord. But we have met before, on my first visit to Bentham Park many years ago. I helped Eleanor hide a grass snake under your pillow."

"So that *was* you, my dear sister! You denied it so prettily that I was fool enough to believe you."

Eleanor said briskly, "I should have chosen an adder instead. Still, your early arrival will work to my purpose. Miss Bennet must learn to waltz before tomorrow evening."

"And you need me to take the gentleman's part," said Lord Charles promptly. "Knowing that I am always happy to be of service to a lovely young lady, with or without torches –although preferably without snakes – you immediately thought of me."

Giving his arm a mock slap, Eleanor said, "You are a rogue! I immediately thought of you because you walked into the room just after I decided to teach her to waltz."

He pressed a hand to his chest dramatically, opening his clear blue eyes wide with mock innocence. "I am crushed, dear sister!"

"You could not be crushed by a coach-and-four running you down in the street. And do not try to work your wiles on Lizzy; she is my friend."

"Utterly heartless," he said mournfully with a glance at Elizabeth, who could not help smiling.

Eleanor rang the bell. "In the meantime, I will see if your room is ready yet."

"Of course it will be ready," he said with an engaging smile. "Our *dear* stepmother would never allow any room to be in anything but a state of perfect readiness."

"She is nothing if not efficient," Eleanor said darkly. "Will an hour be sufficient time for you to tie a cravat to your satisfaction?"

He appeared to ponder this. "It will depend upon the quality of the mirror, but you may be assured that the anticipation of dancing with my Juliet will preclude any delay."

At Eleanor's instruction, a maid led Lord Charles out of the sitting room, though not before he blew a departing kiss in Elizabeth's direction.

Elizabeth shook her head, astonished at the alteration from the perpetually untidy boy she recalled. "Good heavens. Is he always so forward?"

Eleanor leveled a grim look at her. "Charles is charming, witty, handsome, and I love him dearly, but I would not trust him alone with you in a room for even a minute. He is an inveterate rake and enjoys making women fall in love with him, only to leave them once he has had what he wants from them. Do not let him near your heart, no matter what he may promise you."

"I had not planned to," said Elizabeth with amusement, "but I appreciate the warning."

"*One*, two, three, *one*, two, three." Eleanor established the rhythm as she led Elizabeth through the steps. "That's it. You can see how simple it is. Remember, a little rise on the last two steps."

"Is it the same all through the dance? There are no figures or lines?"

"None. You can forget everything you know about reels and country dances. This is completely different, just one man and one woman together for the entire dance. It is wonderfully romantic."

"Oh, lovely," said Elizabeth with heavy irony. "Just what I need, a romance with someone who would never consider me good enough to marry. With luck, no one will ask me to dance."

"It will not be that bad. You may well win an admirer or two."

"Among those coming to this house party? As near as I can tell, anyone lacking a title has a fortune or close connections to the nobility – except for the one who will have eyes for no one but you."

"You may like Captain Bradley. He is not the cleverest of men, but he has a good heart and no undue pride. It is not his fault that his father is an earl. And I will warn you which gentlemen are not to be trusted."

"Apart from Lord Charles?" Elizabeth teased.

"Apart from me?" Lord Charles's elegant tones sounded from the door to the ballroom. "I had hoped you would not even notice any gentlemen apart from me, my dear Juliet."

Elizabeth gave him an arch look as she rose from her curtsey. "I had never realized that it was so difficult to pronounce 'Miss Bennet.' If you wish, I could instruct you in how to say it in return for your assistance with the waltz."

He laughed. "And deprive me of the chance to call you Juliet? Never. But how are your waltz lessons coming?"

"She is doing very well," said Eleanor. "I was about to show her how to turn while doing the steps."

"That is *my* job, fair sister." Stepping close, he caught Elizabeth by the waist, tugging her toward him.

"Lord Charles!" Elizabeth exclaimed reproachfully, pulling away from him.

Eleanor laughed. "You really have never seen a waltz, have you? You put your right hand in Charles's left. Now your left hand rests on his shoulder, like so." She moved Elizabeth's hand into position. "Then Charles..."

Lord Charles interrupted. "Then Charles has the pleasure of doing this." He put his hand back on her waist with a slight smirk.

The sensation was shocking. Elizabeth turned to Eleanor. "You must be joking."

"No, my dearest Juliet, she is not. And what is even better is that we stay this way through the entire dance."

No wonder the waltz was thought so improper! It was practically an embrace. Lord Charles's eyes laughed at her discomfort, making it clear he had no objections to the position. Elizabeth said tartly, "I can tell this dance was invented by a man."

"Enough of that," ordered Eleanor. "You are not in your little country town any longer. Now try the steps in place. Charles will step forward while you step back."

Feeling unusually awkward, Elizabeth tried to do as instructed. Good Lord – was he trying to put his leg between hers? She stepped backwards quickly, then had to remember what to do with her feet. How could she pay attention to her steps with a man standing so close to her – especially when he was taking advantage of his position to admire certain of her assets? She tried to focus instead on Eleanor's counting and not to think about what the ladies of Meryton would say if they could see her now.

"Very nice," said Lord Charles. "Now, keep doing those steps, but allow me to lead you."

Elizabeth strongly suspected the only place he wished to lead her was into temptation, but she swallowed her retort before she made herself look any more provincial than she already did.

His hand pressed more firmly against her waist. "Now turn with me. That is correct. And again." When she stumbled, he said, "You are doing very well. You should have seen me when I first tried to waltz. My partner declared me a menace."

Once he stopped trying to flirt with her, Lord Charles proved a good teacher, gradually coaxing her into taking wider turns and moving more rapidly. To Elizabeth's dismay, Eleanor went to the pianoforte at the end of the room and began to play. Elizabeth had felt safer with her friend only a few feet away from her, but she had to admit that hearing the music made the dance easier. Gradually she relaxed into the rhythm of the movement, though the warmth of Lord Charles's hand against her back continued to disturb her. At least the gentlemen at the dance would be wearing gloves. Elizabeth strongly suspected that her partner had deliberately omitted that part of his attire.

When Eleanor reached the end of the music, Lord Charles released Elizabeth and bowed. "You are a natural dancer, my sweet Juliet.

May I hope to have the honor of your hand for tomorrow evening's waltz?"

"No, you may not!" said Eleanor tartly. "Elizabeth should take the opportunity to dance it with someone else. *You* can find some other unfortunate woman to practice your wiles on."

"You are as cruel as you are fair, dear sister!" He took advantage of Elizabeth's laughter to reclaim her hand long enough to place a lingering kiss on it.

Darcy wondered at Paxton's long face as they rode away from Bentham Park. "I thought that went rather well. We are invited to return, and you may even have a chance to dance with your lady love."

Paxton seemed to shake himself out of his reverie. "Yes, it did, and I thank you. I wonder where Eleanor was today."

"Since we saw very little apart from Lord Bentham's study, I imagine she could be almost anywhere in that massive pile. It makes Pemberley look like a cottage."

"Rather overdone, yes. Incidentally, my dear friend Edward with whom I like to race – who is he?"

Darcy gave him a sidelong glance. "Lord Bentham's eldest son, of course."

"Huntingdon? Good lord, he would have shot me at dawn if I ever called him Edward."

"Edward Carlisle, Viscount Huntingdon - but I would not joke about shooting at dawn. It was hushed up, but he had to flee the country after killing a man in a duel."

"Good God! What happened? I had heard he went abroad, but I assumed it was by choice!"

"The other fellow accused him of cheating in a race. Edward had no choice but to challenge him. He was prepared to accept an apology or a delopement, but the other man shot to kill, and so did Edward."

"But why did he go into exile? Dueling may be illegal, but I doubt any jury would convict under those circumstances."

"Ordinarily, yes, but the other man's father apparently had extensive connections and was prepared to bribe half of London if need be to obtain a guilty verdict. I expected Lord Bentham to counter him, but instead he sent Edward a letter telling him to leave the country and never return. It is not an accident that I have had little contact with Lord Bentham these last four years, despite his efforts to keep me as part of the family." If he had to tolerate Lord Bentham now, at least he could have the satisfaction of knowing he was helping Paxton. Given the Marquess's attitude, it seemed unlikely he would be able to do anything for Edward.

"I was watching Lord Bentham closely. He was very shaken by what you said. If I had to guess, I would say he knew nothing at all of his son's affairs."

"Were I Edward, I would be in no hurry to write home after being cast off like an old shoe for doing what he could not in honor avoid," said Darcy grimly. "But if Lord Bentham asks you about him, just talk about racing. Edward was a demon for a good race."

"I cannot imagine he will go out of his way to speak to me about anything," said Paxton dryly.

"But he will see you in company, and that is the important thing. Will you be able to warn Lady Eleanor in advance?"

"I will write to her, but she cannot always pick up my letters immediately." Paxton chose his words carefully. "It would be dangerous for me to pay too much attention to Eleanor while we are at Bentham Park. She suggests I should pretend to be smitten with her friend. That way I have an excuse to stay near her."

"Have I a role in this charade? I warn you, I may have done well enough today, but I have little talent for disguising my feelings."

"And well I know it! Fortunately, your only role is simply to be the grandson of an earl and a friend of the family, and thus compensate for the inferiority of my company. That should come naturally to you."

"Do you find me proud and disdainful then?" The words slipped out before Darcy had a chance to stop them.

His friend gave him an odd look. "You do not disdain a man on the grounds of his birth, at least."

Darcy's mouth twisted. "Thank you for the faint praise."

"I did not mean it that way. It is true that you can be disdainful, but it is usually when someone is foolish or ill-mannered. You have never treated *me* with disdain."

So Elizabeth had some basis for her opinion after all.

Elizabeth did not see Lord Charles again until dinner, when he managed to monopolize her attention as often as possible, despite Eleanor's efforts to separate them. Fortunately, he seemed to have realized that Elizabeth did not care for the extravagant compliments common among the *ton,* and chose instead to converse with her in a more sensible manner, inquiring about her home and her travels. When he was not engaging in outrageous flirtation, Elizabeth found Lord Charles pleasant company.

She might have given him no more thought, but when the ladies withdrew, Lady Bentham placed a gloved hand on her arm. "Miss Bennet, you would be wise to avoid encouraging Lord Charles. He can have no honorable intentions towards a woman of your station."

Elizabeth thought it was a pity that Mr. Darcy was not there. He would have enjoyed joining in the chorus reminding her of her low connections. "I believe I have already made it clear to Lord Charles that I am not interested in becoming his latest conquest."

"You would do well to trust in those who know him better. He does not give up easily when he wants something."

Her smile becoming forced, Elizabeth said, "I thank you for your concern and advice, Lady Bentham."

Her ladyship nodded a gracious acknowledgement before rejoining Eleanor.

Chapter 3

Bentham Park, June 6

My dear Aunt,

As you can see, I have arrived safely at Bentham. Apart from that, this visit has been quite unlike any other. So much has changed here! Almost all of the staff I knew are gone. The nursery wing has been completely redecorated so that it can now be used as guest bedrooms. More than anything else, the atmosphere is different – whereas I used to find it relaxing here, now it seems like someone is always watching to see if I make a mistake. My place has also changed. Instead of being immediately sent off to play with Eleanor as would have been the case years ago, I have been plunged into the maelstrom of life among the nobility. Rather than my old bedroom in the nursery wing, my new room is in the main part of the house. Eleanor and I are expected to spend much of the day with her stepmother instead of off on our own, and we dine formally with her family at night. We steal a little time to ourselves in the early mornings and late at night, but I definitely prefer the old days!

I did solve the mystery of my invitation. Lord Bentham was the one to give Eleanor permission to invite her 'little friend', though he seemed rather surprised on my arrival to discover that I was no longer fourteen years old. Unfortunately, he did not discuss this plan with his wife, who was not pleased to discover that such a low connection would be appearing just before a long-planned house party. Sometimes it seems that the only thing she cares about is the family's status in the ton*! Still, she is apparently determined to make the best of my arrival by playing the role of Cinderella's fairy godmother. As a result, I have a closet full of Eleanor's less stylish gowns, a vanity covered with borrowed face paints and jewelry, and my own maid who oversees my transformation every morning. Lady Bentham's efforts to assure that I do not feel the part of the poor relation among the lofty guests may look like generosity on her part, but I suspect she is more motivated by a desire that I not prove an embarrassment to her. She even loaned me her own second-best diamond hairpins because, as she says, 'The details are the most important in making a good first impression.' Naturally, I spend half my time searching out mirrors so that I may reassure myself that I have not lost her hairpins!*

Her ladyship also condescended to have her secretary write out a list of all the guests at the house party for me, including the proper forms of address for each. Apparently she believes I was raised in a barn along with the horses and cattle, and that I learned nothing during the years I shared lessons with Eleanor! You will be pleased to hear that I thanked her very politely for her consideration, although Eleanor and I had a good laugh over it later. Knowing Lady Bentham, I was not surprised to discover that her invitation list had been carefully selected to include wealthy and powerful aristocrats with offspring who would be suitable company for 'the young people' – namely Eleanor and her brother, Lord Charles – while she and Lord Bentham spend their time among their parents. Given that Lady Bentham is but three years older than Lord Charles, one must wonder a little at that!

I dislike admitting it, but I was grateful for my borrowed plumage when the guests began arriving yesterday, as their travelling clothes were superior to my best gown. First I was introduced to Sir Henry Matthew Dalgliesh Boyd from Jersey, who managed to inform me twice within five minutes of the heroic role he played when that island was invaded by the French in 1781. His fashionably dressed daughter, Miss Boyd, contrived to look faintly embarrassed but also proud of her father. Lady Mary Huggins, the daughter of the Earl and Countess of Alford, looks to be a few years older than I am, but has a warm smile for everyone. I do not yet have much sense of Miss Elliot, the daughter of a baronet, but Eleanor received her quite coolly.

Although I am playing the role of Cinderella, I do not see much promise for finding my prince among the single gentlemen. Sir Richard Newbury, on being introduced to me, raised his quizzing glass to his eye and took a leisurely and impudent survey of me. I had thought no one could be more rakish than Lord Charles, but Sir Richard may outdo him. Captain Bradley is a jocular, heavyset man in his mid-thirties who greeted me with the same respect he showed the other young ladies, although I suspect that may be because he cannot tell us apart. I did take a liking to the crusty Admiral Worthsley, but I doubt my parents would be pleased to discover I was being courted by a man old enough to be my grandfather!

I can see you frowning in impatience, dear aunt, because I have failed to answer the question foremost in your mind, though I find it difficult to believe anything is more pressing than diamond hairpins. Despite her frantic letter, Eleanor is perfectly well, but if I am playing Cinderella, her role is that of the tragic lover. She does not wish to marry the foppish lordling that her father has chosen for her, preferring instead a gentleman who is unacceptable to the family because of his low connections. I am offering what consolation I can, although there is little anyone can do in the circumstances.

And now I must go, as Cinderella must be made ready for the ball, or at least the informal dancing to take place this evening. Since there will be no prince there for me, I promise you that I will take care not to lose either of my slippers – or my hairpins!

Yours &c.,

E. Bennet

Darcy did not anticipate finding any pleasure in spending an evening of dancing and cards at Bentham Park, but he tried to disguise his distaste from Paxton. On their arrival, they found the first set of dances had already started. Lady Bentham was leading the set, but Lord Bentham approached Darcy immediately. "Welcome! I am glad you could join us, Darcy. Come, Charles is in the card room and anxious to see you."

Darcy glanced at Paxton, who appeared to accept Lord Bentham's lack of notice without distress. His friend said, "Go ahead, Darcy. I will not intrude on a family reunion." No doubt he preferred to remain where he would be able to see Lady Eleanor.

Although he had little interest in seeing Charles, Darcy was content to go to the card room. He was in no mood for making the acquaintance of young ladies. They only reminded him of what he had lost in Elizabeth, and none of them could hold a candle to her liveliness of spirit and arch wit. But that was enough thoughts of Elizabeth – he would not allow her ghost to haunt his every moment. Firmly he put her from his mind.

"Darcy!" cried Lord Charles Carlisle. "What brings you to this godforsaken corner of the country? Never mind; you are just the man I need. Come join us and perhaps my luck will turn. God knows I deserve some good luck!"

Darcy tilted his head in acknowledgement and took a seat across from Lord Charles. Pulling out the handful of coins he had brought for this purpose, he spread them in front of him. "You may do your worst."

The next half hour passed tolerably enough. Darcy ignored most of the banter between the other three men until Lord Charles pushed his cards away. "That will have to do for now," he proclaimed. "I must attend to my latest flirt. After all, I have only a fortnight to make her fall in love with me; and the sooner that is accomplished, the sooner I will be enjoying her favors." He smirked at the other men's guffaws when he traced out with his hands the shape of a well-endowed female. "I have some very particular plans for that young lady."

Bradley looked up over his elaborately knotted cravat. "I say, Carlisle, she *is* a gentleman's daughter, don't you know."

Lord Charles's smile widened. "When has that ever stopped me before? I need some amusement to alleviate the utter tedium of this house party. The Season cannot start soon enough for me."

Newbury drawled, "And *I* say you will not manage to seduce her. She does not seem the sort to fall prey to your blandishments."

"Too virtuous, don't you know," added Bradley helpfully.

Lord Charles tapped two fingers on the table. "Would you care to place a bet on that, gentlemen? I would be happy to take your money along with her virtue."

"One hundred guineas says you cannot enjoy her before the end of the house party," said Newbury without hesitation.

"Agreed," said Lord Charles. "Who else is in? Bradley? Darcy?"

Bradley looked up from counting his coins. "One hundred from me as well."

Darcy shook his head, trying not to let his distaste show. He knew of one girl of good family who had disappeared from the *ton* after Carlisle had set his sights on her, and another whose reputation was ruined. "I bet only on sporting events," he said evenly.

Lord Charles laughed. "There will be sport aplenty for me in this case! But I must not keep the young lady waiting. I bribed the musicians to make this set a waltz. Perhaps I can discover a few of her charms during it – after all, a man's hand might happen to slip from her waist, might it not?" He pushed back his chair.

The other two made to follow him. Darcy, with no desire to watch Carlisle take advantage of an innocent girl, went to observe the other game for a few minutes, but the table was full and none of the players showed an inclination to leave. As the strains of the waltz began to drift in from the next room, Darcy decided it should be safe to emerge from the card room now. Perhaps he could find Paxton and convince him to play a few hands of cards, unless he had managed to win the hand of his ladylove for the waltz.

Making his way into the parlor, Darcy scanned the room for Paxton while avoiding the eyes of the matchmaking mamas. Damnation – his friend was already waltzing, his expression dreamy. Darcy's lips tightened. He had no patience with lovers at the moment.

A light, rippling laugh reached his ears, making his blood run suddenly hot. He knew that laugh. It had haunted his dreams for months. Surely he must be mistaken. What would Elizabeth Bennet be doing among such elevated company?

His heart thudded painfully against his chest as he slowly turned his gaze in the direction of the laughter. For a moment he froze, his body gone rigid at the sight of her light, pleasing form moving gracefully in the turns of the waltz.

Elizabeth was here, in another man's arms, another man's hand splayed against her waist. Bile rose in Darcy's throat when he saw the object of her delighted laughter. She was gazing up into the admiring countenance of Lord Charles Carlisle.

"I had not expected the honor of waltzing with you tonight, my lord," said Elizabeth archly.

"I understood from Eleanor that the final dance was to be the waltz, so I believed I was safe in asking you for the third set," Lord Charles said, his voice pitched low. "I cannot be held responsible if the musicians change their plans, even if I am delighted by it. Obviously it was fate that we should waltz together."

She gave him a skeptical look. He had not seemed surprised when the music began. "Perhaps the musicians miraculously guessed at your desire, and did not wish to offend their employer's son."

He smiled, but made no denial. Instead, he said in a voice intended to be overheard, "I have waltzed with many women, but never with one who seemed to dance on air as you do. I would not have expected such accomplishment in one so young. You must have waltzed frequently."

"You flatter me," said Elizabeth dryly. "I am somehow certain you are aware that I have never danced it in public before tonight."

His look of feigned astonishment would have made an actor proud. "I do not believe it! You must have received the nod from the patronesses of Almack's long ago."

Elizabeth glared good-naturedly at him, aware that he had trapped her neatly, since she could not admit to having practiced it with him privately. She had no choice but to make the appropriate response. "I have not received their nod at all, since I have never been to Almack's, nor am I likely ever to go there. And as for dancing it elsewhere, the waltz is still considered too scandalous for the sort of country assembly I frequent."

He leaned his head closer to her than propriety allowed. "You will dance it at Almack's some day, and it will be in my arms," he breathed, too quietly for anyone else to hear, as the hand at her waist slipped slightly lower. Then, more loudly, he added, "You must have an excellent dancing master."

"He has a very high opinion of himself, so I feel certain he would agree with your estimation, my lord," she said tartly. "Tell me, Lord Charles, would the patronesses of Almack's approve of the position of your hand?"

He laughed, but his fingers ceased their subtle exploration and returned to rest lightly on her waist. "The patronesses might not approve, but they would recognize that sooner or later every gentleman meets the temptation he cannot resist."

In vain have I struggled. It will not do... You must allow me to tell you how ardently I admire and love you. Those heartfelt words, so unlike Lord Charles's practiced flirtations, echoed in her ears. What a pity that they had come from the ill-tempered Mr. Darcy, while the affable Lord Charles did not mean a word he said! Still, it was enjoyable to flirt with him, as long as she did not allow too much impudence on his part. "I have no doubt that you are an expert at meeting temptation, my lord."

His hand tightened on her waist, pulling her closer to him until their bodies almost touched. "Not such a temptation as you, Miss Bennet."

Although the sensation was not unpleasant, Elizabeth chose to enjoy it only for a moment before pretending to stumble and stepping firmly on Lord Charles's toes. "Oh, how clumsy of me!" she said with an excess of sweetness. "Forgive me; I am not accustomed to dancing in such a crowded room."

Since there were only four other couples dancing, he could hardly mistake her meaning.

He chuckled, the pressure of his hand easing. "You are even more tempting when you blush so prettily, Miss Bennet. Tell me, is it the crush around us or just the company that makes such lovely roses bloom in your cheeks?"

Oh, he was good! She lowered her eyelids, hoping to discourage further conversation so that she could enjoy what remained of her first waltz. "There are many things that can make me blush, sir, but it is not always for myself that I blush."

His laugh was teasingly intimate. "Ah, my dear Juliet, how you enchant me!"

She hoped he would cease his attentions at the end of the waltz, but Lord Charles remained at her elbow, murmuring provocative nothings in her ear, until she pleaded thirst and sent him to fetch her a lemonade. Once he left, she lost no time in attaching herself to Miss Elliot. She would have preferred Eleanor as her bodyguard, but her friend was absorbed in a tête-à-tête with her swain, and would not thank Elizabeth for interrupting.

Miss Elliot tapped Elizabeth's arm with her fan. "La, Miss Bennet, you are quite the belle of the ball! It is not every lady who is singled out for notice by the charming Lord Charles."

"He is charming, that cannot be denied," said Elizabeth. "He is also as impudent as he is amiable."

Her companion tittered. "Of course he is! What else would you expect from a hardened rake? I hope you are wise enough to know that his attentions to ladies are always fleeting. Do not fall into the trap of hoping for a proposal from him!"

"I could hardly expect serious interest from his lordship's son," she said coolly. Did she really look like such a fool that everyone assumed she could not recognize him for what he was? She just might scream if one more person warned her against Lord Charles. She pretended to watch the reel being danced at the other end of the room.

"If any woman is to win Lord Charles, it will be through entrapment," Miss Elliot said. "I would not advise trying that, however, unless you are in a position to embarrass him in front of the *ton*. If he were found in a compromising position with a lady lacking powerful connections, he would simply laugh and walk away. He has done it before."

"How fortunate, then, that I have no plans to entrap him! *You* would no doubt be in a much better position than I to make the requisite protest. Perhaps you should try it," Elizabeth said with a false sweetness.

"Do not laugh, Miss Bennet; if Lord Charles should end up as his father's heir, as appears likely, there are many women who would be willing to take that risk for the chance to be a marchioness."

Elizabeth decided that Eleanor would just have to tolerate the interruption. "I will wish all of them the very best of luck. If you will be so kind as to excuse me, I think Lady Eleanor wants me."

Eleanor caught her arm as she approached. "Lizzy, may I have the honor of introducing you to Mr. Paxton? He is our nearest neighbor, although we do not often have the pleasure of his company. It is a delightful surprise that he has joined us tonight. Mr. Paxton, this is my dear friend, Miss Bennet."

Mr. Paxton bent over her hand, giving her a sly wink as he straightened. "Lady Eleanor, I had not realized your friend was the lovely lady I have been admiring from afar tonight. It is a very great pleasure, Miss Bennet."

"The honor is mine, Mr. Paxton." Elizabeth glanced at Eleanor, concerned about how she might feel on seeing her beloved flirting with another woman, but she seemed supremely untroubled, going so far as to cede her chair beside Mr. Paxton to Elizabeth and taking a seat on her other side.

"Lady Eleanor tells me you are visiting from Hampshire," he said. "I hope you are enjoying your visit to Yorkshire.

Elizabeth hid a smile as she saw him glancing at Eleanor even as he spoke to her. "My home is in Hertfordshire, but I cannot deny that the scenery here is lovely. I have always been fond of visiting Bentham Park."

Eleanor turned to Elizabeth. "My stepmother tells me she plans to invite Mr. Paxton and his friend to join us for our picnic."

"That is good news," said Mr. Paxton quietly. "I had been unsure if she would include me again. Ah, and here is *my* friend!"

Elizabeth looked up to see a phantom from her imaginings, one who did not look at all pleased to see her. "Mr. Darcy!" she exclaimed, hardly believing her eyes. What in the world had brought *him* there? His name had not been on the list for the house party, of that much she was certain.

If it were possible to bow in a curt fashion, he did so. "Miss Bennet, may I entreat the favor of your hand for this dance?" He sounded as if he were a judge pronouncing a death sentence.

It took Elizabeth a moment to find her voice over the pounding of her heart. "It would be my pleasure, sir."

Mr. Paxton said, "You are already acquainted?"

"We have met," Darcy said.

His poor manners were enough to set Elizabeth's spirits to teasing. "Oh, yes, we have encountered one another before, enough for me to know that it is quite an extraordinary event for Mr. Darcy to invite a lady to dance. I do hope he is not falling ill."

His lips tightened, a look quite unlike the sort of smile that had formerly come over his face when he gazed at her. "I am in perfect health, Miss Bennet."

"Then you must allow me to introduce *my* friend, Lady Eleanor Carlisle," Elizabeth said brightly. "Lady Eleanor, may I present Mr. Darcy to your acquaintance?"

"Lady Eleanor and I are also old acquaintances." Darcy bowed to her with none of the curtness he had shown Elizabeth. "You have changed a great deal since our last meeting."

Eleanor's curtsey was all that was elegant and feminine, despite her look of confusion. "I am afraid I cannot recall meeting you before, sir."

"That is hardly surprising, since you were perhaps four years of age at the time, while I was all of eleven. I spent the summer with your family many years ago along with my sister, who was but an infant at the time."

"Oh, I *do* remember you! You were the one who claimed to have picked all the flowers from the garden border even though I was the one who did it."

Darcy cleared his throat, looking uncomfortable. "It seemed the least I could do since you knew no better."

"Then Edward could not bear it that you were being more noble than he was, so he said it was him, not you, and the two of you began quarreling about which of you had done the wicked deed."

He dipped his head in acknowledgement. "As I recall, your grandmother questioned us regarding what kind of flowers we had picked, and when neither of us could answer, she turned to you and told you not to pick flowers without permission ever again. I was certain she must have magical powers of perception and was very careful with her ever after."

"That was wise of you, since she does have a knack for knowing everything! But the musicians are about to begin, and I see my next partner coming this way. Perhaps we can speak further later on."

"It will be my pleasure, Lady Eleanor." Darcy's eyes swung back to Elizabeth. He held out a gloved hand to her. "Shall we take our place?"

Numbly she set her hand in his and allowed him to lead her onto the floor, wondering why he had asked her to dance when he seemed so displeased with her presence. She would have thought he would avoid her, not single her out. Was he deliberately trying to make her uncomfortable? "You took me quite by surprise, sir. I was unaware of your presence here."

"Until half an hour ago, I assumed you were in Hertfordshire. You had said it was your plan to return there after your stay in Kent." His words had an almost accusing quality.

"That had been my intent, until I received a letter from Lady Eleanor begging me to come here."

He looked down at her with an unreadable expression. "*You* are Lady Eleanor's friend?"

"Is it so shocking that a peer's daughter would associate with someone with my low connections?" she shot back.

"You misunderstand me. Perhaps I should have asked if you were *that* one of Lady Eleanor's friends, the one she sent for, just as Paxton urgently requested *my* company."

Now it was Elizabeth's turn to feel shocked. "*You* are the one that he asked…Oh, dear." This was beyond embarrassing. It was mortifying. How could she work together with *Mr. Darcy* to chaperone Eleanor and Mr. Paxton?

"I had other business here as well, so it worked out conveniently."

With a start, she realized the music had begun, and they had not taken their place in line. "Shall we join the set?"

The corners of his mouth twitched but without humor. "This is a waltz, Miss Bennet."

"No, it cannot be. There was but one waltz on the schedule." Even as she said it, she heard the distinctive waltz rhythm, making her feel twice a fool.

"*That* was before Lord Charles Carlisle bribed the musicians to play one earlier," he said darkly. As if it took effort, he took hold of her waist.

"Oh." Elizabeth's cheeks grew warm, recalling the liberties Lord Charles had attempted during their dance. She had hoped no one would notice his behavior, but if Mr. Darcy had been watching her as closely as he had in the past, he was unlikely to have missed it. Now she had to put her hand on his shoulder, which suddenly seemed a far more intimate action than it had with Lord Charles. Experiencing an uncharacteristic urge to flee, she raised her hand and carefully rested it on the superfine linen of his coat. There – if she focused on the fabric of his coat and avoided looking in his eyes, it was hardly embarrassing at all. "I should warn you, Mr. Darcy, that I am not an accomplished waltzer. This is only the second time I have danced it, but I will do my best not to tread on your feet," she said in an attempt to lighten the atmosphere.

"You have the advantage of me, madam. Although I know the dance, this is the first time I have performed it in public." His hand pressed against her in a cue to begin.

Something she could tease him about – that was a relief! "Truly? *My* lack of experience stems from the fact that it is not performed at the sort of country assemblies that I frequent. But what is your excuse? You certainly cannot have lacked for opportunities, nor for eager partners."

"All the more reason why I choose not to waltz." The words could have been playful, but his tone was flat, almost insulting.

From her meager experience, he seemed to lead well, and she suspected he would have cut a good figure as he did so, had his expression not been quite so dark. How was she to make him out? When a man who had previously professed ardent love to a woman asked her to waltz, one might reasonably expect it to be a sign of courtship, but this had none of the hallmarks. If anything, he appeared to be undergoing punishment.

"Lord Charles is not a man to be trusted," he said abruptly as they spun around the room.

Not that again! So he *had* seen her earlier waltz. "I will take your opinion under advisement," she said coolly.

"I am not jesting, Miss Bennet. He is a dangerous man and not above taking advantage of...." Darcy broke off, as if he had suddenly realized he was about to say something inappropriate.

What gave him the right to decide with whom she should spend her time? "I thank you for your concern. Perhaps it will reassure you to know that I am well aware that he is a rake and that he is only amusing himself with me."

"If that were all, it would not matter, but he delights in making trouble and cares little for the consequences to anyone else."

Elizabeth had reached her limit with his scowls and warnings. "You may consider me duly warned," she said sharply.

His breath hissed through his teeth in evident frustration, but he said nothing further. It was just as well, since Elizabeth doubted her own ability to make a temperate answer. What was it about this man that he could infuriate her in a matter of minutes?

At least one of her questions had been answered. She had wondered what Mr. Darcy thought of her after she refused him, whether he had been angry or hurt, whether he still cherished tender feelings for her or whether those sentiments had turned into hatred. Well, now she knew. He despised her and thought her a fool to boot.

She swallowed hard, then stumbled as she missed a beat in the dance. To anyone else, she would have made a joke at her own expense; but with this man, she could find no humor in it. Her failures no doubt just reinforced his disdain for her. Her arm was so tense that her shoulder began to cramp.

Oh, if only she could just walk away from him! That would never do. She needed to concentrate on her dancing, to make her feet move in time to the music, and to keep at least a bit of a smile, however false, on her face. Taking a deep breath, she focused her gaze on his shoulder and forced herself to relax. To relax? All she wanted to do was flee, but instead she had to keep moving in concert with him, turning in circles, his powerful body just inches from hers. No wonder the waltz was considered so risqué! The room spun around her, the candles just a blur of light. The only solid thing was the gentleman whose hand rested on her waist. At least he, unlike Lord Charles, did not attempt to take advantage of the possibilities inherent in that position; but then again, she doubted he had any desire to do so.

A few minutes before, she had been grateful for his silence, but now she recognized the danger in it. Silence left too much opportunity for thinking and feeling. Even quarrelling would provide some distraction. There must be some neutral topic of conversation! "Have you known Mr. Paxton long?" she asked, pleased that her voice was steady.

"We met at Cambridge. He was one of the few there who took their studies seriously. He was one of the finest scholars of his year."

She raised a teasing eyebrow. "Along with you, no doubt?"

"I cannot be the judge of that." His voice was tight.

"In that case, I will have to ask Mr. Paxton. What of Mr. Bingley? Was he a scholar as well?" Immediately she wished she had not mentioned him, as memories of the last time Mr. Bingley's name had come up between them intruded.

"Bingley attended Oxford, and I did not make his acquaintance until afterwards."

"A tactful answer, sir!"

Darcy's hand pressed against hers as he whirled them in a tight turn, apparently to avoid another couple. Elizabeth's head spun a little with the movement. To regain her balance, she focused on his face. Looking directly into his eyes for the first time, she felt a shock that raised goose bumps on her arms. Had they always been so dark and unfathomable, or was it just the shadows that danced across his countenance in time with their movement? His eyes held her captive, and she could not look away. If it were not for the slight sardonic twist to his lips, she might have thought he still admired her.

Somehow that idea made her angry once more. "Why did you ask me to dance? Clearly it was not for the pleasure of my company, and we have already established that you do not enjoy the waltz."

His lips pressed together, and for a moment she thought he would not respond at all. "Must I have a reason?" he asked, his voice toneless. "I was invited here to dance, and you are the only lady with whom I have an acquaintance – a recent one, at least."

She raised a mocking eyebrow. "I had forgotten. You are the singular gentleman who believes no one can be introduced in a ballroom."

Darcy's jaw tightened and a pulse throbbed in his throat, but he did not reply, instead averting his eyes from her.

Elizabeth's stomach began to rebel, less from the circles they spun in than from a pang of guilt. Mr. Darcy had never been one to allow her to have the last word, yet he had just done so for the second time tonight. She had been so caught up in her reaction to his presence that she had hardly considered how difficult this meeting must be for him. The memory of their bitter conversation in Hunsford still haunted her, and she was not the one whose love had been spurned in a harsh manner and with false accusations. Her anger had made her needlessly cruel then, yet tonight he had made the effort to be civil, if not amiable, in asking her to dance. She should be feeling sorry for his pain, not baiting him. He had more than enough reason to resent her as it was.

On impulse, she said, "I owe you an apology. Your appearance here tonight took me by surprise, but that is no excuse for incivility."

That made him look at her again, the lines of his face softening a bit. "You have nothing for which to apologize. It is a difficult situation."

"You are very generous," she murmured, hoping the room was sufficiently dim to hide the color that rose in her cheeks.

"I was also unaware that you would be here, but I had half an hour to become accustomed to the idea before speaking to you. I doubt I would have behaved with any credit otherwise."

Why was he being kind to her? She certainly did not deserve it. Perhaps he was trying to make the best of a bad situation. If they were to be thrust into each other's company through the machinations of Eleanor and Mr. Paxton, it would be easier for all concerned if they could be on civil terms. "Perhaps we could start this conversation over from the beginning. I might comment on the fine weather we have had of late."

The corners of his mouth quirked. "It has rained for the last three days, Miss Bennet."

She arranged her face in stern lines. "Mr. Darcy, if you are going to allow *facts* to interfere with a perfectly good topic of conversation, our situation will be desperate indeed!"

The sound he made was almost a laugh. "It is a foolish obsession of mine, the *facts*. Perhaps we are better off simply enjoying the dance."

She wrinkled her nose at him. "It would be a pity to dislike your first waltz."

"Indeed it would be."

Elizabeth's breath left her in a rush as he drew her closer to him and led her through a series of turns that left her dizzy. There were still half a dozen inches between them, but it seemed far too intimate, especially in the darker corners of the room. It had not felt like this when she had danced with him at the Netherfield ball, but that was before she knew he admired her. All she had cared for then was to torment him about Mr. Wickham. When had she developed this tendency toward cruelty? True, she had not known of his vulnerability to her then; she had not even thought that a man like him could *have* vulnerabilities, as if his pride and his fortune would do away with any human frailties.

They managed to remain civil for the remainder of the dance. Still, Elizabeth was relieved when Mr. Darcy returned her to Eleanor and Mr. Paxton.

Eleanor congratulated Elizabeth on her waltzing. "If I had not known you only learned it yesterday, I would have thought you quite proficient. I do not know how they came to play two waltzes, though. My stepmother will not be pleased."

"She must take it up with your brother," said Elizabeth. "Apparently it was his doing."

"I should have known!" Eleanor exclaimed.

Mr. Paxton spoke quietly to Darcy. "You are a success. We are invited to join the party for a picnic the day after tomorrow in the Abbey ruins."

"Fortunately, it is not difficult for me to play the part of my grandfather's grandson," said Darcy. Pretending indifference to Elizabeth Bennet was far more difficult.

Chapter 4

MISS ELLIOT SLIPPED into the seat next to Elizabeth at the breakfast table, though there were several other places available. Even her morning dress was of the finest muslin, and her hair was as carefully dressed as if she were attending a ball. After exchanging a few comments about the food, Miss Elliot said, "You have a talent for finding highly eligible men as dance partners, Miss Bennet. Have you known Mr. Darcy long?"

"Not long. We became acquainted in the autumn when he was visiting a neighbor in Hertfordshire." Had it really been only eight months since she first met him? It seemed so much longer. With a polite smile, she added, "If you intend to warn me that Mr. Darcy is also a rake, I am afraid I will not believe you."

Miss Elliot tittered. "Mr. Darcy? Not at all. He does not pursue ladies; they pursue *him*."

"So I have observed." Elizabeth thought of Miss Bingley's constant efforts to attract his attention.

"Is it any surprise? He is a remarkable catch – wealthy, yet not predisposed to gamble his fortune away; of good family, yet without parents to interfere with his choice of bride. The woman who marries him will be mistress of her own home with no mother-in-law to interfere."

Amused by the characteristics that Miss Elliot apparently valued in a potential husband, Elizabeth said, "Has he no faults, then?"

Miss Elliot appeared to consider this. "He has not been well received in the *ton,* but it is nothing that could not be remedied by the proper sort of wife. One may safely assume he will choose his wife carefully. Since he is very conscious of his rank and his duty to his estate, he would not consider marriage to a woman without equal rank and dowry."

Elizabeth had to hide a smile at this. "Not to mention that such a woman must be truly accomplished."

"Precisely." Miss Elliot gave her a warm smile, no doubt for having taken her hint. "He is not the sort of gentleman from whom one has to worry about improper advances, but it would be wisest not to hope for anything more."

Opening her eyes wide, Elizabeth said, "I am fortunate, then, to have made the acquaintance of someone who knows so well what Mr. Darcy would want in a wife. Tell me, are there any other gentlemen you would like to warn me about, or do you prefer to wait until you see me waltzing with them?"

"Pray excuse my interference. It was kindly meant." With a haughty look, Miss Elliot stood and crossed to the other side of the table.

It might even have been true. After all, a naïve girl could find herself in difficult straits in company this elevated.

Lady Mary Huggins spoke quietly from her other side. "Do not let it trouble you, Miss Bennet. Miss Elliot is in a difficult position."

Startled, Elizabeth turned to her. "*Her* position is difficult?"

"She has a spendthrift father, no brothers, and a taste for the finer things in life. If she does not make a good marriage, her future will be one of genteel poverty. She has been on the marriage market long enough to be feeling desperate."

Elizabeth laughed. "Oddly enough, I also have a spendthrift father and no brothers, but I would rather live in genteel poverty than marry a man without affection and respect. She is welcome to both Lord Charles and Mr. Darcy."

Lady Mary patted her hand. "I am glad to hear it. I agree with you, but not all women are as brave as you. I do not know whether I could make that choice."

"You do not appear to be hunting a husband," Elizabeth said boldly.

"No, I am not, but that is because I have the good fortune to have an inheritance of my own. I have no need of a husband to support me, but I still feel sympathy for those young ladies who are less fortunate. If they do not marry well, they will be poor; and if they are poor, they will lose all their friends in the *ton*. It is a hard choice to make. At least Miss Elliot does not resort to trickery to win a husband; that is a point in her favor."

"Trying to warn me off does not count as trickery?"

"Oh, no, my dear. I speak of the sort of woman who tries to lure an eligible gentleman into a position that appears to be compromising, then demands a proposal to restore her honor."

Miss Boyd, who had taken Miss Elliot's place, joined in the conversation. "It is true. Some women have had great success using that method." Her eyes flickered to the head of the table where Lady Bentham was conversing with the Earl of Alford.

Elizabeth's eyebrows shot up. Eleanor had never mentioned anything of the sort to her. "Surely a beautiful young woman would have no difficulty attracting the interest of a man old enough to be her father, even without trickery."

"A widower with three sons has little impetus to remarry, since there are many beautiful young women in the world who do not insist on a wedding ring as the price of their favors; however, there is a grave shortage of eligible titled gentlemen, especially ones who have not wasted their fortunes away, and a great many ambitious young women. Some are cleverer than others," said Miss Boyd.

"You seem very knowledgeable of all this."

Miss Boyd lowered her voice. "We came out during the same Season, and it became apparent she would stop at nothing to achieve her goals. She first had her sights set on Lord Bentham's eldest son, who was an even greater prize than his father, but he was so heavily pursued that he was always careful to be chaperoned by one of his friends to avoid such entrapments. As I recall, Mr. Darcy was often one of those chaperoning him."

Elizabeth laughed. "I imagine Mr. Darcy would strike terror into the hearts of those entrapping females!"

Miss Boyd gave her an odd look. "Mr. Darcy often needs someone to protect him as well."

Elizabeth could not imagine that, but she had come to some of her own conclusions about Mr. Darcy after their dance. Since she could not confide to Eleanor that he was the ill-tempered man who had proposed to her, she would have to make every effort to be polite and amiable to him. It would be uncomfortable, but if he could be civil after all that had passed between them, so could she. She just hoped they never had to waltz together again.

Darcy had dreamed of Elizabeth the previous night. It had been inevitable, he supposed, after the shock of seeing her the previous day. They had not been pleasant dreams; when Elizabeth had not been berating him for all his sins, both real and imagined, he had been struggling in vain to reach her as Lord Charles Carlisle mercilessly used her passionate nature to destroy her. If Carlisle so much as said a word about her today, Darcy feared his reserve would break. But, just as in his dream, there would be nothing he could do. He could not confront Carlisle over his intentions toward Elizabeth without questions being asked about his own relationship to her. His attempt to protect her could just as easily ruin her.

Of course, Elizabeth wanted nothing to do with his protection in any case. She had made that clear enough. He ought to just walk away, as he had wanted to do when he first saw her at the dance. But the idea of Carlisle using his well-honed seductive skills on Elizabeth made his gut churn.

The solution had seemed obvious. He would do his duty and warn her against Carlisle, and then he would leave Bentham Park and never return. On discovering the last dance was to be another waltz, he decided to extend his protection one last step by dancing it with her. It was the only way to make sure Carlisle did not have the opportunity to paw her again.

His plan had one terrible flaw. Despite starting the dance still furious with Elizabeth, he had failed to foresee the effect of gazing into her fine eyes and holding her pleasing shape in the near-embrace of a waltz, his hand resting intimately on the curve of her waist. In the space of a few minutes, he was back under her spell. Her power held him captive.

Still, he might have been able to free himself if she had not apologized. The genuine sadness in her eyes had crumbled his defenses. By the end of the waltz, there was no doubt he was every bit as much in love with Elizabeth Bennet as he had been two months ago.

Explaining the acquaintance to Paxton was no easier. The last thing Darcy wanted was for his friend to connect Miss Elizabeth Bennet with the woman who had refused his offer of marriage, so his encounter with Elizabeth had to appear to be a pleasant surprise. It would have been hard enough in any case, but with Paxton waxing eloquent about what good fortune it was that Darcy had a previous acquaintance with her, and how much this would facilitate spending time as a foursome, it was well-nigh impossible.

One thing was for certain. Darcy intended to employ every tool at his disposal to make certain Elizabeth was never alone with Carlisle. He preferred not to think about the nights when he would be three miles away. With his elder brother absent, Carlisle was heir apparent to Bentham Park; surely it would not be impossible for him to obtain a key to Elizabeth's room, and then.... Darcy swore under his breath. If he let his thoughts stray in that direction, he would go mad.

Darcy and Paxton arrived shortly before the party was to set out for the ruins. The pretense of participating as one of the group made it impossible for Darcy to approach Elizabeth immediately. Naturally, Carlisle was by her side, whispering in her ear. Blood pounded through Darcy's veins. Fortunately for the sake of his sanity, Lady Eleanor deliberately interposed herself between her brother and Elizabeth.

Darcy could not face Carlisle directly until his blinding fury was under control. Pretending to attend to the conversation around him, he kept stealing glances in Elizabeth's direction. He stiffened when Lady Bentham requested Lady Eleanor's presence, thus leaving Elizabeth unguarded again, but almost immediately the fashionable Miss Elliot was there, laying her hand flirtatiously on Carlisle's arm. Relief swelled through him. Miss Elliot might be vain and self-centered, and was no doubt simply trying to attract Carlisle's notice herself, but if she kept him away from Elizabeth, Darcy was prepared to be beholden to her.

"Darcy, there you are," a deep voice boomed from behind him.

Initially annoyed by the familiarity, Darcy revised his estimation when he turned to see the corpulent figure of his host approaching him. "Lord Bentham," he said, hoping this interruption would not distract him for long from observing Elizabeth.

"I want to hear more of what you have been doing these last years. You may ride with me in the curricle to the ruins. It is a fine stroll for all these young people, but my old bones prefer to let the horses do the work!"

Darcy nodded his acquiescence, but inwardly his frustration continued to mount. How could he make certain Elizabeth was safe from Carlisle when he was trapped listening to Lord Bentham's stories?

The day was warm and sunny, just as Lady Bentham had said it would be. No doubt her ladyship had commanded the weather in her prayers, Elizabeth thought. It was easy to imagine Lady Bentham giving orders to the Almighty. That idea might amuse Mr. Darcy after some of his aunt's eccentricities in that regard.

Darcy did not prove to be among the party of young people walking to the ruins, which unsettled Elizabeth. Mr. Paxton was there, so where was Darcy? Had he decided to remain behind at Mr. Paxton's estate to avoid her presence? It was likely just as well if he did, since Lord Charles seemed determined to stay by her side, despite Miss Elliot's fluttered eyelashes and hints that they could go ahead of the crowd. Since the crowd consisted only of Eleanor, Mr. Paxton, and two other couples, it could hardly be thought to comprise a crush.

The amused glances Lord Charles gave her suggested that he was perfectly aware of the cause of Miss Elliot's requests. Elizabeth supposed that he, like Mr. Darcy, was accustomed to being pursued by beautiful young ladies. She was the one in an unaccustomed role, being noticed by the two most eligible gentlemen despite her lowly status compared to the other guests. At least she did not have to worry about Mr. Darcy's intentions being dishonorable.

They paused for a few minutes where a break in the trees allowed a picturesque view of the abbey ruins, stone arches towering above a winding silver river. While Miss Boyd and Lady Mary chose to rest on the stone benches provided there, Elizabeth took the opportunity to inquire of Mr. Paxton whether his friend would be joining them today.

"He is here already." Mr. Paxton had to tear his gaze away from Eleanor to respond. "I believe he is driving down to the ruins with Lord Bentham. I imagine we will see him there."

So Mr. Darcy preferred the elevated company of the Marquess to that of the rest of them! No, that was not fair. Given that he did not see himself as too grand a personage to befriend Mr. Paxton or Mr. Bingley, she could not accuse him of looking down on the company. If he was avoiding them, it was because of her. She could hardly blame him for that, but it made her stomach clench.

Lord Charles sidled closer to her. "You seem very interested in Darcy."

"Only in his absence. I tremble with fear that Lady Bentham will discover that we walked all the way to the ruins with an uneven number of ladies and gentlemen. We must be prepared with an excuse if we hope to win her forgiveness any time in the next decade," she said solemnly.

He laughed. "I see you have learned the rules for survival at Bentham Park! Never fear, I will tell her that I counted for two gentlemen."

She raised an eyebrow. "You are ambitious, sir."

His slow smile was an invitation. "Are you only just discovering that, Miss Bennet?" he said smoothly.

What an incorrigible flirt he was! Fortunately, Eleanor's preoccupation with Mr. Paxton did not cause her to miss the interchange. Elbowing her brother in the ribs, she said, "That is enough, Charles! Lizzy, will you walk with me? Mr. Paxton is asking how we met, and I am sure he would like to hear your side of the story."

"Sisters," said Lord Charles mournfully. "I suppose I should thank God that I was only cursed with one of them."

Elizabeth, already turning to join the others, looked back over her shoulder. "I have *four* sisters myself, but I have been accustomed to consider them a blessing." Most of the time, at least, when they were not flirting with officers or otherwise embarrassing her.

Mr. Paxton gave her an amused look and said, "So, is it true that Lord Bentham tried to buy you when you were eight years old?"

Eleanor said indignantly, "That is not what I said!"

Paxton grinned at her. "No, but I have my suspicions all the same.'

Elizabeth laughed. "Lord Bentham meant well, truly. Eleanor had been in a serious decline. The doctors said it was likely consumption, which had caused her mother's death, and there was nothing they could do. Of course, she was not ill at all, simply lonely and grieving. Then I appeared quite by accident, told her not to be stupid and to get out of bed and play, and I challenged her to try – well, something acrobatic and quite unladylike. Eleanor never could resist a dare. The rest is history."

Her friend shook her head with a smile. "You are leaving out the best parts! My nurse raced in, frightened by the loud thumps coming from my room, only to discover me rolling around on the floor, wearing a pair of breeches I had pilfered from my brother's room. Horrified, she called for my father, who was frantic when she said something was wrong with me. When he found us sprawled on the floor and laughing, I said, 'Papa, see what Lizzy taught me to do!' Then I did a somersault."

"Oh, the expression on his face!" Elizabeth shook her head at the memory. "I thought I was in the most dreadful trouble. Instead, he marched me down to the sitting room, full of callers in mourning clothes, and he said, 'Who does this child belong to?'"

"And when her aunt claimed her, my father said, 'I would like to keep her,'" Eleanor added.

"My poor aunt is still mortified by this story! There she was, faced with the Marquess whom everyone said was crazy with grief for his wife, with no idea why he was demanding to keep her niece. She barely knew him, and he probably would not even have recognized her as one of his forty-two cousins, so she dared not argue with him. Instead, she suggested a compromise whereby she would bring me back the next day to visit. Eleanor overheard this somehow, came flying out and threw herself at her father, sobbing, 'Don't let them take Lizzy away! I'll die if she goes away!'"

Mr. Paxton snorted. "That sounds like you!"

Eleanor elbowed him. "It had the effect I desired. Her aunt said she could stay overnight, so I took her hand and we raced off to make more mischief. In the end, she stayed for a week before her aunt absolutely insisted that she had to leave. I cried, crawled back into bed, and stayed there."

Elizabeth took over the story again. "On my return home, I told my family all about my new friend Eleanor, but neglected to mention that she was *Lady* Eleanor, since that hardly mattered to me. A fortnight later, my father was utterly bewildered to receive a letter from no less a personage than the Marquess of Bentham, formally offering me a place in his household." When Mr. Paxton shook his head in apparent disbelief, she added, "You must understand that it made perfect sense from Lord Bentham's point of view. If there had been a doll he could buy to lift Eleanor's spirits, or a medicine that would have helped, he would have acquired it instantly, even if it cost more than diamonds. Since I had four sisters, he assumed my parents would be perfectly happy to give him one of their daughters." He had been correct as far as Mrs. Bennet was concerned. Elizabeth still remembered her mother's raptures over the invitation, and the arguments between her parents over it. Eventually Mr. Bennet had been persuaded that it was unwise to displease such a powerful man and agreed to a one-month visit.

"How typical!" Paxton said. In a quiet voice he added, "Lord Bentham seems to have difficulty discerning that other people might not agree with his wishes."

"Oh, he understands they might not agree," said Eleanor. "He just assumes that it is only because they lack his greater understanding of what is best for them, and that if he insists on having his way, they will thank him for it later."

"In this case, I *am* happy he insisted," said Elizabeth. "I loved the time I spent with you." One month had grown to two, the first of a series of long visits to Bentham Park and occasionally to the London townhouse where they had first met, till she was spending almost as much time as part of Eleanor's household as her own. Apart from some homesickness at first, she had been content with the situation. She took lessons alongside Eleanor, whose tutors opened new realms to her, and she was fascinated by the wider world open to the daughter of a peer.

Unbidden, a memory arose of Mr. Darcy saying, "*You* cannot have a right to such very strong local attachment. *You* cannot have been always at Longbourn." How surprised she had been that he could discern, even so many years later, that she had once spent time in a different world! But even she could not deny that it had left its mark. When she first met Eleanor, Elizabeth had been as wild as Lydia later turned out to be, though with somewhat better judgment. She had learned greater control from observing the mannerly adults at well-organized Bentham Park, so different from the chaos of Longbourn.

"You were a regular visitor here for a time, were you not?" Lord Charles had come up from behind them and now walked beside her. Apparently he had been listening to their conversation.

"Yes, for six years," she said lightly, as if it were not a painful subject. "I would come here when you and your brothers were at school. In fact, the same carriage that took you to Eton each term would then collect me and bring me to Bentham Park, with the process reversed at the end of the term. Other children I knew were sent off to school; I was fortunate enough to be sent to Bentham Park instead." She had rarely caught glimpses of Lord Bentham or any of the *ton* during these times since she kept to the schoolroom with Eleanor, who was still too young to be in company.

"I would far rather have stayed here than going to Eton! But that would explain why I do not remember seeing you after your first visit. Why did you stop coming here? Did your family wish to keep you at home?"

A flash of old pain stabbed at her. "Your father remarried."

"Oh. I *am* sorry. I should have realized it." A shadow passed across his face.

She should have stopped there, but the words spilled out of her mouth. "Apparently she persuaded your father that it was a *degradation* for the daughter of a Marquess to keep such *inferior* company, and that my presence would damage her good name and act to her disadvantage as she entered society." She made no attempt to disguise her bitterness. Both she and Eleanor had assumed their arrangement would last for years. Eleanor had talked about their first Season as if it were a given that Elizabeth would be sharing it with her. Instead, suddenly there were no more long trips to Bentham Park, only a plan for a brief visit when Eleanor came to London, and not even that during Eleanor's first Season. Elizabeth knew about that year only from Eleanor's letters.

Lord Charles curled his lip. "How very like her. And how very *convenient* for her that it left Eleanor without an ally."

Her brows furrowed, Elizabeth shot him an odd look. She was not certain what he meant, but he was making too much of it. Lady Bentham simply did not wish to associate with those who were beneath her, and it had cost Elizabeth dearly.

It had been a bitter loss at the time. Although she loved her family and Longbourn, being deprived of Eleanor's company and the greater stimulation she received at Bentham Park had left Elizabeth bereft. Her mother's constant agitation and the antics of Lydia, Kitty and Mary, which had seemed amusing when she had the opportunity to escape them, now grated constantly on her nerves. Even her dear Jane could not soothe her, for despite Jane's sweet nature, she lacked Eleanor's daring and could not offer Elizabeth the kind of stimulating partnership she enjoyed with her friend.

Only the anticipation of her planned week in London with Eleanor had offered her any consolation, but when the great day finally arrived, Elizabeth discovered that her playfellow and partner in mischief had been transformed into a proper young lady. For the first time, she was aware of the difference in their status and that others would see her as a sort of poor relation taken in for reasons of charity. From time to time, she would catch glimpses of rebellion in Eleanor's eyes, but they were quickly dampened. It was almost a relief when the visit ended, though the grief of losing that part of her life had remained with Elizabeth for months.

But she was not made for low spirits. She was eventually able to throw herself into life at Longbourn and only thought of her Bentham Park days as the remembrance brought her pleasure. She could recognize the benefits, and knew she had been fortunate to have had the opportunity, even if it ended sooner than she liked. She eventually found a challenging friend in the much older Charlotte Lucas, and she grew closer to her father. He was happy to keep her at Longbourn, since she was now old enough to be amusing to him, and her education at Bentham Park had made her an entertaining companion.

The pain of it was still there, just buried deep. Poor Mr. Darcy could not have known what a tender spot he hit when he spoke of the degradation of marrying so far beneath him. His references to her inferiority, so similar to Lady Bentham's accusations that had led to her banishment from Bentham Park, had cut her to the quick. But that horrible evening in Hunsford was the last thing she wished to remember, so she turned to Eleanor. "Those were good days, were they not?"

Eleanor bit her lip. "I wish they had never ended. I have never forgiven her for it." There was no need to ask to whom she referred.

The remainder of the walk passed with lighter topics of conversation. It was Elizabeth's first opportunity to converse at length with Mr. Paxton, and she was pleased to discover that he seemed an intelligent young man with a sly sense of humor, not afraid to tease Eleanor or to laugh at himself. He displayed none of the sense of superiority she had seen so much of at Bentham Park on this visit. Given how much Eleanor detested social pretense, it was not difficult to see why she would find his manners appealing.

The ruins were larger and more imposing than Elizabeth remembered from her last visit. She would have to return to explore them another day when she could appreciate the history and imagine when monks had roamed among them. Now the ancient stonework was bedecked with flowers and greenery in honor of the guests, with elaborate displays of fruits, pastries, and cold meats on cloth-covered tables. Servants hovered in the background so that the fine ladies and gentlemen need not be troubled to bestir themselves in the slightest at this picnic.

Amused, Elizabeth said to Eleanor, "Your stepmother has outdone herself."

Eleanor shrugged, the corners of her mouth turned down. "She glories in impressing others with her wealth and power, and does not see the meaningless extravagance." She glanced at Mr. Paxton.

He gave an embarrassed smile. "Lady Eleanor knows me well. I fear I am more a practical landlord than an elegant host, Miss Bennet."

Glancing from one to the other, Elizabeth said warmly, "I have always thought the success of a host was measured by his graciousness and manners rather than by his elegance and display of wealth."

Eleanor beamed at her, and then said quietly, "I told you she would understand."

They continued their pleasant conversation while the remainder of the party gathered. Elizabeth was determined not to watch for Mr. Darcy, though it took an inordinate amount of concentration to keep her eyes from drifting toward the carriages arriving on the gravel lane. She forced herself to focus on what Mr. Paxton was saying about recent events in the Peninsular War, a subject that would have caused any of the other ladies of the party to turn pale and fan themselves, but Eleanor engaged in a lively debate with him, keeping her voice quiet and calm to avoid drawing anyone's attention.

It did not seem fair that Mr. Darcy should take up residence in her mind. After Elizabeth had refused Mr. Collins' proposal of marriage, he had not impinged upon her consciousness as anything more than an embarrassment. Why was it she could not forget for a second that Mr. Darcy was nearby? She had barely noticed him most of the time until that night that he had made his ill-fated offer to her. He had not changed; only her understanding of him had altered. Why in the world could she not simply put him out of her mind for the space of a few minutes? Her resolve finally failed her when the servants began bringing around platters of food. She had expected him to join them by then. Taking the opportunity of being handed a plate to look around, she spotted him near the entrance to the ruins, engaged in conversation with Miss Elliot.

Her throat tightened, but she told herself it was only the natural result of recognizing again how deeply she must have wounded him. Of course, Miss Elliot was his social equal, and no doubt a more suitable companion for him than she was. Perhaps her harsh words had merely served to convince him that it had indeed been a mistake to associate with a woman so far his inferior. She blinked hard, blindly taking a forkful of meat to disguise her reaction. After all, why should she care what company he kept? He was nothing more than an ill-tempered man who had once admired her.

"Miss Bennet," said a deep voice by her elbow, and she turned to see Lord Charles holding two glasses of champagne. He held one out to her. "I thought you might be thirsty after such a long walk."

She might not trust him, but it was a relief to see a gentleman who was willing to smile at her. She took one of the glasses. "Thank you, though if you knew me well, you would be aware it was a short walk for me. I am a great walker and often will walk several miles for the sheer pleasure of it."

His smile widened. "Then perhaps I can convince you to take a stroll around the ruins after you have dined. They are more extensive than you might think."

No doubt they were also full of secluded crannies where he might hope to get her alone, but she would deal with that when it arose. Right now she was happy for the distraction. She handed her barely touched plate to a servant. "In fact, if you would like to go now, I find I have no appetite today."

"I am sorry to hear it." His eyes drifted down her body in a way that suggested he was speaking of a different sort of appetite. "Shall we walk then?" He offered her his arm.

Looking him in the eye, she folded her hands behind her back. "I would enjoy a walk, thank you."

He dropped his arm, his eyes full of laughter. "As you wish, Miss Bennet, but pray take care. The ground can be uneven here."

"I believe I can manage not to embarrass myself. I am more practiced at walking than at waltzing."

"You will never embarrass me," he said gallantly.

"Not even by my inferior birth?" she teased.

"If I did not know better, I would think you were a duke's daughter at the very least, which reminds me that I have not yet told you how lovely you look today. Your dress suits you."

"Thank you," she said in a tone of irony. "It belongs to Eleanor. Your stepmother did not wish me to disgrace her by appearing in my usual apparel. The gloves are also Eleanor's, and the diamond hairpins are your stepmother's second best. My shoes are my own, but that is only because Eleanor's do not fit me."

"If Eleanor were wearing it, she would not make me think of sunshine and fairies dancing, or that she moved with the grace of a wild gazelle."

Elizabeth gave him a dubious look. "I imagine men look at their sisters differently than other women regardless of what they wear."

"Ah, my Juliet, I would be proud to be seen with you whatever you wore."

"I am *not* your Juliet, and I imagine that if we were in London, you, like any other gentleman of your rank, would prefer to be seen with ladies of the *ton*, not a country miss." Men like Darcy would, at least.

"Perhaps I am not like any other gentleman of my rank. I pride myself on forming my own opinions, so it is not unusual for me to disagree with the conventional wisdom."

"So I have noticed," said Elizabeth with a laugh. "For example, you are the only person within miles who has not warned me against spending time with you."

He threw back his head and laughed. "Have they indeed? I wonder if I should be surprised that you have apparently not heeded their advice. Perhaps you also prefer to form your own opinions."

That tendency was what had led her to believe George Wickham's lies. "It depends on the circumstance. If you were, for example, to approach me when I was alone in a room, you would discover just how quickly I would heed their advice; however, I doubt there is anything you can say in public that would endanger my peace of mind."

He glanced at her sidelong, a smile playing around his lips. "Be careful, Miss Bennet, or I might take that as a challenge."

Crinkling her nose at him, she said, "That might be entertaining, I suppose, but you are starting at a disadvantage."

"I am?" He raised an eyebrow.

"The warnings were not to set my cap at you, or to think that your attentions toward me might be leading to a proposal. As I am quite aware of how ridiculous the idea of you proposing to me is, you cannot entice me with that. Besides, any continuing connection between us would require me to have further dealings with your stepmother, which is a very active deterrent."

"That is what I like about you, Miss Bennet. You make me laugh."

"Much like a Christmas pantomime, I expect! But I must tell you that I am unutterably bored with this entire matter of your questionable attentions to me, so I pray you to speak of something else." She said it with such sweetness and archness as to make it impossible to take offense.

"Your wish is my command. What shall we discuss, then?"

"Whatever you like, I suppose."

Given the way his eyes flared, Elizabeth wondered if that response had been a wise one. But when he spoke, he said, "Tell me, then, is something troubling Eleanor?"

She looked at him in surprise. "Should you not be asking *her* that?"

"Perhaps, but I doubt she would tell me. Eleanor keeps her own counsel, and while I may be her favorite brother, it is only in the way that Wellington has a favorite regiment in the enemy army. But I *am* concerned for her, so I am asking you."

Elizabeth shrugged, uncomfortable with the question. "I do not know why you would think something is troubling her."

"And there is the answer to my question, for if nothing were troubling her, you would have said so without hesitation."

He was quick-witted; she would have to give him that. "Perhaps she is troubled by having so many interfering brothers," she said with a sly smile.

"Whether you believe it or not, Miss Bennet, it is sometimes within my power to help my sister, and on occasion I might even be moved to do so." Despite his flippant words, there was an air of sincerity.

Although she doubted anyone could help, perhaps he had enough sway with Lord Bentham to stop the betrothal, or at least delay it. There was no reason she had to mention the existence of another man. "I believe she is less than happy that her betrothal is happening so quickly."

"I cannot blame her, although in *some* ways she could do much worse than Lord Deyncourt." His lips twisted as if he found the idea distasteful.

"She also says it is not as bad as it could be, just that it is too soon. It is different for gentlemen – you bring home a wife, but nothing else changes. When a woman marries, everything is changed; she leaves behind her family, her home, and everyone she knows to live with strangers, all of whom are accustomed to each other but not to her. It can be a frightening prospect, especially when one does not know one's husband well."

To her surprise, he seemed to ponder that. "I had never looked at it that way before."

"I do not know if it is possible, but a little delay might put her mind at ease."

"I see. I hope she is not still pining after that Paxton fellow."

"Mr. Paxton?" Elizabeth did her best to inject surprise into her tone. "They are friends, but that is all." Eleanor had said something about having her brother ask her father about the marriage possibility, had she not? This would not be the right time to focus Lord Charles's attention on the matter. Perhaps a little distraction might help both Eleanor and her. "If anything, I think she might develop a bit of a *tendre* for his friend Mr. Darcy, but it hardly matters."

"Darcy would be an acceptable match for her, I suppose," he said thoughtfully. "Not what we had hoped for, but I can see several advantages to it."

Now what had she done? It was bad enough that everyone thought Mr. Paxton was courting *her*. What would they do if the family started to believe that Eleanor should marry Darcy? This was starting to sound like one of Shakespeare's plays about mismatched lovers. All that they would need was a scene where she and Eleanor disguised themselves as each other to be married to the correct man.

But that would mean Elizabeth herself would be married to Mr. Darcy! What in the world was she thinking? Quickly she said, "I do not think it is anything of note; after all, they just met a few days ago, and I believe Mr. Darcy has no particular interest in marriage at the moment." That part was true, at least. He must be grateful now that she had turned down his proposal.

"A pity; it would be such a simple solution. But perhaps I can think of a reason to give to my father why Eleanor's marriage should be delayed."

"That it is causing her worry is not reason enough?"

"Oh, no. Mere sentiments do not count to him. He is more likely to be swayed if I say that I have heard a rumor about Lord Deyncourt being in debt to moneylenders, and if he would give me some time, I could likely find out the truth of it before we have tied Eleanor to a spendthrift who would be forever dunning us for money."

"Surely you would not say such a thing about an innocent man!"

He shrugged. "It would make no difference since I would eventually report back that there was no truth to the rumor. It is the only way to manage the old man – to concoct a story for why such-and-such should happen, then to encourage him to think it was all his idea in the first place." Lord Charles lowered his voice. "He is stubborn, but rather gullible. I learned the trick watching my stepmother. She is a true proficient at it."

How could he speak so easily about deceiving his father to a mere acquaintance? Admittedly, she had just prevaricated to him about Mr. Paxton, but that was hardly the same thing as deliberately lying to one's father to achieve a desired end. She had been starting to let down her guard to him when he expressed his worry about Eleanor, but this was a reminder that he did not share her values.

She realized he was watching her. "I have shocked you, have I not? It is the fashion to hide one's failings whenever possible. I prefer to be honest about mine. My father is an odd mixture of parts – easily persuaded by others, yet autocratic if confronted directly. On occasion this means that he makes poor decisions. If I were always to tell him the truth, he would dismiss me out of hand, and oftentimes innocent people would suffer for it. I do not have trouble squaring it with my conscience."

Increasingly uncomfortable with the intimate nature of this conversation, Elizabeth gave him a playful look and said teasingly, "Of course, some of your detractors would tell me that is because you have no conscience."

His smile in response looked somehow tight. "They may believe that if it gives them comfort. I find life too complex for simple answers like that, especially when it includes situations like Lord Deyncourt's interest in Eleanor, which is both complex and disturbing."

Tilting her head, Elizabeth said, "I have heard Eleanor's opinion of him. The worst seems to be that he is a fop and she has nothing in common with him, but it appears you find more in him to object to. Is there something she should know about him?"

"She is probably better off not knowing, though she will discover it soon enough."

She crossed her arms across her chest. "Well?"

He smiled down at her. "What?"

"You obviously wish me to ask what this secret is, but my surest means of disappointing you is to ask nothing about it."

He looked away for a moment, his brows furrowed. "In fact, I am only attempting to stay in your good graces. If I told you what it is, you would accuse me of trying to shock you or to despoil your innocence."

"Since I almost always think that of you, it seems quite likely that this would be no different," she said with a laugh. "But if it will make you feel better, I will acquit you in advance of any such intentions – but only on this particular subject." Despite her teasing air, she wanted quite badly to know what had affected his opinion about Lord Deyncourt.

"Very well, if you must know, he is her lover."

"How dare you!" she cried indignantly. "He is nothing of the sort. Eleanor does not even *like* him."

"I am not speaking of Eleanor." His expression oddly sober, he held her gaze as if trying to communicate something.

If not Eleanor, whom could he mean? She knew no one in the *ton* except her fellow guests, and it would be too dangerous for an unmarried woman to take a lover. Then, with a shock, she realized whom he meant, and blushed furiously. He had been right about one thing – he had indeed shocked her. "Surely she would not..." she said weakly.

"Why not? Most married women in the *ton* take lovers."

"Does your father know?"

He considered this. "I doubt it. He would not have agreed to the match with Eleanor if he did. He is too old-fashioned for that sort of thing."

Her eyebrows flew up. "And you are not?"

To her surprise, he looked as if she had slapped him. "We would not be having this conversation if it did not trouble me. I especially do not like the idea of *her* having the power to influence Eleanor's husband."

Elizabeth could hardly believe they were having this conversation. "I did not mean to imply...oh, I do not know what I mean!"

"Perhaps you understand better now why I am willing to deceive my father to delay the betrothal. Eleanor would be better off married to someone like Darcy who is not subject to my stepmother's wiles. But I have no say in that since *my* situation with my father is also complex. If I were his heir, he would listen to me, but neither of us knows whether I am or not."

This seemed a much safer topic. "That would seem to be a simple question, in as much as you have an elder brother."

"I do, though whether he is still alive is another question."

"He is travelling abroad, is he not?"

"That is one way to put it. I suppose Eleanor told you that?" At her nod, he continued. "She has never wanted to face the facts when it comes to Edward. The truth is that he is in exile."

"In exile?"

"Four years ago he killed a man in a duel. He fled the country before he could be charged with murder. He went to Europe initially, and as far as we know, he is still there, but we have heard nothing since his first month there."

"He does not write to you?" Somehow this silence seemed more shocking than a duel.

"No, but I cannot blame Edward for that. My father told him never to contact us again. Edward obeyed him, and as a result, we do not know where he is, how he is managing to live, or even if he is still alive. It is disturbing, to say the least."

"He cannot write to any of you? That seems very harsh."

Lord Charles shrugged. "My father was furious with him, more about the events that led up to the duel than the duel itself. My brother had always been rash, but it was a shock to discover he had become dishonest."

"Really?" Elizabeth injected a touch of skepticism in her voice.

"Yes, really. You have no doubt been told horror stories about my depravity, but what he did – or what they said he did – is something even I would not do. He cheated in a contest with another man. Pardon me; I should not have said even that much. You are so easy to talk to that I forgot myself." He seemed genuinely shaken.

"I am not offended," she said gently. "You sound as if you were uncertain of the truth of it."

He took his time about answering, looking up toward the sky for a short time, then down at his boots. "At some level, I cannot believe it. The brother I knew would never have done such a thing. If I had not been told it by so many sources, I would say it was a lie. Of course, you might say that I am just choosing not to believe it, but my brother was a good man. Not perfect, but not a liar and a cheat."

"It sounds as if you miss him."

"I do. And I miss knowing what is in my future. It was all planned out – Edward was the heir, I was to go into the military, and my younger brother was for the church. But after Edward was exiled, my father bought a commission for my younger brother instead, while I have no purpose, since I am neither heir nor able to pursue a career. If Edward does return someday, I do not know what I will do."

"What would you *like* to do?"

He spoke without hesitation. "I would like to be a diplomat. War only exists when there is a failure of diplomacy. That would seem to be the best place to put our efforts."

She smiled, though she could not help thinking that a diplomat's life would be much more comfortable than a soldier's, and wondered how much that influenced this spoiled young nobleman. "I imagine you would make a good diplomat, though you might have to change your ways to avoid jeopardizing relationships with our allies."

He laughed. "How right you are. But the only other thing I would enjoy doing would cause my father to have an apoplexy on the spot, so it is better for me to think of diplomacy."

It was clear he hoped that she would ask. "And what is that?"

"You must not tell a soul, or I will never live it down." His eyes took on a faraway look. "I would like to breed dogs."

Elizabeth was so startled by this response that she almost tripped over a small stone. "Really, my lord?" she asked with a laugh. "Somehow I imagine you would miss the excitement of London."

He seemed surprised at the question. "I have never liked London. I prefer the countryside, and there is nothing I enjoy more than working with dogs. All of the Carlisles are mad for animals, and I am no exception. And now you are laughing at me."

"Just surprised and confused. If you dislike London, why do you live there, even when the Season is over? You have a country home here, one of the most beautiful in England."

"Aye, there's the rub." The bitter twist of his lips was back. "Bentham Park is beautiful, but it comes with the price of living with my father and stepmother. My father expects me to live either here or in London. Since I cannot live with them, London it must be."

"Yet you are here now and do not seem unhappy."

"I was commanded to return for this house party, so I have done so. And you would accuse me of wild flattery if I told you that the only thing that makes it bearable is your company and that of Eleanor, so I shall not say it, even if it is true."

"Most people would say that my charms pale beside those of Bentham Park," she said lightly. "While I have no particular fondness for your stepmother, and I would be happy never to hear another of her etiquette pointers or lectures on the importance of my deportment, I fail to credit that she could drive you from your home."

His lips pursed as if he had tasted something sour. "You know, I assume, how my father came to marry her?

"I have heard rumors," she said carefully. When he raised an eyebrow, she added, "One person told me she trapped him."

"It was at a soiree given by a very fashionable hostess. My father was given a message that someone needed to speak to him urgently in the library, and when he went there, he found her in a state of dishabille. He chose to be chivalrous and offer her the protection of his name. He did not realize she had done it intentionally."

"An unfortunate beginning, I agree."

"*That* is not the unfortunate part for me. Entrapments happen; it is part of life, and at least she is young, pretty, and capable of handling her role as Marchioness. However, under ordinary circumstances she would not have been able to gain entrance to an event of the sort my father would attend. She was only at the soiree because *I* brought her there."

"Oh, dear." She had not expected that.

"It was not a coincidence. She did not possess the connections needed to enter the exclusive circles where the wealthiest nobles travel. But she *could* approach me, since I am only a second son. She was charming, lovely, and most attentive to me; I was young and gullible. When she said she wished to meet my family, I thought it meant that she cared for me. I brought her to the soiree so that she could meet my father. She made an excuse to leave me for a few minutes, and the next time I saw her was when my father announced his engagement to her."

Elizabeth winced. "I am sorry to hear it. It is no wonder you are uncomfortable with the situation."

He shrugged. "Fortunately, I was not so enamored of her that I could not recognize she had done it all deliberately. Had I any doubts, they would have been put to rest when I discovered my brother Edward had received an identical message at an earlier event to which I had taken her. Women were always trying to trap him, and he saw through it at once, so she had to settle for my father. And *that*, my dear Miss Bennet, is why I do not like coming to Bentham Park."

"That is understandable." In truth, she hardly knew what to say. The story itself was less shocking than that he had told her such a personal and painful tale. Their brief acquaintance did not merit such confidences. It reminded her of Mr. Wickham, who had poured out his fabricated tale of woe at their first meeting, and she had failed to see the impropriety of it. This seemed different, though. Lord Huntingdon did not seem to be trying to influence her views as much as explaining his own.

"And on top of it all, she dislikes dogs." He sounded indignant now.

"I beg your pardon?"

"She dislikes dogs. I do not mind my father having a beautiful young wife, even if she is extravagant, and she seems to try to make him happy. But she *dislikes dogs*. Can you believe it?"

She laughed. "It seems you find that more disturbing than all the rest!"

"Sometimes I think it is," he said, half under his breath. "What sort of person dislikes dogs? I hope *you* do not dislike them, Miss Bennet."

"I would not dare to tell you if I did! But you may rest easy, as Eleanor can attest that I am quite fond of them. She had a spaniel named Maisie who was our constant companion for years."

"I remember her. She slept in Eleanor's bed. Maisie's brother Herodotus was mine, and I would make myself ill with missing him when I went off to school. My grandmother still has some of their descendants."

"I have seen no dogs at Bentham Park on this visit."

"*She* thinks dogs do not belong in the house. She and my grandmother fought constantly about the dogs. My grandmother left after my stepmother hired a new kennel-master who was unkind to the dogs, and she took the family spaniels with her. Eventually my father shut down the kennel altogether, and his two hunting dogs are cared for by the gamekeeper. We used to have the finest kennels in Yorkshire."

"I take it your father is not as mad for animals as the rest of you?"

"Oh, he is! Sometimes I think my father only hunts so that he can be with the dogs. But I can guarantee one thing: no matter whether Edward inherits or I do, Bentham Park will be full of dogs again." He said it with an odd ferocity.

"And your stepmother will be living in the kennels?" suggested Elizabeth with a laugh. While she still would not trust Lord Charles alone with her in a room, she had to admit that today she had found him more likable. When he shed his pretenses and flirtation, he had greater depths than she expected.

"Do not tempt me!" he said with a smile.

Chapter 5

UNDER ORDINARY CIRCUMSTANCES, Darcy would have been interested to hear tales of his father's youth. These were not ordinary circumstances, though; and when the tales consisted primarily of recounting details of cricket matches that took place long before he was born, it was all he could do to remain civil to Lord Bentham. The carriage ride had been short, but the wait for the carriage had stretched forever after Elizabeth and the others disappeared into the gardens on their way to the ruins. His mind kept presenting him images of Carlisle beside her, talking to her, touching her, coldly calculating the seductive potential of each look and word.

By the time the carriage reached the ruins, Darcy felt as if he had eaten rocks for breakfast. Lord Bentham was still speaking to him, but Darcy could not stop himself from looking over his shoulder in an attempt to locate Elizabeth. She was not in his line of sight, but he saw Carlisle chatting with Miss Elliot. Hot relief flooded through him. Nothing terrible could have happened in just this half hour when they were in company with so many other people.

His breathing easier, he turned back to Lord Bentham and nodded as if he had been listening to him all along. Fortunately, his lordship did not seem to require any input from Darcy to enjoy his recounting of the past.

Once they dismounted from the carriage, another one of the guests caught Lord Bentham's attention. Darcy took immediate advantage of the opportunity to walk a few paces ahead, hoping for a glimpse of Elizabeth. If he could find Lady Eleanor, Elizabeth could not be far away, but he could not spot her golden hair either. Where had they taken themselves off to?

"Mr. Darcy," trilled a feminine voice beside him. Darcy recognized Miss Elliot's honeyed tones and resigned himself to yet another delay. Miss Elliot would not allow him to slip away easily. Her sights, like those of so many other young women, were set on the position of Mistress of Pemberley. Little did she know that looking for a bride was the last thing he wanted to do at the moment! Even if he wanted one, she would not be the sort he would choose. Her birth was good, but her vanity and artificial charm grated on him even in brief encounters. He could not imagine spending the remainder of his life with her.

He would be civil to her, though, if for no other reason than that he would not allow Elizabeth to catch him being anything less than amiable to anyone. Of course, he had not been amiable with Elizabeth herself when they danced. He had wanted to shake her when she dismissed his warning about Carlisle. One minute furious with her, the next wanting to hold her in his arms and comfort her, the next wanting to...best not even think about what he wanted to do next.

A sharp rap on his arm roused him from his reverie. Miss Elliot held her fan poised to strike again. "Mr. Darcy, I begin to question whether you are listening to me!" she said flirtatiously.

He floundered for a moment. "I was momentarily awed by the magnificence of the ruins." True enough, but only when considering the ruins of his former love for Elizabeth Bennet.

"Oh, the ruins," she said dismissively. "They are very picturesque, I suppose. The sun is quite warm, is it not?"

He was about to reply that he found it pleasantly cool when he recalled that she was speaking the language of the *ton*. A reference to warmth meant that she wished him to offer to bring her a cool drink.

With an inward sigh, he said, "I believe I see a bowl of lemonade over there. Perhaps a drink might refresh you. May I have the honor of bringing you one?" How he *hated* these games!

"That sounds lovely, Mr. Darcy." She batted her eyelashes at him.

At least fetching the lemonade gave him the opportunity to inspect the area. After a moment, he spotted Elizabeth seated with Paxton and Lady Eleanor. Now that he knew she was safe, annoyance replaced his earlier worry. Why could she not simply have listened to his warnings about Carlisle? Was she deliberately trying to make his life difficult? He returned to Miss Elliot and handed her the lemonade with a forced smile.

Miss Elliot now seemed to expect him to partner her for the remainder of the event. Darcy had a sudden urge to plead illness and return to Hillington Hall where he would not have to make dull conversation with a lady with neither cleverness nor humor to enliven their interaction. Alas, he had promised Paxton he would help by coming to the house party, and he still did not trust Carlisle. The thought made him glance over to Elizabeth's group. Elizabeth was no longer there, only Paxton and Lady Eleanor in close conference. With a sense of dread, he began to look around openly, hoping to spy either Elizabeth or Carlisle. Neither was in sight.

His heart pounding, he said, "Excuse me, Miss Elliot. I have only just remembered an urgent message I must give to Mr. Paxton." He bowed and left quickly, before she could say a word. She would no doubt be angry at this cavalier treatment, but he no longer cared.

Darcy strode across the clearing to where Paxton and Lady Eleanor sat in the shadow of the far wall. After the briefest of greetings, he said, "Miss Bennet is not with you today?"

Lady Eleanor gestured to her left, then stopped. "She was right here talking to Charles...." Her voice trailed off for a moment. "Oh, what a beast he is! Come, Geoffrey, we must find them. Pardon me, Mr. Darcy."

"Lady Eleanor, I believe we share the same concern," Darcy said urgently. "I will look for them as well."

She gave him an assessing look. "I will go with you. Geoffrey knows the ruins well enough to search on his own. We can start with the cloisters."

Had he not been so worried, he would have been impressed by Lady Eleanor's assertiveness. Instead, he led off in the direction she indicated, ducking his head to step through a low stone arch.

Lady Eleanor peered into a dark corner. "They have not been gone long, so they cannot be far."

How many minutes were required to compromise a woman's reputation? If Charles Carlisle was involved, Darcy suspected it was a very short time indeed. The next doorway led into a room where the arched roof was still intact, supported by rows of columns. Enough light came in through the empty window openings to show that no one was there.

"Watch your step here," warned Lady Eleanor, pointing to a half-buried lintel. "This takes us into a corridor that runs the length of the abbey."

It was like a maze, the twists and turns causing him to lose all sense of direction. The shadows finally gave way to bright sunlight as they entered a roofless chapel. Darcy halted abruptly as he spotted the two figures at the far end. Elizabeth was sitting on a fallen pillar while Carlisle towered over her, one booted foot resting on the pillar just inches from her. His hands clenching into fists, Darcy forced himself to remain where he stood. He did not trust his temper, or rather he trusted too well it would lead him into a situation best avoided.

His companion seemed to have no such reservations. Lady Eleanor stalked toward the two of them. "Charles, how absolutely *lovely* of you to show Miss Bennet the ruins," she said in a voice laden with irony. "Especially after I most particularly asked you *not* to do so."

Straightening, Carlisle laughed and chucked his sister under the chin. "Since when do I take my orders from my *little* sister?" he said lazily. "Besides, there is no harm that could befall us here. There are dozens of people within calling distance, not to mention servants swarming everywhere." He turned an intimate smile on Elizabeth. "Besides, your Miss Bennet is quite able to keep me in my place."

Elizabeth stood and dusted off her hands, then paled as she caught sight of Darcy. "Of course, I have not yet figured out what your place is, though I am quite certain it is not in a church, ruined or not."

Lady Eleanor motioned to Darcy. "Would you be so kind, sir, as to conduct Miss Bennet back to the party? I have a few things I would like to say to my brother. Alone."

Lord Charles raised an amused eyebrow. "What a shockingly bossy wench you have become, Eleanor. I think I will join Miss Bennet and Darcy instead."

Raising her chin, Eleanor said, "If you would prefer that I speak my piece in front of them, we can do it that way. I would simply prefer not to embarrass either Miss Bennet or Mr. Darcy with our private business."

"Oh, very well. Miss Bennet, I will see you again *very* soon."

Elizabeth looked from one of them to the other, then gave Darcy a long, serious look. "I can see that any hope of a peaceful day is in vain, so perhaps returning is my best option. Mr. Darcy?"

He nodded, unwilling to trust his voice, and gestured silently toward the corridor.

As soon as Darcy and Elizabeth had disappeared, Charles crossed his arms and

spoke in a tone of insufferable patience. "Well?"

"There is no need to bother with that. You know what I have to say. I want you to leave Elizabeth alone. She is my friend and I do not want her to be hurt for your amusement."

"My dearest Eleanor, I have no intention of hurting her. She is a lovely girl. Although you may not believe it, I enjoy talking to her."

She stared at him with wordless fury for a minute. "You are truly despicable. I am ashamed to be your sister, not that I suppose it means anything to you. All you care about are your so-called friends. I thought you had learned something from what happened to Mary Lynley, but you just do not care, do you?"

"There is no need for dramatics. I did not force Mary Lynley to do anything she did not wish to do, and I am sure she would say the same."

"That is very easy to say, is it not, when you know full well she will never say anything again!"

He gave a deep sigh. "She made the choice to leave London. It is hardly the end of the world."

She marched over to him until she stood just inches away. "You really do not know, do you? You never even bothered to ask what happened to her."

"Very well, I never asked, but I can see that you wish to tell me, so let us get this over with. I have better things to do than to be lectured by my little sister about matters which she does not understand."

Eleanor took a deep breath, then spoke slowly and clearly. "Mary was taken from London last spring, and two months later she took her own life."

He grew suddenly pale and still. "I do not believe you. She would not have done such a thing."

"Feel free to make your own inquiries, and you will discover the truth. What did you expect her to do when she found herself abandoned by you and then cast off by her family when the evidence of what you did could no longer be hidden? You stole her future and then her life, all for a few minutes of pleasure. I hope it was worth it to you." She spat out the last words, then shook her head slowly. "But you really do not care. Well, stay away from Lizzy. She deserves better than to become your discarded toy." Her voice was shaking by her last words, and she ran off without looking at him.

Her brother watched after her, his lips tightly pinched.

84

"So, Mr. Darcy, you seem to have decided that I needed to be rescued," said Elizabeth as they left Carlisle and Lady Eleanor alone in the ruined chapel.

Darcy had not yet mastered his fury at Carlisle, making it that much more difficult to answer Elizabeth with patience, especially when she had chosen to disregard his warnings. "In my opinion, you did, and Lady Eleanor appears to have agreed with me."

Her nostrils flared. "Did it never occur to you that I am perfectly capable of taking care of myself?"

His temper snapped. "Did it never occur to *you* that he is stronger than you are? He is not one of your tame fellows from Meryton. Perhaps he could not persuade you to reckless behavior, but your refusal would not stop him from taking what he wanted."

"There were more than enough people who would have heard had I called for help." Her face was white.

"Being within hailing distance of others is of very little use when his hand is clamped over your mouth, and merely being seen in that position by anyone coming to your aid would be enough to ruin you. Do not think Carlisle is above taking advantage of that fact." Damn it, he knew better than to say things like this to any woman, much less Elizabeth, but he seemed unable to stop the words from pouring forth.

The stubborn set of her jaw showed that she still did not believe him. "I have no desire to hear another word from you on this subject." She began walking faster.

His longer legs kept up with her easily as he burned with helpless fury. How could she be such a fool? No one could be that naïve. He had seen her take risks before – long walks alone through the countryside, showing no hesitation in being alone in a gentleman's company – but what he had taken as boldness now seemed more like foolhardiness. Almost as foolish as a woman with no prospects turning down a proposal from one of the most eligible men in England.

The passageway branched ahead, and he indicated the pathway to the right. That was how he and Lady Eleanor had come, was it not? His sense of direction was excellent, and it was odd that he would even have to consider the choice for a moment. Today, however, that sense of direction failed him since, after turning a final corner, they found themselves in a doorway facing out onto the riverbank. "My apologies; I must have taken the wrong turn," said Darcy.

"It is easy to do. Shall we try again?" Her voice was clipped.

"Of course. I must have missed something." He glanced up at the sun to regain his orientation. Yes, that was it, he had lost track of the direction.

As they re-entered the ruin, Elizabeth looked as if she would like to be anywhere but by his side. Small wonder, given how he had spoken to her! What had happened to him? He prided himself on control of his temper, but even the slightest glimpse of Elizabeth in Carlisle's company set his blood boiling. No matter how hard he tried to ignore it, he could hear Carlisle's drawling voice in his mind, detailing with great specificity his plans for Elizabeth's seduction. And since Elizabeth did not seem to take his warnings seriously, what could he do? Carlisle would never back down on his wager, and Darcy could hardly challenge him to a duel for making a bet. Elizabeth would certainly not thank him for making his interest in her known. No, his only choice was to wait until it was too late, no matter how agonizing it might be.

In the meantime, all he was accomplishing was to drive Elizabeth further away from him. She still had her arms wrapped around her as if to protect herself. Perhaps he should apologize to her, no matter how much against the grain it went. After all, he had been attempting to protect her! But if he did not, she would consider it as one more example of his ungentlemanly conduct. He cleared his throat. "Miss Bennet, I hope you will permit me to apologize for the intemperate nature of my words earlier. Since I have seen the unfortunate results of Lord Charles's predilection for making mischief...well, I will say no more on that subject except that I would have responded in much the same manner if I had found him with my sister."

Elizabeth's shoulders seemed to relax, although she still did not look at him. "Would your sister be more temperate in her response to you?"

He struggled to find an answer that would not seem a criticism of Elizabeth's response. "Georgiana looks up to me more as a father than a brother," he said finally. "In truth, the situation would not have arisen, since I would not have permitted her to remain at the house party given Lord Charles's presence."

She shot him a look out of the corner of her eyes. "It is unfortunate for you, then, that I am not so tractable."

Under the circumstances, it was more than unfortunate; it was a potential disaster, but saying so would not accomplish anything. "You have livelier spirits than Georgiana."

Fortunately for Darcy's sanity, they encountered Paxton just a few minutes later. After one look at Darcy's stormy face and Elizabeth's flushed one, Paxton fell into step beside Elizabeth and began calmly pointing out features of the ruins to her. She seemed grateful for the safe direction of conversation.

"You seem very knowledgeable about the abbey," she said.

Paxton inclined his head. "It has long been an interest of mine. Eleanor and I played hide-and-seek here when we were children. The sense of antiquity must have affected me, for I found myself studying the history of the dissolution of the monasteries at Cambridge. When I was home, I would come to draw the ruins, though perhaps I should not admit to that. I did not have an invitation." He smiled confidingly.

"It sounds unobjectionable," said Elizabeth. "But if you came down the lane, it must have been obvious in any case."

He shook his head. "When we were children, Eleanor's parents did not want her to spend time with me, so I was accustomed to using hidden ways. My lands are on the other side of the river, and there was a rock fall years ago that left large boulders in the river. We called them our stepping-stones when we were young, though even then they were more treacherous than real stepping-stones. More than once I slipped and had a soaking."

"And once," came Eleanor's voice from behind them, "he hit his head on one of the rocks, and I had to drag him to the shore and bind his wounds. My nurse was scandalized when I came home soaked to the skin and with my petticoat torn to rags."

"How did you explain that?" asked Elizabeth with a laugh.

Eleanor shrugged. "I told her my brothers had thrown me in the river because I was following them. It sounded enough like something they would do that she accepted it."

"They must have denied it, though," Elizabeth said as they stepped out into the main clearing.

"I do not recall. Most likely she never thought to ask them since no one would have punished them for it anyway. They were incorrigible little savages."

As far as Darcy was concerned, at least one of them still was an incorrigible savage, now full-grown and more dangerous. He still did not trust himself enough to speak to Elizabeth. How could he be civil to her when she had ignored his warning and put herself in danger? And now she was angry with *him* for his interference, even though Lady Eleanor had been the one to confront Carlisle. Perhaps Elizabeth thought he had convinced her friend to intervene.

This entire pointless endeavor was making his head ache. How had it turned from a matter of providing an entrée for Paxton into one where his primary goal was to protect Elizabeth, preferably without murdering Carlisle? Elizabeth did not even wish to be protected, any more than she wished him to love her. Around and around, everywhere he looked, love and its evil twin, lust, were causing heartache rather than happiness. It was all swirling together into a mass of fractured color. He closed his eyes against the burning glare.

Paxton's voice seemed to boom in his ear. "Darcy! I say, Darcy, are you ill?"

Ill? Everything was ill. The world was ill. "Just the sun," he somehow managed to say despite the invisible knives driven into his skull.

"One of your megrims?"

Darcy moved his throbbing head slightly in agreement. It felt like a major accomplishment.

"Should I take you home?"

"There is no need." Even the thought of mounting a horse made his stomach churn.

Elizabeth's melodious voice flowed past him, a channel of calm in the storm. "My sister and my father have spells like this." Her features swam before him, her fine dark eyes looking at him with concern. Speaking quietly, she said, "Perhaps we should go back into the ruins where it is dark and quiet. Would that help?"

He thought he thanked her, but perhaps it was only in his mind. She took him gently by the arm and led him into a blessedly dark and cool passageway.

"Would you like to sit?" Elizabeth pointed to a recessed bench.

He lowered himself onto it, then carefully leaned back and closed his eyes. Resting his head against the wall, he felt the soothing chill held by the rough sandstone blocks even on a summer's day. It helped to diminish the throbbing in his head to a more bearable level.

"Is there anything I can bring you for your present relief, sir? Some wine, perhaps?" Her voice echoed in the close space, even though she spoke softly.

Darcy had almost forgotten Elizabeth's presence. Embarrassed, he opened his eyes. Between the darkness and the blurring of his vision, he could not see her clearly, but it did not matter. He had memorized her appearance long ago. "I thank you, no. Pray return to the others and accept my gratitude for your assistance." This was not how he wished to appear to her – weak and in pain.

Her skirts rustled as she sat on the other end of the bench. "I am glad to assist. Jane and my father both suffer terribly when the megrim is upon them."

"You do not have them?"

"No, fortunately I have been spared that."

"They often run in families. My sister has had them since she was a child." Speaking was hard work, but the sound of her voice was soothing, and for once she did not sound angry with him.

"I am sorry to hear it, though it must be some relief to her to have a brother who understands and does not believe it to be merely a nervous temperament."

"Perhaps." It was a painful point. His father had often told him to control himself rather than let the megrim get the best of him, as if he had any choice in the matter. "Mine are usually not severe enough to interfere with my activities. This is worse than most." Why was he telling her these things?

"It happens to Jane when there is a change in the weather. When she takes to her bed, my mother orders all the laundry to be brought inside since it is as good as a guarantee of rain in the offing. Perhaps for you it is the sun, not rain."

"This is unusual for me. Most often it happens in crowded rooms, when there is too much noise or too many people talking. Gatherings, balls, assemblies, and the like." He did not want to mention that anger was the other thing that often brought on an attack. He had learned to control his temper because of it, but it did not work where Elizabeth was concerned. His last bad megrim had been after their quarrel at Hunsford.

"You and my father have something in common then. That is why he rarely attends events. Even the noise in our household is often too much for him, so he stays in his library."

"I envy him that. Oftentimes my position requires me to attend events that I would prefer to avoid. I have learned to manage it, but it is not a pleasant experience."

She was silent so long that he turned to look at her, but her gaze remained fixed on her hands. Finally she said, "The first time I saw you was at an assembly in Meryton. Was that an unpleasant experience for you, then?"

He winced with the memory. "Very. I do not know how I managed to dance at all that evening. The room was spinning around me." When she did not reply again, he said, "Why do you ask?"

She hesitated. "You did not appear to be enjoying the occasion."

"I have little talent at disguising my sentiments at times like that."

"I am surprised you agreed to attend so much of the house party under the circumstances."

His mouth twisted. "Paxton is an old friend, and I would do more than that on his behalf." Megrim or not, he had the sense not to tell her that he had no choice once he discovered Carlisle's plans.

"It often helps my father if I put pressure on certain parts of his hands. The apothecary taught me to do it. It must sound impossibly forward, and I do not mean it that way, but if you would like, I could try that with you." She sounded hesitant.

"Miss Bennet, believe me, I know enough to acquit you of any forwardness toward me," he said dully. "You are the only female of my acquaintance from whom I need not fear entrapment."

"Forgive me," she said stiltedly. "No doubt you have been long desiring my absence. I will trouble you no further."

He could feel the movement of the air as she stood. The prospect of her leaving made his head throb anew. "Pray forgive me, Miss Bennet. I should not have said that. I appreciate your concern and am happy to try any remedy you suggest."

She stopped, but it was a long minute before she turned to face him. "Are you certain that is what you wish?" Her voice was flat.

"Yes." He gestured to the bench beside him. "What should I do?"

"If you will give me your hand then."

Managing somehow to restrain himself from saying that he had tried to do just that in April, he held out his hand silently. She put hers beneath it for support, then used her thumb and forefinger to press on the flesh that stretched between his thumb and his index finger, rubbing back and forth in small circles.

It could hardly be called a personal touch since they were both wearing gloves, but it was oddly soothing. If he were to close his fingers now, he would be holding her hand. How ironic that the one time Elizabeth Bennet was actually willing to touch him, he was too far gone to feel desire for her! Still, he could enjoy the pleasure of having her care for him, however briefly, and that he could watch her with no need for disguise.

Her pressure became firmer, and to his surprise, the pain in his head began to recede. It was still there, but it was somehow more tolerable. "That does help," he said.

He could see the corners of her mouth turn up in that familiar arch smile. "You need not sound so surprised."

"Frankly, anything that can ease a megrim is little short of miraculous in my mind."

"Here, let me try your other hand." She sounded amused, as well she might. "Try closing your eyes while I do it."

He obeyed, not least because of the danger inherit in looking at her lips. He must be feeling better if he could even think of wanting to kiss her! It was a pity her concern for him would never run that far. At least they were not quarrelling. That was an improvement. He wondered if it had occurred to her that if anyone were to discover them at this moment, her position would be quite compromising. Alone with him in a dark corner, holding his hand – no, it would not look innocent, even if it was. But he liked the pressure of her fingers on his hand, so he said nothing.

Apparently her mind was working along similar lines because she said, "It may comfort you to know that Lord Charles offered to show me this room, but I insisted on remaining outside. I am not quite as foolish as you may think."

"You should not be here with me now."

"Mr. Darcy, I know enough to acquit *you* of any plans to force yourself on me," she said with amusement, releasing his hand. "You must be feeling somewhat better if you are worried about appearances."

"It is not only appearances I worry about. Lord Charles has boasted publicly of his plan to...his plans for you, and has wagered two hundred guineas that he can win your favors. I hope you will pardon my bluntness, but I thought you should know."

He could almost feel her withdraw into herself, and he damned himself for once again saying the wrong thing, and just as they seemed to have reached some sort of peace. "Once again I must apologize to you, Miss Bennet. I did not mean to upset you."

She shook her head silently, folding her hands tightly together. "Who is aware of this...wager?" Her voice was unusually level.

"Several of the gentlemen attending the house party. He may have told others without my knowledge. And if you are angry at me for telling you this, you have the means for revenge in your hands. If it is discovered that I told you this much, there will be no gentleman here or in London who will not give me the cut direct. Revealing a bet is a violation of the code of honor."

Her laugh was a mirthless sound. "The code of *honor* – and this from gentlemen who are placing bets on whether my reputation can be ruined? Excuse me, Mr. Darcy; I find I suddenly have no taste for company."

When Elizabeth began to lead Mr. Darcy away, Eleanor glanced at Geoffrey. "If we follow, everyone will think the four of us are together."

His eyes lit up, and he lost no time in escorting her through the same archway, but where the others had turned right, Geoffrey pointed to the left, where they followed the outside wall of the abbey to the woods that backed on it. The path into the forest was one they both knew well, and as soon as the trees hid them from the abbey, they joined hands and laughed.

"A few moments of freedom – more precious than gold!" Eleanor said as she stepped into his embrace. She rested her face against his shoulder as his arms tightened convulsively around her. "Oh, how I have missed you!"

He pressed a kiss on her forehead. "My love, you have seen more of me in the last few days than ever before."

"True, but it is still not enough! It is so odd to see you at Bentham with my family and friends, and my father actually speaking to you on occasion. I keep pinching myself to prove it is real."

"You can thank Darcy for that. He is responsible for my presence. Your father is only tolerating me because he wants Darcy here."

"Well, then, I will be forever grateful to him. It has been heaven to be with you without fear of discovery – though I would like it even more if I did not have to keep a constant eye on my brother to keep him away from Elizabeth!"

"I wonder why Darcy was so concerned for Miss Bennet's whereabouts," Geoffrey said idly. "It is not like him."

"Perhaps he knows Charles too well."

"Darcy always makes a point of paying as little attention as possible to women so as not to raise their expectations. He was in love with a woman once, one who was socially inferior to him. Perhaps that is why he is protective of Miss Bennet – she may remind him of the woman who rejected him."

"And Elizabeth once refused the proposal of a wealthy landed gentleman, so there may be similarities."

Geoffrey looked at her, arrested. "You do not suppose that..."

She shook her head. "No, it cannot be. She said the gentleman she refused was very ill-tempered, and you have said that Mr. Darcy is very temperate and good-natured."

He smiled. "A pity – it was such a good theory. Then again, if I were only to judge Darcy by his behavior last night and then today, I might agree that his temper was not well regulated. Or perhaps it is only my own wish to solve Darcy's romantic difficulties that makes me consider it."

She looked up into his eyes. "Well, I imagine that if there is anything to it, we will know soon enough. After all, they are alone together in a dark place."

"And *we* are alone together in the woods."

In response, she pulled his face down to hers once more with unmistakable meaning.

It had taken Elizabeth the better part of a quarter hour to convince the maid that she wished to pack her own trunk, and even then it was only by promising never to breathe a word of it to anyone. Not that she was likely to do anything of the sort since she would be happiest if she never spoke to anyone at Bentham Park again, but she needed something to keep her busy. Without work to distract her, she would go mad.

She left out her brown muslin, the drabbest item in her wardrobe, to wear the following day. Dirt from the stagecoach would not show on it, and she had no wish to look attractive. That was what had brought her Lord Charles and Mr. Darcy.

The sound of the door opening made her look up from folding one of her last dresses. It was Eleanor, of course, still dressed for the picnic. "What happened?"

"It is traditional to knock," said Elizabeth sharply. This confrontation was inevitable, but she intended to stand her ground.

Eleanor closed the lid of the trunk and sat on it. "I was afraid you would not answer. Your maid came down to the picnic to tell me you were preparing to leave. Were you planning to go without even telling me?"

Elizabeth shook her head, her anger deflating. "No. I just did not wish to tell you in front of everyone." Not to mention that, at the time, she had still been angry with Eleanor for interfering when she had been with Lord Charles and for assuming that she, like a child, needed protecting. Even harder to forgive was the humiliating truth that Eleanor had been right, and she *had* needed to be protected. How could she have been starting to like Lord Charles?

"I could kill him! What did he do to you?"

"Mr. Darcy? Nothing." Nothing except make her realize what a fool she had been yet again. It was not his fault that she kept trusting the wrong men despite his warnings.

"Of course not. Charles."

"*He* did nothing but talk to me." Of course, he had also proved how very successfully he could manipulate her as well. It left a bitter taste in her mouth.

"You expect me to believe you are running away because Charles *talked* to you?"

"No, I do not expect you to believe that."

"Are you planning to give me any reason at all?"

Fortunately, she had prepared for this. "After I left Mr. Darcy, I overheard two gentlemen talking about your brother's bet – two hundred guineas on whether he could seduce me by the end of the house party. Apparently it is common knowledge among the men."

"What else?"

Elizabeth rounded on her. "Is that not enough? That all the gentlemen here are amusing themselves over the question of whether your brother will succeed in ruining me?"

"Lizzy," said Eleanor in a calming voice, "surely you already knew that my brother was hoping to seduce you."

"Of course I did!"

"And that everyone else knew it and was watching to see if he succeeded."

She had not thought about it in those particular terms. "Yes, but not that they were making a sport of ruining my life, and laughing about it!"

"They are not laughing at you but at Charles's games. At least one of them must think you will fend him off. Two hundred guineas, you say? You should be complimented. Charles is an accomplished seducer, and why would someone bet against a sure thing?"

"That was probably Mr. Darcy," Elizabeth said scornfully, "since he already knows I am not impressed by wealth or titles."

Eleanor raised an eyebrow. "I doubt it. If Mr. Darcy were the sort to bet on a woman's loss of virtue, Geoffrey would not consider him a close friend. Unless, perhaps, you have some knowledge of reprehensible actions on his part?"

"No," Elizabeth said flatly. She had been wrong about those, too.

"What would you expect the gentlemen to do?"

"They could have tried to stop him from doing it, or at least from bandying my name about like some sort of...some sort of...." But here her imagination failed her.

"Did you not tell me you were sick of everyone telling you to stay away from Charles? What was that, if not trying to stop him? Do you expect gentlemen who have just met you to offer to fight a duel over you? Certainly some of the men here are rakehells like Charles who care only for their own pleasure. They may be encouraging him and laughing about it, but that is what rakehells do. They have probably bandied about the name of every unprotected lady they have met. Certainly this is not the first time Charles has done something like this."

Mr. Darcy had warned her to stay away from Lord Charles, and she had been angry with him for it. She had thought she knew better than he did. "Has he always been like this? You used to like him, I thought."

"He changed when he grew up. He was the only one of my brothers who ever had time for me, and I loved him for that. But he was always Edward's shadow, wanting to be just like him, and when Edward went into exile, Charles just...turned into what he is now. As if he had to prove that he could be as bad as all the other rakehells in the *ton*. I hate it."

"I am glad not to be part of the *ton*, if tolerating this sort of behavior is the price of it." Exhausted, Elizabeth sat down on the side of the bed.

Eleanor sat next to her and put an arm around her shoulder. "You *cannot* leave now. Can you see how that would look? Everyone would assume that Charles had succeeded and you fled in shame. If word reached your family or friends, you would be ruined, even though you are perfectly innocent. Do not let Charles do that to you, I beg of you!"

"I cannot stay for more of this humiliation, knowing they are taking pleasure in the hope of ruining my life!"

"*You* have not been humiliated. Charles and the other rakes are the ones who have done something wrong. You have to show them that he could not fool you. You must cut him in front of them, poke fun at him, laugh condescendingly at his attempts to charm you. Choose one of the other men to flirt with just to prove how little Charles means to you. Then they will all see that he has no power over you," Eleanor said cajolingly. "I have faith in you."

Elizabeth covered her face with her hands. Eleanor was right; she did have to stay. Facing Lord Charles would not be a problem since she no longer felt anything but distaste for him. It would be hard not knowing who else was involved, but she could manage. No, the one she was afraid to face was Mr. Darcy. He had watched her make a fool of herself over Wickham, and now, instead of learning her lesson from that episode, she had believed herself capable of handling an even worse scoundrel, despite Mr. Darcy's specific warning. He must think her as silly and vain as her younger sisters, ready to believe any man who pretended to admire her – and he would be perfectly justified in that opinion.

Chapter 6

THE EVENING PROVED anticlimactic. Elizabeth had prepared herself to ignore Lord Charles, which also meant keeping her temper in check, but he did not appear either at dinner or afterward when the gentlemen rejoined the ladies and tables were set up for whist. In some ways, Elizabeth was sorry for his absence since it just delayed the inevitable meeting and left her more time to worry over it.

When the ladies withdrew, Lady Bentham made a point of sitting with Eleanor and Elizabeth. After inquiring regarding Elizabeth's enjoyment of the picnic, she said, "I saw you speaking with our neighbor Mr. Paxton. What do you think of him?"

Elizabeth forced herself not to glance at Eleanor. "He seems a pleasant gentleman whom I would like to know better."

Eleanor said demurely, "I hope you may have more opportunity for conversation with him, but it may be difficult since my dear brother seems quite enamored of your company."

In a quiet voice, Lady Bentham said, "Has Lord Charles been troubling you, Miss Bennet?"

"I could never call the company of such a gentleman troublesome, but I admit he is somewhat persistent." Taking her cue from Eleanor, Elizabeth pretended to be embarrassed by this admission.

"I see," said Lady Bentham. "Perhaps I will have a word with him. Tomorrow is the fishing party, and all the gentlemen will be enticing trout rather than ladies. As for the following day, I think you would enjoy seeing the famed gardens at Rosedale Park, Miss Bennet. The owners welcome visitors as long as they come in small parties. Perhaps Mr. Paxton and Mr. Darcy might agree to escort you and Eleanor there."

"That sounds delightful," said Elizabeth. "I am very fond of gardens."

"Excellent! I will make the arrangements tomorrow."

As her stepmother swept off to visit with her guests, Eleanor whispered, "Thank you."

Darcy was fortunate to have the excuse of the megrim to explain away his somber countenance that evening. He could not pretend to anything close to his normal spirits, and Paxton would have questioned him had he not believed the cause to be his illness. The day had been like boxing with an opponent who overmatched him, suffering one body blow after another. Now Elizabeth was packing her trunks to leave Bentham Park, and he was the one who had driven her away. Would Lady Eleanor be able to stop her, or would that all-too-brief encounter in the darkness prove to be the last time he ever saw Elizabeth Bennet?

Neither lady was present when he and Paxton stopped at the house on their way home, so he was left in suspense, unable to mourn her absence or even to understand what had distressed her so much. After all, he had been trying to help her. Nor were the ladies in evidence the following morning when the gentlemen presented themselves to join the fishing party. As if he wished to spend the day among all these men who only reminded him that he did not know what had happened to Elizabeth! He had been dreading spending the day in Carlisle's company, unable to speak his mind, but what occurred was even worse: Carlisle was not among the fishing party, and no one seemed to know his whereabouts. He could only hope to God he was not with Elizabeth. To top it all off, he could not even have a moment's peace since Lord Bentham had again chosen him as the recipient of his unending stories about his youthful adventures with Darcy's father.

By the end of the day, he was at the limits of his tolerance, and he still had no idea what to say or do if he saw Lady Eleanor and, dear God, Elizabeth again. Those minutes together when he had been the recipient of her sweet gentleness had only made him crave more of her compassion. Had he already lost his chance?

Under any other circumstances, he would have begged off visiting Bentham Park after the fishing expedition, but the hope of discovering whether Elizabeth had departed drew him there. Darcy told himself firmly it was only because he did not like remaining in suspense. Besides, it would please Paxton to have the opportunity to see Lady Eleanor.

Inside the house, the ladies had arranged themselves decoratively around the saloon, but Darcy knew immediately that Elizabeth was not there. He could feel it in the air, and her absence made his stomach clench. So that was the end of it, after all these months.

Lady Bentham stepped forward to greet them, asking after the fishing. After a little general discussion, she turned to Paxton. "Miss Bennet was telling me she has heard much praise of the gardens at Rosedale Park."

It was all Darcy could do not to interrupt and ask her ladyship what she meant, but Paxton said smoothly, "They are quite impressive. It would be a pity for her to miss them when we are so nearby. Perhaps I should ask her – and Lady Eleanor, of course – if they would like to make an excursion there. I am sure Darcy would enjoy the gardens as well, would you not, Darcy?"

Even with this direct a cue, Darcy almost stumbled over his words. "I would be delighted to escort Lady Eleanor and Miss Bennet there." At least he had managed to remember to mention Lady Eleanor first.

"What a splendid notion!" Lady Bentham said, as if she had not all but ordered them to do precisely that.

Paxton said, "I do not see Miss Bennet or Lady Eleanor here today."

Of course! Darcy had not even thought to look for Lady Eleanor. Elizabeth would be with her friend.

"My daughter has a touch of a headache and has remained upstairs. All the excitement yesterday may have been too much for her delicate constitution. I believe Miss Bennet is keeping her company."

Delicate constitution? From all Darcy had heard from Paxton, Lady Eleanor was capable of climbing to the top of the tower at the ruins without any ill effects.

"I am sorry to hear it," said Paxton. "I hope it is nothing serious."

"I am certain she will be well by tomorrow. In fact, it appears that she is coming down after all."

Lady Bentham was correct. Lady Eleanor stood in the doorway, Elizabeth slightly behind her. Darcy had known from Lady Bentham's words she had not departed, but he had not quite believed it until he saw her. His breath rushed out of him, carrying worry away with it. Then he noticed she was avoiding his gaze. He would have to find a way to make amends.

Paxton made their excuses to Lady Bentham, expressing his intention to deliver the invitation to Miss Bennet immediately. It was not as simple as that, of course, since everyone seemed to wish to speak to Lady Eleanor, and naturally Miss Elliot had to trail across Darcy's pathway until he had no choice but to speak to her.

Finally the crowd around Lady Eleanor abated, allowing Darcy and Paxton the opportunity to approach the ladies. Elizabeth seemed to be looking at Paxton as she curtsied, but Darcy knew better. She was avoiding looking at *him*, and Paxton was her only other choice.

Elizabeth offered her hand to Paxton, who bowed over it. "Miss Bennet, it has come to my attention that you have never seen the famous gardens at Rosedale Park. I wondered if you might do me the very great honor of agreeing to join me in an excursion there, accompanied, of course, by Lady Eleanor and Mr. Darcy." He gave her a quick wink.

Lady Eleanor, her voice just above a whisper, said, "So you have been given your marching orders."

Paxton turned his smile on her. "Even so, Lady Eleanor."

"An excursion sounds like a lovely idea." Elizabeth gave Paxton the arch look Darcy knew so well. "Would you not agree, Lady Eleanor?"

On her agreement, the party returned to its usual habit, with Paxton looking at Elizabeth but speaking to Lady Eleanor. Elizabeth still had not looked at Darcy. This could not continue; her displeasure wrapped around his chest and restricted his breathing.

Darcy moved closer to her. "Miss Bennet, I wonder if I might seek your advice on a small matter."

Her whole figure seemed to grow tense. "And what might that be, sir?"

He took a deep breath. "I am considering having new calling cards printed."

Finally she looked at him, though her expression implied he belonged in Bedlam. "New calling cards?" she asked dubiously.

"Yes, but these, in addition to my name, would also say, *I apologize, Miss Bennet, for distressing you with my ill-chosen words.* That way I could simply hand you one on those frequent occasions when it seems to be required."

Her lips pressed together, but the sparkle in her eyes suggested she might be repressing a smile. "And why would you seek my opinion on such a matter? It sounds as if your mind is made up."

"I cannot decide how many cards to order. Do you think two hundred would be sufficient, or should I bespeak a thousand?"

Now she was definitely smiling. "You are ambitious, sir. The house party is almost half over. You would have to work hard indeed to offend me a thousand times in the remaining days."

"True, but I do seem to possess a remarkable talent for it. Still, it might be prudent to plan ahead, given the frequency with which we seem to cross paths. After all, we have only met in Hertfordshire, Kent and Yorkshire so far. There are still thirty-six counties where we have not met."

"Only thirty-six? I take it you do not anticipate travelling to Wales, Mr. Darcy."

"Not at present, so you may go there in perfect safety."

"Well, then, if you order only two hundred cards, that will be five or six cards per county. Do you think that would be sufficient?"

"An excellent point. Based on experience, it might not be enough. There are some offenses that might require two or even three cards."

"You need not concern yourself..."

The butler's voice interrupted her, announcing in stentorian tones a new arrival. "The Dowager Marchioness of Bentham."

Eleanor spun to face the newcomer, an expression of heart-felt delight on her face, clearly only just restraining herself from running to her grandmother. Darcy also turned toward the older woman. It was remarkable how little she had changed since he was a child. Then his attention was drawn by the absolute silence in the room, everyone frozen as if in a tableau.

Finally, Lady Bentham swept forward. "Welcome to Bentham Park, my lady," she said in honeyed tones.

The dowager honored her with a dubious look that swept from her head to the hem of her gown. "Why, I thank you, Lady Bentham." Her voice could have frozen the ocean. "I hope this is not an inconvenient time. I see you have guests."

"Though we are, as always, *delighted* to see you, we do have a house party at present. Pray allow me to present some of our guests." Lady Bentham took her mother-in-law's arm and began to escort her around the room, starting on the side opposite Darcy.

Apparently Paxton had not been exaggerating the enmity between the two women. Still, a great-aunt he had not seen for years could not compete with Elizabeth Bennet for Darcy's attention. What had she been about to tell him? He turned to her, but she was watching Lady Eleanor, who in turn focused on the Dowager Marchioness.

When the dowager reached Admiral Worthsley, her voice rose enough to be audible across the room. "Why, Worthsley, you old buzzard! Where have you been keeping yourself all these years?" Had she really called him an old buzzard in public? She had always spoken her mind, and evidently that tendency had not diminished with age.

Darcy stared as the Admiral who, clearly pleased to see the older woman, answered genially. "England is still at war, your ladyship, so I have not spent as much time enjoying the beauties of the countryside as I might have wished."

Lady Eleanor rocked back and forth on her feet as if trying to resist temptation, but she stayed in place until her grandmother reached them. Casting her eyes nervously at the present Lady Bentham, Lady Eleanor leant forward to kiss the older woman's cheek. The dowager was having none of it, though; she hugged Lady Eleanor tightly.

Lady Eleanor's eyes were misty when the embrace ended. "Grandmama, I am so pleased to see you!"

Her stepmother's eyes flashed. "My dear, would you be so kind as to introduce your friends to our new guest?" Her voice had a chill in it.

"Grandmama, may I present Mr. Paxton to your acquaintance? You must already know Mr. Darcy, and of course you remember my friend Lizzy."

The dowager took a step back and examined him. "Why, Fitzwilliam Darcy, this is a surprise! When you wrote that you were coming to Yorkshire, I did not realize it was to Bentham Park." Clearly this intelligence displeased her.

For once, an accusation he could defend himself from! "In fact, I am visiting my old college friend Paxton. I had no idea he lived so nearby. We are here only for the day."

She nodded, apparently satisfied by this. "You have grown quite tall. Your mother always said you would be tall. I will have to accustom myself to looking up at you."

"This is a fortuitous meeting. I had originally thought you still resided here, but when I learned otherwise, I planned to call on you next week."

"Well, we must sit down and talk, you and I; but first I must converse with my granddaughter. Lady Bentham, I assume you have no objection if I borrow Eleanor for a short time?"

Lady Eleanor's smile was as bright as her stepmother's was artificial. "Of course not," said Lady Bentham. "The west sitting room would be convenient."

The dowager wasted no time, leading Lady Eleanor toward the door. Just before they left the room, Lady Bentham called after her, "Eleanor, do you mean to leave poor Miss Bennet all alone?"

Poor Miss Bennet, who had not seemed the slightest bit disturbed over her friend's departure, looked up in astonishment. "I thank you, my lady, but I am quite comfortable here, and I have no wish to intrude."

The cool glance froze Elizabeth now. "Eleanor is your hostess and has duties as such." It was patently obvious that Lady Bentham was trying to avoid allowing her stepdaughter to be alone with her mother-in-law, and she had left no opening for Elizabeth to refuse.

Darcy looked after Elizabeth's retreating form, damning the interruption. When would he have the chance to speak to her?

No sooner had the three women arrived in the west sitting room than the Dowager Marchioness turned to Elizabeth. "It has been a long time, Lizzy. Or must I call you Miss Bennet now?"

"Of course not," said Elizabeth warmly. She had been a little hurt that the dowager had not seemed to notice her before. During her years visiting Bentham Park, Elizabeth might not have seen Lord Bentham often, but the Dowager Marchioness had been a regular visitor in the nursery wing and the schoolroom, and Elizabeth had enjoyed her acerbic commentary. "But you are here to speak to Eleanor. Pray do not concern yourself about me in the slightest. I plan to sit in the corner and read quietly."

"There is no need," said Eleanor. "You already know all my secrets – unless perhaps Grandmama is planning to tell me some of hers." Her smile showed her view of the likelihood of that.

"Not at all. You know that I prefer to be direct, and since I have no doubt that we will be interrupted soon, I will be even more so today. Eleanor, I had a surprising visitor this morning. Your brother came to see me."

"My brother? Which one?"

"Charles, of course, who under any other circumstances could not be bothered to spend time with an old lady. He came to tell me that he was worried about you and to ask me to use my influence to delay, if not stop, your betrothal."

Elizabeth stared. Once again, she had thought she understood Charles Carlisle, and again he had surprised her. After learning of his bet, she would never have expected him to actually try to help Eleanor.

Eleanor's mouth dropped open. "He did?" Her voice squeaked.

"Yes, I have said so, have I not? Is it true, my dear? Has he cause to worry?" She laid her wrinkled hand over Eleanor's.

Eleanor glanced at Elizabeth. "It is true. I do not wish to marry Lord Deyncourt, and if I must do so, I would rather wait as long as possible."

The dowager nodded. "Have you spoken to your father about this?"

"Yes, but he will not cross his wife in this or any other matter."

Frowning, the older woman said, "Charles also suggested that you might be open to a different marriage."

Eleanor stiffened. "He did?"

"There is no need to keep questioning things I have just said, young lady. Is it true or not that you wish to marry young Darcy?"

"Mr. Darcy? No, of course not. I do not know where he came by that idea."

Narrowing her eyes, the dowager said, "You do not like Darcy, then? When I saw you standing together, I thought Charles must be right."

"Oh, I do like him, and he is far superior to the man I am to wed. Indeed, he would make an excellent husband, except that he knows perfectly well that I am in love with his friend."

"A pity; it would have solved two problems at once. And who is this friend of his?"

"He is the other gentleman that was with us, Mr. Paxton."

"Paxton – he is not related to that merchant that bought Hillington Hall?"

Eleanor winced. "His son. That is why I cannot tell Father. Geoffrey is only here on sufferance because he is Darcy's friend; otherwise he would not be welcome."

Distaste pursed her grandmother's lips. "Nor was his father before him. It is not what I would have hoped for you."

Lifting her chin, Eleanor said, "I love him. He is the only man who truly understands me and does not wish for me to be a decorative puppet in his sitting room. He was educated as a gentleman, and you can see he is perfectly presentable. If only you knew him, you would understand!"

"What if he is only interested in your dowry?"

"He has no need of it. His income is almost as large as my father's."

"He would gain enormously by your connections."

Eleanor jumped to her feet, wrapping her arms around herself. "I am sorry you disapprove, but you need not say these things." Her voice was flat. "I will not be allowed to marry him. I only told you because you asked."

"My dear, I admit I would have preferred it to be Darcy or someone of his ilk, but I am not completely backward in my ways. I am aware that there are impoverished highborn gentlemen who are suddenly deciding that the amount of a dowry is more important than the source of the money for it. It is not as unacceptable as it would have been in my day, but still..." She gave a deep sigh. "If he is what you truly want, I will do what I can, but it will likely not be enough."

Eleanor threw her arms around her grandmother and burst into tears.

"I wish I knew what they were talking about," Paxton muttered to Darcy for at least the third time.

"We will find out soon enough, I imagine."

"Eleanor has often said that her grandmother would like me. I think she forgets that the dowager refused to acknowledge my parents' existence. One time, when I was very young, I ran in front of her in church, and she looked at me as if I were some species of particularly offensive insect. She would be horrified if she knew the truth."

Although his friend spoke quietly, Darcy glanced around to ensure they were not overheard. "Perhaps, and perhaps not. She may dislike the idea, but there is someone she dislikes even more." He cast a significant glance toward Lady Bentham. "A common enemy can create unexpected allies."

Out of the corner of his eye, Darcy saw the dowager enter, followed by Elizabeth. The older woman did not appear distressed, but neither did she appear pleased. At least Elizabeth was smiling as the two strolled directly to their corner of the room.

The Dowager Marchioness inclined her head to the two gentlemen in response to their bows. "Darcy, I will be leaving soon as I have no doubt already overstayed my welcome here. I hope you *will* call on me during your visit."

"You may count on it, madam."

She turned her bird-like gaze on Paxton. "Perhaps your friend would like to join you."

Paxton's eyes widened, but he showed no other sign of surprise. "I would be honoured, your ladyship."

It was such a glaringly odd thing for her to say that Darcy could guess what must have passed between Lady Eleanor and her grandmother. "Is it not late in the day for you to undertake such a long drive home? You will be travelling in full dark."

She gave a bark of laughter. "There does not appear to be an invitation to remain here forthcoming. Besides, travelling on a dark road is less dangerous than what I would face should I chose to remain. You need not worry; I have lanterns on my carriage and there is an inn at which I can stop should it prove necessary."

Beside him, Paxton took a deep breath, his face pale but determined. "If it pleases your ladyship, my house is but three miles from here, and I would be honored if you chose to stay the night there. I am sure Darcy would enjoy your company."

Darcy silently applauded his friend's courage. Clearly he expected to be rebuffed. His desire to wed Lady Eleanor was driving him to extreme lengths.

With a sharp look, she said, "Thank you. That would be lovely."

"I understand you are acquainted with my granddaughter, Mr. Paxton."

Paxton raised his chin slightly. "I have that honor, yes."

"What do you think of her?"

"In what way?"

"What do you find to admire in her?"

He paused. "The proper answer to that would be to speak of her beauty and her accomplishments, but while she has these in abundance, I have known ladies more beautiful and more accomplished. What I admire about Lady Eleanor is that she is perfectly, exactly herself."

"What precisely does that mean? Are we not all ourselves?" She sounded annoyed.

"No, I think not, especially young ladies. They are taught deference, manners, and how to present themselves in public until they turn into identical languorous ladies with an identical air of boredom. Lady Eleanor can put on that mask of deference and of world-weariness, but she does not allow it to rule her. She likes to laugh and even to skip when she thinks no one is looking. She may be deferent in public, but inside she is still the little girl who pushed me into the river because I agreed with her when she complained of her brothers' cruelty to her. *That* is what I admire about Lady Eleanor."

The dowager's face showed little reaction. "You admire her for being a hoyden?"

"No, I admire her for being strong enough to remain true to herself and not to the *ton*'s idea of what a perfect lady should be – and also for her ability to act the part of a perfect lady when she so chooses." Paxton's tone was defiant.

"What did you do when she pushed you into the river?" Now she sounded almost amused.

Paxton's lips curved in a reminiscent smile. "I splashed water at her while she stood there like a proud little queen and told me that *she* was allowed to criticize her brothers but *I* was not. Of course, this also was while your late husband was still alive and had forbidden her on pain of a beating to so much as speak one word to me. I also admire her for speaking to me anyway."

"For disobedience?"

"For doing what she felt was right, even though it meant breaking rules. But that was many years ago. I do not believe she would disobey her parents now." His voice had grown cool.

"And why is that?"

He seemed to reflect for a minute. "I believe you would have to ask Lady Eleanor why she fears disobeying them."

She chuckled. "Oh, I do not think I have any need to ask her that. Darcy, you are very quiet tonight. Are there no young ladies that *you* admire?"

He favored her with a haughty glare. "I will happily discuss whatever you like, as long as it is *not* on that subject."

"My! You are every bit as testy on the subject as Matlock warned me you would be. Had your heart broken, did you?"

"Did he tell you that? He has lost his reason." Darcy had forgotten about the dowager's uncanny ability to discern the truth.

"That slowtop? I hardly think so. He said you were being unreasonable on the subject of marriage and requested my assistance in convincing you to see the matter differently."

Darcy snorted. "You are wasting your time. I do not intend to marry, nor do I intend to permit my relatives to lecture me on the subject."

To his surprise, she acquiesced to his request and returned to speaking of topics that were more neutral until she announced it was time for her to retire. Darcy gravely bade her good night but remained where he was.

As soon as the sound of her footsteps faded away, Paxton slumped down in his chair, covering his face with his hands. "This must be how heretics felt after facing the Inquisition."

Darcy laughed. "I expect so. You held your own very well, though."

"I did nothing but babble. I feared she would see through any attempt at prevarication and order me shot at dawn."

"She does give that impression, I grant you."

"I could hardly believe she was actually here and speaking to me. I feel as if this evening has taken a year off my life!"

"You did not show it, which is fortunate. I believe she liked your frankness."

"Do you?"

"If she had not, she would have given you a set-down you would never forget."

"I still cannot believe that Eleanor told her. I would rather trust a dragon to protect my pile of gold." Paxton let out an explosive breath.

Darcy said slowly, "I may be mistaken, but I believe she is trying quite hard to give you every chance to prove yourself. I am rather surprised by it – she was born a Fitzwilliam, and the Fitzwilliam women are not known for their ability to bend to circumstance – but I think it a hopeful sign." In the meantime, he was grateful that she had not had a significant chance to observe him in Elizabeth Bennet's company. The dowager's sharp eyes might have seen too much.

Rivulets of water meandered down the panes of the mullioned window in the breakfast room at Hillington Hall. Normally Darcy did not mind rain, but this would delay the planned trip to the gardens at Rosedale Park, which would leave Elizabeth alone all day at Bentham Park with Charles Carlisle. Good God, if only she had listened to him this time and would be more careful! He just wished he could be certain. She had not seemed angry with him at the end of the previous day; then again, he knew just how well she could disguise her sentiments when she chose.

The Dowager Marchioness entered with a sweep of skirts. "Ah, there you are, Darcy. No Mr. Paxton this morning?"

"He already breakfasted and has left with his steward to deal with a problem. He should return soon." Privately Darcy thought Paxton had been glad for the distraction. Having the older woman in his house was making him unaccountably nervous.

"Does he do his duty for the estate and the tenants, then?"

Darcy gave her a dry look at this almost indecently direct question. "He seems attentive to their needs – more so than some nobles I could name. May I bring you a plate of food?" Any other woman would serve herself, but somehow he doubted his great-aunt would deign to do so.

"Thank you." She waited while a footman pulled out her chair. "A roll and some cold meat would be lovely. I assume the noble in question is my son. You need not tell me of his failings; I am well aware of them."

Dropping a roll onto a fresh plate, Darcy looked back over his shoulder. "I never doubted it. You were always aware of estate matters."

"You are very prickly this morning. Is something troubling you?"

He set the plate in front of her. "Paxton is not a trained dog who is aping his betters. In my experience, the sons of tradesmen can be as intelligent and articulate as those gentlemen with bloodlines that span centuries; and in many cases, they take their responsibilities more seriously. They are less reckless than the young bloods who gamble away their fortunes without a second thought and consider carousing to be their purpose in life."

"I need no sermons read to me, I thank you. My question is why *you* came here to promote a match against the wishes of your own relatives."

Darcy took a slow sip of coffee before responding. "I came here to visit Paxton, knowing nothing of this situation, and I am not so much promoting it as giving my friend the opportunity to make his own case when he would otherwise not be permitted to do so. I doubt I could influence Lord Bentham one way or the other."

"I will not argue with you there, especially since his dear wife seems less than fond of you – an honor which I share. What does she hold against *you*?"

He hesitated, then said, "I know something she would rather I did not, but it is perhaps better not to discuss it."

"Ha! Now I *must* know what it is. I insist that you tell me."

From experience, Darcy knew arguing with her would be an exercise in pointlessness. "It dates to before her marriage, when she was still Miss Reed. She was determined to marry into the nobility, and Edward was her prime target. He narrowly avoided a trap she set in hopes of forcing him to marry her. Lord Bentham inadvertently walked into the next trap in his son's place, so he was the one to compromise her rather than Edward. He did the honorable thing, and it never seemed to occur to him that she had planned the whole affair; but I was witness to her anger over having trapped the wrong man."

The dowager frowned. "It still made her Marchioness of Bentham and mistress of Bentham Park."

"Yes, but only as long as he lives. Any children she might have with him will not inherit, and she knows full well that Edward has no fondness for her. She will have no power once he inherits."

She looked thoughtful. "Well, that explains a great deal. I cannot imagine she would be happy with this possible match between Eleanor and your friend Paxton."

"I cannot say. I barely know her. For that matter, I barely know Lady Eleanor, but from all I have heard she is a woman who knows her own mind."

The Dowager Marchioness cackled. "That she is! I am very fond of Eleanor. Unlike her brothers, *she* has both mettle and sense. You do not need to convince me that Paxton is more sensible and upright than my grandsons, since most men are. Still, Charles may be beginning to show signs of improvement."

Darcy choked on his sip of coffee. When he regained his breath, it took all his self-control to keep silent. He did not trust himself on the subject of Charles.

"Nothing to say for yourself?"

Carefully choosing his words, he said, "Edward is my friend. I do not care for Charles's choice of amusements."

"Do not speak to me of Edward! What a disappointment he proved to be." Her lip curled.

So Edward had fallen into the dowager's bad graces as well. Darcy had thought her more sensible. Although his temper flared, he managed to hide it under the guise of standing and offering to bring her more tea.

So the division in the family was to continue. He only hoped Edward would not be pained further by it. He had suffered quite enough already.

Chapter 7

THE SUN CAME out the following day, allowing the postponed visit to Rosedale Park to proceed. Darcy drove Paxton to Bentham Park in the curricle, assuming they would all ride together in a larger carriage to Rosedale, but Lady Bentham had different ideas. In order to accommodate a maid travelling with Lady Eleanor, she suggested the use of two carriages. With no real grounds for protesting this plan, they started off in tandem, the ladies in the carriage followed by the gentlemen in the curricle.

It was hardly a surprise when the carriage pulled up several miles from Bentham and Lady Eleanor emerged, claiming the closed vehicle was giving her a headache. Darcy wondered what Lord Bentham and his wife would think of this if they found out, since presumably Lady Eleanor's maid was under instructions to report any irregularities to them, but he handed over the reins of the curricle to Paxton without protest and took Lady Eleanor's place in the carriage. He was not going to complain about an arrangement that allowed him to be with Elizabeth, even if it was under the close chaperonage of a maid.

Inside the carriage, Elizabeth lacked some of her usual sparkle. Her bonnet lay beside her on the seat, leaving her hair uncovered. Her face looked wan, and while perhaps that was merely the light, her smile of welcome seemed forced. Perhaps she had not in fact forgiven him, despite their discussion of calling cards. He damned the Dowager Marchioness for interrupting that conversation just when they might have made some progress.

He greeted her cautiously and received a polite response, but nothing more. Once the carriage was in motion, the clatter of the wheels was loud enough to make conversation across the seats difficult. Since he was obliged to sit in the facing seat, there was little he could do about it. She seemed most interested in looking out the window, which gave him the freedom to rest his eyes on her.

How should he approach her, given her uncertain mood? Silence was easy now, but once they reached Rosedale, it would be just the two of them walking together, since Paxton and Lady Eleanor would want their privacy. Should he ask directly if he had offended her or take the safe road of simple courtesy and innocuous topics of conversation?

For the moment, he decided to follow her lead and say nothing. Instead, he took the rare opportunity to drink in her appearance. Sunlight poured in through the window, exposing the chestnut highlights in her dark curls. He rarely paid much attention to women's coiffures, but hers was the exception. As always, the ringlets that bounced against her cheeks were full of life, constantly in fluid motion, unlike those of so many ladies whose hair appeared set with shellac. Her hair had fascinated him almost since the beginning – the way stray curls kept escaping at the nape of her neck, and the bright luster that somehow matched the sparkle in her eyes.

In his dreams, she often appeared with her hair down, an image he had imagined so often that it should have become familiar and dull, but instead it always produced a rush of longing that tested his ability to keep his hands to himself. His intense fascination with her hair had only become more fervent in their meetings at Bentham Park, where she had taken to wearing jeweled hairpins that protruded beyond the knot of hair at the back of her head. In Hertfordshire and Kent, he had never caught sight of the hairpins that must have been tucked deep inside her coiffure. Now his most urgent fantasy had become one in which he slowly removed those very pins, allowing her luxurious locks to spill around her shoulders, turning the careful order into disorder that would give him the opportunity to run his fingers through the silken curtain of her hair as he took possession of those enticing lips. A surge of desire raced through him at the thought. Had she so much as smiled at him at that moment, he doubted he would have been able to restrain himself from touching her. Perhaps it was just as well that she was so subdued. It was the only thing holding him in check – that, and those tempting hairpins.

He had to force himself to look away from her until his arousal was back under regulation. Though not easy, given the temptation before him, it was an exercise with which he had extensive practice. Mentally conjugating verbs in ancient Greek had proven to be a far more useful skill than he had ever expected it to be in his days at Cambridge. Today he made it through all the verb classes in indicative, subjunctive, and imperative, and was well into the optative mood before he deemed it safe to look back at Elizabeth. Perhaps English verbs needed an optative mood as well, an entire set of grammatical rules devoted to the expression of hopes and wishes. He had a great many optative thoughts regarding Elizabeth Bennet.

After a half hour or so, he took a gamble and raised his voice to point out a highland on the side of the road. "It is one of the moors. They are more common to the east, but there are a few in this part of Yorkshire."

She seemed interested, craning her neck to look out the window past the maid sitting beside her. "How can you tell it is a moor?"

"The vegetation on the moors is dark, and you can see the dark line toward the top of it. Also, the moors here are generally at higher elevation, often on a plateau."

"I see. Thank you."

And that was the end of the conversation, but at least she had been willing to interact with him. If only he could stop worrying about her mood! The more he thought about how to please her, the more he seemed to annoy her.

When he handed her out of the carriage at Rosedale, her smile seemed more genuine as she turned her face up to the sun. Flexing her fingers, she gave him a curious look. "Is something troubling you, Mr. Darcy?"

"Not at all. I was wondering the same of you since you seemed unusually quiet."

Shaking her head as if to clear it, she said, "I am not fond of riding in closed carriages – too much noise and motion, not enough air, and so much of the scenery hidden from view. That is all. I apologize if I was dull company."

"Hardly, Miss Bennet." After all, she should know by now that he was perfectly content just looking at her, at least as long as he did not let his eyes stray toward those dangerous hairpins.

As he had expected, once they entered the garden gate and started down the lime avenue, Lady Eleanor and Paxton quickly fell behind. They did not catch up even when Elizabeth stopped for several minutes to admire the subtle variations in hue and shape between the various trees in the arboretum. Her face now reflected the liveliness that nature always aroused in her. Perhaps this outing would be more pleasant than their previous encounters.

The path curved, taking them along the top of a slope. After they reached a small terraced overlook, Elizabeth turned to take in the prospect, resting her gloved hands on the stone parapet in front of her. Darcy longed to place his hand atop hers, but while his imagination saw her smiling up at him as he did so, he knew her true reaction would be quite different. He clasped his hands firmly behind his back.

Her face was turned slightly away from him, gazing across the valley to a series of ridges that faded into blue shadows at the horizon. No matter how fine the prospect, nothing could take Darcy's attention from her, so it did not pass his notice when she shook her head slightly.

"You seem deep in thought, Miss Bennet," he said with great care.

She released a breath that turned into a sigh. "Those hills seem so peaceful. From here we can see only their beauty, yet in reality, the people who live there have no fewer troubles than we do. Perhaps there is someone standing there looking out as us, thinking how fine it would be to escape into the distance."

Darcy's chest tightened painfully. Was he the one she wished to escape from? He had thought they were making progress, but perhaps he was mistaken. If so, it would be best to know now. He had to take several deep breaths before he dared to speak, and even then, it was a long moment before words came out of his mouth. "Would it be best if I left you to enjoy the peace of the garden on your own? I have no wish to impose my company upon you."

Her head swiveled toward him, her countenance a mask of puzzlement. "I beg your pardon?"

The heat in his face turned to fire and his stomach churned. "You wished to escape, and I do not mean to burden you with my presence."

Her finely arched brows drew together for a moment, but then her expression cleared. "Oh, for heaven's sake! I was thinking of Eleanor and Mr. Paxton, and how there is no escape for them. I wonder sometimes if we are doing them a disservice by allowing them this time together when it can only lead to further heartbreak."

Mortification now warred with Darcy's other emotions. How vain he must have seemed, to assume she was speaking of him! But at least she had corrected him, rather than taking advantage of his offer to leave her alone. That was definite progress. "Perhaps it allows them to store up some happy memories to sustain them in the years to come."

She gave him a sharp look, making him wonder if she knew he was speaking of himself as well as the couple who trailed behind them. "I hope so," she said, but sounded doubtful. "There can be no happy ending for them, can there?"

"Since her father has refused his consent, and she will not marry without his approval – no, it seems fairly hopeless." Just as *his* cause was hopeless. How empty the world seemed without hope!

"Of course." She turned away and began to walk again. He caught up in a few short strides.

They remained silent until they had rounded the corner into the formal gardens, past the artfully constructed ruined temple occupying a picturesque spot, but Elizabeth had little interest in it. Usually ladies seemed to be fond of such follies, but Elizabeth never followed the fashion. Perhaps it was the utter artificiality of it that lessened its appeal for her.

She paused, though, as they passed between several mounds of low-growing shrubs covered with purple flowers. Bending down, she rubbed the tips of her fingers along a set of blooms, then raised her hand and sniffed it. With a puzzled expression, she looked more closely at the blossoms.

"Is something the matter?"

"No, just that this plant is new to me. I thought it might be related to lavender, but it lacks the scent."

Darcy gave the flowers a perfunctory glance. He had no particular interest in horticulture, and his knowledge of decorative flowers was cursory at best. This, however, seemed somehow familiar, but it was a moment before he could place it. "Odd. I have never seen it cultivated before, but it appears to be heather. It grows wild on the hills here in the North, though not so densely as this. It thrives in the moors where the soil is poor, and it provides fodder for sheep. I am surprised to see anyone planting it in a garden, though it does add color to the hillsides in summertime."

"My aunt has told me of it, although she did not mention the sheep." She sounded amused.

Elizabeth could not possibly mean the silly Mrs. Phillips he had met in Meryton; he doubted she had been more than thirty miles from her home in her life. But it was a chance to demonstrate that he taken to heart her words about his manners. "Has she travelled to the North, then?"

"She was born and raised in Derbyshire and misses it to this day."

"I take it this is not your aunt who lives in Meryton. I would have noticed a Derbyshire accent."

Now she wore a delightfully arch expression. "No, it is my Aunt Mary Gardiner who now lives in London."

He knew from her look that she must be teasing him, but he was baffled as to the source. "Where is she from? Derbyshire is a large county."

Elizabeth's smile widened. "She is from a small market town by the name of Lambton. Perhaps you have heard of it."

So that was it! "Of course. As you are no doubt already aware, it is not five miles from Pemberley."

She ran her fingers along the side of the hedge they were passing. "I have heard something of that. My aunt is full of praise for the grounds of Pemberley."

"I am honored," he murmured automatically, though inwardly he was appalled. There were few families of any note in Lambton. Elizabeth's connections must be even lower than he had thought. For heaven's sake, her aunt might be related to his tenants! That would be an embarrassment. Yet even as he thought it, he knew he would not consider it an impediment if only, only, only Elizabeth would marry him. But it was best not even to think about that, or most likely he would say or do something that would offend her yet again. "Although Lambton is a pleasant town, I have visited it only rarely and can claim few acquaintances there." Surely that was safe to say!

"My aunt has not lived there these last twelve years, so I doubt you would have met her in any case. You might have known her father, as he held the living there."

"A clergyman?" Darcy struggled to recall the name of the previous incumbent in Lambton. It was one of the Darcy family livings, so he ought to know. A young man had taken it over a decade ago, but who had preceded him? He had met all of those whose livings came from Pemberley, even when he was a boy, and his father had insisted he learn the names of everyone associated with the estate. It began with a C, he thought, but at the moment the only name beginning with C he could think of was Carlisle. Or was that actually it? "Would that have been a Mr. Carlisle?" he asked slowly.

Elizabeth raised an eyebrow. "You have a good memory."

"As in Lady Eleanor Carlisle?"

"Yes, she is a cousin of sorts. My aunt's father was one of Eleanor's great-grandfather's sixteen children. The present Lord Bentham is one of her forty-two Carlisle cousins." An amused smile hovered on her lips.

She had caught him out again. He had been assuming her aunt's origins to be humble, yet she turned out to be the granddaughter of a Marquess. One of a great many grandchildren of that particular Marquess, it was true, but still of noble blood. "Is that how you came to know Lady Eleanor?"

"Yes. We met in London as children when my aunt Gardiner paid a condolence call after the death of Eleanor's mother, and we became fast friends. Eleanor had been in a decline ever since her mother became ill, so when it was seen that my presence cheered her, the commandment came down that I was to be invited for an extended stay regardless of my questionable connections. As the only daughter among four children, Eleanor was starved for female company, especially of the sort that could stand up to her brothers."

Another piece of Elizabeth's life he had not known! He was hardly better than a stranger. He knew only what he had seen in Meryton and Rosings. If he had met Elizabeth here for the first time, he would have assumed her to be of good family, and he would never have known of her family's embarrassing behavior. What did he truly know of most of the women he met?

"I must admit that I do not understand *your* connection to the Carlisles, Mr. Darcy, apart from that you visited them as a child and that they seem to take an unusual interest in your activities."

"Sometimes I am not certain that *I* understand it either," said Darcy with a touch of irony. "It is complex. There have been ties between the Carlisles and the Fitzwilliams for many generations. Lord Bentham's mother is the sister of the late Earl of Matlock, and thus aunt to the current Earl and my late mother, but there were bonds of friendship that were as strong as blood ties. Lord Bentham was my father's closest friend, and his first wife was a dear friend of my mother, so naturally our families were quite close. My father was desolate after my mother's death, so my sister and I were sent here for the summer to escape from the mourning atmosphere at Pemberley. For many years, I looked on Lord Bentham as an unofficial uncle."

"But no longer?"

It was silent except for the birds chirping and the sound of Darcy's heels striking the gravel path. After a long pause, he said, "We did not see eye to eye on some matters regarding his eldest son, who was my particular friend, along with my cousin Colonel Fitzwilliam. That was four years ago. His son is now in exile and my cousin has been on the Continent most of the time since then, so there has been little reason for contact between us."

"That must have been a difficult time, losing both your friends and your unofficial uncle so soon after your father's death."

Her words, though delivered with sympathy, nonetheless felt more like she had applied live coals to his chest. How could she have known what that year was like? The topic of his father's death was still too painful for him to discuss openly, and he would remember if he had said anything to her about it. Perhaps Eleanor...no, of course not. He must have mentioned it in that bitter letter he gave her at Hunsford. He had been in such agony that night that one more painful recollection made no difference. But she had remembered it all this time and thought of it enough to put it together with this new information, not simply dismissed it as unimportant to her life. Did she truly think about him to that extent?

He cast a glance in her direction, but she appeared to be looking at the flower borders. Forcing himself to take a few breaths, he said, "It was difficult at first, but I developed a new circle. I spent more time with

Paxton afterwards, and he introduced me to Bingley. And, as you know, I do see Richard – Colonel Fitzwilliam – from time to time."

Elizabeth's lips curved in a smile of reminiscence. "My trip to Kent was also a reunion of sorts. Charlotte – Mrs. Collins – was my dearest friend until she married and moved to Hunsford. I missed her, but her absence also made me closer to my sister Jane, and I am glad of that."

Something about her gentle tone soothed a wound he had not realized was still open. Or perhaps it had just re-opened with his visits to Bentham Park, where he should have felt at home and instead felt at odds with everyone. During the last four years, he had managed to avoid thinking of Edward most of the time, but at Bentham he could not forget that Edward ought to be there, and there was a great emptiness in his life where Edward used to be.

He was so caught up in his thoughts that he did not notice at first that Elizabeth had stopped walking. Her attention seemed to have been caught by a bushy plant covered with unimpressive yellow flowers. She stood still a few feet away, as if frozen. As he retraced his steps to join her, he discovered what had caught her attention. A large butterfly, yellow with black markings, rested on a fringe of greenery.

He felt a weight on his arm and looked down to see Elizabeth's gloved hand gripping the sleeve of his coat, silently warning him against movement. He was more taken aback by the fact that she was voluntarily touching him than he could be by the presence of any insect.

"It is a swallowtail," she said in a hushed voice. "I have always wanted to see one, but they are very rare outside the fens."

"I did not realize you had an interest in butterflies." It seemed fitting somehow, since her movements were so much like those of a butterfly.

"My father makes a study of them, and I used to follow along when he was in search of new specimens. He taught me all about them."

"It is a pity he is not here today."

She shook her head. "No. I am glad he is not. He would want to capture it for his collection. I could not bear to see the life snuffed out of such an elegant creature."

Darcy had been watching her intent expression more than the butterfly, so when she glanced up at him as if to gauge his response, their eyes met, creating an ineffable tension. It was as if there were a cord connecting them, and he was falling into the darkness of her fine eyes. The amazing part was that she did not immediately turn her gaze away. He forgot to breathe.

He was the one who looked away first. This was too dangerous. Her eyes could tempt him into doing things he must not do and saying words he must not say, especially when Paxton and Lady Eleanor were just a short distance behind them. To preserve his appearance of equanimity, he said the first words that came into his mind. "Those red spots at the base of its wings look almost like a pair of eyes." But it was not the colorful mock eyes on the butterfly he craved, but the brightness that gleamed in Elizabeth's eyes.

"Yes, they do," she said softly as the butterfly began to dip toward the tiny yellow flowers, sipping at the nectar within them. "How odd that it can drink from a plant so bitter. Rubbing those leaves on my skin would give me blisters, but it does no harm to such a delicate creature, and a tea made from the leaves can ward off pestilence. Nature can be very perplexing, can it not?"

"What is it?"

He felt more than saw her gaze flutter over him. "Rue. Mad Ophelia's favorite."

He quoted, "'There's rue for you; and here's some for me. We may call it herb-grace o'Sundays. – O, you must wear your rue with a difference...' I have always wondered what she meant by that."

The butterfly chose that moment to take flight, making loops in the air until it disappeared over the tall brick wall that surrounded the garden. Elizabeth watched it until it was out of sight, then began to walk again. Her eyes cast downwards, she said, "I suppose we all wear our rue differently."

For perhaps the thousandth time, Darcy wished he could see what she was thinking. What did she rue? Did she regret believing Wickham's lies? Or did she regret some of the things she had said to him? Or possibly...no, it was best not to think about that.

After passing a rock garden, the path led them up several steps to a pergola covered with green leaves, with pendulant violet blossoms hanging from the lattice overhead. Darcy looked back over his shoulder. Paxton and Lady Eleanor were perhaps a hundred paces behind them, looking deep in conversation. He could not be sure, but Paxton did not look pleased. Darcy was torn between sympathy for his friend and a sense of envy that at least Paxton knew his love was requited, which was more than Darcy himself could claim. It was yet another thing not to think about.

He had no choice but to move closer to Elizabeth as they entered the narrow pergola, but she showed no sign of objection. Her nearness was intoxicating, even more than when he had waltzed with her. The pergola stretched ahead of them for some distance with pillars on each side, like the aisle of a church down which they must walk. Darcy gave a mental wince at the thought. This might be the only aisle he would ever walk down with Elizabeth, but he was not prepared to give up hope yet.

It was darker here, with only a little light filtering through the leaves, and the flowers overhead gave off a heavy, sweet scent that seemed to cloud his senses like opium. It was as if they had walked into a strange land where nothing was the same, some underworld from the ancient myths. He allowed himself a brief moment to pretend that in this odd flowery world Elizabeth might actually care for him, tasting the ephemeral sweetness of his dream as he gazed down on her bonneted head.

His reverie was shattered when she said his name with the sort of firm determination that indicated some kind of rebuke was about to come. He wondered what he had done this time to upset her. Cautiously, he said, "Yes?"

She looked up at him, fragments of filtered sunlight dancing across her face and the dark curls that framed it. A thought flitted through his mind, wondering if she would taste of flowers like the scent that surrounded them. His eyes caressed the familiar curves of the lips he had so often surreptitiously admired.

When she parted those rosy lips, apparently to say something, a jolt of fierce, possessive desire shot through him, overthrowing his reason. He forced himself to concentrate on what she might say. Another misunderstanding could ruin this tentative truce of theirs. But no words emerged from those tempting lips. Her fine eyes were fixed on him in bewilderment, and somehow he knew, just as he knew that Elizabeth Bennet would always hold his heart in her delicate and expressive hands, that for the first time she was aware of what lay between them. Was she feeling as drugged as he by the heavy scent of flowers, or was it just her presence that overwhelmed him? All he would have to do was to lean down and brush his burning lips against hers and.... No, that way led to madness. Better just to savor the moment, to revel in the awareness of her shallow breaths and darkened eyes, and to hope that this moment lasted forever.

But he could not resist her completely. Raising his hand, he brushed the back of his fingers lightly against her skin. It was as soft as a flower petal, and his hand lingered at her jawline, unwilling to give up the prize it had discovered. As his index finger found its way to the tender skin just beneath her chin, he heard a hitch in her breathing that sent a sharp lance of desire straight to his loins. If only he could pull her into his arms, pressing her soft curves against him as he claimed those tempting lips....

The sound of approaching voices made Elizabeth jump back like a startled doe, her eyes darting everywhere except at him. A fashionably dressed older couple was coming towards them, laughing over some shared thought. How could they be laughing when his world had just shifted on its axis? For once, Elizabeth's agitation did not trouble him, since it only provided proof that she now knew what it was to desire him. A mixture of triumph and sweet relief surged through his veins.

The couple was only a few feet away now. The gentleman acknowledged them with a bow. "You must be the visitors from Bentham Park. I am Sir William Taylor."

Darcy returned the bow. "Fitzwilliam Darcy of Pemberley, at your service. May I present Miss Bennet, a guest at Bentham Park? Lady Eleanor Carlisle is just beyond the pergola."

"Your gardens are very impressive," said Elizabeth, her cheeks still flushed. "I have never seen such a happy grouping of formal and informal plantings."

"The credit must go to my wife, Lady Janet," said Sir William with evident pride. "She designed almost all of it."

Lady Janet smiled warmly. "With a great deal of help from the gardeners, of course. You are fortunate to come when so much is in bloom." She gestured to the pergola as she spoke with a light Scottish accent.

"Yes, it is very lush," Elizabeth said. "Some of these plants I would have expected to see only in the South, though Mr. Darcy tells me that at least one of them is native to this area." She gave him a bewitching smile that made his heart skip a beat.

It took him a moment to collect himself. "I believe Miss Bennet is referring to the heather. I have never before seen it cultivated in such a manner."

Lady Janet was obviously pleased by his observation. "That was one of my experiments. Our head gardener thought I might as well decide to grow weeds, but even he has come to like it. It blooms so profusely in the moors where the soil is poor that I wanted to see what would happen if it were in better soil and kinder conditions. It looks quite different here from its cousins on the moor."

"I have certainly never seen it grow in attractive groupings like that."

Elizabeth said, "I was very taken with it, though I have never seen the wild version."

"Oh, you must visit a moor while you are here, Miss Bennet," exclaimed Lady Janet. "They have a wild beauty all their own, although I must admit to a certain amount of prejudice since they remind me so much of my home."

"I would love to see one." Elizabeth's face was alight with interest.

Just then Paxton and Lady Eleanor joined them. After Darcy had made the introductions and the requisite compliments paid to the garden, the Taylors continued on their walk, and Darcy turned to Paxton. "The moor we passed en route – is there a lane going up into it?"

"I believe so."

"Would you object to making a brief stop on our way? Miss Bennet has never seen one of our heather moors."

Lady Eleanor and Paxton exchanged skeptical glances. Lady Eleanor said, "There is nothing to see, just a wasteland."

"Still, the moors have a certain stark attraction, and it would be a shame for Miss Bennet to miss the opportunity to see them while she is here."

Paxton said, "It should be simple enough. Darcy, perhaps you and Miss Bennet could go ahead in the curricle, and we will plod along behind and meet you just beyond the moor. Your greys can easily make twice the speed of the carriage."

"If that is acceptable to the ladies, I would be happy to do so." It might please Elizabeth as well, since she would be happier in the open curricle than in the closed carriage.

"I have my maid, so there will be no difficulty if Geoffrey rides with me," Eleanor said, looking delighted by the idea. Darcy suspected that the maid would be riding in front with the coachman.

Chapter 8

ELIZABETH'S PULSES WERE fluttering at the idea of travelling alone with Mr. Darcy in the curricle. It was respectable enough as long as they were on a well-travelled road, but were moors not supposed to be empty, desolate places? If she declined, it would seem as if she did not trust him. While she might be unsure of what she wanted from him, she was certain he would never impose himself upon her. He could have done so easily in the past had he so chosen. Her cheek tingled where he had touched her. How could the merest touch of a man's fingers produce such intense sensations?

She allowed Mr. Darcy to hand her into the curricle. The seat was higher than she was accustomed to, allowing her to look over the backs of the matched greys. Darcy paused beside one of them and made a slight adjustment to the harnesses, speaking quietly to the horse as he did so. The domestic moment made her smile.

Swinging up beside her, Darcy shook the reins and the curricle began to move. He kept the horses at a brisk trot until they reached the main road, then encouraged them to a canter. "If this is too fast, I hope you will tell me. We will still be ahead of the others even at a trot, but this will give us more time." He spoke loudly to be heard over the wind whistling past them.

Elizabeth found the speed exhilarating. "Will it not tire your horses?"

"The greys? They are racing stock. They could go a good deal faster than this on a better road."

The noise of the road provided an excuse to remain silent, which was fortunate since she knew not what to say. Once again, she did not know what to make of him. She should be counting her blessings that Sir William and Lady Janet had interrupted them in the pergola. What had she been thinking? It was all well and good for her to attempt to be civil with him, but what in Heaven's name had made her speak so openly to him, both about her worries for Eleanor and then in that ridiculous discussion of rue? It was true that the flower-laden pergola would have to rank high in a list of romantic settings, but that was absolutely no excuse for what had almost happened there. However much she might hate to admit it to herself – and certainly would *never* admit it to anyone else – she knew the truth. If he had tried to kiss her then, she would not have stopped him, and she did not know why. He was annoying, ill-tempered, proud, and demanding, and she had no intentions toward him – or at least she *should* not. But when he had touched her face, she had wanted more – more of him, more of that hot sensation that seemed to rush deep into her. Oh, what was wrong with her today?

Somehow his feelings for her seemed to have unexpectedly stood the test of time and survived the trial of her bitter refusal at Hunsford, something she would not have believed possible. But why should it matter that he was more constant than she would have expected? Naturally she was sorry for his pain and disappointed hopes, but that was no reason to give any consideration to a man who did little but vex her. Perhaps it was just this odd intimacy into which they had been thrust by Eleanor and Mr. Paxton. Being the only two people admitted into their secret made for a peculiar situation. But given their own past, how could she expect any sort of normalcy in their interactions?

She had also caught a glimpse of a new side of him today when he had told her about his history with the Carlisle family. In the past, he had been haughty, cold, angry, and insolent; but when he spoke of his friends leaving him, his eyes had been full of loss. It was understandable; she herself had struggled first over losing Eleanor, then years later over her disillusionment with Charlotte's decision to marry Mr. Collins. How much worse it must have been for Darcy to discover that his childhood friend had been a cheat and a liar! She could not imagine Darcy would have accepted that behavior, so he must have lost his friend even before he went into exile. Apparently it had occasioned him so much pain that he could not bear to have any contact with Lord Bentham.

How had her sympathy toward him at that moment transmuted into a desire to relieve that pain in his eyes? It made her vulnerable to him in a new way she could not understand. Perhaps it was only the romantic setting of the gardens that had made her so susceptible to his mood.

All of her rational thoughts, though, were inadequate to convince her body to abandon its new awareness of the gentleman holding the reins beside her. She could feel every one of the inches that separated them. How easily he could reach past them to touch her hand or her arm! He would not do so, of course, but she still could not forget the possibility, or stop herself from imagining it. The brush of the air against her skin made it tingle as if she were blushing from head to foot, and she felt aware of his nearness each time the curricle lurched to one side or the other. It was ridiculous to feel so sensitive to his presence when nothing had happened! All he had done was to look at her as if he wanted to kiss her, and touched her face one time. He had not even tried to take her hand, yet that small interchange was still enough to have changed everything between them.

Why had she agreed to go to the moors alone with him? She could have insisted that the others remain with them, but she had not. Only in the most secret recesses of her soul could she admit it was because she wanted him to touch her like that again, his intense gaze probing her, and to feel how it made her entire body come to life.

Finally they reached the section of road where the moorlands rose to one side. "I saw a lane on the way that looked to lead up to the moor," said Darcy.

"Are the moors always on higher ground?"

"I am no expert, but the ones I have seen are usually at an elevation. There is something different in the soil there."

"It looks steep."

"No doubt, but the horses can manage."

"But not at a canter, I venture to guess! I take it you are a racing enthusiast?"

"I? Not in particular. Paxton dearly loves a race, but I prefer other sports."

"Yet you own a fine racing team, at least from what I have heard Mr. Paxton say."

"I doubt there are many finer, but it is not owing to my efforts. They were entrusted to me by their original owner when he could no longer care for them. I hope to be able to return them to him in the near future. In the meantime, Paxton has enjoyed keeping them in racing fettle during my visit. Look, there is the lane. You may wish to hold the rail; this might be a bit rough."

The lane was, in fact, little more than a grassy track, but Darcy's handling of the team allowed them to avoid the most uneven ground. When the lane began the winding ascension to the moors, the curricle was at such an angle that Elizabeth was forced to lean forward. Although the slope was steep, the horses did not seem unduly troubled by their load. She hoped the descent would be as simple.

As they rounded a large rock formation, the wind abruptly picked up, tearing at the ribbons of her bonnet as the moors were dramatically revealed before them. An expanse of uneven dark ground covered with small scrubby plants seemed to stretch to the horizon, a startling change from the verdant valley they had just left behind. It was simultaneously desolate and invigorating – or perhaps the invigorating part was the wind that whipped across the plateau. In the valley it had been no more than a pleasant breeze, but here she could hear it whistling over the untamed ground.

There was no sign of humans or habitation, only a few dots of white indicating the presence of grazing sheep. The horses ambled along the track which seemed to lead nowhere in particular. She turned to Darcy, only to find him watching her with a certain intensity that made her pulses flutter. "It is like a primeval landscape," she said.

"Untouched by man," he said. "The heather is just beginning to bloom in the more protected spots. In another month it will be a sea of purple."

A gust of wind threatened to tear Elizabeth's bonnet from her head, but she caught it just in time. "That must be an impressive sight."

"It depends on your point of view. Most locals would, like Paxton and Lady Eleanor, tell you the moors are monotonous, but I find there is something untamed about them."

The expression in his eyes made her look away in embarrassment. "Are the moors in Derbyshire similar to this?"

"The ones in the High Peak are, but Pemberley and Lambton are located in the dales. Heather grows in barren spots on the hills there, but not in great quantity as it does here."

"I have heard a great deal about the beauty of the Peak."

A faint smile touched his lips. "There is nothing that can compare to it."

"I have never seen it, of course, only heard of it from my aunt. Later this summer I will be travelling to the Lakes with my aunt and uncle, and that will be my first time in the mountains. I have tried to imagine it so often."

"I hope it meets your expectations," he said in an oddly formal voice.

The track turned to climb a slight incline where some exposed rocks showed at the top, then came to an abrupt end. Darcy reined in the horses. "I wondered where this track led. It looks like we will need to proceed on foot from here." He swung out of the curricle in a smooth movement, then came around and offered her his hand as she carefully descended the high steps.

"What is it?"

"A stone circle, if I am not mistaken. I imagine the locals come here for celebrations."

"A stone circle? Like Stonehenge?" Excitement rose in her at the unexpected treat.

He laughed. "Yes, but much, much smaller."

"I have never seen Stonehenge, so I have no grounds for comparison and will be impressed in any case."

When Darcy offered her his hand once more to cross a rock in the pathway, she was almost shockingly aware of his touch and the strength behind it. She had to focus her attention away from him when they reached a small cleared area. The circle was made up of perhaps a dozen standing stones, none reaching higher than Elizabeth's waist, but was nonetheless impressive in its antiquity and solitary splendor on the moor. In the middle of the circle, Elizabeth slowly spun around, taking in the atmosphere of the site. "Do you suppose it was built by Druids?"

"I cannot say, though it seems likely." Darcy remained just outside the circle, his attention focused on Elizabeth more than the stones.

Another gust of wind snatched Elizabeth's bonnet, this time managing to tug it off until it hung by its ribbon behind her head. "Oh, bother!' she exclaimed as a thick lock of curly hair slipped out of its knot. Crouching down, she searched through the grass for the hairpin that had been pulled out with the bonnet.

Darcy knelt beside her. "What are you looking for?" He ran his gloved fingers over the loose peat.

"A hairpin." Elizabeth parted a clump of grass with her fingers. "I would not worry, but it is one of Lady Bentham's. My own hairpins are not fine enough for Bentham Park. Oh, there it is!" She reached out for it just as Darcy stretched out his own hand, and their fingers met with a shock.

Neither moved for a moment, then Darcy carefully picked up the hairpin and handed it to her, his fingers skimming her palm as he did so.

Despite her gloves, Elizabeth felt a burning sensation where he had touched her. Almost involuntarily she raised her eyes to meet his.

It was like the moment in the pergola all over again, except this time she was not in a formal garden with Eleanor and Paxton nearby, but completely alone with him on a deserted windswept moorland, her bonnet blown off and her hair half down. She should feel frightened given her vulnerable position, but somehow she knew he would not hurt her. Instead she felt her insides turn to liquid from the knowledge of his desire for her.

Tugging off his glove, Darcy reached out and touched her hair reverently, letting it flow through his fingers. Elizabeth's stomach flip-flopped as the sensation of his hand in her hair made her long to be closer to him. What was wrong with her? She should not be allowing him to touch her in any way, even if it was just her hair. Though truth to tell, it would not sound particularly compromising if anyone heard of it. Even the ladies of Meryton were not so silly as to say, *Why, she is quite ruined! A man has touched a lock of her hair!* The thought made her smile mischievously.

The slight movement was enough to draw Darcy's attention back to her face. A look of shock crossed his features, then his hand left her hair to caress her cheek. With his forefinger, he lightly traced the shape of her lips, leaving a burning trail of sensation behind.

Elizabeth could not have moved had her life depended on it. Her flooded sensibilities rooted her in place, and the depth of his dark eyes mesmerized her, especially as he began to lean closer to her. At some level she recognized he was about to kiss her and she should stop him, but it seemed unbearable to do so.

His eyes were warm as he put a finger under her chin. There was an endless moment when she seemed to have forgotten how to breathe, then his lips were moving gently on hers, filling her with a burning sensation, yet seeming to pull her very soul from within her.

So this must be desire! Whatever it was, it certainly was pleasurable, and the astonishing feeling of his warm mouth caressing hers made her skin tingle. Who would have thought that her lips could be so sensitive, or that they could send pulses of heat throughout her body? It lasted only a few seconds, and when he drew away, she felt as if she had lost something precious.

She did not know what to expect from him now, but she was shocked when he suddenly withdrew. His hands dropped to his sides as he straightened and rose to his feet, his expression forbidding. Dismayed, she stood as well, even though he had not offered her his hand. She had thought he would be pleased. What had she done to anger him?

He spoke grimly, enunciating each word. "I am not Charles Carlisle."

At this patently obvious statement, she looked at him in puzzlement. "Of course you are not."

He gave her a burning look, then strode away to the curricle without a word. Concerned, she lifted her skirts to hurry after him, but he was already adjusting the harness when she arrived. "Mr. Darcy, I am sorry if I have offended you, but...."

He interrupted, but kept his eyes fixed on the horses. "You have called me ungentlemanly, but I do *not* lure young ladies to isolated places in order to make love to them."

"It never occurred to me that you did," she said more gently. "I would not be here with you otherwise."

"And now I have proved that you were unwise to trust me."

"Not at all. All you have proved is that even an honorable gentleman can be overcome by temptation, and that it might happen as easily in an isolated place as anywhere else. If you were untrustworthy, you would persist with your attentions even if I had told you to stop – and if you tell me that is what you would have done, I will not believe you."

His jaw seemed to unclench slightly. "You make it difficult to argue the point, Miss Bennet."

She decided to press her advantage. "And a word of advice, sir. If you ever *do* wish to impose yourself on an unwilling woman, I strongly advise against doing so immediately after handing her a long, sharp hairpin."

An unwilling smile tugged at his lips. "In *my* case, Miss Bennet, that hairpin is better employed in holding your hair in place."

Though a little offended by this, she decided it was best to turn the insult into a joke. "Yes, I suppose I would look better without half my hair falling down!"

His head bent so far that his forehead almost touched the back of the horse. In a strangled voice he said, "It is not unattractive. Rather, it attracts me far too much. We should go back; the others will be waiting for us."

Elizabeth blushed. "I require only a few minutes to repair the damage. You might wish to keep your back turned if you prefer to avoid seeing even more of my hair down." Without waiting for his reply, she ducked behind the curricle where she was more protected from the wind, then pulled out the remaining hairpins. Shaking her hair free, she ran her fingers through it several times to bring it into some kind of order.

That was when she realized Darcy had not turned his back. He was lounging against the curricle only a few feet from her, his arms firmly crossed across his chest, his eyes fixed on her with a burning look that made her breath catch.

He gave a crooked half-smile. "You did not say what I should do if I *did* wish to see it. Forewarned is forearmed."

The goose bumps on her arms had nothing to do with the wind. Feeling hot and cold at the same time, she managed to arch an eyebrow, hoping her expression would prevent him from guessing how thoroughly nonplussed she was by the way he was looking at her. Given the sensation created in her from the touch of his eyes, it might as well have been his hands that were running through her hair and over her body. The almost visible control he was exerting over himself charged the atmosphere.

The correct thing to do would be to bind up her hair as quickly as possible, but Elizabeth was not ready to give up this moment, so she shook out her hair again before parting it into sections with deliberate slowness. Lingering as she looped up one section at a time, she thrust each hairpin in place. "Better?" she asked archly.

He gave her a long look. "No, but perhaps safer."

She did not know what to expect from him next, but he merely handed her into the curricle and drove down into the valley, giving no evidence that anything unusual had occurred between them. It was disappointingly anticlimactic after the power of their connection on the moor. Perhaps he was as uncertain of what he wanted as she was. Certainly he had given no hint a proposal was forthcoming. She knew now that he was still attracted to her, but it did not follow that he had any intention of renewing his offer for her. Of course, she was not sure that she wished him to. Discovering that she enjoyed his touch was not the same as loving him, was it?

His long, tapered fingers held the reins loosely. He had not replaced his gloves, and her eyes were drawn to the strength of his hands, the shape of his knuckles and square fingernails. Those fingers had touched her face, and she could still feel where his touch had traveled along her cheek. She had never given a thought to a man's hand before, but she realized his were beautiful, tempting her to run her own fingers along his, learning every line of them. What was wrong with her? She had seen men's hands many times before. Why did her stays feel suddenly too confining, as if her skin could not stand the touch of the stiff whalebone against her ribs and breasts?

She had to look away. They were traveling down the steep slope at the edge of the moor. Darcy appeared completely in control of the horses and the curricle moved steadily, but her position felt oddly precarious, as if she might somehow fall. It was foolish to feel afraid, but she held on tightly to the seat until they reached the valley.

Her heart was still racing as they followed the lane, passing between fields bordered with dry stone walls. A shepherd and his dog herded sheep two fields away, and the main road was in sight when Darcy surprised Elizabeth by pulling the horses to a stop.

"Is something the matter?" she asked.

Without answering, he rummaged underneath the seat and brought out a leather bag, from which he withdrew a small sheath. Pulling out one of the short stable knives commonly used to trim reins, he passed it to her, hilt first. "Would you be so kind as to hold this for a moment, Miss Bennet?"

"Of course." If there was a problem with the harnesses or reins, it was not obvious to her.

"This is a populated area, would you not agree?"

Mystified, she said, "I suppose so." She turned over the knife in her hand, but saw nothing unusual about it.

Warmth kindled in his eyes. His voice was husky as he said, "Since I do not have a hairpin to give you, I hope the knife will prove an adequate substitute should you feel the need to defend yourself." And before she could even comprehend that statement, he slid closer to her until she felt his thigh pressing against hers. Cupping her cheek with his hand, he turned her face toward his and captured her mouth in one swift motion.

Their kiss on the moor had been gentle and tentative. This one was something else altogether, like the difference between lighting a candle and kindling a bonfire. This time his kiss staked a claim, smoldering with the same urgent hunger she had seen in his face as she arranged her hair, but now he had loosened that tight restraint that had kept him in check earlier. His teeth nibbled on her lower lip, probing and questing, stimulating and provoking her until she gasped, surrendering her mouth to his possession.

She had caught glimpses of people kissing like this, but how could she have known that it would be so consuming, that his probing tongue would unleash cravings she had no notion of controlling? Her instincts knew what to do, and she met his sweet torment half way, her hands rising involuntarily to grip his shoulders as if he were the only solid thing in her world.

His hands roamed down to her back, pulling her close to him until she felt the hardness of his chest pressing against her. Had she truly believed the waltz was like an embrace? It had been nothing compared to this heated intimacy, a thirst that yearned to be quenched, yet instead grew fiercer by the second. She knew she should not be allowing this, but instead of pushing him away, she arched against him.

A shudder ran through him. "Elizabeth," he whispered raggedly. "This would be a good time to use that knife."

"I know." Even she could hear that her voice throbbed with longing, and she had to force her fingers to release his shoulders. Flushed with embarrassment, she straightened, already aching to be touching him again, and too embarrassed to look at him.

His self-possession seemed equally tested as he moved away from her. After staring at the horizon briefly, he rubbed his hands over his face. He took a deep breath, then slowly released it. "Good God, Elizabeth," he said quietly, then he muttered something under his breath.

"I beg your pardon? I could not quite hear what you said."

He gave her a look she could not interpret. "I said, 'Aorist passive subjunctive plural.' The conjugation is different in Attic Greek and Homeric Greek, you see. It is more challenging that way."

Elizabeth's eyebrows shot up. "Perhaps I was not paying adequate attention, but I seem to have missed when we started discussing Greek grammar."

"Greek grammar is an extremely useful thing to know, Miss Bennet. Someday I will tell you about it." He flicked the reins, and the obedient horses resumed their pace. "Although I am fond of the moors, I must say I have never been so happy to leave an isolated place before."

She considered a teasing answer, but that could lead into a discussion she was not ready to have, not while they were alone together in a curricle and she still ached for his kiss. She should say *something*, but after her display on the moor, not to mention her passionate response to his touch, it would seem *Missish* at best and hypocritical at worst to reproach him. She compromised by testing the edge of the knife on her finger. "I hope you realize this is quite sharp, Mr. Darcy," she said.

"If it were not, the stable boys would have to answer for it. I suppose, though, it is not quite the thing when we are in motion." He handed her the sheath just as they reached the road.

She slid the knife into the sheath, looking up at him through her eyelashes. His attention remained on the road as he urged the horses to a canter, but she thought she could detect a pleased look on his face.

Darcy counted the trip back to the valley as a success. He had handed Elizabeth into the curricle and sat in the driver's seat beside her without incident. He had not commented on the deliberate torture she had inflicted on him when she let down her hair, nor had he ripped out every one of those damned hairpins and thrown them as far as he could into the heather, nor had he said anything that could be interpreted as even remotely forward. Of course, he had only managed it by promising himself the reward of a kiss at the end, but all the same, it was an accomplishment.

And that kiss! He suspected it might not have happened quite so smoothly had he not taken her by surprise, but still, there was no denying that she not only permitted it to continue, but responded to it with an unexpected fire. While it might not be the same as reaching an understanding, it was damned close to it, and certainly she was seeing him in a very different light than she had even a few hours before. That little display while she put her hair up had made that clear. She would not have gone out of her way to arouse his interest if she did not want it aroused – and, by God, she *had* aroused him!

It was just as well that the other carriage was not far down the road, or he might have repeated the experiment. That would be a mistake; better that he should leave her wanting more than give her the chance to push him away. No, he should keep his mind on Greek conjugations, and after that kiss, he needed the most difficult irregular verbs.

Still, when he sighted the others and slowed the horses to a walk, he felt regret that this special time was ending. As he glanced down at Elizabeth, the discovery that she was watching him made his heart pound.

When her tongue darted out to touch her lips, he thought his heart might leap out of his chest, and certainly other parts of his body were leaping as well. If only he could kiss her again! But it would not do, not when anyone in the carriage could see them. Instead, he carefully placed his hand over hers as it lay on the bench between them.

Her expression did not change, although a flush warmed her cheeks. She turned her hand over so her palm was against his, and he felt the light pressure of her fingers. It was beyond belief. Elizabeth had deliberately taken his hand. She had changed her mind about him. Triumph and heart-felt delight surged through him.

The sound of crunching gravel warned him that someone was approaching rapidly. Thank God for Edward's brilliantly trained horses who had known to stop even when their driver was completely distracted!

Elizabeth dropped her eyes and withdrew her hand, leaving his feeling unbearably empty. Darcy had to tear his gaze away from her to see Paxton striding toward them, his expression stormy. Lady Eleanor was nowhere to be seen.

Darcy had barely exited the curricle when Paxton spoke without any preliminary. "Darcy, it is time for us to leave. Perhaps Miss Bennet should join Lady Eleanor in the carriage."

This incivility was so unlike his friend that Darcy hardly knew how to reply. "Is Lady Eleanor unwell?"

"Lady Eleanor is quite well," Paxton snapped, his tone implying that his opinion of her was in very ill health indeed. "Are we going?"

Confused, Darcy looked from his friend to Elizabeth and back. "Of course, if you wish, but we must see the ladies back to Bentham Park."

"*You* may do so if you wish." Paxton made the slightest of bows to Elizabeth. "Miss Bennet, I hope you enjoyed the moors." Despite his attempt at civil words, his anger was apparent.

"Very well," Darcy said coolly. He could not imagine what had brought his usually affable friend to this extremity, but he had no intention of parting from Elizabeth on this note, not after what had just happened between them. He offered her his hand to assist her out of the curricle. "I will join you shortly, Paxton."

With a sharp nod, Paxton turned away.

Concerned, Darcy walked Elizabeth to the carriage with the intention of apologizing for his friend's poor manners, but her attention was immediately turned toward Lady Eleanor, whose flushed face and tight lips revealed her distress. Lady Eleanor usually appeared so calm, almost placid, that it looked as incongruous as if she had suddenly sprouted wings. Elizabeth put an arm around her friend, but Lady Eleanor shrugged it off as if in irritation. "I am perfectly well!" she snapped loud enough for Darcy to hear.

To Darcy's surprise, Elizabeth cast a look at him over her shoulder. Was it concern, distress, or a request for assistance? If only he understood her better! Her friend's face had gone from flushed to white. Obeying his instincts, he entered the carriage as well.

"Is there anything that might aid you in your present distress? Shall I fetch Paxton?" Darcy asked Lady Eleanor. When she shook her head without looking up, he said to Elizabeth, "Pray excuse me. I will return presently."

He found Paxton pacing beside his curricle, his expression grim. "Are you ready?" his friend demanded.

With a reproving gaze, Darcy said, "Lady Eleanor is unwell."

"And no doubt sent you to give me that very message to prevent us from leaving!"

"Not at all," Darcy said, "but you may depart whenever you please. I plan to see the ladies to Bentham Park, and will find my way back to Hillington Hall from there."

"She is undeserving of your sympathy, Darcy."

"That may be, but it does not follow that I should leave Miss Bennet in a difficult situation."

Paxton's lips twisted. "Do as you will, then."

Whatever Lady Eleanor had said to him must have been dreadful indeed to provoke this sort of behavior. Nodding, Darcy moved past him to the ladies' carriage. While he was still giving instructions to the coachman, he heard Paxton urging the greys into a canter.

Elizabeth did not know whether to be sorry or grateful that Mr. Darcy accompanied them home. She was glad to know there would be someone to turn to, apart from Eleanor's useless maid, should Eleanor's illness become worse; and she supposed that even without his presence, Eleanor would not tell her what had happened until they reached the privacy of her room. Still, she would have paid dearly to learn what had upset Eleanor now rather than later. She had not thought Mr. Paxton the sort of man who would cause a lady such distress, but she had been wrong about men before.

The thought made her glance at the man sitting opposite her. Heat flushed through her again at the remembrance of what had just happened between them. What had possessed her to behave as she did? Certainly it had not been a conscious choice, or even a reasoned response. No, it was far more primitive. When Darcy touched her, she resorted to pure instinct. She could not manage a coherent thought when he was so close to her.

Not that he seemed to be paying the least attention to her now! Instead, Darcy was looking out the window as if the passing countryside were of greater interest than the sight of a marquess's daughter blinking back tears, but she supposed it was the most tactful thing he could do. He seemed to feel her gaze on him, since his eyes shifted to her. Caught, she gave a slight shrug, to which he responded with a sympathetic look and the tiniest of nods before once more turning away.

Between her concern for Eleanor and her disconcerting awareness of Mr. Darcy, it seemed a long time before the carriage turned into the tree-lined drive of Bentham Park. Fortunately, Mr. Darcy had thought to mention to the driver that he should avoid the main doors, so none of the other guests observed them as he handed them out of the carriage. The few servants in the vicinity knew better than to stare or remark on Lady Eleanor's tear-streaked face.

Elizabeth addressed herself to Mr. Darcy. "Thank you for accompanying us. I hope it did not inconvenience you."

"Not at all, Miss Bennet. No doubt the stablemaster will allow me to borrow a mount to return to Hillington Hall." He hesitated. "Is there any message you would like me to carry?" Although he spoke to Elizabeth, his words were clearly meant for Eleanor.

Eleanor drew herself to her full height, which was still half a head shorter than Elizabeth. "There is no message."

Mr. Darcy bowed silently to her, then shot a significant glance at Elizabeth. "I wish you good day, then."

With her chin in the air, Eleanor said in her most aristocratic manner, "I hope you enjoy the remainder of your stay at Hillington Hall, Mr. Darcy."

Elizabeth's mouth was suddenly dry. Eleanor's dismissal made it clear she did not expect to see him again. Would the quarrel between Eleanor and Mr. Paxton mean she could no longer see Mr. Darcy? Something deep inside her tied into knots at the thought.

His face grew white, but he managed another correct bow. "Pray accept my best wishes for your future happiness, Lady Eleanor. Miss Bennet."

She knew she should say something, but her mind was a complete blank. When he turned and strode away, her gaze followed him involuntarily. Shaking her head to clear it, she supported Eleanor at the elbow. "Come, let us go inside."

Eleanor, her shoulders now slumped, allowed Elizabeth to lead her. Although resolutely trying to push thoughts of Mr. Darcy from her mind, Elizabeth could not resist taking one last look at him before stepping over the threshold. To her surprise, he had stopped and now faced in her direction, clearly watching her. Elizabeth's skin tingled alarmingly, and she had to force her eyes away from him. Eleanor needed her attention now. Her own confused feelings could wait. Indeed, waiting was the only choice she had.

They climbed the back staircase to avoid curious eyes. Once in the privacy of Eleanor's rooms, Elizabeth dismissed the maid and closed the door firmly behind her. By that time, her friend was already lying prone on her bed, sobbing into her pillow. She had not even removed her bonnet and gloves.

Feeling oddly numb, Elizabeth sat beside her and rubbed her hand comfortingly on Eleanor's shoulders. "Can you tell me what happened, dearest? Was he cruel to you?"

"Cruel? Only in that he would deny us any future!"

Elizabeth chose her words carefully. "It is hard to have a future when you are to marry another man."

"Of course it is! And what choice do we have but to make the best of it? Not Geoffrey, though – no, he says that after my wedding day everything between us must end, and he will have no more contact with me!" Her voice choked up with sobs.

It was hard to argue with that, and Elizabeth did not understand her friend's reaction to it. "I take it you do not agree?"

"How can I?" Eleanor turned red eyes toward her. "I cannot put him aside like a plaything I have tired of. He is part of my soul! Or at least I believed he was."

"But once you are married..."

"Once I am married, that man will own my allegiance and my body until I produce his heir, and then he will no longer care what I do or with whom I do it as long as I am reasonably discreet. Oh, why does Geoffrey not understand?"

Certain things that had puzzled Elizabeth suddenly began to make sense – Eleanor's docility about marrying, her seeming indifference to the impending separation from her lover. Apparently she viewed it as a temporary inconvenience, not a permanent division between them. Elizabeth was both shocked by her easy acceptance of adultery and her expectation that everyone else would understand it as she did. "Is that what provoked your quarrel today?"

Eleanor nodded miserably. "I assumed he knew, but apparently it never crossed his mind, and he is determined to be such a... such a fool about it. Is his precious morality more important to him than I am?"

"He loves you. Perhaps he could not bear to share you with another man, to watch you marry another man, to bear his children. Perhaps that would be more painful than to give you up entirely."

"Yet he wants *me* to give up my entire life for *him*! My family, all my friends – they would refuse to receive me if I married him. I know *you* would not cut me, but all the others...I would never see my home again, never touch any of my belongings again, never move in the society I am accustomed to again. *He* would lose nothing apart from the ability to move in certain circles where he is hardly welcome anyway. Oh, how can he ask it of me?"

"Has he reproached you for your choice to marry Lord Deyncourt?"

A sob escaped Eleanor. "Not in so many words. He *says* that he understands I must obey my father, but I can tell he does not. Men think nothing of what a woman gives up when she marries; they expect us to leave everything behind while everything stays the same for them."

"He will need an heir as well. How will you feel when he marries?"

"I shall *hate* it, of course, but I shall not blame him, as long as his heart remains mine."

"And what of his wife? Will she accept so easily that her husband loves another?"

"Do not look at me like that, Lizzy! I have no wish to hurt anyone; you know that. But since my father will not consider Geoffrey's suit, there is no hope for a solution that would be happy for everyone. And it will be nothing but misery for me, for I will never see him again, and now I will know that he despises me as well."

Elizabeth patted her arm. "I am certain he does not despise you. He is angry, yes, but that does not mean his feelings for you have changed."

"But how can he *not* despise me? Sometimes *I* despise myself. Every other girl in the world is happy to follow her father's wishes. Why cannot I do the same?"

"Where in the world did you come across that idea? When girls happen to agree with their fathers, they are happy to follow his wishes, but not if they disagree – or perhaps you think women should have no minds of their own?"

"I might be happier if I did not have a mind of my own," muttered Eleanor. "Are there so many girls who do not wish to marry their father's choice? Everyone tells me it is a great personal failing and that I should pray for forgiveness and humility."

"Allow me to guess – this 'everyone' of whom you speak would be your father and your brothers?"

"And my stepmother."

"Of course. All the people who would benefit if you are happy with whatever you are given. I have four sisters, and I can tell you there is nothing at all natural about wishing to follow your father's commands! While I cannot advise *refusing* your father's commands, my dear, there is no reason whatsoever that you should *like* it."

Eleanor raised her head to stare at Elizabeth. "Are you serious? You would not be ashamed if you did not wish to please your father above all else?"

"If I *did* wish it, I would take to my bed instantly because it would be a certain sign that I was seriously ill! It is as ridiculous as if I said you should be ashamed not to agree with everything *I* say simply because you are my friend. This is what comes of not allowing you to go to school or spend time with other young ladies! Do you truly think your father has chosen your husband-to-be based solely on what is best for you? Or is he thinking of what is best for *him*?"

"Should *I* not want what is best for him, too? He is my father."

"You are his daughter, not his possession. He can force you to do whatever he likes, but he cannot make you *think* whatever he likes. You are a person, not a puppet." Elizabeth could see from her friend's dubious expression that she was not convinced. "Have you never spoken to the other young ladies in London? Do they all wish for nothing but to please their fathers?"

"They never talked about that, just about which gentlemen were the most handsome or richest and how to catch their eye. That had no interest for me because I only wanted Geoffrey, and I dared not say so. Now I have lost him as well." The tears began to pour down her cheeks once more. "I have loved none but him, and now he hates me."

"Just because you quarreled does not mean he no longer loves you." Elizabeth wished she knew the right thing to say. Encouraging a rapprochement with Mr. Paxton would be asking for more heartbreak, but it seemed cruel to allow her to believe he had rejected her forever. "He was invited to hunt with the other gentlemen tomorrow, was he not? We can walk down by the stables in the morning, and perhaps you will be able to steal a moment with him to explain." And perhaps she would be able to see Mr. Darcy, at least from a distance. She needed to do some serious thinking between now and the next time they spoke together.

Chapter 9

THE FOLLOWING MORNING Elizabeth and Eleanor haunted the wilderness walk near the stables, but no one arrived from Hillington Hall. When the hunters rode out without Darcy or Paxton, Eleanor announced her intention to retire to her room and write letters. Since she made no mention of an invitation to join her, Elizabeth knew to whom the letter must be.

Left with sudden free time, Elizabeth was seized by the urge to take a long walk of the sort there had been little opportunity for during her stay. Before anyone could take notice and insist that she join the other ladies indoors, she set off down the path to the abbey ruins. The exertion elevated her spirits, but could not stop the question in her mind of why Darcy had not come for the hunt, given that it would offer the opportunity to see her afterwards. That Paxton would not wish to attend did not surprise her; he did not strike her as a man who easily put aside his principles. But why would Darcy stay away?

Surely after yesterday he would wish to see her, would he not? There must be a reason for his absence. Perhaps Paxton was so disturbed by his quarrel with Eleanor that Darcy felt it unwise to leave him alone, or he might think it not worth the time to spend half the day hunting for the prospect of a few minutes' conversation with her at the end. While her vanity did not like that possibility, her reason could not argue with it.

Despite the intention of taking a leisurely survey of the ruins, Elizabeth found that her feet led her to the dark room where she had sat with Darcy during his megrim on the day of the picnic. Since there was no one to observe her this time, she curled up on the bench, pulling her legs under her. Was that the day that her view of him had begun to change, or was it even earlier? That moment during the waltz when she realized she was hurting him – that she even *possessed* the capacity to hurt him – had been a revelation, as had the experience of losing herself in the dance with him. Looking back, she could finally admit what she had not allowed herself to at the time. She had not wanted the waltz to end, not when she felt safe and warm spinning around the room in his arms.

But whenever it might have been, she had indeed changed toward him. Some of her reservations about him were not yet resolved, but she had seen enough to assure her of his basic honorability and trustworthiness. He had certainly demonstrated his constancy and willingness to forgive. Yes, if he should make her another offer, she would know what to respond. And if he did *not* make another offer...That idea sent a cold shiver down her back.

The next day would be a better test of his intentions. Darcy and Paxton had been invited to join the house party on an excursion to York Minster. Unlike the previous day, this would allow extended opportunities for interaction, perhaps even for private conversation. But once again her hopes were destined to be disappointed as neither gentleman appeared. Her first flutters of disappointment were disregarded as she attended to Eleanor, whose countenance had become increasingly dull since the previous day when Elizabeth accompanied her to the tree where she and Paxton left their messages for one another. The letter Eleanor had placed there the previous day was still in the hiding place, and there was nothing waiting for her there, the first time such a thing had occurred.

Elizabeth's only relief at first had been the continued absence of Lord Charles. No one seemed concerned about his disappearance without a word, assuming that since his valet was also missing, they were no doubt together on some errand he preferred to keep private. Elizabeth thought he had most likely discovered some other mischief to get into, and wondered whose life he was trying to ruin now.

But when the party returned from the outing to York, Lord Charles was once again ensconced in his favorite chair reading the newspaper with a half-empty snifter of brandy beside him. In his usual smooth manner, he greeted the returning party without any reference to his absence or sudden return. Elizabeth's heart sank when she heard his voice, and she instantly turned to say something to Lady Eleanor. Afterwards, she could not remember what she and her friend had conversed about, only that it gave her an excuse not to look in Lord Charles's direction. It made little difference to her self-consciousness, since she imagined she could feel the weight of his gaze on her in any case.

With the absence of Darcy and Paxton, Elizabeth knew it would be difficult to avoid conversing with Lord Charles. In hindsight she could see they must have deliberately taken turns to avoid leaving her in a position where Lord Charles could approach her, giving him less time when he could hope to have a tête-à-tête with her. And fool that she was, she had allowed his approach!

She would no longer be deceived by him, though. Even during his absence she had not felt safe, and had instituted the precaution of requesting that her maid sleep in her room at night. A locked door no longer seemed an adequate defense. She had told the puzzled maid that one of the gentlemen had made an indecent proposal to her and she felt safer not being alone at night. Elizabeth wondered whether the maid's easy acceptance of this explanation was owing to the absolute obedience of the servants at Bentham Park or to her knowledge of Lord Charles's ways. She suspected it was the latter.

In any case, it was not within her ability to prevent Lord Charles from approaching her when they were both in company. She said as little as possible to him on those occasions without direct incivility. He had the temerity to look injured, which made Elizabeth seethe inside.

It did not help matters when Darcy again failed to make an appearance on the following day. This time she could not conceive of a possible excuse except that he regretted what had happened between them on the moor. She told herself it was for the best, that she should not have allowed herself to soften towards him. She should be grateful that Darcy, unlike Lord Charles, had at least done his wooing in private. But nothing could ease the sick feeling in her stomach that his absence had engendered. Had Darcy felt some fraction of this when she had rejected him? Doubts pulled at her heart as well as her conscience.

At least the end of the uncertainty was in sight. Darcy and Paxton had long ago accepted an invitation to the Midsummer Eve dinner that was to mark the end of the house party. There had been nothing tentative about this plan. Several neighbors had been invited to join the company, and the house party guests were to depart over the next two days. If Darcy did not attend the dinner, she would know he did not intend to return, regardless of the kisses and intimate looks they had shared. The idea made her ill. She would have to forget him, no matter how difficult it might be.

Darcy had spent three days questioning his motivations and was no closer to an answer than when he had started. Paxton's damned quarrel with Lady Eleanor had put him in an impossible position with conflicting expectations and demands from too many people. "I cannot simply refuse to attend the dinner at Bentham Park," he said for at least the third time. "I am sorry it puts you in an uncomfortable position, and I will give Lord and Lady Bentham your excuses. But I cannot offend my relatives, however distant, simply because Lady Eleanor offended you." Not to mention that he would cut off his right hand rather than leave things unsettled with Elizabeth after their time on the moor.

"Go, then, if you must," Paxton growled. "But if *she* speaks to you, I want to know nothing of it, and I hope you will tell her nothing of me."

"I will do my best." Try as he might, Darcy could find no anger in himself toward Lady Eleanor for her assumptions. From an intellectual point of view, he could see objections to the idea of a woman marrying with the intention of later infidelity, but since such arrangements were the rule rather than the exception among the *ton*, he could hardly fault Lady Eleanor for assuming Paxton would think the same. So why did the assumption which seemed natural in Lady Eleanor feel repugnant if he considered applying it to Elizabeth? Despite his understanding of Lady Eleanor's position, he could comprehend Paxton's as well. It would be intolerable if Elizabeth were to tell him that she was marrying another, but offered to take him as a lover later. Not that she was ever likely to agree to an affair, but the very idea of being with her when she was married to another man made him want to rend his skin open with his fingernails until he bled. No, he understood Paxton's distress all too well.

Of course, he was only telling his friend part of the truth about attending the dinner. He was indeed obliged on family grounds to honor his promise to dine at Bentham Park, but it was Elizabeth's presence there that made it impossible for him to stay away. The memory of the look on her face after he kissed her haunted him. What would have followed had they been able to see one another the next day? Could he finally have told her of his feelings in a way that would warm her heart rather than drive her away? Or perhaps it was only a momentary softening on her part, and a few minutes' reflection would bring her dislike of him back to life. He could not bear to leave Yorkshire without some sort of resolution.

When Darcy came downstairs after dressing for dinner with unusual care, he was greeted by the surprising sight of Paxton in evening wear. "Will you be coming after all?" Darcy asked.

"I realized you were right. We accepted the invitation and I should honor it. It would be discourteous to leave the party one man short."

Darcy studied his friend for a moment. "I hope you are not planning anything that could embarrass you later."

Paxton gave a mirthless laugh. "Hardly. I assure you that if I speak to *her* at all, no one will be able to fault my manners."

"Are you certain you wish to do this?"

"Of course I do not *wish* it, but I will not let the Carlisles have the satisfaction of scorning me because I did not attend when I had promised to do so."

"I understand." Darcy only hoped that Paxton's presence would not interfere with his opportunity to speak to Elizabeth.

Elizabeth had been uncharacteristically nervous all day. She would have liked to attribute her anxiety to Eleanor's distress, but she was perfectly aware that, had there been no question of Darcy's absence, she could have borne the strain of her friend's moods somewhat better. Eleanor picked at her food and had grown a little paler with each day, although no one but Elizabeth seemed to notice. That morning, at Eleanor's request, she had gone to the message tree without her. On receiving the intelligence that her last letter still remained there untouched, Eleanor burst into tears and told Elizabeth to leave her.

Lady Bentham had other plans, however. She sent a maid to demand Eleanor's immediate attendance at the festivities in preparation for Midsummer Eve. Shortly thereafter, a perfectly coiffed Eleanor with a perfectly false smile and perfectly swollen red eyes appeared to join the rest of the house party in gathering greens to decorate the doorway. Not that any of Lady Bentham's guests would dirty their hands with actual labor, of course; piles of already cut birch branches and greenery were neatly arranged along the woodland walk for the convenience of the guests who could choose their favorite pieces and indicate to the servants precisely where they were to be hung.

From Eleanor's demeanor, one might have thought it the culmination of her dreams of pleasure. She examined one pile after another, prettily exclaiming over the merits of one branch versus its neighbor. The other ladies seemed equally excited by this mundane task, leaving Elizabeth to wonder whether it was a particular treat for them to be allowed to participate even this far in the revelry. She certainly had not expected Miss Elliot to lay aside her fashionable languor to join in the activity, but she had done so.

Lord Charles's familiar voice interrupted her thoughts. "For you, Miss Bennet." He held out a bouquet of vervain, ferns and St. John's

Wort he must have gathered himself, given the lack of formal arrangement.

She raised an eyebrow, surprised he would take so much trouble when she had been all but refusing to speak to him since his return. Unfortunately, she could not ignore him in front of all the other guests. "How kind of you," she said without meeting his eyes.

He pressed the bouquet into her hands with an oddly eager look. "They say that if you put some of these under your pillow tonight, you will dream of the man you are to marry."

Unbidden, the image of Darcy rose before her. She had almost forgotten her anxiety over him in the activity, but now it came back to her with gut-clenching force. "I imagine it is preferable to a grass snake under the pillow," she said coolly.

"I hope flowers will be a more pleasant awakening for you, although I have to confess, I rather liked the snake. I kept it for a week in an old trunk that I filled with grasses and twigs, but then one of the maids found it and started to scream. I told you that all the Carlisles are mad for animals – even snakes." He smiled at the memory.

If he thought this would soften her toward him, he was wrong. "How very fitting, my lord." She turned to Eleanor and began talking of the plans for dinner.

Chapter 10

IT WAS EARLY YET when Elizabeth went down to dinner, anxious for the time to pass and to give her an answer to the question of whether Darcy and Paxton would come. Perhaps they had already sent their excuses. Lady Bentham might have seen no reason to inform her daughter and the least important of her guests. The room was already half full when Eleanor appeared, looking every inch the noble lady. Only when she was sitting beside Elizabeth did it become apparent she had employed face paint to cover the circles under her eyes. Her voice was pleasant but brittle as she exchanged pleasantries with Miss Elliot. Her eyes kept darting toward the door.

If the gentlemen did not arrive in the next ten minutes, they were not coming, and Elizabeth would need to forget Mr. Darcy. She could not help glancing at the clock on the mantel, only to discover that a mere minute or two had passed since she had checked it last. Scolding herself for her silliness, she resolutely turned to Eleanor and entered into a conversation with Miss Elliot on the latest styles.

Eleanor's sharp, indrawn breath made her look up. There, in the doorway, stood Mr. Darcy, with the shape of Mr. Paxton behind him. Relief flooded through Elizabeth, and for a minute she could not tear her eyes away from him as he conversed with Lord Bentham. Feeling the heat in her cheeks, she forced herself to look away.

It was only a few minutes, but it seemed an eternity until Darcy crossed the room to join them. Bowing, he said, "Lady Eleanor, Miss

Elliot." Turning to Elizabeth, he paused. "Miss Bennet." His voice sounded somehow different.

When Elizabeth looked up from her curtsey, her eyes met his with an almost palpable shock. She was accustomed to finding Darcy gazing at her at unexpected times, but something about his look today seemed to search deep within her with an almost intolerable intimacy. It made her glad to resume her seat, since her legs felt distinctly wobbly.

Eleanor's practiced social voice interrupted the moment. "Will you not join us, Mr. Darcy? We have not had the pleasure of your company these last few days."

He bowed again and took the seat next to Elizabeth, his nearness causing her to flush, even though she had been seated just as close to him on several occasions in the past. "I would have liked to have been here sooner, but certain matters at Hillington demanded my attention. I have regretted that it cost me the opportunity to be in your company, Lady Eleanor. I hope you will forgive my absence."

Unable to repress the urge, Elizabeth murmured, "No calling card, sir?"

The warmth of his gaze would have set tinder ablaze. This time Elizabeth was glad when Eleanor's voice gave her an excuse to look away, relief that she had not lost his regard overwhelming her.

"I do hope your business was resolved to your satisfaction." Eleanor's voice had a tight edge, making Elizabeth suddenly aware that Paxton had not accompanied Darcy when he joined them. He was across the room with his back to them, apparently deep in conversation with Captain Bradley. Paxton had never before failed to make his way to Eleanor's side at the earliest opportunity. He might as well have forsworn Eleanor to her face.

Darcy did not pretend to misunderstand, but he glanced significantly at Miss Elliot. "It is a problem between two parties that defies a simple solution, but I have done what little was in my power."

Eleanor did not respond immediately. Seeing her friend swallowing hard, Elizabeth stepped in to fill the silence. "It is always trying to mediate disputes, since I find often the solution can only come from communication between the principals. Why, I recall a disagreement that was resolved only when I received a *letter* which made me realize I had misunderstood certain events." Would he understand her emphasis on 'letter' was a hint that such a letter existed?

Darcy seemed to be struggling with himself. "Did the letter *soon* make you think better of...the other party? One never knows with a letter if the recipient will, on reading it, give any credit to its contents."

Normally Elizabeth would have laughed, but tonight she felt incapable of it. "Not immediately, I am sorry to say. My opinions tend to be decided ones, and, like most people, I dislike discovering that I am in the wrong. It took several readings to convince me I had not been in possession of all of the facts of the matter." Now she was able to manage an arch smile. "Over time, I even forgave the writer for having been right when I was wrong."

A slow smile grew on his face. "That was generous of you. Of course, most disagreements are not simple; usually I find there is error and misunderstanding on *both* sides."

Miss Elliot snapped her fan shut, apparently tired of being excluded from a conversation she did not understand. "Mr. Darcy, it is a shame you missed our excursion to York Minster. It is an astonishing sight, much larger and more awe-inspiring than it looks in the engravings. I have never seen its equal. Have you had the opportunity to visit it?"

Darcy shifted in his seat, as if suddenly recalling where he was. "Not since I was a child. I cannot say I appreciated it then, since I was more interested in exploring the city walls with my cousin Huntingdon so that we could pretend to be knights defending the city from attacking hordes of barbarians."

"I assume your defense must have been successful," said Elizabeth solemnly, "since I noticed no signs of barbarian hordes when we were there."

With a warm look meant for her alone, Darcy said, "It pains me that you would doubt the ability of two young boys armed with sticks to defeat a barbarian horde."

Abruptly Eleanor rose to her feet. "Excuse me. I find I am too warm sitting here." With quick steps she crossed the room to Paxton and Captain Bradley.

"Well!" exclaimed Miss Elliot. "I would have said the room was a little cool."

Darcy started out of his chair as if to follow her, then seemed to realize the inappropriateness of his action. "I hope Lady Eleanor is not ill," he said.

Seizing on the excuse, Elizabeth said, "Perhaps I had best join her."

But there was little she could tell by observing Mr. Paxton with Eleanor. He was perfectly polite, though he acted as if she were the merest acquaintance. Elizabeth did not know what to make of it – whether he was acting out of hurt or anger, or whether he wished for a reconciliation. Eleanor grew paler.

At least Elizabeth would have the opportunity to obtain some answers from Mr. Paxton once dinner began. Lady Bentham, who was not one to allow her guests to seat themselves as they pleased, would not miss the opportunity to put him next to Elizabeth. It was such a certainty that when Elizabeth found her place card beside the near-deaf Sir William, she did not bother to look at the card on her other side.

She was startled when Lord Charles took the place beside her. With a baleful look, she said, "I believe you may be in the incorrect seat, my lord."

He smiled at her warmly, as if he had forgotten all her coldness of the past three days. Gesturing to the place card in front of him, he said, "My name is here."

With a frown, Elizabeth glanced up the table where Paxton was seating himself between Miss Elliot and Eleanor, near the head of the table where Lord Charles and Darcy would usually be found. Lady

Bentham would never have chosen this seating arrangement. "You switched the place cards." Her voice was low and accusing.

"I needed to speak with you, and it did not seem that you would permit it at any other time."

"So you decided to force the issue. How charming."

The servants began placing the covers in front of them, causing Elizabeth to subside rather than to have her speech overheard.

"You are completely safe here. I can do nothing but speak to you. What harm can come of that? You have enjoyed my company in the past."

Tempting as it might be to make a sharp retort, Elizabeth forced the words back. Quarreling would just draw attention to them, and the less anyone noticed his presence beside her, the happier she would be. He had trapped her well; she had no choice but to converse with him at least a little, but she need not do it on his terms.

"I am not worried," she said lightly. "From the look on your stepmother's face, I do not doubt that you will regret your foolish action." Indeed, Lady Bentham was eyeing Lord Charles with evident distaste. Apparently she had no difficulty discerning who was to blame for the disruption of her carefully planned seating arrangement.

"She is the least of my concerns – and you are the greatest of them. When I left last week, you and I were friends, but since my return, you want nothing to do with me. What happened? Has Eleanor been telling you stories about me?"

There was a bowl of ragout by Elizabeth's place, and she took her time spooning some onto her plate. When she deemed the silence had lasted long enough, she said, "What think you of books, my lord? Have you any particular favorites?"

He lowered his voice. "Pray, Elizabeth, do not do this to me, I beg you."

She cocked her head to one side. "I do *not* recall granting you the right to make free with my Christian name."

"My apologies. I should not have said that. It is how I think of you, and it slipped out."

"Not as your Juliet?" Hopefully the scorn in her voice would give him pause.

"Juliet came to a tragic end. I want to make you happy."

His lies infuriated her. "*I* derive great enjoyment from reading. One learns such interesting things from it. I was reading the Gospel according to St. Matthew earlier. It is quite curious how things can strike one differently on re-reading a text."

He smiled. "I assume this has some lesson for me in it."

"I have always thought Judas Iscariot wanted the thirty pieces of silver because he was poor. I wonder if we would think differently of him if it turned out that the thirty pieces of silver were only an added incentive. Perhaps he *enjoyed* betraying our Lord. Which would be worse, do you think – betraying him for money or for pleasure?"

"I do not know what you have been told, but I have not betrayed you, nor do I intend to do so – ever."

"I know you will not, for *I* will not give you the opportunity. Which do you suppose has greater value – thirty pieces of silver or two hundred guineas?"

He did a creditable job of looking puzzled. "It would depend on the size of the pieces of silver, I suppose, but my guess would be that few coins of the time were the equivalent of even one guinea."

She smiled at him with absolutely no warmth. "Indeed, it is all about relative value, is it not? I am complimented that *my* life has such a great monetary value in comparison to that of our Lord. You see, your sister has no need to tell me stories about you when all I needed was to eavesdrop on the conversation of so-called gentlemen." Deliberately she turned away to face Sir William. Laying a hand on his arm to gain his attention, she pointed to the ragout and began to loudly praise its merits. Frustrating as it was to attempt to communicate to him, at least when Sir William looked baffled by what she was attempting to say, he was not pretending.

There was another benefit of giving the old man her attention. Darcy sat two seats beyond him, and she could take comfort in seeing his profile. When he turned to speak to the lady on his left, his eyes caught hers.

She could read nothing in his expression since the candles were just beyond him. Was he aware of her proximity to Lord Charles? Sitting on the same side of the table, he might be oblivious to it; but somehow it did not seem likely, given his tendency to watch her. What would he be thinking? He could not possibly think she would listen to Lord Charles's blandishments now, could he? Given her past foolhardy behavior despite his warnings, she could not blame him if he did, but she did not feel anger radiating from him as it had in the past. She tried to indicate her displeasure with the situation in her expression, but had no way to know if he comprehended her meaning.

Darcy directed a significant glance past her up the table. Although reluctant to turn back toward Lord Charles, Elizabeth followed his gaze to where Eleanor and Paxton sat. Her eyes widened on seeing her friend's wooden countenance. Was that a tear running down her cheek? Elizabeth would have sworn Eleanor could keep her countenance in face of an invading army should she so choose. Paxton seemed completely unconcerned, dividing his conversation between Eleanor and Miss Elliot on his other side. With a surge of anger, Elizabeth wondered what he could have said to her friend to cause her such distress.

"Miss Bennet," said Lord Charles gently. "Is something troubling you – apart from me, that is?"

"Nothing, I thank you," she said.

"I do not believe you."

Elizabeth shrugged. "Believe what you like, my lord. You will anyway."

"Pray, could we begin this conversation anew? I truly do not mean to anger you."

This was pointless. She could not keep sniping at him for the two hours that dinner was bound to last, not while also worrying about

Eleanor and knowing Mr. Darcy sat only a few feet away. "Very well," she said ungraciously. "I have no objection to a civil conversation over dinner, as long as it does not touch on personal topics."

A look of warmth suffused his face, one which she would likely have found charming only a week before. "Thank you. I have missed talking to you, more than you know."

"Pray do not waste your time with flattery, my lord."

"Actually, that was the pure, unvarnished truth." Something in his voice, a certain bluntness, a lack of his usual artificiality, made Elizabeth look at him in surprise. "I *have* missed talking to you, whether you believe it or not."

Unsure how to respond to this new approach, she simply shrugged lightly and returned to her food.

He leaned closer to her, speaking softly near her ear. "I will not attempt to deny that when I first met you, I wanted only one thing from you, and it had nothing to do with conversation. Nor were you the first; it was how I approached any attractive young woman who took my fancy."

Elizabeth's cheeks burned. "Lord Charles, we are in public, surrounded by your family and friends!" she hissed.

"No one is paying any attention to us, and you have left me no other option if I am to speak to you."

"You believe you can whisper in my ear during dinner without any effect on my reputation? I am not a fool!"

"If your reputation is injured, I stand ready to make amends."

"Do not be ridiculous, *my lord*. We have had this discussion before, and I repeat, I am *not* a fool."

"You are very far from a fool, and that is precisely why I have so enjoyed our time together. You seek nothing from me, and that is more rare than pearls. I had forgotten how to spend time with an unmarried woman from whom I do not have to fear entrapment."

"If you are trying to engage my sympathies, it is not working."

"I am *trying* to do something that I have little practice at, and that is to tell you the truth."

She shook her head with a smile. "Lord Charles, the only thing you are trying is my patience. If you hope that this approach will succeed where your earlier ones have failed, you are wasting your time."

"What will it take to convince you to listen to what I have to say?"

"You cannot buy good faith." Elizabeth glanced at Eleanor again. Her friend's complexion was white and she was biting her lip hard enough that it must be causing her substantial pain. Impulsively, she said, "If you wish to do something useful, you should look to your sister."

"If it is your wish." His brows furrowed, he turned toward the head of the table, then his breath hissed out between his teeth. "She cannot stay here, but I cannot take her away without a reason. Will you help me?"

As far as Darcy was concerned, dinner was nothing more than a dull interval serving as advance payment for enjoying a few minutes in Elizabeth's company after the gentlemen rejoined the ladies. He had at first been concerned to see her sitting next to Carlisle, but it was clear from her expression that she was no happier about it than he was. So long as Elizabeth was decided against Carlisle, there was no need for him to worry. As he had cause to know, she had no difficulty refusing unwanted attentions.

At least he had thought so until she unexpectedly left the table clinging to Carlisle's arm as if she required his support. She had not seemed unwell earlier. Was it possible Carlisle had slipped something into her wine to reduce her resistance? Darcy would not put it past him. Fury threatened to choke him. And now Carlisle was taking her out of the dining room, and she would be alone with him. Darcy's fingernails dug into his palms. If only his fingers were wrapped around Carlisle's neck!

It was intolerable to think of Elizabeth, unwell and helpless with a man who was determined to take advantage of her. No, he would not allow himself to feel rage; he could not afford a megrim right now. Swallowing hard, he willed himself to remain calm. It was a singularly ineffective exercise.

His every muscle tightened with the desire to follow them, but it would be the height of bad manners for him to leave the table without a reason, and it would make people ask questions. He had to stay there and remain civil while Carlisle took advantage of Elizabeth. No, that was ridiculous! How could he allow Elizabeth to suffer because others might think him ill-mannered?

Without conscious decision, he found himself on his feet and moving toward the door. The front hall was empty. Where would Carlisle have taken her? He would not dare to take her to his bedroom, not in front of the servants, so it must be a public room. But which one? The main saloon was closest, but it was empty, as was the library. Where could they be in this ridiculously huge house? When he was eleven, he had known every room. Perhaps the grand gallery? He strode past two startled-looking footmen without a second glance.

The echoing gallery was dark and silent. The music room was somewhere hereabouts, but where? Then he heard the faint sound of a woman sobbing, and he took off at a run in the direction from which it came. Flickering light came through a large doorway. The old orangerie, of course. He should have known the damned blackguard would take her somewhere secluded. He raced inside, ignoring the humid air and the greenery surrounding him. He was going to pull Carlisle off her and thrash him within an inch of his life.

Darcy skidded to a halt when he reached the circle of benches in the center of the orangerie. The light of a large candelabra revealed Carlisle leaning back against a table, looking quite at leisure, a lighted cheroot in his hand. Confused, Darcy looked beyond him, only to discover Elizabeth seated on one of the benches, her arms around Lady Eleanor, who was sobbing uncontrollably.

His breath rushed out with relief at finding Elizabeth safe and apparently unharmed. It was a moment before he realized the incongruity of what he had discovered. "What is the matter?" he asked Elizabeth.

She gave him a meaningful look. "I suspect you can guess."

So sitting together had not solved their problems as he had hoped it might when he had switched his place card with Paxton's. His endeavor had apparently made matters worse instead.

Carlisle took a long draw on his cheroot, then blew out smoke in a straight line. "You have fortunate timing, Darcy. You are just the man I wish to see."

"I am?"

"Yes." Carlisle tapped the ash from the end of his cheroot. "I believe there is something you wish to say to my sister."

Could Carlisle possibly have known of his maneuver with the place cards? That was the only reason Darcy could imagine for which he might be expected to apologize, but that would be to Lady Bentham, not to Lady Eleanor. He glanced at Elizabeth to see if she understood, but she looked as puzzled as he did. "I do not take your meaning."

"Come, Darcy, I am not a fool. It is time for you to come up to scratch."

What was this nonsense about coming up to scratch? Why would Carlisle wish him to propose to Elizabeth? This made no sense. Then he recalled Carlisle's first words about having something to say to his sister. He shook his head. "You misunderstand the situation. There is nothing between Lady Eleanor and me."

"I had thought *you* too honorable for this sort of game, Darcy. Why did you switch the place cards if not to avoid sitting with her? Look what it has done to her. Now you come racing after her like St. George in search of a dragon, no doubt in hopes of finding her alone. Unless you wish to answer to *me*, you need to say your piece."

Good God, was Carlisle threatening to call *him* out? If it were not such a serious matter, he would have been tempted to laugh. "I was not even aware that Lady Eleanor had left the dining room."

"Somehow I doubt you were eager for a rendezvous with *me*," Carlisle drawled.

Darcy opened his mouth to retort, then realized his danger. He still had no right to protect Elizabeth, and claiming to do so would ruin her reputation. Finally he said, knowing it was already too late to deflect Carlisle's suspicions, "I left the dining room for a few minutes and I heard someone crying."

To his astonishment, Elizabeth said testily, "Oh, just tell him the truth. Mr. Darcy and my father are friends, and he has been trying to prevent me from being alone with you. I imagine he thought we needed a chaperone."

Breathing a sigh of relief, Darcy merely nodded. Her explanation could still endanger her reputation, but the way she said it had stripped out any implication that he was interested in her himself.

Carlisle did not appear appeased. "And how does your friendship with her father explain your switching the place cards?"

"*You* were the one who switched the cards!" cried Elizabeth. "You as much as admitted it to me."

"So I did, but in this case, my dearest Miss Bennet, I was not the *only* person who switched them. Or perhaps you care to deny *that* as well, Darcy?"

"I would advise you to take more care in how you bandy about my honor, Carlisle. I do not deny it."

"And what possible reason would you have for doing so?"

"I have no reason to avoid your sister, but I did not desire to sit with Miss Elliot, for reasons I am certain you can guess. Paxton is beneath her notice, so she would not try to entrap *him*." It was the sort of thing Carlisle himself would do, so it would be hard for him to dismiss.

Carlisle tapped one finger slowly on the table as he considered this.

Elizabeth laughed. "I wonder how many other people have been switching place cards. Poor Lady Bentham must be distraught over the wreckage of her seating plan! Now, gentlemen, if you would be so kind as to take your disagreement elsewhere, perhaps I will be able to assist Lady Eleanor."

The dark look that Carlisle aimed at Darcy told him that this was not over yet.

Elizabeth watched them depart with relief. The last thing Eleanor needed was another quarrel.

"Are they gone?" Eleanor's voice trembled as she raised her head from Elizabeth's shoulder.

"Yes, dearest."

"I should have said something, but I could not face Mr. Darcy, not like this, knowing that he would tell Geoffrey about it."

"What did he do to you?"

"Geoffrey?" Eleanor choked back another sob. "Nothing. Nothing at all."

"He would not speak to you?"

"Oh, he *spoke* to me. That was the worst. He talked to me as if I were an ordinary lady of the *ton*, as if I had no thoughts in my head beyond lace and the next ball. He even told me not to trouble my mind with men's business when I mentioned something about the war." Tears began to flow down Eleanor's cheeks once again.

Elizabeth winced. "I am so sorry, my dear. That was cruel of him."

"Oh, I wish he had not come! Why did Darcy have to move the place cards? *He* at least would not have treated me so." Her voice dropped. "Then again, I would have said that Geoffrey would not have, either."

"He said nothing else?"

Sniffing, Eleanor dabbed at her eyes with a lacy handkerchief. "Yes," she said dully. "At the very beginning, just as we sat down, he leaned toward me and said, 'It is him or me. You cannot have both.' He is still determined to have nothing further to do with me."

"At least if you marry Lord Deyncourt," said Elizabeth carefully.

"I have no choice!"

"Eleanor, dearest, listen to me. What do you stand to lose if you refuse him?"

"Everything! My family would disown me, I would never be able to return to my home, even as a visitor, and I would be cast off by the *ton*."

Elizabeth had survived exile from Bentham Park and emerged the stronger for it. "Your stepmother would certainly never speak to you again, but I cannot see *that* as a serious loss. Your grandmother would not reject you. Your brothers are old enough to make their own decision, and if they are as perpetually short of money as you say, they might see the wisdom in visiting their sister with the wealthy husband. As for the *ton*, I have yet to hear you speak of it with any pleasure. Losing your home and your father would be high price indeed, and if that is harder than losing the man you love, then you are making the right decision."

"You do not understand! If I refuse to marry Lord Deyncourt, they will lock me in a room with nothing but a Bible until I am so weak from hunger and afraid for my life that I will do anything they say. They have done it before."

"Oh, my dear! I am so sorry." Despite herself, Elizabeth was horrified. She had not thought even Lady Bentham would go so far or that Lord Bentham would permit it. No wonder Eleanor had seemed to lose her spirits after her father's remarriage!

"I have no choice. Even marrying Lord Deyncourt is better than that."

"They cannot lock you up if you leave without their knowledge." Elizabeth would have been hard pressed to say if she were more shocked by what Eleanor had told her or that she herself was effectively counseling elopement.

Eleanor shook her head. "I am not yet of age. They would simply come after me and bring me back, and then it would be even worse."

Chapter 11

ELIZABETH HAD SEEN no point in hurrying back to dinner where she would be saddled with Lord Charles' company and Eleanor would be exposed to more coldness from Mr. Paxton. Still, after half an hour of comforting her friend in the orangerie, she thought it was time to return before their absence became too conspicuous. When she said as much to Eleanor, her friend announced that she had no intention of going back. She would go to bed instead, and plead a headache in the morning.

Although this seemed certain to draw disapproval from Lady Bentham, Elizabeth thought it unwise to mention it. Instead, she accompanied Eleanor up to her rooms and offered to stay with her, but her friend said she would prefer to try to sleep. This left Elizabeth with little choice but to turn her reluctant feet toward the dining room.

She was relieved to discover that the second remove was already ended and the servants were setting out the desserts. Although she did her best to enter inconspicuously, both Darcy and Lord Charles seemed to have been watching for her. Toward Darcy she gave a smile she intended to be reassuring, then adopted a cooler demeanor as she approached her seat.

Lord Charles said silkily, "May I hope you are feeling better, Miss Bennet?"

"I am, thank you. A little rest was all I needed. I appreciate your assistance."

"I was happy to be of service." He shot a significant glance toward Eleanor's empty chair.

Elizabeth rubbed her fingers together lightly as she debated how to answer. "I considered simply resting for the remainder of the evening, but I have been hearing for days about the amazing confections the cooks have planned for tonight, and I could not bear to miss them."

He nodded to show his understanding. "Do you have a taste for sweets, then?"

"I have become quite partial to ices during my stay here. I find them most refreshing." They were also a safe topic of conversation, as was the extensive array of decorative desserts and the model of Bentham Park done all in spun sugar and sweetmeats. It was enough to keep her conversation with Lord Charles untroubled until it was time for the ladies to withdraw.

Even after Elizabeth finally returned to the table, Darcy found the remainder of dinner dull, and the interval with the gentlemen after the ladies withdrew was just one more delay until he had the opportunity to speak to Elizabeth again. Since this was the last of his invitations to Bentham Park, he had to find a way to ask her for a private meeting. His body suffused with warmth at the thought. This time she would not refuse him. Even in the unlikely event that she asked for time to consider his offer, he thought her final verdict would be positive. After all these months, it would finally be settled, and Elizabeth would be his.

These reflections were far more satisfying than attending to the usual conversation that passed between the gentlemen over port, so he paid little attention to what was said and barely noticed when Lord Bentham left the dining room. His thoughts were too full of Elizabeth and the warm smiles she had bestowed upon him before dinner.

A footman interrupted his reveries to inform him that Lord Bentham requested his presence in his study. Shaking off his reveries, Darcy wondered what he wanted. Paxton had not received the same message, so it might be more questions about Edward. He rapidly revised that estimation when he discovered Lord Charles Carlisle was in the study as well.

Inwardly he groaned. Not more of this nonsense about him and Lady Eleanor! Carlisle had not said a word to him on the way back to the dining room. Darcy had hoped he had dismissed that ridiculous notion, but apparently he was not that fortunate.

"Darcy! Do come in." Lord Bentham gestured to a seat. At least he sounded friendly. "Would you care for some port? I have a particularly fine vintage here."

"Thank you." Darcy accepted a glass, less out of interest in the contents than because it would seem rude to refuse.

"Charles and I have just been discussing my daughter. I have not failed to notice that you have sought out Eleanor's company more than once since your arrival, nor that she has seemed particularly happy in your company, and unhappy in your recent absence."

How could he explain that he sought out not Eleanor, but instead the woman who was always by her side, and that Eleanor was not pleased to see *him*, but his own companion? "I enjoy Lady Eleanor's company as well, but I assure you it is nothing more than that. She has not shown me any sign of particular regard. I view her as a distant cousin, nothing more."

Lord Bentham leaned forward. "Darcy, I will be frank with you. You are no doubt aware I have an unofficial understanding with Deyncourt about her. It has not yet been formalized, as I thought it best to give Eleanor some time to accustom herself to the idea. I know him to be a decent man, but she does not wish to marry him, though she is unable to give any reason for her dislike. While I think she could be happy with the position he can offer her in the *ton*, you are family and not without advantages of your own. Most importantly, she seems to like you. It need hardly be mentioned that she would be an excellent match for you, and it would further cement the ties between our families. What do you say?"

Taking a sip of port gave him a few seconds to think. "I am honored that you would consider me as a suitor for your daughter, but I must confess I am not at present marriage-minded."

Lord Bentham leaned back and exchanged a glance with his son. "Perhaps you ought to consider becoming marriage-minded. It did not pass unobserved when you and Eleanor disappeared together for a substantial length of time at the picnic."

Darcy set down his glass of port. "I do not know where you obtained that idea, but it is not true."

"I have reports from three different people, one of them my son, that you did exactly that." Lord Bentham's voice was distinctly cool.

Carlisle drawled, "You were alone with her when you came upon Miss Bennet and me in the cloister."

"I had been alone with Lady Eleanor for all of perhaps two minutes at that point, accompanying her as she was seeking Miss Bennet. If that is enough to compromise Lady Eleanor, perhaps I should consider whether *you* compromised Miss Bennet by being alone with *her* for a substantially longer time!"

Lord Bentham said, "Miss Bennet's reputation is of no importance to me. After all of you returned to the picnic, you left again, accompanied by both Miss Bennet and Eleanor. Miss Bennet returned alone a few minutes later. Neither you nor Eleanor returned for some time."

This was ridiculous. Bentham must have servants watching his daughter's every move. Had Parsons been completely invisible to them, unimportant because his fortune was from trade? In a clipped voice, he said, "I admit that I did retreat to a quiet place for a period of time. I cannot tell you where Lady Eleanor was, but she was *not* with me."

"There are too many coincidences here for me to credit one more." Lord Bentham's eyes bored into Darcy.

After five years as Master of Pemberley, Darcy was immune to pressure of this sort. The harder question was how to deal with this. Given Edward's situation, demanding satisfaction for the insult to his honor seemed a singularly poor idea, but he could walk out and refuse to return. Still, if Bentham truly believed his daughter had been compromised, he was within his rights to be questioning Darcy, and it would not be wise to leave him in a position to make public accusations. He did not wish to betray either Paxton or Lady Eleanor, but he could also not allow his honor to be questioned.

"Since you appear disinclined to believe my word," he said frostily, "I would respectfully request that you send for your daughter, who will tell you that I was not with her during that time."

"I already spoke to her, and she says she *was* with you."

Darcy bit off a retort. Lady Eleanor was no doubt trying to protect herself, and likely did not realize what her father planned to do with the information. "Then Lady Eleanor is confused, because I was *not* with her at that time."

"You ask me to take your word over that of my daughter, my son and several witnesses?" Lord Bentham said. "Darcy, I do not wish to be at odds with you. I said nothing after the picnic because I judged you to be trustworthy, and I believed I could rely on you to do the proper thing if you somehow managed to engage her fancy. I rather liked the idea, in fact. Although Eleanor may not realize it, I do not like to see her unhappy, and I went to some lengths to find a husband for her who would not mistreat her. But if she found an eligible gentleman whom she preferred, I would not be displeased."

"I appreciate your honesty, sir. I can only repeat that I have the greatest of respect for Lady Eleanor, but I have done nothing to compromise her, and I am quite certain she has no interest in marrying me. If you ask her, she will tell you the same."

Carlisle said, "She did not deny it in the orangerie."

"She was distraught. If you wish to take her silence as consent, then she must also have consented to a duel between us."

Lord Bentham slapped his hand down on his desk, making the wineglasses jump. "What is this?" he roared.

"Nothing, Father," said Carlisle dismissively. "Darcy was making a jest."

Darcy raised an eyebrow. "I was *not* jesting, but I have no intention of engaging in a duel with your son." He might still decide to murder Carlisle with his bare hands, though.

"That is quite enough!" snapped Lord Bentham. "Darcy, I had hoped we could resolve this amicably. Let me be very frank with you. You were seen not only walking into the woods together, but also kissing her."

"That is ridiculous!" Darcy exclaimed. "I have *never* touched your daughter."

Carlisle drawled, "Tsk, tsk, Darcy. And you pretend to be so honorable."

"Who claims to have seen this?" snapped Darcy.

"Charles saw you leave together, and two of my servants followed her. Eleanor is an heiress; I do not leave her unprotected."

The servants no doubt reported that the tall, dark-haired gentleman kissed Lady Eleanor, and Lord Bentham did not even consider the fact that there were two tall, dark-haired gentlemen in the party. From the back, he and Paxton were similar in appearance, though no one would confuse them when their faces were visible. They both tended to choose coats in sober colors and with a conservative cut, and from the rear, no one could see the difference in their waistcoats.

He had no choices left. "You seem to forget that Mr. Paxton was also a member of our party. He can explain all of this."

Lord Bentham's lips curled into a sneer. "I am ashamed of you, Darcy. Trying to cast the blame on your friend, when you know full well that my daughter would never allow that creature to touch her. Enough is enough. If you did not want to marry, you should have thought of that before kissing her."

"My father is too kind to you, Darcy." Carlisle's voice was hard. "You have a sister as well, and I will defend *my* sister's reputation just as you would defend yours. You have besmirched my sister's reputation. If you are unwilling to marry her, then *I* will make certain every gentleman in London believes that I have ruined *your* sister. You can challenge me if you like, but even if you kill me, the damage will be done."

Darcy could hear the clock on the mantle ticking. He needed to be cool and rational. Strangling Carlisle would not help the situation. Forcing down the impotent fury that filled him, he tried to consider his options. Lord Bentham had no reason to believe him over his daughter if Eleanor said he was with her, and given her desire to hide her connection to Paxton, he strongly suspected she had done so. Paxton's testimony would mean nothing to Lord Bentham, nor would Elizabeth's. There was no way out of this. "Carlisle, I did not think my opinion of you could sink any lower, but you have just proved me wrong. Very well. I was *not* with your daughter in the woods, and I did *not* kiss her, but you leave me no choice. I will offer her my hand." And he would pray she refused it.

The Marquess waved to a footman who bowed and disappeared. "I am pleased you are seeing sense, Darcy," he said genially. "You will be glad of it later, once you have time to think it through. You like her, and you could not possibly make a better match. Your father would be pleased both by the connection and to add her dowry to the Pemberley coffers. Frankly, I cannot understand why you did not jump at the opportunity."

If all he had cared about was Pemberley and his family, he might have. "Perhaps it is because you are forcing me to break my word to another lady," he said icily. "My father would *not* have wished me to do that."

"Ah, is that how the land lies? That makes more sense." Lord Bentham had the gall to sound sympathetic. "Well, I am sorry for you, but protecting my daughter must be my first priority."

A discreet knock heralded Lady Eleanor's arrival. She took a few steps into the room as the footman held the door open for her. "You sent for me, sir?" she asked in a subdued voice, then looked startled as she took in the presence of the other two gentlemen.

Lord Bentham said gently, "You have done nothing wrong, my dear. I simply have a question to put to you."

Lady Eleanor paled noticeably. "I will do my best to answer."

"This is quite simple. Darcy has expressed a desire to offer you his hand. He is not the match that Deyncourt is, but if you would be happier with Darcy, it is good enough for me. What do you say?"

She turned a look of utter astonishment on him. "Is this true?"

Unable to trust his voice, Darcy nodded his assent. All she had to do was to refuse, and this nightmare would be over.

"But you know..." She did not need to finish the sentence.

"Yes, I know." His voice was clipped.

She looked down, her lashes fluttering as she blinked rapidly. He supposed this must be as much of a shock to her as it was to him. If only she had not told her father that he had been with her in the woods! But it still would have made no difference. Lord Bentham would have believed his servants.

The Marquess held out his hand to her. "It is up to you, my dear," he said gently. "If you prefer to marry Darcy, so be it. If you would rather wed Lord Deyncourt, we will forget this ever happened."

A trickle of icy fear ran down Darcy's back. If it were just a question of whether she wished to marry him or not, she would almost certainly refuse. But being offered it as the only alternative to a match she disliked was a different matter. He balled his hands into tight fists as he watched her chewing her lower lip in indecision. If she only asked for time to think about it, he could explain everything to her. He could live with anything, as long as she did not agree.

Finally she looked up and turned to her father. "Yes," she said, her voice perfectly steady. "I would prefer to marry Mr. Darcy."

As the ladies settled in the drawing room, Elizabeth found it strange to be in a group without Eleanor. She took an empty chair beside Lady Mary Huggins, who asked after her health in a very kind way. Having practically forgotten she had feigned illness to leave the table, Elizabeth hesitated a moment before answering that the heat in the dining room proved too much for her, but a little fresh air had restored her completely.

Miss Holmes, the daughter of a neighboring family who had been invited to dine with them, said, "I was worried when first you took ill, and then Lady Eleanor. I am glad it was not something in the food."

"I do not believe Lady Bentham would allow anyone to become ill after dining at Bentham Park," Elizabeth said with mock solemnity, causing Miss Holmes to smother a giggle.

Lady Mary said, with more of a wicked sense of humor than Elizabeth had expected from her, "I was more concerned that Miss Elliot might have an apoplexy when the two most eligible gentlemen in the room left to care for you."

Elizabeth laughed. "I can imagine. She wants their attention and I do not, so naturally the men flock to me, logical creatures that they are! I would happily spend time with you instead, but as it is, I have hardly managed more than three words to Miss Holmes until now."

Miss Holmes flushed. "I hope you do not think I was avoiding *you*. Lord Charles is usually by your side, and I *do* avoid him."

"I can certainly understand that!" Elizabeth said with a laugh. "I only wish I could avoid him as well. I would be much happier for it."

"It is not like that," said Miss Holmes earnestly. "I am fond of him, but for the sake of my reputation I cannot be seen with him, even in public. We were friends in our younger days, and later he would flirt with me, though always within the bounds of friendship. But when he fell in with bad company a few years ago, people saw our closeness in a different way. Simply having our names linked has harmed my reputation, so I have no choice but to ignore him now."

"I am sorry," Elizabeth said, and meant it. Apparently the warnings that Lord Charles's interest alone could harm her reputation were true. "It is unfair that you should be blamed for his rakish behavior."

A sad smile lit Miss Holmes's face. "Pray do not say anything to him. He does not know, and I do not want him to feel guilty."

"I will not say anything, but I do not believe Lord Charles is in the habit of feeling guilty about anything!"

"Oh, but he does! He plays the part of the rake, but underneath it, he is a good man. He was very different before he went to live in London, and I do not think he could have changed in his essentials."

Elizabeth almost stared at her. This was praise most opposite to her ideas. That Lord Charles was not a moral man had been her firmest opinion, and his behavior to her had supported that conclusion. But there had been times when she thought she had caught a glimpse of another person beneath his façade, so perhaps there was something to what Miss Holmes was saying. Still, good young men had grown up to be dangerous before, and Lord Charles clearly had no morals where she was concerned.

Sensing her confusion, Lady Mary said, "*I* am quite grateful to you, Miss Bennet, for keeping Lord Charles occupied. Lady Bentham seems to have decided that I would make a fine wife for him. Since I have no desire to occupy that position, it would be awkward if he actually took a liking to me."

"Really? She said something before the house party that led me to believe you had expressed some interest in the idea," Elizabeth said.

"Not at all! Though I did say something she may have misinterpreted. The *ton* is so talented in finding hidden meanings in everything they say that she may have read more into it than I meant. How typical of me! I am far too direct for the *ton*."

"What was it you said, if I might ask?" Miss Holmes asked.

"Something to the effect that I had heard a great deal about the beauties of Bentham Park, and I hoped to see it myself someday. And that is precisely what I meant, but she must have heard it as a hint, which would explain our sudden invitation here. I had hoped it might be for another reason, but I was mistaken." She sighed. "I do wish to be on good terms with her, but she does not make it easy."

Elizabeth nodded. "No, she certainly does not – though Miss Elliot seems to like her well enough!"

The conversation proved livelier than Elizabeth had expected, making her wonder whether Eleanor's presence served to subdue some of the other young women. She was grateful for the distraction, since it kept her from dwelling on the moment when the gentlemen would join the ladies. If she could be secure of having the opportunity to speak to Mr. Darcy, she would have been looking forward to it, but it seemed certain that Lord Charles would try to make the most of the opportunity to trap her into conversation. Darcy would most likely join them, if nothing else to prevent her from being alone with Lord Charles, but they could have no real conversation under those circumstances.

To her surprise, when the gentlemen arrived, neither Lord Charles nor Darcy was with them. She had a moment of fear, recalling Lord Charles's none-too-veiled threats to Darcy in the orangerie, but that was foolish. Darcy would not fight him over something as ridiculous as an imagined attachment to Eleanor, and besides, duels took place at dawn, not after dinner.

Mr. Paxton was the last to enter, his eyes flickering about the room, no doubt wondering if Eleanor might have returned. On failing to discover her, he came to sit by Elizabeth. "I hope you are better, Miss Bennet. I understand you felt somewhat faint earlier." While polite, his words lacked his usual warmth.

"Quite well," she said, wondering if he was looking for information on Eleanor. Surely Darcy would have told him what had happened. "I hope all is well with the other gentlemen. You seem to have lost Mr. Darcy as well as Lord Charles."

He shrugged. "Darcy is discussing some urgent business with Lord Bentham, though what urgent business can arise during a dinner party is beyond me. Is it always like this here – people disappearing and reappearing throughout dinner? I have never seen such behavior."

"From Lady Bentham's expression, I expect she never imagined such a thing occurring in her domain either." Elizabeth lowered her voice. "Why, I think that if I went too close to her, I might shrivel up and blow away simply from the sour look on her face!"

"No doubt Lady Eleanor will have to answer later for her disappearance," he said, his voice remote.

Elizabeth felt a flare of anger. After all, he was the cause of Eleanor's disappearance! "Perhaps so, but then again, she is no stranger to being the subject of Lady Bentham's displeasure. That might trouble her less than the displeasure of those whose opinions she cares more for."

He gave her a long look. "Personally, I would have said there is very little that could penetrate Lady Eleanor's self-possession."

"You would be much mistaken in that case," she said with a sting in her voice. "I may not always agree with Lady Eleanor, but I do not doubt the depth of her feelings."

He had the grace to look slightly ashamed. "I will bow to your greater knowledge of these matters."

It was going to be an unpleasant interlude if they continued in this line of conversation, so Elizabeth said, "Tell me, how long have you been acquainted with Mr. Darcy?"

Paxton seized on the new topic with evident relief. "We met during my first month at Cambridge. Darcy was in his last year, so our paths would not have crossed much; but as it happened we shared a fencing master. Darcy was his prize pupil. On my first day there, one of the young nobles was making the usual sort of comments about me to his friends, how I handled my epee as if it were a hammer, and so on. Monsieur Franchon overheard this, and before anyone could move, his sword point was at the young man's throat. He said, 'In my salon, we judge a man only by his skill with a blade.' He called for Darcy and told him to put me through my paces so he could watch."

"What happened?"

Paxton smiled in remembrance. "It was clear to me in a few minutes that Darcy could have dismembered me any time he pleased, so I was sure I was failing. Naturally, that only made me fight harder and use every fancy move I knew. Apparently I acquitted myself creditably, for Monsieur Franchon took me aside for some private tutelage afterwards, then had Darcy drill me. I did not know at the time that Darcy could have dismembered any man there apart from Monsieur Franchon himself."

"So you became friends?"

"After Darcy had drubbed me thoroughly, yes. I thought the world of him and could not comprehend why he bothered himself with someone like me, but later he told me he liked my attitude, that I fought back harder when I knew I was losing. He had no patience for pretentious lordlings, as he called them."

So Darcy liked people who fought back? Perhaps that explained why he had noticed her in the first place. Elizabeth considered that interesting piece of information. "I would have said he has no patience for anyone who is pretentious."

Paxton laughed. "Oh, yes! The things I have heard him say over the years to people who he believes are above themselves!"

Even though she was not facing the doorway, Elizabeth sensed when Darcy appeared in the doorway. Turning, she found his gaze on her, but the look in his eyes was one she had never seen before. He wore his haughtiest expression, just as he had at the Meryton assembly where she first had seen him. Eleanor was on his arm, looking up at him with a smile, no hint of redness in her eyes now.

Lord Bentham, who had preceded them, clapped his hands for attention. "My dear friends, I have joyful news. Although it will not be officially announced for some weeks, I want you to be the first to share my happiness in the engagement of my daughter, Lady Eleanor Carlisle, to Mr. Fitzwilliam Darcy."

The room suddenly darkened around Elizabeth. Surely she must have misheard, but as everyone began to gather around the couple to offer their congratulations, she knew the truth. The words stabbed like a knife through her, making her throat tighten as if she would never breathe freely again. Engaged to Eleanor? How could it be? His attentions to her, his kisses, the look in his eyes at the gardens – all had meant nothing, and now she was cast off completely, without even a word of warning or farewell.

Paxton was saying something to her, but she could make no sense of it until his hand descended on her wrist, pressing hard. "Miss Bennet," he said deliberately. "Have I told you how very lovely you look tonight?" At her baffled stare, he whispered fiercely, "Do not give them the satisfaction. Look at me. Flirt with me. Show them you need nothing from them."

It made no sense, but nothing made sense anymore, so she did as he said. Pasting a false smile on her face, she fluttered her lashes at him. "Why, Mr. Paxton! I did not expect such flattery from you."

"It is not flattery, madam, to praise what is beautiful; and nothing becomes a woman more than her natural honesty and modesty. Your directness, your desire to follow your heart, make you more admirable than the greatest beauty of the *ton*. You, I feel certain, would never value status over affection, nor injure those who believed in you by putting riches before sentiment." Had she not known better, she might have thought him to be admiring her in earnest. It was only his pointed words, no matter how light and admiring his tone, that gave away his bitterness.

She could not blame him. Paxton had far more right to be angry than she did. Darcy had never made her any promises, nothing but a proposal that she had rejected months ago. He was free to do whatever he liked, and it was a good thing she had found out his true character before it was too late. The man she had thought him to be would never have betrayed a friend by offering for his beloved, but she supposed it was all in a piece with Darcy's disregard of her sister's feelings for Mr. Bingley. With a deliberately warm smile, she replied archly, "Such sweet nothings, sir! But it is an admirable sentiment. I have often thought that a gentleman's breeding could be told by how much his friends could trust him."

"Precisely my thought, my dear Miss Bennet. I am delighted to find we are of one mind on this topic."

"I hope we will always be in such excellent accord, sir."

Lord Charles's drawl came from behind her. "Is this an accord to which a third may be admitted?"

Elizabeth jumped. In the agony of betrayal, she had completely forgotten Lord Charles's existence. Just what she did not wish for –

another deceitful man! "My lord, pray allow me to offer my congratulations on your sister's engagement," she said coolly. "I know it is something you hoped for."

"Yes, I did hope for it. Darcy took some persuasion, but I fancy he is now quite pleased with the situation. It is a better match than he could otherwise have expected."

"His mother was the daughter of an earl. I imagine he could have married whomever he wished." A bubble of resentment rose inside her.

"The daughter of an impoverished earl, not the exceedingly well-dowered daughter of a Marquess. It is a coup for him, you may be certain."

"Darcy has always been an excellent strategist," said Paxton with just a hint of a bite. "I think I shall give my good wishes to the happy couple and then be on my way. I imagine the celebration will go on for some time, and I have a long day ahead of me tomorrow. Lord Charles, would I ask too much to beg the loan of a horse? That way I can leave the carriage for Darcy."

"Of course," Lord Charles said, now all affability. "Tell the stablemaster you spoke to me."

Elizabeth privately thought Paxton had the correct idea. Perhaps she should retire early as well. That way she could pretend to be asleep if Eleanor sought her company later on. Tomorrow she could make some excuse why she must return home earlier than expected. "Pardon me, Lord Charles, but I must congratulate them as well." She took Paxton's arm almost before he could offer it. "Shall we?" she asked with a brilliant smile.

He covered her hand with his free one. "Indeed, my dear, it will be my pleasure."

Despite his relaxed air, she could feel the rock-hard tension in his arm. The few paces it took to reach the new couple felt like a desert that must be crossed, and then Paxton was shaking Darcy's hand with every evidence of pleasure.

Elizabeth doubted she could manage as much, so she settled for a polite smile. "My congratulations, Mr. Darcy. You are a very fortunate man."

Now that she was closer, she could see new lines around his mouth. His eyes were full of pain and seemed to plead with her. "I thank you, Miss Bennet. I hope we will have the opportunity to speak more of this soon."

Could he possibly think she would still be available to him now? If he was sorry to lose her, he deserved every moment of pain it gave him. Without answering, she moved on to Eleanor, to whom she offered an embrace. "Eleanor, dearest! You have been so sly, not saying a word of this to me. I hope you will be very happy."

Beside her, Paxton bowed correctly. "Indeed, Lady Eleanor, I wish you and Mr. Darcy all the happiness you deserve."

Eleanor's cheeks flushed. It was not hard to hear the hidden message in the clichéd words. "Thank you, Mr. Paxton. I am glad to know I will carry your good wishes with me."

Then they were past and into the freedom of the front hall. Paxton's face flickered in the light of the blazing Midsummer Eve bonfire outside the great windows. Although Darcy and Eleanor could not have seen them there, he bent over Elizabeth's hand in an attitude of intimacy. Elizabeth said softly, "You *do* have *my* best wishes, Mr. Paxton. You deserve better than this."

"As do you," he said gravely. "I admire your courage. It is Darcy's loss."

So he knew. She had wondered earlier, but now it was beyond doubt. Had Darcy said something to him, or was it just his own observation? There was no point in being coy. He deserved her honesty at least. "Thank you. I daresay we have both learnt something tonight about those who consider themselves our superiors."

He nodded abruptly, as if he could not trust himself with words. "Good night, Miss Bennet."

Her heart heavy, Elizabeth walked toward the grand staircase, only to find Lord Charles lounging against the balustrade. "A touching farewell, Miss Bennet. You should set your sights higher than Paxton though."

Anger bubbled up inside her, anger at both Darcy and Lord Charles for toying with her. "I do not plan to set my sights on Mr. Paxton or any other man. Why should I? Shakespeare said it best: *Men were deceivers ever.* Now pray let me pass. I am very fatigued."

He looked at her searchingly. "If I do, will you be willing to hear me out tomorrow?"

All Elizabeth wanted was to reach her room before she started to cry. "If you wish," she said dully.

He reached up and touched her cheek with two fingers, his lips curled in what she might have called a tender smile had it been on another man's face. "Then good night, my sweet. Until tomorrow."

Elizabeth went up the stairs with dignity, although she wished she could pick up her skirts and run. Run away from Lord Charles, run away from Darcy, run away from Bentham Park and all the lies that filled it. Tears were already sliding down her cheeks when she reached her room. Locking the door behind her, she leaned back against it and slid down to sit on the floor, her knees bent up to her chin, uncaring that she sat in complete darkness. Covering her face with her hands, she let the silent sobs come.

When had this happened? How had she allowed herself to come to care so much for him? At first she had wished nothing more than to be rid of him and his ill temper. When she had finally admitted there was more to him, her desire had been to part on cordial terms. Then, that day at the gardens, something had changed – and she had felt that somehow she *knew* him in a different way than she had in the past, and she had wanted to feel that connection to him again. But how had that turned into love without her even knowing it? How had it reached the point where the news of his engagement to another woman was a crushing blow, one from which she could not imagine recovering?

But the man she thought she loved did not exist. She needed to remember that. The man she had believed him to be, the man who valued honesty and loyalty, was nothing but a mirage. That man would not have wanted to marry the woman his friend loved, no matter how large her dowry or extensive her connections. She had deceived herself about Darcy, just as she had deceived herself about Wickham and Lord Charles. Never again would she trust any judgment she made about men!

Not only had she lost Darcy, but Eleanor as well. For all their disagreements, Eleanor was an old and valued friend, almost another sister, but this time Elizabeth would be leaving both Bentham Park and her friendship with Eleanor behind. She could not blame Eleanor for agreeing to marry Darcy; after all, Elizabeth had gone to great lengths to make certain her friend knew nothing of Darcy's role in her life. Eleanor could not know that her decision would hurt Elizabeth. But she could not imagine visiting Mrs. Eleanor Darcy, or seeing her with her husband. Eleanor would never visit *her*, of course. It had always been the other way around. She would never see Eleanor again, and she did not know if she could bear even to correspond with her and to hear about her life with Darcy. The very thought made her ill.

Eleanor and Darcy, Darcy and Eleanor – the refrain pounded in her head. She needed to get into bed so she had an excuse not to see Eleanor tonight. Tomorrow she would be able to handle it better. The pain would be less. It would have to be. She could not imagine living with this agony. Stumbling to her feet, she felt her way to the bed. She did not even trouble herself to change into a nightdress, merely removed her slippers with shaking hands, then pulled the counterpane over her.

Chapter 12

THERE WAS NO QUESTION in Darcy's mind that Paxton was avoiding him. Not that he could blame him, but how was he to explain himself to his friend when he could not even find him? First he had left Bentham the previous evening without even a word to Darcy, then when Darcy returned to Hillington, the butler insisted that Mr. Paxton had not yet returned. Darcy might have believed that had he not spotted an unfamiliar horse in the stable whose saddle bore the Bentham arms. Over the objections of the butler, Darcy had pounded on the door of Paxton's suite of rooms, saying loudly that he knew he was in there, but there had been no reply.

In the morning, Darcy had arisen earlier than usual – not that he had slept much in the interim – to be certain he did not miss Paxton at breakfast. The platters of food were untouched when he arrived, but Paxton never appeared. Finally he tracked him down in one of the outbuildings where he was meeting with his steward.

It took all of Darcy's restraint to make a polite request for a moment of Paxton's time. Paxton barely looked up from the account book he was studying before saying, "I have a great deal to do today. Perhaps later."

"You cannot spare me even half an hour?"

"Not at present. Perhaps this evening, if you are not otherwise engaged." Paxton said the last two words with evident scorn.

"I hope you realize that things are not always what they seem. My advice is that when something unexpected happens, you should always investigate further, because there may be more to the story than you know." It was all Darcy dared to say in front of Paxton's steward and two gardeners. When Paxton neither looked at him nor responded, Darcy left without a word, fuming. He was expected at Bentham Park to go over the marriage settlements. It was his duty, so he might as well get it done with.

In the morning, there was a pall of smoke in the air from the bonfires that had burned all night. Elizabeth had to force herself to follow her morning routine of stopping in Eleanor's rooms on her way to breakfast. Determined to disguise her low spirits, she entered with a smile on her face. The maid was still doing Eleanor's hair, and she seemed, if not the joyous bride-to-be, at least pleased to see Elizabeth. They talked of inconsequential matters until Eleanor dismissed her maid.

"You must have been up late last night celebrating with your family," said Elizabeth brightly.

Eleanor made a face. "Far too late."

"Your announcement took me quite by surprise. Was it not just a few days ago that you told your grandmother that you did not want to marry Mr. Darcy?"

"That was nothing against Darcy, simply that Geoffrey would be hurt if I married his friend. Now that Geoffrey has spurned me, there is no reason I should not marry Darcy. He is better than that fop Lord Deyncourt." Eleanor shuddered. "Given that I must marry someone of whom my family approves, I am happy for it to be Darcy. He is a man I can respect who will not wish me to be something other than what I am. Very few women are so fortunate."

"You no longer care if Geoffrey is hurt by your marriage?"

Eleanor's face lost its animation. "He will not be hurt. He made it clear that he wants nothing to do with me. Why should he care whom I marry?"

"Do you not think that his anger at you shows that he cares very deeply?"

Her lips tightening, Eleanor said, "It shows only that I proved a disappointment to him and that he means to waste no further time on me." Her strong words were belied by a quaver in her voice.

"I do not think him as fickle as that, but given that you are marrying Mr. Darcy, perhaps it is best that *you* do." Elizabeth was proud that her own voice had not shaken. "Mr. Darcy is a sly one, though. I had not realized he had the slightest interest in you."

Eleanor stretched languorously. "He probably did not. It was my father's idea, and it is very hard to refuse my father when he has his mind set on something.

A heavy stone seemed to have taken up residence in Elizabeth's stomach. "It was not his idea to make you an offer?"

"I expect his loyalty to Geoffrey stood in the way. Although we had no time to speak privately, Darcy said something about being put in an impossible position and sounded unhappy about it," said Eleanor indifferently. "No doubt he was speaking of Geoffrey. He seemed to accept it, though. I am a very good match for him, after all."

"Naturally, your family would be a desirable connection for him." Elizabeth wandered to the window, more out of a desire to hide her face from Eleanor than of any wish to admire the view over the gardens. Was it terrible that she wished Darcy to be bitterly unhappy? "I assume the two of you have some plans for the day?"

"He said he would call at some point, but nothing beyond that. My stepmother will no doubt wish to discuss wedding plans."

Spots of color showed in the walled garden beneath the window where early roses had begun to bloom. "Have you already chosen a date?"

"First we must decide on the announcement. Darcy insists that we wait until he can inform his sister in person, and he appears in no hurry to do so."

"He plans to remain here for now?"

"Apparently so."

Then she must be the one to depart. She had thought it through during the long, sleepless hours. She would stay two more days. If she left immediately, Mr. Darcy would know why, and she would not give him that satisfaction. She had lost enough on this trip; she would at least leave with her pride intact.

Wedding plans were not on Lady Bentham's agenda for the day after all, and apparently neither was Eleanor. She ignored her stepdaughter whenever possible, her displeasure obvious. Evidently the match with Mr. Darcy was not to her liking. She could not make any direct complaint since the new match was of Lord Bentham's making, but no one was in any doubt of her opinion.

When Mr. Darcy eventually arrived, the icy greeting he received from Lady Bentham did not seem to trouble him. Elizabeth did her best to ignore him, which was not an easy task when Eleanor kept trying to bring her into the conversation. She could not avoid looking at him altogether, and saw several pained glances he sent in her direction. She had no sympathy for him; he had chosen money and prestige over love, not caring that she was left without either. As the day wore on, he seemed to spend more and more time with his gaze fixed on the floor.

After an hour or so of this torture, one of the footmen came up behind her and said quietly, "There is a caller for Miss Bennet."

"For me?" She could not imagine who could be seeking her out here.

"Mr. Paxton awaits your pleasure in the entrance hall."

Eleanor's head snapped toward her, and even Mr. Darcy looked her way. Elizabeth said, "Well, I must not keep him waiting." She curtsied and made her excuses to Lady Bentham, then walked sedately to the hall, feeling Eleanor's eyes boring into her back the entire way.

Paxton stood before a portrait of an elderly gentleman in judge's robes. "Miss Bennet, thank you for seeing me."

"Would they not announce you?"

One corner of his lips turned up. "I did not ask, and it was not offered. Nor was I offered a place to sit, but at least I was allowed in the door, which is more than I would have merited a fortnight ago. I should count my blessings."

"This is intolerable! You were a dinner guest here yesterday."

"Ah, but that was when I had Darcy by my side. But the manners of those at Bentham Park are of little interest to me. I hoped I might convince you to walk about the grounds with me. It is a very fine day."

Although somewhat bewildered as to why he would wish for her company, Elizabeth agreed and sent a maid to fetch her bonnet and gloves. It was odd how quickly it had begun to seem natural to be waited on hand and foot, but leaving Eleanor and Darcy behind did not seem natural.

Paxton led Elizabeth through the front door. "What is your pleasure, Miss Bennet? The woodland walk or the ruins? It would probably be best to avoid the gardens lest my presence pollute them."

"The ruins, then." They set out across the lawn to the path to the abbey.

"You seem surprised to see me," he said quietly.

Elizabeth tilted her head to look at him. "Though we have spent many hours in company together, I have rarely had the opportunity to speak to you separately. Still, I must thank you for rescuing me from the drawing room. I was not enjoying the scene being played out."

"I would imagine not, and I am glad to have spared you from it for a time. But you are correct; I do not know you well enough to pretend that I came to check on your well-being. The truth is that I wanted your company because you are the only person in the world with whom I need not pretend."

"There is something to that," she agreed. "I take it you and Mr. Darcy have not resolved matters between you?"

"What is there to resolve? I have been perfectly civil to him, but have avoided giving him the opportunity to speak to me alone. He tried to tell me that this was not what it seemed, but how could I credit that? Either they are betrothed or they are not."

"How long can you continue that?"

"Long enough. I plan to leave tomorrow on an urgent visit to a sick aunt in London." His dry tone told her it was nothing but an excuse.

She laughed. "I hope her illness is not serious."

"Oh, it is very serious, so serious that it put her in the grave two years ago; but I am sure she would appreciate a visit and some flowers by her headstone. She is better company than I can expect at Hillington."

"At least Mr. Darcy attempts to speak to *you*. He only casts longing looks at me, as if I should have pity for him." She did not attempt to hide her bitterness. "I must ask one question, though. How did you know about me? Did he tell you, or was it a guess?"

"He told me once about a woman who had refused him. That was before he knew you were here, of course. He never mentioned your name, but when I saw the strength of his reaction to you, it was not difficult to put the pieces together. *Your* sentiments were more of a mystery. Although I could see you were not indifferent to him, I was not certain until last night when Lord Bentham made his announcement. Then it was plain in your expression." He paused. "I am sorry. For your sake, I wish your feelings had not been engaged."

"Did you share your suspicions with Eleanor?" If he had, then Eleanor's behavior meant something completely different.

"I raised the question once, but she seemed unconvinced, so I allowed the subject to drop. I thought you and Darcy had enough stumbling blocks to work through without the two of us watching you."

"Eleanor's understanding of these matters is sometimes quite different from mine. Apparently, she saw no impediment to accepting Mr. Darcy since she believed you had lost all interest in her."

"Lost all interest!" he exploded. "How could she think that?"

"It is a mystery to me, but Eleanor seems to have little faith that anyone would appreciate her for anything beyond her dowry or her birth."

"And you seem to think the same of Darcy, but I assure you, he is *not* indifferent to you." He made a sound that was almost a laugh. "May I tell you one of the truly reprehensible things I imagined last night?"

"What was that?"

"You will enjoy this. It was one of those midnight fantasies that makes perfect sense at the time but is ridiculous by light of day. I thought of making you an offer just so I could see the look on his face when he discovered how it felt to have the woman he loved marrying another man." He smiled at her in rueful amusement. "See, I told you it was truly reprehensible."

She gave him an arch look. "Overall, I cannot recommend it as a way to choose the future partner of your life, but I must confess I might enjoy seeing his face as well."

This time his laughter sounded genuine. "Well, I have no intentions of offering for any woman for quite some time, if ever, but I am sorry I did not have the chance to get to know you better, Miss Bennet. I hope we will have the opportunity to cross paths again someday."

"I fear it is unlikely. We have only two acquaintances in common, and I do not anticipate that I will visit either of them in the future."

"Nor I," he said in a heartfelt voice. "Well, perhaps I will call on you someday in Hampshire... no, wait, it is Hertfordshire, is it not? Where is your home?"

"It is near the market town of Meryton in Hertfordshire, not ten miles from the Great North Road."

"There you are! I pass by it regularly."

Elizabeth knew that this was a game of make believe, and that he would never come to Longbourn. Neither of them would want any reminders of this time, but it was comforting to pretend they were not quite alone in the world with their losses.

Clocks, Darcy decided, were an invention of the devil, especially the one sitting on the mantel opposite him, the ornate one almost overpowered by the detailed sculptures of shepherds embracing their lady loves. Were it not for that particular clock, he would not know that Elizabeth had been out walking with Paxton for an hour and thirteen minutes. Despite their many years of friendship, Paxton had been unable to spare one minute to speak to Darcy, yet he could find seventy-three minutes for Elizabeth, whom he barely knew. That gave Darcy seventy-three minutes to castigate himself for listening for the sound of the door opening to herald their return, seventy-three minutes of wondering what Paxton was telling Elizabeth about him, seventy-three minutes of recalling just how much cause both of them had to detest him. One such minute could be an eternity of pain, and seventy-three of them surely must count as torture.

During each of those minutes, he had somehow managed to smile and make polite conversation with people *he* detested, those same people who had robbed him of his chance for happiness. To be fair, he did not detest Eleanor; she was almost as much a victim of this whole mess as he was. What could not be mended must be endured, and he needed to prepare for the strong possibility that he might not be able to extricate himself from this engagement. He had very few potential allies; Edward might support him in breaking the engagement, but he had no power with his father; and his uncle Lord Matlock would be enthusiastically in favor of the match.

If he had to marry Eleanor, he needed to treat her with the respect due to that position. And that meant not dwelling constantly on Elizabeth, not taking his pleasure by resting his eyes on her or delighting in her arch remarks, and not wondering what she was thinking and saying to Paxton for seventy-three interminable minutes.

The sound of the door closing gave him a brief moment of relief, but Elizabeth still did not return to the company. It was only natural for her to wish to freshen up after her walk, so he granted her thirty minutes for that task. When she did not appear after forty minutes, he tasted bile in the back of his mouth. Fifty minutes. An hour. An hour and a half. God, he detested that clock!

It was nearly two hours before Elizabeth finally joined them. Despite his resolve, Darcy drank in the sight of her. His heart thumped in his chest as her light and pleasing figure passed in front of him. She had changed her dress, and now she wore silvery satin slippers with light blue shoe-roses, unlike the tan kid half-boots with black leather lacings she had worn earlier. Those must have become dusty during her walk with Paxton. Where had they gone? The gardens, the ruins, walking along the river? Had she kept her hand on Paxton's arm the entire time? Had she laughed for him in that arch manner that caused the corners of her eyes to tilt up in an elfin way?

He had not heard a word anyone had said since Elizabeth appeared in the doorway. This was unacceptable. Turning his head toward Lady Eleanor, he concentrated his complete attention on her.

Lady Eleanor's shoulders looked tense. "Did you enjoy your walk, Miss Bennet?" she asked.

"Very much, thank you." Elizabeth sounded relaxed and happy. "It is a beautiful day and Mr. Paxton's company was quite entertaining."

"I had not realized he intended to call on you today."

"I believe it was a spur of the moment decision. His plans have changed unexpectedly, so he came to bid me farewell. His aunt is gravely ill, and he is leaving to visit her in the morning. He thinks it unlikely he will return to Hillington before Christmas."

Paxton's aunt was dead, damn his eyes! It was an excuse, and Paxton was taking care to make sure he knew it. Beside him, he heard Lady Eleanor swallowing hard.

Lady Bentham said, "What a pity that your acquaintance should be cut off so abruptly."

"I prefer to think of it as an interruption. He said that he hoped to call on me when I return home. After all, it is only twenty miles from London, and what is twenty miles of good road? Would you not call it an easy distance, Mr. Darcy?"

Was she mocking him by throwing his own words back at him, or was she deliberately trying to torment him with images of Paxton laughing with her at Longbourn? "A very easy distance," he said without looking at her.

Eleanor said nothing, but Darcy noticed the knuckles of her folded hands were white. Did Elizabeth not realize she was hurting her friend? He could understand why she might be angry at *him*, but Eleanor had done nothing to her. Perhaps her anger was on Paxton's behalf. Could Elizabeth truly have begun to care for Paxton? He gritted his teeth against a wave of nausea at the thought.

Just when he thought matters could get no worse, a few minutes later Lord Charles Carlisle crossed the room and took the vacant spot beside Elizabeth on the loveseat. Stretching his legs out in front of him, he asked her a question that Darcy was unable to hear over the conversation with Lady Bentham. At least Elizabeth knew enough not to listen to him – or did she? Since that day in the ruins, Darcy had seen her cut him several times, but today she was responding to his question with animation and apparent pleasure. This time there was nothing he could do to stop it without appearing grossly rude to Eleanor. All he could do was to watch out of the corner of his eyes and feel the loss of one more ray of hope with each laugh and arch comment Elizabeth directed to Carlisle. If Carlisle succeeded in his plans for Elizabeth owing to Darcy's inaction....Darcy could not even allow that thought to finish. But if Carlisle moved one inch closer to Elizabeth, Darcy would not be held responsible for the consequences. There was only so much a man could bear.

Finally the room began to empty as the occupants left to dress for dinner. Not having anticipated staying for dinner, Darcy could make no such preparations, so he hid in the library and tried to pretend an interest in the volumes on the shelves.

Elizabeth was more than ready to quit the company and remove the falsely sunny expression she had kept on her face for the last hour. She excused herself from Lord Charles before making her escape.

His hand caught her wrist. "Miss Bennet, last night you made a promise to hear me out today."

It was not the sort of thing she was likely to forget. Why did he think she had tolerated his company this long? "We have been conversing for the better part of an hour, sir!"

"What I have to say cannot be said in front of a drawing room full of people."

"I cannot be alone with you!"

"You were alone with Paxton today for over an hour." His mouth was set in a line.

If she did not know better, she would have thought him jealous. "We were walking in public where anyone could see us, not closeted in a room." It was probably better not to say that she had no worries about Paxton making inappropriate advances to her.

"Can we be alone if we also remain where anyone could see us?"

She stared pointedly at his hand until he released her. "Very well." It would probably be simpler to listen to his seduction attempt than to fight about it.

"Then we can talk here, if that will suit."

Glancing around, she saw that the others had indeed departed, though there were still a few people in the entrance hall. "With the door open."

He smiled gently. "With the door open. I know you will not credit this, but I have no intention of compromising you."

"You are right. I do not credit it, but I will attempt to pretend that I do." She chose a chair in direct sight of the door. "Very well, my lord, I am listening."

Naturally, he pulled up a chair so that it was only inches from hers. "Thank you. You do not know how hard it has been for me these last few days when you would not speak to me. That I deserved it, I cannot argue. But pray bear with me; I am going to try to be completely honest, which is something I have done little of these last few years."

Elizabeth raised an eyebrow. "I have no trouble believing *that*."

"It is a compliment to you that I undertake it." He took a deep breath. "Very well. When I first met you, my plan was precisely what you thought. I wanted to seduce you, and I thought that whatever difficulty it caused you would be your own fault, and only show what a fine fellow I was. No, pray, Miss Bennet – I am trying to say something important here. I quickly learned that the usual flattery and blandishments did not work on you as they did on the girls in the marriage mart, perhaps precisely because you were *not* in the market for a husband. So I had to change my tactics, and I discovered you responded best when I simply talked to you in a serious manner about things that mattered to me. That is when my plan began to go awry, for I discovered that I *liked* talking to you that way." He gave her a sheepish look. "I have never much cared about what ladies had to say before."

"I will grant that you are not trying to paint yourself in an overly favorable light." She was not taken in, but she was becoming curious about where he planned to take this extraordinary confession. Most likely he hoped to play on her sympathies.

"I liked listening to you as well. It was like a puzzle, learning the person who lay behind the pretty face and attractive figure, but my goal did not change until that day in the ruins. I told you things that day I had never told anyone before. Then Eleanor told me..." He broke off with a frown. "Darcy, this is a private conversation."

Startled, Elizabeth looked up to see Darcy standing in the doorway, holding a book and looking displeased. How much of the conversation had he already heard?

"Then pray continue it," said Darcy coolly. "Pay me no mind. I will simply sit over here and read."

"Miss Bennet's reputation is in no danger from me," Lord Charles said.

Darcy gave him an incredulous look. "You will have to forgive me if I fail to believe the leopard has changed his spots."

"Perhaps the leopard cannot change his spots, but it does not follow that he cannot change the leopardess' name."

"Not that again!" exclaimed Elizabeth, rising to her feet. "I do not care to be mocked by either of you."

Lord Charles blocked her way. "Pray, Miss Bennet. I apologize if you were offended. That was not my intent. I would greatly appreciate it if you were to allow me to finish what I was telling you."

With no great civility, Elizabeth said, "Oh, very well." She tried not to watch as Darcy chose a seat across the room from them, far enough away not to overhear quiet conversation, but in direct view of Elizabeth. It was almost humorous.

"I appreciate your tolerance, Miss Bennet. Now, where was I? Ah, yes. Eleanor told me the same story she no doubt told you."

"I cannot recall her telling me any story about you, but no matter."

He lowered his voice. "It involved one of those young ladies whose feelings I did not take into consideration and who left London to deal with the consequences. It turns out that she...." He paused and rubbed his hand across his mouth. "Pardon me. I find this difficult to speak of. She took her own life. That is what Eleanor told me, and it disturbed me greatly. Eleanor has been known to exaggerate things for her own purposes, and I hoped this was one of those cases. You will recall I left Bentham for several days after that. I needed to determine the truth of the matter. As it happens, Eleanor had not exaggerated." He blinked several times, then looked toward the window.

Despite herself, Elizabeth felt some pity for him. Even if he was selfish and shallow, it did not necessarily mean he was heartless, and clearly this had shaken him deeply. "I am sorry to hear it."

"I am not the one who deserves your sympathy. I would like to tell you that I fell on my knees in repentance and vowed to dedicate my life to her memory, but I did not. In truth, I barely recall what she looked like. What haunted me was that when I thought of her fate, I saw not her, but you -- in misery over my callous treatment of you, being rejected by your family because of what I had persuaded you to do, your body floating in the mill pond." His voice had fallen to a whisper, but now he sat up straight once more and his usual mask fell back into place. "Suffice to say that it caused me great distress. I hurried back to Bentham, needing to see that you were alive and well. My original plans for you were completely cast aside by that point. I only wanted to talk to you and to hear you laugh. Somehow I thought it would give me some sort of absolution – as if anything could do that. When I returned, you were alive and well, but refusing to speak to me, and looking at me with scorn in your eyes that I knew I deserved. It is still there now."

Elizabeth looked from him to Mr. Darcy, who appeared to be engrossed in his book. She had misjudged him as well at first, then slowly learned to trust him, only to have that trust betrayed. It had been a harsh lesson about letting down her guard with a man. Men spent their entire lives looking out for their own best interests, and it should be no surprise that they continued to do so. "Lord Charles, you have been through a painful experience. For that I am sorry, and if it has convinced you to reconsider your behavior, I applaud you. But I would be foolish if I did not consider the possibility that you might be playing on my feelings, attempting to elicit my sympathy and trust in an effort to disarm me precisely so you could take advantage of me in the same way that you did to that poor girl."

His eyes widened as if she had slapped him, and a flash of anger crossed his face, then was quickly banked. He took several ragged breaths. "That is understandable, I suppose, since a fortnight ago, I might well have done precisely that. While *I* know that is no longer true, you cannot see into my heart to know it, and you would indeed be foolish to give immediate credence to a man with my history. All I can hope is that you will allow me the opportunity to prove to you that I have changed."

"All I can offer is to grant you the benefit of the doubt, but to what purpose? I will be leaving Bentham soon and I think it unlikely we will cross paths again. It seems you have little to gain, unless you still have hopes for your original plan."

He took a deep breath, and then spoke all in a rush. "Miss Bennet, you are quite lovely, but there are many other lovely ladies in the world. I would not have bared my soul like this for the sake of a night's pleasure. I am not making you a proposition but a proposal."

What a fool she was! She had almost believed him up to this point. "My lord, we have discussed this in the past, and there is absolutely nothing you can say to me that would convince me you are sincere. It is very easy to make a promise, and just as easy to break it." She pushed herself to her feet and made for the door, avoiding the eyes of Mr. Darcy who had looked up from his book at her raised voice.

Lord Charles was there immediately, blocking her route. "Perhaps you will believe this. Darcy, may I have your attention? I need a witness." He took her hand between both of his and pressed it to his lips. "Miss Bennet, will you do me the very great honor of becoming my wife?"

How dare he toy with her! She snatched her hand back. "I will *never* believe you. Now pray let me pass."

He did not move. "I have made you an offer of marriage in front of a witness of good family. I cannot withdraw it. Tell her, Darcy."

There was a brief silence, and then Darcy said in a strained voice, "In that much he is correct. For what it is worth, he appears to mean it."

It would be hard to determine which of the two gentlemen angered her more. However, if she had learned one thing from the disaster of Darcy's proposal at Hunsford, it was not to allow herself to lose her temper. Digging her fingernails into her palms, she said, "If you are in earnest, my lord, then I thank you for the compliment of your affections, but fear I must decline."

He smiled tenderly at her. "You still do not believe me, do you?"

"Why *should* I believe you? You have known me for all of a fortnight, you know nothing of my family except that it is far inferior to your own, and you expect me to believe you have fallen so much in love with me that you are willing to degrade yourself by marrying me? Perhaps you mean it at this particular instant, but when you return to your right mind in an hour or two, you can thank God on your knees that I did not take you seriously."

"It is not just this instant, Elizabeth; I have been trying to tell you this for three days, but you have not been willing to hear me out. I cannot blame you for failing to trust me when everything in my past gives you no reason for trust, but I assure you, I will keep repeating this question tomorrow and the next day, in front of whomever you choose, until you do believe me." Placing a finger under her chin, he leaned forward.

She jumped backwards with an angry retort on her lips, but before she could say a word, Darcy interposed himself between them. "Carlisle, Miss Bennet is distraught. Perhaps if you allow me to speak to her separately, she will be able to see reason."

Now Elizabeth knew which one of them she hated more. Lord Charles looked puzzled for a moment, and then his brow cleared. "Ah, yes. You are a friend of her father's."

"Indeed." Darcy, clearly lacking an understanding of how close she was to striking him, took Elizabeth by the elbow and led her to the other side of the room.

"Kindly unhand me! What right have *you* to counsel *me* about marriage?" she hissed.

He paled. "I was forced into making that offer, Elizabeth. You, of all people, must know it was not what I desired! I am doing my utmost to delay making it public in the hope I can find a way out of it. I have *not* given up."

Her heart seemed to leap from her chest. Could it be true? Or was it just wishful thinking on her part? His reason made no sense. "How could you be forced into making an offer? Did they hold a pistol to your head?" she said scornfully.

He winced. "No. The pistol was at my sister's head. I could not allow them to ruin her life, even if it meant hurting you. I have been looking for an opportunity to tell you this."

She wanted so badly to believe him, but all she had suffered in the last day came to the forefront. "And since Lord Charles decided to propose to me, this seemed like the best time." He could not miss the cutting edge on her voice.

He glanced at Lord Charles. "No, but for *once*, pray *listen* to me. If you refuse his proposal, you make it in his best interest to do something to force you into marrying him. For God's sake, do not do that!"

She would have dearly loved to ignore anything Darcy said, but she could not miss his implication. "You think I should accept him?" she said in disbelief.

"No, of course not! Tell him you need time to think it over. Let him think he can change your mind with a little persuasion."

How dare he look at her like that when he was to marry Eleanor? And how she hated to admit that he might be right. Without a word, she turned her back on him and walked slowly back to Lord Charles, her heart pounding. "My lord," she said, striving for calmness, "This is so unexpected. I am overwhelmed by the honor of your offer. Would you be so generous as to allow me a little time to consider it? Mr. Darcy has reminded me that he knows you far better than I do, and that I should not allow myself to be swayed by third-hand reports and rumors."

Lord Charles took her hands in his. "Of course you may take time to consider, my dearest. I should have realized that this would be too much to take in all at once." Glancing over to where Darcy stood, he said, "Thank you, Darcy."

"You need not mention it," said Darcy coolly, returning his attention to his book.

Although Elizabeth wished for nothing more than to return to her room and hide her head under a pillow, there was something she needed to do first. She did not know what to make of Darcy's words, and Eleanor was the only one who might be able to answer her questions. Stopping at her friend's rooms, she found Eleanor alone, wearing nothing but a shift, quietly brushing her already perfectly smooth hair in front of a mirror. Her maid, who should have been dressing her for dinner, was nowhere to be seen.

Eleanor only glanced at her briefly on her entrance, then resumed staring in the mirror. Crossing behind her, Elizabeth took the silver-handled hairbrush and ran it through Eleanor's golden hair. "You seem out of sorts," she said quietly.

Meeting her eyes in the mirror, Eleanor said flatly, "How could he stop loving me so quickly? Or did he never love me in the first place?"

"Paxton? He has not stopped loving you, not for a minute."

"Then why did he come to see *you*?"

"Because *I* am the only person he can talk to about you. Confiding in Darcy is out of the question, and it is too painful for him to see the two of you together. We spent most of our walk speaking of you. You are all he thinks about."

"He is not courting you?"

Elizabeth laughed. "Lord, no. And I have no romantic interest in him either. I am just the only one to whom he can unburden himself."

"It would be so much easier for him if he loved you instead of me. He could just go to your father and ask for your hand, without any need to hide."

Elizabeth put her hands on either side of Eleanor's face. "Yes, it would be much easier for him if he loved me, but *you* are the one he loves."

"Even after I quarreled with him?"

"Even then. Tell me, did *you* stop loving *him* after your quarrel?"

The shadow of a smile began to form on Eleanor's face. "No, of course not. But he was already so angry with me even before this engagement, and now it must be even worse."

"It is not you he is angry with, but Darcy. You told him all along that you would wed the man your father chose for you, so he is not surprised you are doing so. He thought Darcy planned to help him in his quest to marry you, and instead Darcy is marrying you himself. Paxton is understandably bitter about that." Elizabeth began brushing Eleanor's hair again, but encountered a tangle. Eleanor winced as she tugged at it.

"It is not as if Darcy had decided to offer for me of his own accord. My father and brother put him up to it."

Elizabeth chose her words with care. "He told me they threatened to harm his sister in some way if he did not make the offer. Is that true?"

Eleanor's eyes widened. "I cannot say. I was not present at the time. Why would they do such a thing?"

"That is what I cannot understand." In her mind, Elizabeth heard Darcy's earlier words – *If you refuse him, you make it in his best interest to do something to force you to marry him.*

"Why would he need to be threatened? I am an excellent match for him. Perhaps it is his loyalty to Geoffrey."

Coming to a sudden decision, Elizabeth said, "Or perhaps his heart is engaged elsewhere."

Eleanor swiveled to face her. "I hope not. I would never wish to cause him the heartbreak I have known with Geoffrey. Surely he would have refused if that were the case!"

"Not if he feared for his sister," Elizabeth said slowly. "He is her guardian, and he takes that responsibility very seriously." She was not certain which of them she was trying to convince.

Eleanor frowned. "I will ask him. I would like him as my husband, but not at that price."

Elizabeth swallowed hard. "You need not ask him. It is true."

"How do you know? Did he tell you?"

"He did not need to." Elizabeth looked down at the brush in her hands. "He and I had just come to an understanding when all this happened."

Eleanor's face grew as white as her shift. "Oh, no! And you... Oh, Lizzy, I would *never* have agreed to it if I had known! Pray, you must believe me!"

"I know that, and while the news distressed me, I was not upset with *you*. He was the one who had abandoned me without a word."

Tears gathered in Eleanor's eyes. "I am so sorry! I have ruined everything for you. How you must hate me!"

Setting down the brush, Elizabeth caught her friend's hand in hers. "I could never hate you, dearest Eleanor. You could not have known.

I never told you because you were already suffering so much from your quarrel with Geoffrey, and I did not wish to say anything until I was certain."

"I will *not* stand in the way of your happiness! I shall tell my father that I have changed my mind and will not marry him – that I have decided I would rather marry Lord Deyncourt."

"Wait! You should speak to Mr. Darcy first. If you suddenly change your mind, your father may assume that Darcy asked you to do it, and that could endanger his sister."

Eleanor frowned. "You are right. I must somehow make it clear that he had nothing to do with my change of heart. But I *will not* marry him – that much I can promise you."

Chapter 13

WHY HAD HE AGREED to stay for dinner? Darcy could have been gone by now instead of facing endless hours more of Lord Bentham and his wife, not to mention his betrothed, to whom he had so little to say. Then there would be the pleasure of watching Carlisle making up to Elizabeth. What a hopeless situation!

Nor could he stop being haunted by the look of anger and hurt in Elizabeth's eyes when she reminded him that he had no right to say anything to her about marriage. She was the last person in the world he wished to injure. At the same time, a shameful part of him rejoiced in knowing she cared enough about him to be hurt by his sudden defection. But had she believed him when he told her that he had been forced into it? She still seemed so angry, and rightly so. He still hoped to find a way to escape the betrothal, but it was only that – a hope. He needed to prepare himself for the very real possibility that he might have to marry Eleanor.

Then there was the question of Paxton, who clearly had no intention of allowing him to speak. Did all their years of friendship not entitle him to a chance to defend himself? After all, Paxton's suit was doomed regardless of whether Eleanor was engaged to Darcy or to Lord Deyncourt.

But it made a difference to Darcy. Unbidden, the image of Elizabeth rose before him, with all the wrenching pain of loss, but that was not the only problem he would face if he married Eleanor. There was the matter of her family; Lord Bentham might wish for improved ties, but Darcy did not. If he could not engineer a way to break the betrothal, he would have to talk to Eleanor regarding his expectations about her family soon. He supposed he had no particular objection if Eleanor wished to visit her father and stepmother, but he needed to make her understand that he would not be joining her on such occasions, nor did he wish to entertain them at Pemberley.

Then there was Edward – another problem to be solved. If Eleanor resented Edward as much as the rest of her family did, she was not going be happy to discover her brother might be spending a great deal of time at Pemberley in the future. It was hardly reasonable to expect her to keep his presence a secret from her father. If Darcy could barely tolerate Lord Bentham now, it would be a disaster when the Marquess discovered that Edward was with Darcy. What a tangled muddle they had created!

Devil take it – the windowpanes were shattering into tiny diamond fragments. Damn his megrims! And this time he could not ask Elizabeth to work her magic to ease his pain. Instead he would have Eleanor, and he needed to become accustomed to that idea.

Elizabeth had not been surprised when Eleanor said she would not come down to dinner owing to a return of her headache from the day before. But yesterday's headache had been fictional, and judging by Eleanor's pallor and pinched brows after their discussion, today's was likely genuine. Elizabeth only wished she could avoid the meal as well, but even if Lady Bentham accepted her excuses, Lord Charles would not.

Even so, the atmosphere at dinner was stiff. Most of the house party guests had left, leaving only Lady Mary and her parents, Lord and Lady Alford. It was harder to disguise tensions in the smaller group. Darcy seemed withdrawn and uninterested in speaking to anyone, not even returning the tentative smile Elizabeth offered him. Had he regretted telling her the truth of his engagement, or was he angry with her?

Lord Charles was beside her at every possible moment. To his credit, he did not engage in any of the flirtation she found so displeasing, instead setting himself to ensure her comfort at every turn. It was the first time Elizabeth had been with him since his astonishing proposal, and she found it disconcerting. Having reflected upon it, Elizabeth no longer thought his proposal a trick, but rather that his character had more complexity than was initially apparent. She had heard from both Eleanor, who could be presumed to have a bias in favor of her brother, and from Miss Holmes, who should be biased against him, that Lord Charles had been different before his years in London. Now she could see that man still existed, at least to some degree, under the thick veneer of rakish manners. If her presence was helping that part of him emerge, she did not wish to discourage it; but she would have no interest in marrying him, even if she had no affection for Mr. Darcy.

She stole a glance at Mr. Darcy. He sat between Lady Mary and her mother, although he was not conversing much. His attention seemed focused on his plate, but he did not appear to be partaking of the food before him. His thoughts were a mystery to her, and they would have to remain that way for now. It might be some time before Eleanor could find a way to break off the betrothal, and even then, Darcy would have to wait a decent interval before showing interest in her. Since they could not go back to where they were, Elizabeth had decided that her only option was to pretend he was nothing more than an old acquaintance, at least until such a time when he could pay court to her properly. She did not like the idea, but could see no other choice.

When the ladies withdrew after dinner, Elizabeth decided Eleanor had the right idea. Claiming a headache of her own, she excused herself for the night. Her headache was not fictional either – it had been christened Charles Carlisle, though his distant cousin Fitzwilliam Darcy could claim a share in it as well.

Two gentlemen, two major difficulties. Oh, how she wished her sister Jane were there to advise her! The situation with Mr. Darcy would resolve with time, but Lord Charles would not wait that long. She had to tell him the truth sooner or later, and once she had done that, she would need to leave Bentham Park. That much was clear. But how could she leave? Lord Charles would try to stop her efforts to depart, and even if she somehow managed it, there was nothing to prevent him from following her to Longbourn.

In the end, she decided on a compromise. She would tell Lord Charles that, although she was pleased with the changes he planned to make in himself, she did not feel she could rely on it yet. Her answer for now would be no, but if his feelings for her remained the same in a year, he could ask her again. Some more obliging young woman was bound to cross his path in that time, and he would forget all about her – or so she hoped.

As satisfied with this plan as she could hope to be under the circumstances, Elizabeth was preparing for bed in the hope she might actually manage to sleep tonight when a maid knocked at her door. Lord Bentham wished to see her in his study immediately, it seemed, and his lordship was not pleased.

After a moment of apprehension, Elizabeth realized this might be the end of her problem. Why would Lord Bentham be displeased with her unless he had found out about Lord Charles' proposal to her? If Lord Bentham forbade the match, that would be the end of it.

She had never before entered the sanctum of Lord Bentham's study, and so was unprepared for the imposing sight of his lordship sitting behind the largest desk she had ever seen. It was enough to quail even the bravest of hearts, but she reminded herself that she had done nothing wrong. Well, nothing apart from deceiving him about his daughter's meetings with Paxton. Her palms grew suddenly damp.

He frowned at her. "Miss Bennet. Pray be seated."

She sat in the large wing-backed chair he indicated, feeling swallowed up in it like a child in an adult's chair. "You sent for me, my lord?"

"Yes. Tell me, where is Eleanor?"

"She is in bed with a headache."

Lord Bentham's brows drew together. "Try again, Miss Bennet," he said sternly.

"I do not have the pleasure of understanding you, my lord."

"Eleanor, as I believe you know, is *not* in bed with a headache. Now, where *is* she?"

She shook her head helplessly. "I have no idea."

The massive desk was daunting enough, but when Lord Bentham marched around it to loom over her, he appeared even more formidable. Elizabeth considered herself courageous, but only a fool would not have feared being alone with the furious Marquess.

"Miss Bennet, we have taken you into our home and treated you with kindness and generosity. We have given you opportunities you would never otherwise receive. Is this how you repay us?"

"I am very grateful for all your generosity to me, but I still do not know where your daughter may be. Have you asked her maid?"

He glowered at her. "Her maid also thought she was in bed, but when she went in with a cup of hot milk as my wife had ordered, she found the bed empty, with only a pile of pillows under the bedclothes to make it appear that someone was there. She says *you* were the last to see her."

"This is as much a shock to me as it is to you, my lord." Unfortunately, now she also had a good guess as to where Eleanor might be, and Lord Bentham would not be happy about it. But if Eleanor was determined to break her engagement to Darcy without blame falling on him, it appeared she had found a way to do it.

The study door opened, allowing Lord Charles to stroll in. It was perhaps the first time Elizabeth had felt glad to see him. "Is something the matter?" he asked with a frown, looking directly at her.

Of course! When he realized she was with his father, he must also have assumed that Lord Bentham had learned of his proposal and was taking action to stop it. Before he could say anything to that effect, she said, "Your father had a question for me about Lady Eleanor."

"It appears she has run off." Lord Bentham briefly outlined the situation. "Miss Bennet denies all knowledge of her whereabouts, but it seems highly unlikely that Eleanor would not have taken her friend into her confidence." He glared at her as if it were her fault Eleanor had not told her.

"Allow me." Lord Charles pulled up a footstool and sat on it, facing Elizabeth. Taking her hand, he laced his fingers with hers and leaned toward her. "You are sure she told you nothing?"

"Nothing about this." The intimacy of their position bothered her far more than the questioning.

"When did you see her last?"

"When I went up to dress for dinner, I stopped by her room and we talked. That was just after I spoke to you."

He cocked an eyebrow. "Did you tell her about anything in particular?"

She knew he was asking if she had told Eleanor about his proposal. "Nothing important. We just talked about the things we always talk about."

"Can you remember what was said? There might be some helpful detail that seemed insignificant at the time."

Repeating that conversation seemed a singularly poor idea. "She asked about my walk with Mr. Paxton, what he and I had talked about, and whether I thought he had any serious intentions towards me. That was most of it." All true, and all deceptive.

"Did she say anything about her engagement? Is she happy with it?"

Elizabeth hesitated. "I cannot recall her saying anything in particular about it this evening. When we spoke of it this morning, she seemed pleased to be marrying Mr. Darcy instead of Lord Deyncourt. She felt it would be a good match for both of them."

"So you do not think she ran off because of her engagement?"

"To get away from Mr. Darcy? She gave no sign of distress this morning, and she seemed pleased enough to be in his company today. He spent much more time talking to her than I did. Perhaps *he* might have some idea where she is."

Lord Charles looked up at his father. "It is worth a try, I suppose. We cannot hope to keep it hidden from him in any case."

The Marquess gave an abrupt nod. Releasing her hand, Lord Charles went to the door and instructed an unseen servant to fetch Mr. Darcy.

Elizabeth surreptitiously wiped her hand on her skirt. "Is that all, my lord?"

"You may go," he said absently.

Grateful to escape, she rose to her feet, but Lord Charles blocked her way. "No, pray remain with us. We may need more information from you, and you are part of this now."

Good Lord! Did he mean he considered her to have joined the family already? Apparently Lord Charles was as certain of her eventual acceptance as Mr. Collins had been. Following Eleanor's lead and stealing off into the night was starting to sound appealing.

When Mr. Darcy arrived a minute later, he gave her a brief startled glance, but no other acknowledgement. He also appeared distinctly displeased to be there. "You sent for me?" he said in a clipped voice.

Lord Bentham eyed him beneath furrowed brows. "Did you quarrel with Eleanor today?"

"Of course not. We were in the sitting room with your wife all day."

"You did not see her separately?"

"No. If you doubt me, I can easily call witnesses to account for my whereabouts at all times *today*."

"Now, Darcy, there is no cause to raise your hackles at me. It was just a simple question."

"I did not care for last night's *simple questions*. Is there anything else you wish to question me about, or may I go?"

Although she had seen Darcy make offensive comments in the past, she had never known him to be so deliberately rude. Was he trying to provoke Lord Bentham?

Lord Charles spoke first. "We have a slight problem, Darcy. It appears Eleanor has run off."

"Run off?" Darcy's eyes flew to Elizabeth.

She was half-tempted to laugh. "I know nothing about it."

"Perhaps she went out for some fresh air, and did not wish anyone to know about it. She may well return in a few minutes."

Lord Bentham scowled. "She would not have stuffed pillows in her bed to hide her absence for a night-time stroll."

Darcy raised an eyebrow. "No, I suppose not. What has been done to locate her?"

"We are organizing a search of the estate. The gatekeeper says she did not pass him, no horses are missing, and there have been no carriages on the road. There is nowhere nearby for her to go, so it seems most likely that she is hiding in one of the outbuildings or has injured herself in the dark."

Darcy did not seem to share Lord Bentham's worry, no doubt knowing as well as she did where Eleanor was likely to be. "I hope you discover her soon. In the meantime, I will return to Hillington and hope to receive more positive news in the morning." He sounded bored, but Elizabeth noticed how stiffly he held himself. The poor man must be having another megrim!

"I would prefer you to remain here, Darcy. We may need to discuss matters further when she is found."

If Elizabeth was correct, Eleanor would not be found anywhere on the estate. But if Eleanor had not taken the road to Hillington, how had she planned to cross the river? There had been no opportunity for her to communicate to Paxton, so he would not be there to assist her, and he had made it clear the river crossing was dangerous. Of course, that sort of warning was unlikely to stop Eleanor. Most likely she would be able to manage the stepping-stones, but it was dark outside. Elizabeth's heart began to beat a little faster.

Turning to Lord Charles, she said in a low voice, "I hope you will excuse me for a few minutes. I will return shortly."

He gave her a nod and an understanding smile, no doubt thinking that she needed to visit the necessary. Hurrying to her room, she took out her portable writing desk and opened the inkwell. Fortunately, the pen was newly sharpened.

Sir, my friend has been discovered to have left this house some time ago, and her whereabouts are unknown. I hope she has safely reached her destination. She apparently travelled across the park rather than along the road. If she has not yet arrived, it is cause for concern. A search of the park has already begun.

She read it over quickly. Hardly articulate, but Paxton would understand it, and she did not have time to make it clearer yet still unidentifiable. She blew on it to dry the ink as much as she could, though it would undoubtedly still smudge. Who could deliver it? With a search going on, she could not go out to the stables to find a boy to take it. Folding the paper several times, she found her way to the kitchen instead. It was still bustling with servants handling the remains of dinner. One of the kitchen maids was able to point out a likely boy to her.

She took him outside to give him the note. "You must give this to Mr. Paxton directly, and tell him it is from one of the ladies at Bentham. If you are there and back in an hour, I will give you two shillings."

The thought of such great wealth sent the boy off at a run. Elizabeth looked after him, hoping he was not inclined to gossip. Her reputation was already endangered enough by tonight's events.

Paxton re-read the unsigned note for the third time. It had to be from Miss Bennet; it was not in Eleanor's handwriting, and no other lady at Bentham Park would send him a message. So Eleanor had fled Bentham, and was presumably on her way to him at Hillington. Was Miss Bennet letting him know the search was on, or giving him warning so he could decide how to receive her? It was not as if he would ever turn Eleanor away, though he did have a few choice words about her recent decisions. Perhaps the warning was just that Eleanor's absence had been discovered, so she would know not to return.

She apparently travelled across the park rather than along the road. If she has not yet arrived, it is cause for concern.

Suddenly his stomach felt as if it were full of rocks. "Good God, the stepping stones!" he cried.

"Sir?" Symons eyed him oddly.

"I need a lantern immediately. This instant, Symons!"

"Yes, sir." Symons scuttled off.

Surely Eleanor would not have been so foolish...but of course, she was a daredevil, and had always believed he was exaggerating about how dangerous the stones were now. He prayed she had not tried to cross them. But she must have, if she had not come by road. Devil take it, where was that lantern? Perhaps he should go without it – but no, that was foolish. The new moon had been but a day ago, and he might end up missing her altogether in the darkness. But she could be injured or even dying as he waited!

A footman ran up to him with a lit lantern in hand. "Here, sir."

Paxton grabbed it and ran outside. Holding the lantern high, he sprinted across the broad lawn to the avenue beyond the rose garden. The trees where the park gave way to forest looked different in the dark, branches reaching out like fingers, and it took him several agonizingly long minutes to find the entrance to his pathway. He had gone to some pains to make it unnoticeable so no one would discover he was visiting Bentham, but it worked to his disadvantage now. Finally he spotted the broad beech tree that marked it.

He had to slow his pace as he followed the twists and turns of the narrow path, the undergrowth clutching at the tails of his coat. Was this the right path? Perhaps he had chosen the wrong one and was going in circles. No, he was headed downhill, and that was correct. At last he reached the place where the path widened out as it ran through a small meadow. Now he could move freely, despite the small circle of flickering light cast by the lantern. He cursed as a hillock caught his foot and nearly sent him sprawling.

Down through the copse and into the valley until finally he could make out the line of trees along the riverbank. "Eleanor!" he called and stopped a moment to listen. Hearing nothing except the haunting cry of an owl, he hurried to the river's edge.

The water reflected the pale glow from the lantern. Surely she would not have attempted the stepping-stones in the dark! Treacherous and slippery at the best of times, he would not dare hazard them himself without the light of day, but it had been many years since Eleanor had last crossed them. He always came to her now, and he had never admitted to her how close he had come to falling on those journeys.

He shone the lantern light along the muddy bank. He could make out the stones, but Eleanor was nowhere to be seen. Calling her name again, this time with a degree of desperation, he held the lantern high, trying to make the feeble light illuminate the banks.

Good God! What was that white patch a short distance downstream? There was no path here; all he could do was scrabble along the marshy bank, keeping his eyes on the odd whiteness. He was nearly there when he tripped over a root and lost his footing, crashing down into the shockingly cold water. It was not deep – the water came no higher than his chest – but the current tugged sharply at his clothing. He had dropped the lantern in his fall, and it went bobbing off downstream until the light spluttered out. He did not even pause, just ploughed his way through the icy water until he reached a spot where the white figure lay.

It was the same almost translucent white dress with silver embroidery she had worn the night they waltzed, a thousand years ago, but now the wet fabric was molded to her body. She must have pulled herself out of the water somehow before exhausting herself.

She lifted her head when he knelt in the mud by her side. "Geoffrey," she said weakly. "Is it truly you this time?"

Almost dizzy with relief, he said, "Of course it is me." He gathered her shivering body close, and she cried out in pain. "Are you hurt?"

"Just a little." She touched her hair, and Geoffrey was horrified to see something dark trickling through it. "I thought you were here before. You were a boy again, giving me swimming lessons, but then you vanished when I reached the bank."

"My poor Eleanor! Whatever made you try to cross those stones at night?"

She laughed faintly. "Now I *know* it is you. You are scolding me."

"I will do more than scold you if you ever attempt a foolish stunt like that again!" He had to get her somewhere warm and safe, but where? Bentham Park was closer and would serve to protect her reputation. He could see lanterns moving in the woods there, presumably searchers who could help him, but he would have to get her across the river, not just along the bank. And once at Bentham, they would never allow him to see her. The path to Hillington was twice as long, but there would be no one there who would try to keep him from Eleanor. No, Hillington it would be, and if it tarnished her reputation, so much the better. He was perfectly prepared to marry her to save her from shame, or for any other reason. "Do you think you can walk?"

"I do not know." Gamely, she rose to her feet with his assistance. "See, I am perfectly well." She took one step, and her leg went out from under her.

He caught her just before she fell.

The ground was too marshy to walk safely, especially when carrying a burden, so it had to be the river again until they reached the usual path. Geoffrey stripped off his sodden coat and left it on the bank. It would only weigh him down.

There were long minutes of terror when Eleanor lost consciousness as he forced his way against the current. His relief when she opened her eyes again as he neared the house was tempered when she moaned and clutched at her leg. Each step he took seemed to caused her pain, no matter how smoothly he tried to carry her.

"I am so sorry," he said. "Should I put you down and run to the house for a litter? That might hurt less."

"No, do not leave me!" She wound her arms tightly around his neck as if to prevent his escape.

He was just as glad since he did not know how he could bring himself to leave her side. "You must tell me if the pain grows worse."

"It hardly hurts at all," she said stoutly, but he could tell she was lying. "Your arms must be very tired."

As if he cared how much his arms ached! "I cannot imagine a better cause in which to tire them."

She laid her head back on his shoulder. "All I do is cause trouble for you. I cannot understand why you do not hate me."

"How could I hate you when you hold my heart?"

"Do I still?" Her voice trembled slightly.

"Silly girl, how could you think otherwise? Of course, it is possible that you may hate *me* by the time tonight is over."

"Why?"

They had reached Hillington, and Paxton kicked at the base of the front door in lieu of knocking. Symons opened it so quickly that he must have been waiting beside it, but he could not disguise his astonishment at finding his master soaked to the skin and carrying a dripping young lady who clung to him and hid her face. A footman stepped forward at once, but Paxton shook his head. "Have the fire in my room built up at once, and I will require hot water and tea as quickly as possible. Also, send for the apothecary and tell him that Lady Eleanor Carlisle is injured and requires his services here."

"Will you be needing a lady's maid as well?" asked the shaken butler.

"Excellent thought." Without further ado, he carried his burden up the stairs.

In a faint voice, Eleanor said, "You did not answer my question. Why should I hate you?"

He kissed her forehead. "I did answer in my own way. I just destroyed your reputation, and I did it quite deliberately. I am not going to stand by and watch you marry Darcy or any other man, even if it means dragging you down so low that your father has no recourse but to allow our marriage."

"Oh." She sounded puzzled. "I still do not hate you."

His voice held laughter as he said, "Good. Still, it remains to see if you feel the same when you are more in your right mind." He gently deposited her in a chair beside the fire. Pulling the satin counterpane off his bed without a thought for its value, he wrapped it around Eleanor. "We must get you warm."

That was enough direction for the string of servants that followed them, since in short order Eleanor sat before a roaring fire with her feet in a basin of hot water and warm bricks tucked beside her. Paxton's valet had to beg him to come into the dressing room to remove his drenched clothes and boots. He barely managed to wrap his master in a dry housecoat before Paxton insisted on returning to Eleanor's side.

The housekeeper bustled in with a voluminous nightdress and lady's robe, and Paxton told her what little he knew of Eleanor's injuries. "Do what you can for her comfort. She is not to attempt to walk. Pray inform me as soon she has dry clothes on, and I will carry her to the bed."

"Of course. I will have the blue room readied for her."

"You may ready it for *me*," he said firmly. "Lady Eleanor will sleep here."

"But sir, that is most improper! What will the servants and the apothecary think when they find her in your bed?"

"They will think precisely what I wish them to think."

"But sir..."

"Did you fail to understand my instructions?" His tone was sharper than his usual wont.

She paled and dropped a curtsey. "No, sir."

"Good. And you will make certain that all the staff treat her with the respect due to the future mistress of Hillington."

Her cheeks regained their usual ruddy color. "Of course, sir. On behalf of all the staff, I hope you will accept my congratulations."

"Thank you. I shall be just outside in the sitting room should Lady Eleanor ask for me."

Once the door to the bedroom was closed behind him, he sat at the writing desk and drew out a fresh sheet of paper.

Lady Bentham had ordered them to remain in the privacy of her husband's study with the door closed. "We must keep any knowledge of this from our guests. I will try to distract them, but if they see all of you here, they will know something is amiss."

The searchers were still at work, but had found no trace of Lady Eleanor. Lord Bentham had tried to send Elizabeth to bed, telling her that a tender young thing like her needed her sleep. Elizabeth, with that sweet archness Darcy knew so well, had told him she could not possibly rest with Eleanor's whereabouts unknown, and so she was permitted to stay. Darcy decided not to think too hard about the propriety of a single woman alone in a room with three gentlemen. If it did not trouble Lady Bentham, it would not trouble him. At least Elizabeth no longer seemed angry with him, though she showed him no particular warmth. If only the hammers inside his skull would stop pounding!

The mantelpiece clock had long since chimed one when a servant entered with a letter for Elizabeth. "From Hillington Hall, miss. The boy who brought it said it was urgent."

Did she realize they were all watching her as she inspected the envelope and broke the seal? Presumably it was from Paxton, damn him. Were it known she had received a letter from a single gentleman to whom she was not betrothed, her reputation would not escape unharmed.

Carlisle went to stand behind her. "I do not like it, Elizabeth. You should not be receiving letters from him."

"At this hour, I imagine it is not so much a letter as an urgent communication," Darcy said, his voice sharper than he had intended.

Elizabeth did not bother to look at either of them. "It is a reply from a message I sent him after I learned Eleanor was missing. I thought he might be able to find her, as Eleanor has spoken of crossing the river at the rock fall." Unfolding the single sheet, she glanced briefly at the contents. Something in it made her gasp.

She looked up at Lord Bentham, then down again at the letter and began to read, her voice shaking slightly. "*You will be pleased to hear that I have discovered Lady Eleanor's whereabouts. I am sorry to report that she injured herself in an attempt to cross the river in the dark. Although not life threatening, her injuries are enough to preclude moving her. She is currently at Hillington where the apothecary will be attending to her. If you wish, you may tell Lord Bentham that I will send further information once I have heard the apothecary's opinion. Thank you for informing me she was missing, as she likely would not have survived had I not discovered her when I did. Yours, etc., G. Paxton.*"

Carlisle took it from her hand as if it was his right and read through it. From the set of Elizabeth's jaw, Darcy could guess how much this possessive behavior angered her. It surprised him that she was managing to follow his advice to avoid refusing Carlisle outright; in the last few hours, he had seen half a dozen instances where he had expected her temper to flare.

Odd – he was more worried about that than about returning to Hillington to face Paxton and Eleanor. Since Paxton had sent the note to Elizabeth rather than Darcy, even though it was a flagrant breach of propriety, it seemed certain he had not forgiven Darcy. Eleanor had made her feelings plain by running to him, but she might have planned to return before morning with no one the wiser, and then to go on with the engagement. Darcy was bound to it until she said otherwise, but he was not going to marry an unwilling woman, no matter what threats were leveled at him. He cleared his throat. "That was a good thought, sending word to Paxton. Thank you, Miss Bennet."

Lord Bentham seemed more confused than his usual forceful self. "Why did you think Paxton would know where Eleanor went?"

Elizabeth looked at the floor. "It was a guess, my lord."

Even if Lord Bentham did not now grasp the significance of Paxton's knowledge of Eleanor, he would work it out later. Perhaps it was time for the truth, for his own sake as much as anything else. Darcy said, "My lord, we have not been completely open with you. Your daughter is very fond of Paxton, and he is perhaps her closest confidant."

Lord Bentham shook his head. "Nonsense. She hardly knows him."

"So she has led you to believe. Over the last year, she has met with him clandestinely on a number of occasions, both in London and here. Lady Eleanor invited Miss Bennet here to serve as her chaperone at their meetings. I told you last night that I was not in the woods with Lady Eleanor on the day of the picnic, nor had I kissed her. That was Paxton. Our height and coloring is similar; no doubt your observer confused the two of us."

"She said it was you. Why would she lie to me?" Lord Bentham sounded sadly bewildered.

"She fears your anger. They are in love, but know you would never agree to a marriage between them. You have seen that your daughter has been unhappy, and this is why."

"But *Paxton*? How could she care for *him*?"

Darcy chose his words with care, not an easy feat when the world refused to hold still. "The world is changing, sir. A girl like Lady Eleanor sees young men from good families like hers becoming wastrels and fops, ruining their family's fortunes for the sake of passing pleasures. The tradesmen whom you knew lacked social graces and connections; but their sons, like Paxton, have been raised and educated as gentlemen and they do not take their good fortune for granted. You look at Paxton and see grubby hands; she sees a gentleman she can respect, a responsible landlord, an intelligent man with no interest in gambling for high stakes and drinking himself into oblivion."

"She would not feel the same way when she discovered she was no longer welcome in the *ton*." His shoulders sagged. "And now she is at Hillington. This will be very difficult to disguise."

It was tempting to point out that the easiest solution was to allow the two to marry, but Darcy thought he had pushed as far as he could without risk of sounding as if he were trying to weasel out of the engagement. Instead, he said, "Now that I know Lady Eleanor is safe, I shall take my leave as well. I will send you word in the morning as to your daughter's condition." It was only a few hours until first light in any case.

Elizabeth's dress rustled as she stood. "Perhaps I should go with you. If I arrive before morning, it might appear that I was there as a chaperone throughout."

The possibility of quelling rumors seemed to rouse Lord Bentham. "That is an excellent idea, if Darcy has no objection. Pardon me, I must inform Lady Bentham of this." He shuffled from the room.

Lord Charles looked down at Elizabeth. "I do not like this. You should remain here."

"I will be perfectly safe with Mr. Darcy, and I must go to Eleanor. I cannot leave her there alone, especially when she is hurt."

"Then I will take you."

Darcy gritted his teeth.

"Pray, sir, my reputation would be unlikely to survive a night-time journey with *you*." She gave him an arch look that made him laugh.

Lady Bentham strode in imperiously. "Ah, Mr. Darcy. I have heard the news, and this is what we shall say. After dinner, Miss Bennet went to check on Eleanor. Thinking some fresh air might revive her, they went for a walk. They lost their way in the dark and Eleanor tripped, injuring herself. Seeing the lights of Hillington Hall nearby, they sought assistance there. With Eleanor's injury, we felt it best for her to pass the night there, and we will bring her home in the morning."

Darcy wondered how Lady Eleanor would feel if she knew her stepmother was more concerned about her reputation than her injuries or what had led to her flight. Perhaps it was exactly what she would expect.

Chapter 14

Darcy waited beside the carriage in the blessed darkness as Elizabeth approached, wearing the dark hooded cloak Lady Bentham had insisted upon. He held his hand out to help her into the carriage, but she was looking back over her shoulder at the house. He asked, "Is something the matter, Miss Bennet?"

With a sigh, she turned to face him and took his outstretched hand. "I used to love Bentham Park." Her voice was wistful.

"So did I." He spoke quietly, without intensity, as she ascended the carriage steps, ducking her head to enter the enclosure. She would be discovering now that this carriage had no facing bench, so he gave her a moment to adjust to the idea that he would be seated beside her rather than across from her. Not that he planned to do anything but converse with her – his megrim did not predispose him to romance, and he would not demean her by touching her when he was promised to another woman.

As soon as he joined her, the carriage set off at a leisurely pace. With the uneven, pot-holed roads between Bentham and Hillington, it would be unsafe to outrun the light from the lanterns strapped to the front of the carriage. This was likely to be a slow trip.

"Mr. Darcy, pray give me your hand," Elizabeth said crisply.

He blinked at her, not that he could see her in the darkness. "I beg your pardon?"

"Your hand. You *do* have a megrim, do you not?"

If he had not already been violently in love with Elizabeth Bennet, he would be now. He held his hand out to her. "How did you know?"

"By your expression and how stiffly you moved." She pressed her finger into that particular spot by his thumb.

"Were you aware Eleanor planned to run off?"

She did not answer immediately. "No, but I think something I told her provoked her flight."

"Something you said?" Darcy's megrim was not retreating this time despite Elizabeth's ministrations, but he said nothing. Just having her gentle touch helped.

"I told her everything – what you had said about threats to your sister, and about you and me. She had known you were reluctant, but not why." In an abrupt shift to annoyance, she said, "This is not working."

The pressure left his hand. He was tempted to say it *had* been helping just so she would continue holding his hand, but then he realized she was removing his glove – and her own. She began again, but this time it was her bare finger against his flesh. Megrim or no, a shiver ran down his spine.

Her finger was probing, moving in little circles, until finally she found the spot she wanted and pressed firmly. "*That* is better," she said with satisfaction.

And it *was* better. The knife of pain swirled and dissolved into a cloud, then began to slide down his arm to vanish where she touched him. The relief was so abrupt that he let his head fell forward, his senses swimming. It had not been this intense when she had helped him in the ruins, but they had worn gloves that time. It was probably just as well; if he had felt this strange melting and melding in his body then, he might have assumed it was witchcraft. "It is a good thing I proposed to you in Hunsford; otherwise you might think I only wanted to marry you because of this. Georgiana is going to *adore* you."

"You might wish to be careful, sir," she said, but her voice seemed to smile. "People's tongues sometimes become unguarded at this stage."

Good God, had he actually *said* that? Well, it was too late now; he could not take it back. "I will keep that in mind. Thank you."

She shifted her finger slightly, and now his head felt like it was floating, or that it would be if it were not so firmly attached to his neck. She said, "Obviously all those match-making mamas have been teaching their daughters the wrong skills. There is no magic to it; I could show anyone how to do it."

"It would not be the same." He was grateful she had taken it with amusement. He had no business even mentioning marriage when he was engaged to Eleanor. Had Elizabeth not said something about that, something important, just before she turned his brain into jelly? Oh, yes. "What did Lady Eleanor say when you told her?"

"She was very distressed. Horrified, actually. Then she said she would not marry you, and that she would find a way to end the betrothal in a way that no one could blame you. It seems she did not waste any time about it."

This time the enormous rush of relief had nothing to do with Elizabeth's magic touch. Eleanor would refuse to marry him! He had been hoping for that since he heard of her flight. If she were determined to end the engagement, then he truly would be free. "She has my deepest gratitude. I am reaching the limit of my tolerance for her family."

"I noticed, although I thought you did quite well."

"I did not murder Charles. That was an accomplishment." It had been one of the worst moments of his life, that brief instant after he realized Carlisle was serious and before Elizabeth answered. If she had accepted him, Darcy would not have been answerable for the consequences.

She laughed, soft and low. "Is the megrim gone now?"

"Not if it means you will stop holding my hand." But it *was* gone. The megrim was gone, his engagement to Eleanor was gone, Carlisle was left behind – and he was alone with Elizabeth in a dark carriage. After thinking he had lost her forever, after torturing himself with images of her married first to Paxton, then to Carlisle, her closeness was as intoxicating as fine wine. "You told Carlisle that you would be safe traveling to Hillington with me."

"Yes, I said that." She sounded amused again.

"I think..." His voice was low and uneven. "I think you may have been wrong."

The air in the carriage seemed to vibrate with tension as she considered this. "Will I be requiring a hairpin?"

"That can be arranged." He found her face with his hands, then pushed back her hood. He ran his fingers lightly over her hair until he discovered the knot. Probing it carefully, he found the end of first one hairpin, then another. There had to be a third and a fourth somewhere – she always wore four. The other two were below the knot, near the tender skin of her neck. Slowly he drew the pins out, one at a time, savoring each moment. At last, her hair tumbled over his hands, down past her shoulders.

It did not matter that he could not see it. He could feel the silky curtain of her hair, tantalizing him with the scent of lavender, begging for him to take possession of it, to plunge his hands into her curls and never release her. Drawing his fingers lightly along her neck with one hand, he dropped the hairpins into his pocket. Triumph surged through him. "On second thought, you do not get a hairpin this time. I intend to keep them myself."

She laughed. "To defend yourself from me?"

"No. Because I do not want you to put your hair back up. I want you just like this." He could hold back no longer. He touched her face, then buried his fingers deep into her hair, luxuriating in the softness of it. The utter darkness making all his other senses more acute, he was aware of each quick breath she took until he captured her mouth with his own.

The sweet taste of her only fueled his need, not only for her, but also to wipe the memory of her time with Paxton and Carlisle's proposal from his mind. It was more than desire, this thirst to possess her; it was the expression of all the agony of the last day, of believing he might have lost her forever. He had thought she was his after he kissed her on the moor, but she had been torn away from him by someone he had once trusted like a father. Now he could never be certain, not even as she pressed herself against him and returned his kiss with a gratifying fervor. If only he could knot his fingers in her luxuriant hair and never let go!

He could not get enough of her, and he no longer cared about propriety. He drew her onto his lap so he could hold her closer and feel the tantalizing pressure of her soft curves against his chest. When her hands stole around his neck, he thought his life might never be so sweet again. Pressing his lips to the sensitive skin of her neck, he traced kisses beneath her ear, her hair falling over his face like a curtain, then he tasted the hollow at the base of the neck. He might have been able to stop there if she had not moaned at his touch, but that little sound left him hungry for more.

His fingertips traced along the line of her collarbone to the neckline of her dress, then he pushed the lacy fabric aside. His breath came in a rush as her bare shoulder was revealed, a piece of her no other man had touched. Dizzy with desire, he pressed his lips to her newly exposed skin, silently marking her flesh as his, only his. Then, before she could protest the liberty he had taken, he reclaimed her mouth, demanding and receiving a response that thrilled him to his core.

He knew he had gone too far, especially since they were not yet engaged and he was still tied to another, albeit only in name. All in all, he thought he had done quite well only to go that far, given how desperately he wanted to tear off her dress and make her his right there in the coach, as much to ensure that she could never marry another man as out of his own desire for her. He would never, ever let Charles Carlisle have her, not if it cost him his life. But he wanted her to know his tenderness for her, not the consequences of his jealousy.

What had happened to his self-control? He had to recover it, had to remember it was enough to have her in his arms, her hair flowing loose around her shoulders, and responding to his kisses. With a great effort, he forced himself to lessen his demands, and began to scatter light kisses across her face.

Then his lips discovered a trail of warm moisture running down her cheek. For a moment he could not comprehend the reason for this, and then he froze in horror. "I am so sorry, Elizabeth. Pray tell me I am not hurting you," he begged.

"No," she said in a whisper. "You are not hurting me. Nothing is amiss. Just...I had thought I would never feel your arms around me again." Her voice cracked on the last word, and she buried her face in his chest, her shoulders shaking with silent sobs.

Instinctively he cradled her to him, whispering words of love and consolation. What a beast he was, thinking only of his need to possess her, and forgetting that she had been injured just as much by Lord Bentham's machinations as he was. How would he have felt, had she been the one to sweep into the room and announce her engagement to some highly eligible gentleman? He would have been devastated. Just listening to Carlisle's proposal had nearly torn him to pieces, and Elizabeth had been forced to live with the knowledge of his engagement to Eleanor for much longer than that. As her sobs stilled, he said, "My sweetest Elizabeth! I do not deserve you."

She gave a shaky laugh. "It is too late to tell me that. I have already decided that you do."

He was too late in more ways than one. The carriage was already drawing to a halt, and Elizabeth was still on his lap, in his arms, her hair spilling over her shoulders. He heard the coachman jump down from the driver's seat, knowing they had only a few seconds before he opened the door.

In a panic, Elizabeth scrambled off him, twisting and knotting her hair, then pulled her hood up over it. Would the coachman be able to guess what they had been doing? She felt as if it must be written across her face in large letters. Somehow she managed a sort of normalcy as Darcy handed her down from the carriage in front of Hillington Hall.

Despite the late hour, there was light shining through several of the windows of the large Palladian manor before them. A yawning footman scrambled to greet them as Darcy opened the door for Elizabeth.

"Is Paxton still awake?" Darcy asked tersely.

"Yes, sir, he is in his suite." Though the young footman tried to say this calmly, it was clear he was disturbed by it. He took Darcy's gloves without seeming to notice Darcy had not been wearing them.

"And Lady Eleanor?"

"Lady Eleanor is... is with Mr. Paxton," he stuttered. In the master's suite? That would account for the footman's shock, or perhaps it was the sight of the unmarried Mr. Darcy arriving in the middle of the night accompanied by an unknown lady.

"Pray have a room prepared for Miss Bennet."

"Yes, sir." He held out his hand for Elizabeth's cloak, but did not look at her.

She removed it reluctantly, hoping the knot in her hair would hold. It would look odd with her formal dinner dress, but she would be happy if it stayed up. "If possible, I would prefer to stay with Lady Eleanor."

"Yes, miss."

"That will be all," Darcy said. He took a candle from the small table. "This way, Miss Bennet." Once they had passed the footman, he turned to inspect her. Gravely he reached out a hand and tugged her dress up where it still exposed her shoulder, then handed her a handkerchief.

She blushed furiously, grateful for the handkerchief that hid her face as she used it to dry her eyes. No wonder the footman would not look at her! She could only pray that Paxton's servants were discreet.

"I suppose I should return these as well," said Darcy. Her hairpins lay in his open palm.

"Thank you." Somehow she managed a weak smile as she inserted them into the floppy knot she had created. At least now it would not fall down. Perhaps everyone would think she had been roused from bed to come here and had not had time to arrange her hair. The diamond hairpins might not fit well with that theory, though.

It felt odd to walk through a grand house in the pre-dawn hours as if they were burglars. She heard a clock chime the half hour, and wondered whether it was half three or half four. The flickers of candlelight illuminated neoclassical plaster moldings, sending grotesque shadows across the walls as Elizabeth followed Darcy up the grand staircase. The house was impressive – not Bentham Park, but very few houses in England would meet that standard – yet at least as large as Netherfield, and she thought that to be Mistress of Hillington would suit Eleanor well.

Darcy waited for her on the landing and gestured to the left. "Through here." Soft light spilled through an open door into a tastefully decorated sitting room, which led in turn into a bedroom lit by two large candelabras and a roaring fire in the fireplace. Eleanor, her complexion pale, lay propped up on pillows in the large four-poster bed, a bandage around her head. Mr. Paxton sat beside her on the bed, holding her hand in both of his. At least one good thing seemed to have come from this evening, as they were clearly not quarreling any longer. Apparently they had also moved into challenging the two new arrivals for lack of respectability.

"Paxton!" Darcy's voice was a rebuke.

His friend looked up, but did not stand. "Oh, it is you. I was beginning to think you were staying the night at Bentham Park. My apologies, Miss Bennet, I did not see you there. Welcome to Hillington."

"What in God's name are you thinking, putting Lady Eleanor in *your* bed?" Darcy demanded.

Paxton gave an exaggerated sigh. "What am I thinking? Well, having carried Eleanor in my arms for nearly a mile in my shirtsleeves, while she wore nothing but a thin wisp of silk that was soaking wet and hid nothing, and having my entire staff witness our arrival in that same state, it is really too late to worry about compromising her. And the *other* thing I am thinking is that Lady Eleanor is no longer any business of yours."

Elizabeth missed Darcy's response as she rushed to her friend's side. "Dearest Eleanor, what happened? Why did you run off?"

Eleanor smiled dreamily at her. "It all became clear after you told me the truth. How could I obey my father when it meant injuring both you and Geoffrey? The only way to free Mr. Darcy was to run off, and I wanted to see Geoffrey so much. It was a fine plan until I tried to cross the river at the stepping-stones. They are much trickier than I recalled. I slipped and fell on the rocks, then into the river. Fortunately," she said, turning a luminous smile on her beloved, "Geoffrey taught me the rudiments of swimming when I was a child, and I remembered enough of it to get to the bank."

"Which was where I found her," said Paxton, "soaked to the skin and bleeding, and more than a little confused."

"You were injured?" Elizabeth prompted.

"Just cuts and scrapes," said Eleanor, "and I turned my knee somehow in the process."

"Some fairly serious cuts and scrapes," Paxton corrected. "A blow to the head, with a gash in her scalp. I believe she lost a significant amount of blood from that, although it was dark and I could not tell for certain, apart from what she left on my shirt. I am also concerned for her knee. I am glad you are here, Miss Bennet, since I can trust your judgment better than that of the housekeeper who was the only female I could find to look at it. She said it was bruised and as big as a melon. And then there is the matter of taking a chill after being wet for so long. Eleanor, you will discover, is still a little dazed from her experience."

"I suppose that explains why this room is as hot as an oven," Elizabeth said. "A good precaution."

"I can assure you that it took no cleverness at all to realize that she needed warmth. She was chilled to the bone." The look on Paxton's face showed how shaken he still was by the experience.

Eleanor laughed. "You were wet, too."

"Yes, but I was carrying you, and that exercise kept me quite warm, let me assure you!" He raised Eleanor's hand to his lips and met her eyes for a long moment.

Darcy cleared his throat. "Pray do not suppose that I object to the proceedings, but in as much as there is still a formal engagement in effect, at least in name, and I am not in a position to release Lady Eleanor from it, perhaps *she* would be so kind as to jilt *me*?"

Eleanor looked at him as if uncertain how he came to be there. "The engagement? Yes, of course."

"Good. *That* is done, at least," said Paxton. "Although I fail to see why *you* could not release *her*."

"Apart from common politeness? The blackmail used to convince me to enter into the engagement is still in place, and I have great faith that Carlisle would be happy to act on it if he has the slightest sense that I withdrew my offer. Therefore, my offer must stand, and the refusal must come from Lady Eleanor."

Paxton said, "Blackmail? Oh, come now, Darcy."

"You may call it what you like, but Carlisle believed I had compromised his sister, so he made it clear that if I did not remedy the matter, he would make a point of ruining *my* sister's name. I know him too well to doubt that he would do it, nor that he could do it with no more than the right words in a single ear. Of course, *you* were the one who kissed Lady Eleanor in the woods at the picnic, but Lord Bentham was told I had done it; and for reasons of her own, Lady Eleanor also told him that I was the one with her at the time. My denials were of no use. I am sorry you despise me for it, but given the choice between the certainty of ruining Georgiana's life or taking away the practically non-existent chance that you could convince Lord Bentham to allow you to offer for his daughter, I would again choose to protect my sister." Darcy's icy tone could have cut through steel.

Paxton looked down at Eleanor, who made no effort to deny the allegation, then back at his friend. "You do not wish to marry her?"

"Of course I do not wish to marry her! Even if I were unprincipled enough to try to steal her from under your nose, surely you know that I have no desire whatsoever to ally myself to Lord Bentham – as I would have explained to you had you allowed me the opportunity!"

"I did not realize someone had seen us kissing," said Eleanor weakly. "I thought he just wanted to know who I was walking with, and it seemed safer to say it was you."

Elizabeth moved between the two gentlemen and held up her hands. "Obviously the two of you have a great deal to discuss, but perhaps Eleanor's sick-room is not the best place for this argument."

Darcy's face softened as he looked at her. "You are quite right. Paxton, perhaps we can speak further downstairs."

"I suppose we must." Paxton eyed Eleanor with regret. "And I suppose I should tell you to sleep and that I will see you in the morning. Miss Bennet, will you inform me should there be any change in her condition?"

"Of course."

Darcy cleared his throat. "And Miss Bennet?"

"Yes, Mr. Darcy?"

"May I speak to you tomorrow – privately?"

"Yes," she said quietly, trying to reassure him with her eyes. "I will look forward to it."

Chapter 15

"SHE WANTS TO BRING Eleanor back in the morning?" exclaimed Paxton. "Did you tell her that she was injured and must not be moved?"

"I did, and I am no happier about it than you," Darcy said. "I think it would be best for Lady Eleanor not to return to Bentham Park at all, but the fact remains that her father has the legal right to do whatever he pleases, and to call on the magistrate if you refuse to allow him to take her."

"Devil take him! Then it will have to be scandal. I would rather not have tarnished Eleanor's name, but tonight has convinced me that the current situation is untenable."

"*That* is abundantly obvious. However, there may be another option. With your permission, I would like to send a rider at first light to the Dowager Marchioness with an urgent request for her presence here. It will be much more difficult for Lord Bentham to insist on removing his daughter over his mother's objections."

Paxton nodded slowly. "An excellent idea."

The next morning, Paxton appeared at Eleanor's door, accompanied by the apothecary. As if there were nothing unusual about it, Paxton strolled into the room and made the introductions. The poor apothecary, clearly shocked, had no idea where to look, but finally gave all his attention to Eleanor.

Under the cover of his questions about her injuries, Elizabeth whispered to Paxton, "You should not be here!"

He looked altogether too pleased with himself. "If I am going to cause a scandal, I might as well do it properly."

The apothecary's pronouncements were much as Elizabeth had expected, that Eleanor must rest and not be moved. He left a bottle of laudanum to ease her pain before he scuttled out, clearly anxious to be away from the shocking scene of Lady Eleanor Carlisle in Mr. Paxton's bed.

Paxton ordered breakfast to be served in the bedroom. It made for an odd party, since Paxton and Eleanor seemed determined to ignore any hint that they should not be holding hands. Elizabeth, who had never been in a bedroom with a gentleman present before, much less in said gentleman's bedroom, was alternately bemused and shocked by this informality.

She wondered where Darcy was, but her main concern was for Eleanor's comfort, since as near as Elizabeth could tell, Eleanor had barely slept at all from the pain. Eleanor steadfastly refused her efforts to convince her to drink the laudanum. "Sooner or later my father and stepmother will arrive to take me away, and I must have my wits about me if I am to oppose them."

Shortly after breakfast, Paxton's butler, Symons, brought the message that there was a visitor for Miss Bennet, giving her a calling card bearing the name of Lord Charles Carlisle. Elizabeth sighed, then handed the card to Eleanor. "I suppose I must see him, but I would request that a maid attend me while I do so," Elizabeth said apologetically.

"Of course," said Paxton, gesturing to one of the maids who came forward and bobbed a curtsey. Turning to the footman, he added, "Pray inform Mr. Darcy that Lord Charles is here to see Miss Bennet."

"There is no need for that," protested Elizabeth. The last thing she needed was an unpleasant scene.

Paxton laughed. "I am doing it for my own sake, not for yours. Darcy would flay me alive if I did not inform him, and I am particularly attached to my skin. I will join you in a few minutes myself to pay my respects to his Lordship." His sardonic tone took away any trace of respect from his words.

She found Lord Charles in a large sitting room. How odd it was to be receiving a guest in a room she had never seen before! The smile he gave her before kissing her ungloved hand looked somehow strange, and it was a moment before she realized that it was a genuine smile, not a calculated attempt at seduction. Apparently he was truly happy to see her.

"My lord, I do not think I have seen you earlier than noon before," she said teasingly. "I hope there is no great emergency to rouse you at this hour."

"You see what a good influence you are on me, my dear! I brought some clothing and necessities for both you and Eleanor. Your maid was kind enough to make the selections."

Surprised at this thoughtfulness, she thanked him. "My clothing is a little worse for wear." She gestured ruefully at her dress that looked as if she had slept in it, as indeed she had. "Eleanor is in even greater need. It is a good thing she cannot walk, since she has nothing to wear but a nightdress belonging to one of Mr. Paxton's sisters that is at least a foot too long for her."

"How *is* my dear sister? Truly injured, I take it?"

She raised an eyebrow at his dubious tone. "The apothecary says she is weak from loss of blood, but the main injury is to her knee. He gave no indication of when it would improve enough for her to walk on, or even if he expected a good recovery, but it is excruciatingly painful for her to move even a few inches in bed. There is a cut on her cheek that may leave a scar."

"My stepmother will not be happy about that. She places great value on a perfect complexion."

Elizabeth did not doubt that, as Lady Bentham had made it clear she did not approve of Elizabeth's own rather tanned complexion. "Do you bring word from Lord Bentham or his wife? Are they still planning to bring Eleanor home today?"

"They were both still abed when I left, so I cannot say."

"I hope they will see reason and leave her here. The apothecary agreed that she should not be moved, and it would certainly be agonizingly painful for her."

"I will do my best to persuade them of that. Is it possible to see her?"

She could think of no grounds to refuse the request, apart from the scene he was likely to discover in the bedroom. Elizabeth instructed the maid to tell Lady Eleanor that her brother would be there presently. Hopefully that would give Paxton and Eleanor the chance to assume a more proper position.

Her error was in failing to consider the propriety of her own position. No sooner had the maid left the room than Lord Charles approached her, a warm, intent look on his face. "How clever of you to dispose of our chaperone. Now we may speak freely."

"As long as it is only speaking you desire, then I have no objection." Frantically, she tried to think of a way to forestall his addresses, but could think of nothing apart from fleeing. Surely she could do better than that!

He took her hand and placed a lingering kiss in the palm of it, his eyes holding hers throughout. "My Elizabeth," he said tenderly.

Every instinct told her to snatch her hand away, but she recalled Mr. Darcy's injunction. "Sir, I must insist..."

Darcy's voice interrupted her. "Not *your* Elizabeth, Carlisle." In a few quick strides he was beside her. To her astonishment, he physically removed her hand from Lord Charles' grip, and then laced her fingers with his own. "I am sorry for any pain it occasions you, but Miss Bennet is *my* Elizabeth." He raised her hand to his lips, his eyes meeting hers with an undeniable warmth that set her pulses fluttering. Had he planned to make this public declaration, or was it the impulse of the moment?

"You may be her father's friend, but that is taking it a bit far, Darcy!" said Lord Charles angrily. "*You* are engaged to my sister."

"*You* are behind the times. Last night, Lady Eleanor, whom you will find upstairs in Paxton's bed, told me she was unwilling to marry me."

Lord Charles' jaw dropped. "In Paxton's bed? I will kill him!"

Elizabeth, still stunned, interposed herself. "My lord, she is in the bed which is his, but not *with* him. I shared Eleanor's bed last night."

"What? This is ridiculous." His face was still stormy, but he no longer sounded out of control.

"In any event," said Darcy, "since your sister had released me from that engagement, I wasted no time in renewing my addresses to Miss Bennet. After some persuasion, she saw reason and accepted me."

Elizabeth stared at Darcy in disbelief. What in God's name was he doing? She could not fault him for claiming they were engaged, since he must have known that she would accept him this time, but to imply that he had forced her into it? She hoped he knew what he was doing. His face wore a small, superior smile, but he was looking at Lord Charles, not her.

Without glancing her way, Lord Charles said tightly, "Miss Bennet, I must request that you be so kind as to leave the room."

"But..."

"Immediately." His voice brooked no argument.

Darcy released her hand, but still did not look at her. "For once, I agree with Carlisle. I will speak to you later, Elizabeth." The sense of violence in the air was palpable.

There was nothing she could do to prevent the inevitable by staying there, so she picked up her skirts and ran. She had to find Paxton and convince him to intervene. Surely he would be able to stop them! She raced for the stairs, but skidded to a stop in the entrance hall at the unexpected sight of the Dowager Marchioness handing her hat and gloves to the butler, another figure hovering in the background.

A loud thumping noise came from behind her, and she cast an agonized glance over her shoulder, then threw propriety to the wind. She hurried to the dowager's side, and with more feeling than sense, cried, "I beg your ladyship, you must come with me immediately! There is not a moment to lose! It is in every way terrible."

"Good God! What is the matter?" The figure behind the dowager spoke, and Elizabeth recognized Admiral Worthsley.

She pointed toward the sitting room. "It is Darcy and Lord Charles. They are fighting." These last words were perhaps not necessary, since they were accompanied by a crash and cursing. "Pray make them stop!"

The Dowager Marchioness needed no further urging, walking boldly in the direction indicated as Elizabeth trailed behind. The sitting room was barely recognizable, with chairs kicked aside and knocked over. Darcy was rising to his feet, a trickle of blood running from his mouth, then his hand shot out unexpectedly to hit Lord Charles in the midriff. That gentleman doubled over just as the dowager, her arms akimbo, cried, "That is quite enough, both of you!"

Darcy, breathing heavily, turned to look at her. Lord Charles took advantage of his distraction to grab his opponent by the cravat and deliver a punishing blow to his jaw. Over Darcy's involuntary groan, Elizabeth heard behind her the unmistakable click of a pistol being cocked.

Admiral Worthsley pointed a pistol at the combatants. "Her ladyship told you to stop," he said in a voice that would not have been out of place on a battlefield.

Lord Charles released Darcy's cravat and took several steps backward, one hand pressing against his side. His right eye was rapidly purpling. "There is no need for that," he said breathlessly.

"Thank you, Frederick," said the Dowager Marchioness. "One accepts the risk of highwaymen when travelling, but who would have thought we would discover savages in a sitting room?" She turned a disapproving look on Darcy and Lord Charles.

Paxton appeared in the doorway. "Good God!" he said, taking in the pistol, the two injured men, and the chaos of his formerly pristine sitting room. "If this is how noble families behave, I am glad my parents were in trade!"

Lord Charles shot him a killing glare. "This is between Darcy and me."

The Admiral snapped, "Then I suggest you settle it like gentlemen, not street vermin!"

"And I do *not* wish to hear who started it," the dowager said briskly. "I heard enough of that when you were children."

Lord Charles glared. "This is not over yet, Darcy."

"You know where to find me, but I will warn you that some things have changed since that day four years ago when Richard Fitzwilliam held me back by force from challenging Piper because I was useless with pistols. I learnt my lesson about relying solely on my sword, and now I am quite proficient with pistols as well." Darcy turned a dark look on the dowager. "I wish I had learned that lesson earlier, for then *I* would have challenged Piper in Edward's place."

"What *are* you talking about, Darcy?" the dowager said irritably. "Edward was the one who cheated, not you."

Darcy turned very slowly to face her, as if he could not believe what he had heard. "No, madam. I judged the race, and Edward did not cheat."

"That is nonsense. Everyone knows he cheated."

"It is *not* nonsense, madam. I was there. *I* was the judge. It was *my* judgment Piper impugned, as well as Edward's honor. Edward's team was easily half a length ahead of Piper's at the finish. Piper wanted to blame his loss on something other than his ham-handed driving or the team he had spent a small fortune on. Before you accuse *me* of lying, I suggest you ask Richard Fitzwilliam for the truth of the matter. He witnessed it as well. Or, for that matter, you can ask Edward. He will be in England within the month."

Elizabeth did not see Lord Charles' reaction as dead silence blanketed the room. The usually intrepid Dowager Marchioness turned pale and seemed suddenly unsteady on her feet. Elizabeth slipped a hand under her elbow. "Pray, my lady, you must sit. Allow me to accompany you to the sofa."

The older woman followed her directions with unaccustomed meekness. Sitting beside her, Elizabeth said, "Is there anything I can bring you for your present relief? A glass of wine, perhaps, or a vinaigrette?" Not that she had any clue where to find such things at Hillington, but certainly a maid could tell her. Two footmen had already begun righting the fallen furniture.

"I never use vinaigrettes. Vile things," said the Dowager Marchioness, the very idea appearing to restore a little of her usual vitality. "I shall be quite well in a moment."

Paxton approached the dowager. "Thank you for coming, your ladyship. I did not expect to see you so quickly."

"Do you think me too old to manage twenty miles in the saddle?" she asked challengingly.

"Madam, I would not be a bit surprised if you could beat the Prince Regent in his prime in a race."

"Hah! It would be no contest."

Elizabeth glanced up to see Darcy scowling, causing a few drops of blood to gather at the corner of his mouth. With a significant look, she handed him her handkerchief, then touched the same spot on her own face. He grimaced, but blotted the blood away, then tucked the handkerchief in his pocket.

"Darcy, sit down before you fall down," said the Dowager Marchioness.

He remained on his feet, his countenance stormy. "Madam, the only thing I would like from you is a list of those individuals who claim that Edward cheated, as I need to have words with them. And if *you* wish for a list of witnesses to the race who can attest that what I say is true, I will be happy to provide it. Sir Francis Leigh was there with his son, as well as Captain Danforth, Lord James Kilbarren, Henry Nash, Oliver Percy, and..."

The dowager cut him off. "That is quite enough, Darcy! I take your point, and you may be certain I will be asking my son where he obtained his information. Now, where did Charles go?"

Paxton said, "As far away as possible, I would venture to guess. He stalked out without a word while Miss Bennet was attending to you."

"Then Darcy will have to tell me what induced the two of you to make fools of yourselves at this hour."

Elizabeth dropped her eyes, flushing, as Darcy said, "That would be a discussion better held in private."

"As opposed to Edward's personal affairs?"

"Madam, Edward's duel took place four years ago. I had no reason to think it anything but old news to everyone involved," he said stiffly. "The reason I requested your presence so urgently was on Lady Eleanor's behalf."

The dowager huffed. "Since Charles, Darcy and Edward are already creating mischief today, why should Eleanor be any different? So, what trouble has she discovered for herself this time?"

"Why limit it to us?" said Darcy sardonically, rubbing his chin where a bruise was beginning to emerge. "This started with *your* son, who decided it would be a clever idea to force Lady Eleanor and me into an engagement which neither of us wanted. That was what led her to run off."

Paxton took up the story next, informing the dowager of the events of the previous evening and Eleanor's injuries. Elizabeth used the opportunity to steal a glance at Mr. Darcy. He was still caught up in his anger, but she only felt the heat of his love. This was quite an unorthodox way to start an engagement, and she would have to tease him about it later.

The Dowager Marchioness listened to the tale without comment, then said, "I will see my granddaughter now. Miss Bennet, perhaps you will be kind enough to take me to her."

"Of course." Elizabeth gave Paxton a teasing look, knowing full well he would have preferred the task, but could not admit to the impropriety of having been in Eleanor's bedchamber in the first place. "She will be glad to see you, and if you could persuade her to take some laudanum, she might be able to sleep a little. She has been refusing it, saying that she cannot afford to be sedated when her parents arrive."

"I always said she was a clever girl. Well, lead on, Miss Bennet."

Chapter 16

DARCY'S JAW ACHED and he suspected that one of his ribs might be broken, given how painful it was to take a deep breath. The knuckles of his right hand throbbed painfully. Carlisle had proved to be a better fighter than he had anticipated. He moved his jaw experimentally from side to side. It could be worse, he supposed.

Paxton shook his head. "Good Lord, Darcy, what were you thinking to take your eyes off your opponent?"

Darcy sighed. "I am not accustomed to ladies appearing while I am sparring, but perhaps we could discuss the deficiencies in my boxing style another time."

"You are an idiot," said Paxton affectionately. "I am assuming you were not the one to start throwing punches. Dare I ask what set him off?"

"Just the usual."

"The usual? That is not much of an answer."

Darcy scowled. "I did not care for his attentions to Miss Bennet, and I told him so."

"And that made him hit you? Remind me to stay away from him in the mornings."

"He has formed an attachment to her, and I made an outrageous and untrue claim. I told him Elizabeth was engaged to me, and implied that she had spent the night in my bed."

"Good Lord, Darcy! I shall have to remember to stay away from *you* in the mornings as well. So you and Miss Bennet did resolve matters between you last night?"

"No."

"No? But you just said..."

"That it was outrageous and untrue. I knew he would be angry, and I wished to make sure I was the one he would lash out at, not Elizabeth."

"Even the engagement part was untrue?"

"You may be assured I would have mentioned it to you if it were otherwise. When did you develop this sudden interest in my views on Miss Bennet?"

Paxton cocked his head to the side, looking searchingly at Darcy. "Since your engagement to Eleanor, when Miss Bennet and I discovered we had a great deal in common."

Darcy allowed a beat or two to pass as he struggled to control a surge of jealousy. "What did you have in common?"

"We both felt betrayed by those we cared for."

"She felt betrayed by me?"

Paxton threw back his head and laughed. "Darcy, have you always been such a slowtop, or is this a new development? Yes, she felt betrayed by you."

"She told you that?"

"There was no need to tell me. I saw her face when Lord Bentham announced your engagement, and *I* am not a slowtop."

"So you are just guessing at her feelings."

"No," said Paxton with some exasperation. "She admitted as much to me. Perhaps you should just talk to her instead of quizzing me. I must write to Lord Bentham with an update on Eleanor's condition."

"Better you than me." Darcy examined his sore knuckles. Writing was not something he cared to do at the moment. Still, that would likely be the worst of it had he not been distracted. His boxing skills were not above average, but Carlisle's were worse. As it was, his head was less than clear.

Symons entered, proffering a tray with a calling card. His look suggested he felt that quite enough visitors had been admitted that day already. "A gentleman calling for Mr. Darcy."

Already? Darcy had assumed Carlisle would return, but not so soon. He barely bothered to glance at the calling card and was already rising to his feet when he realized it was not from Carlisle. Snatching it up, he looked at it carefully for a minute to be certain his eyes were not deceiving him. Head injuries could be tricky, after all. But the name remained the same. "Good God, what is *Edward* doing here?" he asked of no one in particular. "Show him in at once!"

Darcy had longed for Edward's company so often in the last fortnight that he was fully prepared to believe that he had somehow wished him into existence, but the new arrival was unquestionably Edward. A scar now ran down his cheek and he leaned a little on his cane, but Darcy would have known him anywhere. Striding forward, Darcy shook his hand with great warmth. "What a happy surprise! Edward, do you remember Paxton? He was two years behind me at Cambridge."

Paxton shook his hand. "Welcome to Hillington Hall, Lord Huntingdon."

Edward smiled warmly. "A pleasure to see you again, Paxton, but I no longer use either the title or family name. Captain Edward Huntingdon, at your service." Darcy noticed that he bowed like a soldier now, heels clicking together.

"You are welcome by whatever name you choose," said Paxton. "Do sit down, and let me order some refreshments."

Darcy still could not believe Edward was actually there. "You are clearly much improved to be travelling and walking."

"Far better than I was two months ago. The surgeon is very pleased with himself." Edward peered at Darcy's face. "And you - have you been *brawling*?" he asked with disbelief.

Darcy rubbed his chin. It must be starting to bruise. "I am afraid so. Carlisle came out worse than I did, though."

"Which Carlisle?" asked Edward with interest.

"Your brother Charles. I am sorry to say he has not improved in your absence. And it is a long story as to why we fought," said Darcy. "Edward, while I am beyond pleased to see you, what on earth brings you *here* of all places? I thought you planned to go straight to Pemberley."

"I am grateful for your offer of refuge there, and I intend to take advantage of it, at least temporarily." Edward spoke with a confidence he had lacked four years earlier.

"However, there have been some changes in my plans, and it does not suit me to skulk around England as if I had no right here, hiding my presence from my family, so I decided to come to Bentham Park and face my father directly. I stopped here first in hope of finding you, since I do not imagine my conversation with my father will be lengthy. Then I shall go to an inn for the night, and on to Pemberley tomorrow."

"You are welcome to stay here tonight," said Paxton. "Since I already have your sister and your grandmother here, one more Carlisle would be no trouble."

"My sister? Darcy, you said in your letter that no one from my family ever sets foot here. I thought no one would know if I came here first."

"Yesterday at this time, that would have been true," said Paxton. "Today is the exception. Lord Charles has already been and gone, and the Dowager Marchioness and Lady Eleanor are upstairs."

Edward raised his eyebrows. "A party? What is the occasion? It cannot be in my honor, since no one knew I was arriving."

Darcy said, "Your family is in an uproar. Eleanor has fled Bentham, and your grandmother is here to chaperone her and to protect her from your father's wrath. Lord Bentham is not yet furious with me, but he will be soon; and Charles has come within an inch of challenging me three times in the last two days."

"Good Lord! I do have fine timing in coming home for a visit."

"To say the least!" Darcy said.

Paxton handed him a glass of wine. "I was planning to meet with your father later today. Perhaps I should delay my visit to your father until after yours, though, since he will be in a ferocious temper after seeing me. You might prefer to go to Bentham first while he is still in a good humor."

"What I have to tell him will anger him as well," Darcy said. "On the bright side, it would be embarrassing for him to expel all three of us in one day."

Edward snorted. "This sounds ominous."

"It is," Darcy said. "Your father has demanded that I marry your sister. I am going to tell him that I refuse."

Paxton said, "Then I will make matters worse by telling him that *I* intend to marry her, whether it pleases him or not – and I know it does not."

"*Marry* her? *I* cannot believe that my sister is old enough to marry *anyone*! She was not even out yet when I left. And why is she here?"

Paxton grinned. "A great deal has happened recently." Briefly he recounted the events of the previous evening. "So now both your sister and grandmother are in residence here; and perhaps equally important to you – speaking as one racer to another – there is a pair of horses in the stable that I daresay you have missed."

His eyes alight, Edward exclaimed, "The greys are here? Where are the stables?" He rose to his feet, looking around him as if he might find horse stalls in the corners of the sitting room.

Darcy offered to take him to the stables. Paxton chose to stay behind, thoughtfully giving them some privacy. If Edward's leg was troubling him, it was not apparent in the pace he kept on the way to the stables. "Take care, though; the stablemaster here protects those horses as if they were the crown jewels," Darcy said.

"And well he should! They *are* the crown jewels, as far as I am concerned," said Edward.

It was dark inside the stables after the bright sunlight outside, but Darcy had no difficulty finding the proper stalls. With a smile, he stepped back to let Edward through.

Edward's face lit with joy as he entered the stall. Argent lifted his head and whickered eagerly, his ears pricked forward. Silver whinnied in the adjoining stall, dancing in place, quite unlike the exquisitely trained creature he was.

"Oh, my beauties," said Edward, his voice a bit unsteady, as he reached a hand around the horse's neck. Silver turned his head to nuzzle Edward's ear, while Argent leaned over the barrier between the stalls to nibble at his shoulder. "My sweet beauties."

The stablemaster tromped over to Darcy. "What is all this?" he demanded.

Darcy gestured toward Edward. "That is my cousin, who raised and trained them. He has not seen them these four years while he was in the war."

The stablemaster peered inside the stall, then turned back to Darcy. "You should ha' *told* me they was the Viscount's horses," he said reproachfully.

Darcy hid a smile. "I did not realize it would matter."

"Oh, everybody knows 'bout his lordship and his horses. Should ha' been born with four hooves, that one."

From between the horses, Edward said mildly, "I heard that."

"And I'd wager it's not the first time you heard it, milord," the stablemaster said with a laugh.

Darcy cleared his throat. "My cousin does not wish anyone to know he is back yet. He is Mr. Huntingdon to you."

The stablemaster gave him a look that said he might as well have suggested pretending that the king was a beggar. In a low voice, he said, "Don't you worry. Nobody round here ever believed any o' those stories about his lordship."

"Good," Darcy said, though he was not certain what the man was talking about. Surely the locals would not have heard that ridiculous story about cheating!

Edward had found a brush and was combing Silver's flanks. "Not that he needs it," he said apologetically to the stablemaster. "Their coats are in beautiful condition. It has just been so long since I could do it."

A quarter hour passed before Edward could tear himself away from his most prized possessions. "I suppose I ought to see my sister and grandmother as well. They would not be pleased to discover that I gave precedence to the greys!" When he thanked the stablemaster for his excellent care of the greys, Darcy could have sworn the man was glowing with pride.

On their return to the house, Darcy took him upstairs, then knocked on the half-open door of the bedroom. "Lady Eleanor, are you fit to receive visitors? There is someone here who wishes to see you."

Elizabeth came to the door and opened it fully. "Visitors are quite welcome. Eleanor is exceedingly bored of lying in bed." She cast a puzzled look at Edward, but held the door for him.

Darcy leaned down toward her, relishing the scent of lavender in her hair. "Viscount Huntingdon," he said quietly.

"Edward!" cried Eleanor. "Is it really you?"

It was a happy reunion, with tears of joy on the part of the astonished ladies. Elizabeth had to work at convincing Eleanor to remain still to avoid injuring herself further.

The Dowager Marchioness brought an end to the commotion. "Oddly enough, Edward, we were just speaking of you. I am very glad you are here, as we made a rather confusing discovery this morning."

Darcy stepped in at this point, having some idea how Edward was likely to take this news. "You are not going to like this, Edward. In fact, I suggest that you and I discuss it in private."

"Nonsense," said the dowager. "We are his family."

"You are the *ladies* of his family," Darcy said. "This is as vile an insult as can be leveled at one gentleman by another."

Edward's eyes narrowed. "I think you had best tell me about this straight away."

"Very well." Darcy took a deep breath. "We discovered quite by accident this morning that your family has a different view of the events that led up to your duel. In short, they were told that you had, in fact, cheated in the race."

"What?" Edward exploded, jumping up from his chair. "And they *believed* it? This is unforgiveable! Who else believes this? I must know."

Darcy said soothingly, "I can assure you that none of my acquaintances believe it, and when the subject has come up at the club, everyone seems to think Piper was an idiot not to realize you simply had the faster team. There has never been the least hint that anyone believed his assertions. I cannot begin to guess how your family came to their own conclusion."

"I can tell you one thing, which is that *I* will never forgive *any* of them for believing it! That my own father could think me a cheat!"

The dowager said, "We *all* believed it, Edward. At first I said it was utter nonsense, but when your father kept saying it was true, I could think of no reason why he would keep repeating it unless it *were* true. Which of us should have argued with your father, who should know best about these things?"

Edward did not even look at her, instead pacing the room, shaking his head from time to time. His hands clenched and then stretched as if unable to remain still.

"I cannot forgive myself for failing to ask more questions," Darcy said. "Your family's reaction to the duel did not make sense, but it never crossed my mind that they could believe Piper's lies."

"I am the one who should have realized there was a problem. But my father *still* should have known better, and I will not forgive him for it quickly. It has been a very long four years." Edward rubbed his injured leg.

"The question is *how* your father came to believe this," the dowager said. "He would not have come to this conclusion on his own, so someone must have told him. But who and why?"

Darcy had been waiting for this moment. "Your brother Charles is the obvious culprit. He stood to benefit most from your disappearance, and Piper was a friend of his."

Eleanor burst out, "Charles would not do that. He is too cavalier about other people's lives, but he is not malicious."

"He stood to benefit, certainly," said the dowager slowly. "But Charles took Edward's absence badly. That was when his reckless behavior began."

Edward tapped his fingers on his knee. "Has he tried to step into my place?"

The dowager huffed in annoyance. "I cannot tell you one way or the other. I am not welcome at Bentham Park these days, and anything I learn comes from other sources."

Frowning, Edward said, "I do not understand. Why would you be unwelcome? It is your home!"

"No longer. Your stepmother and I are not meant to live in the same house. She managed to make my time there sufficiently unpleasant that I preferred to establish my own household."

"But if neither I nor you are there, who counsels my father? Charles?"

"*She* does," said Eleanor bitterly. "Charles as well, I suppose, but he is so rarely there. and he has his own quarters in London. And he has *not* tried to take on your titles, or to be declared heir."

Elizabeth spoke for the first time. "It is none of my concern, of course, but Lord Charles told me recently that, although he felt he had no choice but to accept your father's verdict, he still could not believe in his heart that you would ever cheat. Pardon me if I am speaking out of turn, but I thought you might wish to know."

Edward turned to her with a puzzled look. After a pause, he said, "Do I know you?"

Eleanor said quickly, "My apologies. Pray allow me to introduce my dear friend, Miss Bennet."

With a curtsey, Elizabeth said, "We last met some twelve years ago, on which occasion I helped Eleanor put crickets in your bed."

Edward laughed. "Well met, Miss Bennet. I can think of no one whom I would rather have put crickets in my bed."

Darcy had heard quite enough of Carlisle men flirting with Elizabeth. Placing his hand over hers, he said with an edge of warning, "And, as of two hours ago, she is also my betrothed."

"Lizzy, you wretch!" cried Eleanor before anyone could offer their congratulations. "Why did you not tell me?"

Elizabeth looked up at Darcy with dancing eyes. "The circumstances were somewhat informal. I thought perhaps I should wait for an actual proposal – and an actual response – before I said anything."

He leaned down until his lips almost touched the tempting flesh of her ear. "Miss Bennet, you wicked little minx, will you do me the great honor of agreeing to be my wife, preferably before you drive me into utter madness? Or must I carry you off and make love to you until you agree?" Tired of denying himself, he brushed his lips against the shell of her ear, and was exhilarated by her quick intake of breath.

Her eyes widened, but her look was one of mock seriousness. "Must I decide between the two options? They both sound quite appealing."

All the blood left his head and rushed to his loins. By God, if there were no onlookers, he would... no, best not to consider what he would do. Instead, he laughed at how neatly she had turned his teasing back on him. "Be warned; that counts as an acceptance," he said softly. At her smile, he turned to the others. "Very well. *Now* we are formally engaged."

Eleanor and the dowager congratulated them, followed by Edward, who still had a preoccupied look. Concerned for him, Darcy turned the discussion back to the previous subject, although he kept his hand on Elizabeth's shoulder, his thumb delicately exploring her back, where no one could see it. Elizabeth could feel it, though – he could tell by her flushed cheeks and quick breaths.

Forcing his attention back to Edward, Darcy said, "We should ask your father where his information came from."

"There is no need," Edward said levelly. "I already know who did it. There is only one person with both the motive and the means."

"Who?" Eleanor demanded.

Edward hesitated, as if unsure whether he should divulge the information. "His wife," he said, with finality. "She can concoct a convincing story, and *she* is the one who stood to benefit from a breach between my father and me."

The room was eerily silent, then the dowager began to nod slowly. "Just as she benefitted from separating me from my son. I thought she just hated my dogs."

"But why..." Eleanor began.

Edward returned to pacing. "She knew I disliked her. She had first set out to entrap *me*, and I had no patience for her or any other fortune-hunter. I especially did not like the way she used Charles to reach me. The final straw came after she married my father, when she began keeping company with that damned fop Deyncourt. I confronted her and told her to end it, and if she did not, I would tell my father. She must have seen the duel as an opportunity to rid herself of me, and she made the most of it."

Eleanor's head had shot up. "What is this about Lord Deyncourt?"

Edward looked away as if he were suddenly uncomfortable. "It is nothing of any importance," he said stiffly.

"It is important to *me*!" exclaimed Eleanor. "Father wants to make me marry him."

Her brother swore softly, then said, "I can guess whose idea *that* was. You need not worry, Eleanor – one way or another, you will *not* marry that man. I will make certain of it."

"But why do you object to him?" Eleanor asked.

Edward stared at his boots, saying nothing. Finally, Elizabeth rose and whispered something in Eleanor's ear.

"No!" cried Eleanor, her face a study in horror. "Are you certain?"

"Lord Charles sounded certain, and I suspect that is why he sought so hard to arrange a different marriage for you." Elizabeth glanced back over her shoulder at Darcy.

Suddenly Charles's insistence on Darcy's engagement to Eleanor took on a different light in his mind. Most likely Lord Bentham would not agree to end the arrangement with Deyncourt unless there was a marriage he wanted more; and for whatever reason, he did seem to want to increase ties to Darcy. Charles must have thought his presence a godsend. It did not excuse his behavior, but at least it made some sense of it.

"Miss Bennet," the dowager said sharply. She cocked a finger to beckon Elizabeth closer.

With an amused look, Elizabeth repeated the process of whispering. The dowager's lips tightened, and then she stood, the tip of her cane hitting the floor with a distinct thump. "That is quite enough. Edward, you need not confront your father about this, because you may be certain I will take great pleasure in doing so myself!"

"No," Edward said. "I must think this through and decide how to proceed."

Symons appeared in the doorway, his lips pursed in disapproval. "Lady Mary Huggins is calling. She is asking for..." He paused, then sighed heavily, as if this were too painful to speak. "For anyone who wishes to see her."

Hiding a smile, Elizabeth rose. "I imagine she is here to see either Eleanor or me. I will go down." But before she could leave the room, Edward moved ahead of her, hurrying out the door without a word. The sound of his footsteps pounding down the stairs echoed behind him.

After a puzzled glance at the others, Elizabeth followed him at a more sedate pace. Darcy caught up with her in several long strides. "I wonder what that was about," he said.

"I have no idea!" She halted on the landing where the stairs turned to face the hall. At the foot of the stairs stood Edward, wrapped in a passionate embrace with Lady Mary. Her cheeks burning, Elizabeth turned away from the spectacle and began to mount the stairs again. "I think we had best go back up, then come down making a great deal more noise," she whispered.

Darcy stopped her by catching her wrist. "I prefer Edward's idea."

Before Elizabeth could even comprehend his meaning, Darcy's arms were around her, sweeping her to him, his mouth descending on hers. Taken by surprise, she was overpowered by the exhilarating sensation of being engulfed in his embrace, her entire body pressed along the length of his. It was a heady pleasure far beyond any kiss in a carriage could be, and it made her forget where they were and who might come upon them at any moment. And his kiss – it seduced her and left her wanting more. Her hands slid around his neck to pull him closer as she moaned her pleasure.

The dowager's deliberate voice rang out above them. "Mr. Paxton, I begin to have serious concerns about the quality of persons you permit in this house."

Paxton laughed. "But their breeding is impeccable, your ladyship. Not a penny of their money comes from trade."

With a gasp, Elizabeth pulled away from Darcy, wishing she could disappear, or at least hide behind him until she determined whether it was, in fact, possible to die from embarrassment. Fortunately, the attention of the newcomers seemed to be centered primarily on the couple below them.

Edward released Lady Mary from his embrace, although his arm remained around her in a quite improper way. "Grandmama, I would like to present to you *my* betrothed, Lady Mary Huggins, the daughter of Major Hug --" He winced before continuing. "The daughter of the Earl of Alford."

The dowager turned back to Paxton. "Perhaps it is something in the air here. This has become an epidemic of betrothals."

"Ours is not new," Edward said. "Lady Mary agreed to be my wife earlier this year. We decided not to announce it until my return to England."

Darcy strode down the stairs to shake Edward's hand. "Congratulations. Lady Mary, I give you my very best wishes. He will make you a fine husband."

"Thank you," she said calmly, her affection for Edward clear in her every look.

A few minutes later, the dowager herded them all upstairs once more. After another round of congratulations were made, Elizabeth asked, "How did this come to pass? You said nothing of it at Bentham Park."

Lady Mary said, "Edward wished to tell his family himself. When my parents and I were invited to Bentham Park, I assumed he must have done so. After I discovered his family knew nothing of it, it seemed wisest to keep it to ourselves."

"But how did you meet?" Eleanor asked. "Edward has been in Portugal all this time."

"And I was there for much of it as well!" said Lady Mary with a warm smile. "My father was Edward's commanding officer until he unexpectedly inherited the earldom. My mother and I travelled with him wherever he was posted."

"I came to know her after I was wounded at Alba de Torres," Edward said. "She and her mother visited all the injured officers to improve our morale. I was quite taken with her, and she seemed to enjoy my company, but she was always careful not to favor any one of the officers over another. Most of us were half in love with her. Then, when the old Earl died and Major Huggins inherited, they returned to England, and that was the last I saw of her for almost two years."

Eleanor asked, "Were you in contact all that time?"

"No, I never expected to see her again. When her father came to Portugal this winter to confer with Wellington, she travelled with him, having missed the simplicity of her old life in the camps. I had just taken a bullet to my leg." Edward slapped the side of his thigh to indicate the spot. "As before, she came to visit the wounded, and seemed glad to see me. We spent hours talking and laughing together, and this time I definitely fell under her spell, but she knew me only as Captain Edward Huntingdon, a gentleman's son with no prospects beyond the Army, while she was an Earl's daughter and an heiress. I considered telling her the truth, but at that point, I thought there might still be a noose waiting for me in England, so Viscount Huntingdon was an even worse prospect than Captain Huntingdon. The situation looked quite hopeless to me. Then I took a fever and was delirious for several days. When I finally came to my senses, I discovered she had stayed by my bedside each day, wiping my forehead and talking to me as I raved – and that the other patients were looking at me oddly." He smiled at Lady Mary.

"When I came to see him the next day, he told me that he could remember little of those days, and he hoped he had not said anything too embarrassing in his delirium." Lady Mary held out her hand to him.

"And she said – completely calmly, mind you – 'Not at all. Mostly you begged me to marry you.' I was mortified, and started to stammer an apology. She put her finger to my lips and said, 'Do you not wish to know what my response was?' That was when I realized the others had gone silent and everyone was watching us." He tightened his hand on hers.

"Well, boy, what did you do?" the dowager demanded.

"What else could I do? I could not understand why she did not simply pretend it had not happened. It seemed unlike her to humiliate me with a public refusal. Since there was nothing I could do about it, I said, 'Lady Mary, I would be happy to hear anything you wish to say to me.' And she leaned close to me and said quietly, 'I said yes, so I hope you meant it.' At that point I decided I must still be delirious, and that I should enjoy it while it lasted, so I said, 'Oh, I meant it!' And then, since I knew it was not real, I kissed her."

Darcy laughed. "I hope her father did not hear about that part!"

"Of course he did. He had been our commanding officer, so no one, including me, would have dared to keep it secret. Fortunately, he found it amusing, and he was surprisingly pleased with the match."

"There is nothing astonishing about that," Eleanor said. "You are one of the most eligible bachelors in England."

"Except he did not know that! He believed she would be happier with a plain Army officer than a noble with connections in the *ton*. So then I had to ask her if she would still wish to marry me if I were the heir to a wealthy Marquess. And she said she would, but that she was very glad I was not a Marquess's heir. I had never imagined that I might have to apologize to my future bride for being the heir to Bentham Park!"

"You did apologize quite nicely, my love," Lady Mary said with a smile.

"Lord Alford did not take the news of my true identity as well at first, since it meant I had lied to him about it for years. Fortunately, Richard Fitzwilliam, who is *his* superior officer, told him it had been his idea in the first place, and he vouched for my character. So once I was well enough to travel, I sold out, and here I am."

The dowager raised a cup of tea in his direction. "And we are very glad of it."

"Indeed we are," said Eleanor.

They talked pleasurably for some time. Darcy himself was in excellent spirits. He was engaged to Elizabeth, who was proving to be every bit as passionate as he had hoped, and Edward was back. The world was a fine place. Even the tight look on Edward's face had disappeared since Lady Mary's arrival.

It reappeared, however, when Symons returned once more, actively frowning this time. "The Marquess of Bentham is here, and he demands to speak to Mr. Darcy. I showed him to the sitting room." He glanced backwards over his shoulder as if fearing he would find Lord Bentham in pursuit.

"He *demands*?" Paxton raised an eyebrow to Darcy. "Shall we go see what he wants?"

Scowling, Edward said, "Do not tell him I am here. I am not ready to speak with him."

Darcy nodded, then left with Paxton. In the passageway, Paxton said, "And to think my parents wanted nothing more in life than to have even one of the Carlisles cross their threshold! Now I am unable to keep them away."

Darcy chuckled. "At least they can no longer pretend to be mere acquaintances!"

Lord Bentham prowled the sitting room like an infuriated tomcat, while Admiral Worthsley relaxed by the fireplace. "What is going on here?" the Marquess demanded at once. "Darcy, you were supposed to send me word this morning about Eleanor. Instead, Charles came storming home looking as if he had been in a prize-fight, insisting that my *mother*, of all people, was here. Then Worthsley puts in an appearance and claims you have something urgent to tell me, but refuses to explain himself. What the devil *is* all this nonsense?"

"I am sorry I did not send word. I was preoccupied by being on the other end of the prize-fight, as well as a few other things." Darcy flexed his hand, wondering if Elizabeth's megrim magic would still work while his hand was swollen. Hopefully there would be no need to find out.

Paxton took a conciliatory tone. "In fact, I was just writing to you with an update of Lady Eleanor's condition. The Dowager Marchioness has indeed honored me with her presence, and she is with Lady Eleanor at the moment. Symons, pray inform her ladyship of her son's arrival, and that we would be delighted if she chose to join us here. And welcome to Hillington Hall, my lord." His manners certainly could not be faulted.

Darcy interposed himself before an explosion could occur. "As for the other matter, my lord, I discovered this morning that your family has been under a misapprehension about the events leading up to Edward's ill-fated duel. That is no doubt what Admiral Worthsley was referring to." Interfering old buzzard! "With your permission, I would like to tell you the truth of what happened that day."

With a scowl, Lord Bentham snapped, "I already know what happened, and I do not wish to hear it again!"

"I beg your pardon, but if you believe your son cheated in a race, then you have been sorely misled." Darcy met his gaze evenly. "I can call witnesses to attest to my version of the affair."

Lord Bentham snorted. "So what is *your* version, then?"

With what Darcy felt to be admirable restraint, he repeated the story of the race and the duel once again.

A visibly shaken Lord Bentham opened his mouth to say something, then closed it again. Finally he said, "Are you certain?"

Darcy exhaled a deep breath. "I am completely certain."

"Why did that man think Edward had cheated?"

"Piper was a poor loser. He had boasted all over London about his new team, how much he had paid for them, and how he would finally best Edward in a race. The horses were nothing extraordinary, of course. Edward did not wish to humiliate him, so he did not use the full speed of the greys, just enough to win by a small margin. It could have been much larger, had he so chosen. No one else present at the race – and there were a number of spectators – felt there had been any cheating. Edward thought the duel would be a formality to allow Piper to save face, but Piper shot to kill, and Edward had no choice but to do the same."

Symons attempted to announce the Dowager Marchioness, but she loftily swept past him. "I cannot believe," she declared to the room as a whole, "this ridiculous muddle."

Darcy was tempted to ask which muddle she had in mind. "I have just been telling Lord Bentham about the events at the race."

"*I* would like to get to the bottom of who started that story about Edward. If no one else believed he did anything improper, how did everyone here come to believe otherwise?" She studied her son with sharp eyes.

Lord Bentham shook his head in bewilderment. "Everyone said it was true."

"You were here at Bentham Park at the time, I believe. Did you receive letters about it?"

"I cannot recall."

The dowager frowned at her son, then turned back to Darcy. "Now, what is this about Edward returning to England?"

Darcy glared at her. If she wanted to force the issue of Edward's presence into the open, she could do it herself. "Several years ago, after Edward nearly died while fighting in Spain, Richard Fitzwilliam and I persuaded him that enough time had passed that he could safely join the British forces without being recognized. I purchased a commission for him in Richard's regiment under the name of Mr. Edward Huntingdon. He was injured again in January in the fighting at Ciudad Rodrigo, and Richard arranged for his convalescence in a private villa. He improved somewhat during that time, but his doctor recommended a protracted rest for him to recover his full strength. We felt a return to his native soil would be the best medicine."

"Why did you not tell me this until now?" asked Lord Bentham sharply.

"Everything I told you when we first spoke was true; I simply omitted the part about his return. Part of my reason for travelling to Yorkshire was to assess whether Edward would be welcomed back by his family. After meeting with you, I judged that the answer was no, so I instructed my solicitor to make arrangements for a small house in the country suitable for a quiet gentleman named Edward Huntingdon. You would not have crossed paths with him."

The Dowager Marchioness said impatiently, "What of the charges against him? Is he not in legal jeopardy?"

"That is a curious point. I had my solicitor look into it, planning to reach a private settlement with Piper's family. It turns out no charges were ever made. Edward has spent four years fighting on the continent for no reason."

The sound of the clock ticking was the only interruption to the silence that greeted this statement. Lord Bentham was staring at the floor, looking more defeated than Darcy had ever thought to see him, and even the redoubtable Dowager Marchioness appeared lost in her own reflections. There was no triumph for Edward's vindication in this moment, only regret.

When Lord Bentham at last looked up, he said tiredly, "You will tell me what sums you have laid out on my son's behalf."

Darcy chose his words with unusual care. "With all due respect, sir, I must decline. Everything I did was done out of affection for my friend, and it was not more than I could afford. He would have done the same for me."

"I can and must repay you!"

What a foolish argument to be having at this juncture! Darcy was about to refuse again, in stronger terms this time, when a better idea struck him. "I have no need of repayment, but if it would ease your mind to do something in recompense, I would ask that you do me the favor of listening to what my friend Paxton has to say." Darcy watched Lord Bentham closely, knowing this had the potential to backfire.

From his sudden pallor, Paxton had clearly not been expecting this, but he managed to rise to the occasion. "My lord, I believe Darcy has already told you that I love your daughter, although no one can express my devotion to her. I know I am not what you have hoped for in a suitor for her, but as you can see, I am well able to provide for her; and if you were to be so generous as to grant your consent to our marriage, I can promise you I will devote my life to making her happy. I have no need of her dowry, so I would ask that instead you use it to help re-establish Viscount Huntingdon to his rightful place in society." He paused to take a deep breath, and when he was not interrupted, he said, "I would be remiss if I did not add that in the process of rescuing your daughter last night, I could not avoid the *appearance* of compromising her, although nothing happened between us that was not required by the circumstances. I can only hope that you will allow me to make matters right by granting your permission for our marriage."

Darcy said, "The apothecary said she would not have survived had Paxton not found her. We all owe him a debt of gratitude for that." And to Elizabeth, who had been the one with the presence of mind to tell Paxton to look for her.

Lord Bentham looked bewildered, as if he had no idea what to do in this situation. "But her place in the *ton*...."

His mother interrupted him. "Personally, I would advise you to keep Eleanor as far from the *ton* as possible. Eleanor is a great deal like me. Your wife has somehow managed to bring her into line, but once she is married and no longer under your control, she will revert to being the same wild Eleanor she used to be. She proved that last night. She will end up undoing all your wife's work to re-establish your family in the highest circles. I say you should marry her to Paxton where she can do you no harm – and before word gets out as to what she did yesterday."

Lord Bentham looked from his mother to Darcy, then at Paxton. "If that is what Eleanor truly wishes," he said heavily, "I will give my permission."

Paxton stood stock-still for a moment, as if he could not believe what he was hearing. "Thank you, my lord. I will never give you cause to regret it."

The Dowager Marchioness bustled into Eleanor's room. "Do you still have that laudanum?" she asked Elizabeth.

"Yes, it is on the bedside table."

"Well, Eleanor, you can drink it now. I have agreed to stay here as your chaperone until you are well enough to return to Bentham Park."

Eleanor's eyes brightened. "Thank you, Grandmama! I cannot thank you enough. Is he very angry?"

"Not now – and it seems the epidemic of betrothals is not yet over. He has given your Mr. Paxton his permission to marry you."

"What?" Eleanor half-shrieked. "Is it true? Tell me you are not teasing me!"

"Yes, my dear, it is quite true, and your young man is absolutely incandescent with joy. I suspect Darcy will have to tie his feet to the floor to keep him from floating away like a hot-air balloon."

Elizabeth reached down to hug her friend. "I am so very happy for you."

To her surprise, Eleanor burst into tears. "I never thought it could happen," she sobbed. "Thank you, thank you, thank you."

"I may have struck the killing blow on your behalf," her grandmother said briskly, "but Darcy is the one who deserves your thanks. He put your father in a position where refusing his permission would have looked downright churlish. It was very clever of him."

"Darcy did? I must thank him!"

"What you *must* do, young lady, is drink that laudanum!"

"Of course, Grandmama. Whatever you say." Eleanor immediately drank off the cup Elizabeth handed her, for all the world as if she had not been fighting it for hours. "May I see Geoffrey?"

"I imagine he will be in later, but not while your father is in the house. By the by, you should tell your young man to keep better track of his property." The dowager plucked a gold cufflink from the counterpane and dangled the damning evidence in front of her granddaughter.

Edward rose from the windowseat where he had been conversing quietly with Lady Mary. "Well? What did his lordship want?"

"Your father? Somehow he heard that Darcy knew something important about you. Charles, probably. Darcy told him about the duel – repeatedly, I might add, at your father's request. I left during the third iteration, at which point I was expecting your father to demand to know how many blades of grass were in the field and the pattern of the waistcoat you wore."

"Did he believe it?"

"Yes. Of course Darcy was quite forceful on the subject, and insisted on telling him the name of every possible witness, as well as everything anyone ever said about it to him. It was fortunate he had so much evidence, since that boy is the worst liar I have ever seen. Young

Paxton had to rescue him several times when your father asked about your whereabouts. He wants to see you – your father, that is, not Mr. Paxton."

One corner of Edward's mouth crooked up. "The question is whether *I* wish to see *him*."

"That is up to you, but *I* will not hide your whereabouts again. I do not hold with keeping this sort of secret."

Lady Mary looked up at Edward. "My love, you will have to see him sooner or later."

His face softened. "I know, my dear. But I must say that later sounds better than sooner."

Under the influence of laudanum, Eleanor finally fell asleep, the lines of pain in her face relaxing at last. When Darcy and Paxton reappeared with the intelligence of Lord Bentham's departure, the others relocated to the greater comfort of the private sitting room just beyond the bedroom, where Darcy reported on the remainder of his meeting with the Marquess. "He did not say anything about his sources of information, but I asked enough leading questions that he should have the answer soon. He says he was at Bentham for hunting season when it happened, and that the news first came via a letter to his wife, but then he refused to say anything further about it."

Paxton had just given directions for a light dinner to be served in the sitting room when Symons appeared once more in the doorway, several lines appearing between his furrowed brows. "Begging your pardon, sir, but we have just received two urgent messages for the Dowager Marchioness of Bentham."

"Yes?" said the dowager sharply. "Where are they?"

"They were both oral messages. The first was sent by Lord Charles Carlisle, who asks that your ladyship proceed to Bentham Park with all speed, and suggests bringing reinforcements. The second, which arrived as I was ordering a carriage to be prepared for your ladyship, was brought by a young boy. He claims to have been sent by the butler at

Bentham Park, who begs for your ladyship's immediate presence, and I am most particularly to tell you that this is not the polite request sort of begging, but the kind done on hands and knees out of desperation." Clearly it pained Symons that any butler might sink to such a state. "Neither gave a reason, though on closer questioning, the boy reported that Lord Bentham is in a towering rage, as evidenced by locking people up and dismissing all the servants."

The dowager raised her eyebrows. "It seems I am going to Bentham Park. Since I am to bring reinforcements, and I also have the responsibility of chaperoning Eleanor and Miss Bennet, I will have to insist that Paxton and Darcy accompany me. Edward may remain if he chooses, since Eleanor is his sister."

Darcy scowled. After the stressful day, all he wanted was some quiet time with Elizabeth and Edward, but clearly that was wishful thinking. Charles had asked for reinforcements, and since he was unaware of Edward's presence, that had to mean Paxton and Darcy. If Charles was asking for *his* help, the situation must be desperate indeed.

Lady Mary said, "I will accompany you as well, since I need to return to Bentham in any case. I am accustomed to seeing battlefields, and I doubt anything at Bentham Park can match that."

Edward sent Darcy a glance that suggested he did not necessarily agree with that assessment. "Very well. I will come, too."

Chapter 17

IF WAR HAD broken out at Bentham Park, it was not obvious as they drove up the long lane. The only sign of unusual activity was the expression of pathetic gratitude on the butler's face when he saw the Dowager Marchioness among their party, quickly replaced by a look of astonishment when he recognized Edward.

Lord Charles strode out into the hall to meet them, his hair uncharacteristically disheveled and his cravat askew. "Thank God you are here! The worst seems to be over, but it has been... Edward!" Astonished, he embraced his brother. "You are a welcome sight. Very welcome, indeed." He turned to his grandmother. "You, madam, are a miracle worker. I have spent the last hour promising my father that I would fetch Edward from Portugal and bring him back here immediately. It was the only thing that would calm him. I do not know how you managed to produce my brother from thin air, but I am very, very grateful for it."

"What has happened here?" The dowager looked stern.

"My father returned from Hillington – at least I think he was at Hillington – in a rage, then confronted my stepmother about something. He kept shouting, to the point where I began to fear for her safety. After a long argument, he forced her into her rooms and locked her in from the outside, then he went on a rampage, horsewhip in hand, and began dismissing all the servants she had hired during her tenure here, telling them to leave and never come back. Since she replaced almost everyone except his personal servants and the butler, most of the staff is gone. They were so terrified that some ran out the door without even collecting their effects. After that, he called for his fastest horse because he was going to ride to Portsmouth that very minute and get on a ship for Portugal, which is how I ended up promising him I would find Edward." He raked his hand through his hair.

"Everything seems quiet enough now," she said suspiciously.

"Desperate measures, madam! I kept handing him glasses of his favorite port, and he would toss them off without a thought until he was so foxed that he no longer had the energy to rage at everyone. Thank God Lord Alford was here! He can certainly bark out orders when he sets his mind to it, and my father actually listened to him eventually. As for the servants, I can only hope the housekeeper is doing something to prevent some of them from leaving, since otherwise there will be no one to cook our breakfast." He paused to catch his breath. "But you may come to the parlor and see for yourself."

In the parlor, Lord Bentham was sprawled on the sofa while Lord Alford spoke to him quietly. Lady Alford hovered nearby, ready to assist. The dowager waved away the butler when he moved to announce them. Edward made a bow in the direction of his father, who blinked slowly at him.

Lord Alford stepped forward, his hand outstretched. "Huntingdon, good to see you once more," he rumbled.

Shaking his hand, Edward said, "A pleasure, Lord Alford. In another few years, I might even believe that failing to salute you is not a hanging offense."

"Hah! I trained you well."

Charles, recalling his duties, said, "Edward, I see you are already acquainted with our guests."

"Acquainted? That is one way to put it," said the Earl heartily. "I've ridden into battle by his side. A fine soldier - the very devil in battle, begging your pardon. He makes Boney's troops turn tail and run."

Lord Bentham wagged his finger slowly at his eldest son. "You," he said, his words slurred. "You are in Portugal."

Edward pressed his lips together to hide a smile. "I *was* in Portugal, sir. I am now in England."

"Oh." His eyes shifted to Charles. "That was quick."

"I do my best," Charles said modestly.

Lord Bentham drew his brows together as if trying to concentrate. "Darcy."

Darcy stepped forward. "I am here, sir."

"I figured it out. It was my wife. Don't know why *you* couldn't see it. Obvious, once I thought about it."

Darcy almost yelped as the heel of Edward's boot came down forcefully on his toe, and he turned a quick glare on his cousin. "Well done, my lord. I knew you would solve the mystery."

"I locked her in her rooms. Told her I was going to send her away." He looked around blearily. "Where is Charles? Oh, there you are. You should hire some new servants."

"Fortunately, Grandmama is here to rescue me from that duty," Charles said. "No one can manage a household as well as Grandmama."

The Dowager Marchioness gave him a sidelong look, then sat down beside her son and patted his knee. "You have done very well, my dear. Now I think it would be best for you to rest here while I find out what has happened to your dinner. Edward and Lord Alford will keep you company and tell you all about Portugal."

Lord Bentham appeared to ponder this for a moment. "Very well. I would like to hear about Port...Portugal."

"Good," said the dowager briskly. "They have some news for you regarding Lord Alford's daughter as well."

"The one who is to marry Charles?"

Charles' head jerked up. "Did I miss something?" he asked suspiciously.

"No, dear, Lady Mary is engaged to Edward, not Charles."

He looked puzzled, then nodded slowly. "That will do as well."

"Good." She pointed to Charles, Paxton and Darcy. "You will come with me."

They dutifully trailed after her. In the hallway, she turned to her grandson. "Good Lord, Charles, how much port did you pour into him?"

"Half a decanter, then another bottle. He had already smashed all the French porcelain his wife had collected, and was chasing after the servants with a horsewhip. And I thought he had mellowed in recent years!"

"You should have dosed the port with laudanum. It works faster that way."

"Indeed. I will keep that in mind should the circumstance arise again, madam." His lips were pressed together in amusement.

She waved the butler over. "How much of the staff is gone?"

"Well over half of the indoor staff, madam. It is possible some may return eventually."

"We will make do. Pray attend to his lordship and his guests."

The butler bowed and disappeared into the parlor.

The Dowager Marchioness gestured to Paxton. "We must remove his wife from here with all dispatch. Mr. Paxton, I hope you will be so kind as to write out a letter for me to my butler at Newiston House, commending Lady Bentham to his care to be kept under lock and key. Also, he should send as many servants as can be spared – and the spaniels. Darcy, you will check on the outdoor staff and discover which of them can do indoor work temporarily. Charles, you will come with me below stairs to speak to the remaining servants. Most of them will not know me, and I will need your authority."

"I cannot imagine why," Charles muttered.

The dowager gave him her haughtiest look. "I beg your pardon?"

"Madam," said Paxton with a laugh, "you have just given orders to a Marquess, an Earl, a Viscount, two gentlemen of property, Lord Charles, and the butler, and you are worried about whether the kitchen staff will listen to you?"

She favored him with a dark look. "*You* are supposed to be writing a letter, young man."

"Ho, there!" A gentleman in riding clothes approached one of the gardeners whom Darcy had already interviewed and rejected for indoor work. "Why is no one answering the door at the house?"

Darcy's head shot up. "Richard? What in God's name are *you* doing here?"

Colonel Fitzwilliam's eyes widened at the sight of Darcy. "The question is what *you* are doing among the gardeners! But never mind that – I am hunting after that scapegrace Edward. Is he perchance here?"

"He is conversing with his father in the parlor, but you might wish to wait until he is done to see him."

"Oh, no," said Richard firmly. "I am going to speak to him right this minute."

Recognizing the signs of temper in his usually affable cousin, Darcy declined to argue. "Very well, but you are walking into a hornet's nest."

"Once I am done with Edward, he will think a hornet's nest is nothing but a walk in the park!"

After dismissing the gardeners, Darcy took him inside, explaining briefly about the lack of staff. The scene in the parlor was mostly unchanged, though the ladies had left and Edward now sat stiffly in an armchair near his father.

Richard did not trouble himself with greetings apart from a perfunctory bow to Lord Bentham. "Damn you, Edward! I have chased halfway across England after you. What in God's name do you think you are doing?"

Edward said, "Calm down, Richard. I am perfectly well. I needed to return here quickly, and there was no time to dawdle with slow carriages in short stages." He took a few steps forward, then turned in a circle. "See – no damage."

"No damage? Ha! I called in every favor I had to get you the finest surgeon in Portugal, and I stayed by you day and night until he could assure me you would keep that leg – *as long as you followed his orders.* I forced you to stay in that damned bed for months to allow the muscles to knit properly so you would be able to walk again. Then, the *minute* my back is turned, you rush off and do *the one thing* he said you should avoid at all costs, not only riding a horse but riding half the length of England! By God, you *deserve* to limp for the rest of your life!"

Edward held his hands out placatingly. "I could tell everything was healed. It is *my* leg, after all."

"And that justifies sneaking out of the inn in Portsmouth and leaving me nothing more than a note saying you were going North? How could you be such a fool? Did you think Lady Mary would thank you for re-injuring your leg in your haste to reach her? Devil take it, if you had not already sold your commission, I would have you court-martialed for disobeying my orders!"

"Enough! Very well, I admit that it was a foolish thing to do, as well as unfair to you; but I *did* stay in that damned bed for six long months doing everything your surgeon said, and I have had *enough* of being an invalid."

Lord Alford laid a hand on Richard's arm. "You need say no more, Colonel. I assure you Huntingdon will be hearing from *me* on this subject," he said in an ominous tone.

Darcy handed Richard a glass of port. "You can *both* take this up with him later. We are *attempting* to keep everyone here calm." He cast a significant glance toward Lord Bentham.

"I hope you added laudanum to that," said Edward dryly.

Lord Bentham looked up, his eyes bleary. "Laudanum? Is someone injured?"

Edward patted his arm reassuringly. "No, everyone is perfectly well. Richard Fitzwilliam is here to see me."

"Fitzwilliam is here, too? Is *anyone* left in Portugal?"

Richard said in an amused tone, "I promise you, sir, Portugal is in good hands."

"Good. Then Edward can stay here. I would like that." Lord Bentham looked around the room as if trying to ascertain who was present, then turned back to Edward and spoke in a confidential tone. "I still miss your mother, you know, even after all these years."

"Yes, Father," said Edward quietly. "I do know."

Darcy looked back over his shoulder at Edward and his father as Lord Alford herded Richard and him from the room. At least that was one problem resolved.

"Are you certain you wish to do this?" Darcy asked Elizabeth for at least the fourth time.

"Yes. You need have no worries; you will be able to see me the entire time."

"And you may be certain my eyes will not wander for a second," he grumbled. "I still do not like it."

She touched his hand lightly. "I know, and I am sorry, but it is something I must do." She could feel his eyes on her as she left him to enter the morning room where Lord Charles sat reading a newspaper, a spaniel sprawled at his feet. The bruise around his eye was beginning to fade to yellow.

His eyes gave a flicker of surprise when he saw her. "Miss Bennet, I had not expected to see you at Bentham today."

"It is a spontaneous visit. May I join you?"

He indicated a chair. "Certainly. I will be happy for the distraction. I have heard enough from Edward about the wars without reading about them in the newspaper."

She could not help but notice the change in his demeanor toward her. In the past, he would have slipped in a compliment or an endearment. "I will try to be more amusing than the wars."

"I doubt you could do otherwise, yet I suspect you did not come merely to keep me company – especially as I can see Darcy glowering in the hall. He is not best pleased by this tête-à-tête, is he?"

"No, he is not, but he will survive. And you are right that I do have something to tell you. I wanted you to know that Mr. Darcy had been courting me for some months before I came here. By the time you made your unexpected offer, I had already decided in his favor and we were very close to an understanding. It was not a matter of choosing him over you, but of already having an attachment to him. Had I met you first, it might have been different."

"You are very kind, Miss Bennet," he said with a certain irony, "but I am well aware that no woman in her right mind would, given a choice, take me over Darcy. He has an estate and a fortune; I have only a courtesy title."

She laughed, which seemed to surprise him. "You do not know *me* well, then! Your prospects played no part in it, nor did his. I turned down two very advantageous offers because I could not respect the gentlemen concerned. Not all women are venal."

"If any woman were to judge a man only on his merits, I am not surprised to find it is you," he said. "May I ask you to indulge me by answering one question?"

Elizabeth would much rather not, but she nodded. "Of course."

"Why did you act as if you planned to accept me?"

Now it was Elizabeth's turn to look away. Reluctantly, she said, "I was afraid that if I did otherwise, you...you might make it impossible for me to refuse you."

"What? And *that* is what you think of me? Miss Bennet, I have committed a great many sins in my life, but I have *never* forced myself upon a woman. I might have pestered you mercilessly to change your mind, but not *that*."

She let out the breath she had been holding. "I am very glad to hear it. I did not like thinking it of you."

"And somehow I suspect Darcy had some role in suggesting it to you," he said darkly. "He always thinks the worst of me."

"A compliment which you seem to return!"

"It *was* him, was it not? I remember – you started to refuse me, then he asked to speak to you, and I thought he had made you reconsider. And *he* was engaged to Eleanor at the time, damn his eyes!"

"I *am* sorry that I misjudged you, and I do realize Mr. Darcy is prejudiced against you. I have also been informed that you are quite a decent fellow, when you are not playing the part of a rake."

"Good Lord, someone actually spoke well of me?" he said with heavy irony. "I must not have tried hard enough to disillusion him."

"Her, actually."

He waved a dismissive hand. "That is meaningless. It just means she hopes to marry me."

With a smile, Elizabeth shook her head. "Shall I tell Miss Holmes that she is incorrect and you have no redeeming virtues, then?"

"Ah, it was Carrie, then? Now *that* I do not deserve."

Elizabeth thought it best to leave this subject as quickly as possible. "Tell me, will you be returning to London soon?"

He reached down to scratch the head of the spaniel. "Not yet. We will all remain here long enough to see Eleanor married. After that, I suppose I will join the army. That is the simplest option."

"I thought you did not want that."

"I am too fond of my creature comforts to enjoy army life, but it is what second sons do, and it is past time that I do my duty – and, if I am not mistaken, you must also do yours." He directed a significant look toward Darcy. "He looks on the verge of apoplexy. To tell the truth, I can hardly blame him."

She was being dismissed. "Very well, I will go attend to poor, long-suffering Mr. Darcy. Good day, then, Lord Charles."

"Good day, Miss Bennet."

On impulse, she touched his cheek lightly with the back of her fingers, then left without a backwards glance. Darcy did look rather apoplectic, but his face softened as she drew nearer. "Happy now?" he asked.

"Yes." She slipped her hand into his arm and walked a short distance from the sitting room. "I know you do not approve, but I have recently developed a certain sympathy for anyone discovering the person they love is engaged to someone else. As you know, I did not always understand the importance of gentleness in refusing an offer, but I would like to think I have learned with experience."

He was silent at first, but then said, "You are quite correct. I am being selfish in not wanting you even to smile in his direction."

"He may receive a few smiles, but you have all my kisses! But on another subject, there is an idea I would like to put to his lordship. Do you think he would be willing to listen to me, or is he still angry that I did not tell him about Eleanor and Paxton?"

"My dearest Elizabeth, so much has happened since then that I doubt he even remembers that omission on your part; but if you like, I can tell him your idea instead. Of course, I omitted the very same information as you."

She thought for a moment. "I think it is better if it comes from me. It is about Lord Charles, an idea for something that might help him, but if Lord Charles discovers the idea came from you, he might refuse it on principle."

"A fair point. It is kind of you to try to help him." Although Darcy did not seem particularly pleased with her kindness, he took her to Lord Bentham's study where his lordship was conversing with his eldest son. After informing Lord Bentham that Elizabeth had an idea to share with him, Darcy excused himself, leaving her with the two gentlemen.

"You have an idea, my dear?" asked Lord Bentham cordially.

Elizabeth took a deep breath. "Perhaps you are aware that Lord Charles fell into the habit of confiding in me during these last few weeks. One time we were talking about his original plan to enter the army. I asked him what he would like to do, had he a choice in the matter. His answer surprised me – he said that he wished he could live in the country and breed hunting dogs." At Lord Bentham's frown, she hurried on. "While that may not be realistic, it occurred to me that you do have an empty kennel that is falling into disrepair, and Lord Charles is in need of occupation outside the *ton* and, in my opinion, to have a goal he can accomplish and feel pride in. The dogs from your kennels used to be the finest in Yorkshire. I thought perhaps you could ask him to rebuild the kennels to their former glory. It would be a temporary project rather than a career, but it might allow him the respite he needs."

Lord Bentham looked at her as if she had suggested that Lord Charles should fly to the moon, but Viscount Huntingdon nodded slowly. "I remember how he all but lived in the kennels when we were young. I have not thought of that in years. And I agree, he needs something to keep him away from the *ton*."

"But could Charles be happy away from the excitement and luxuries of London?" asked Lord Bentham dubiously.

"I do not know," his son replied. "I was surprised to hear that he had lived in London all these years, because, as I remember it, he never liked Town. He found it too crowded and noisy. But perhaps all that has changed, and he is content with it now. It is worth asking him. The question is whether you have an interest in building up the kennels again." It was something of a foolish question given that one spaniel was sprawled at Lord Bentham's feet and another had its head in his lap.

The Marquess stroked the dog's head absently. "It would be good to bring in new dogs, but I still cannot imagine he would want to stay here and *work*."

"If you do not object, Father, I will speak to him. The worst he can do is to say he would rather not."

"I suppose so. I thank you, Miss Bennet, for bringing this to our attention."

"It was the least I could do, my lord." She curtsied and turned to leave.

Lord Bentham's voice came after her. "Miss Bennet, I understand that I should give you my best wishes on your engagement to Darcy."

She turned back slowly to face him. "Thank you, my lord." Under the circumstances, she supposed it was a concession on his part.

"I am very happy that Darcy has re-established his connection with us. On his deathbed, Darcy's father asked me to watch over his son, and it has troubled me greatly that I have not been able to fulfill that duty. When you make your wedding plans, I would be honored if you would consider celebrating the occasion here at Bentham."

Momentarily speechless, Elizabeth could only stare at him. Finally, she stammered, "That is a very generous offer, my lord."

Lord Bentham passed a hand over his forehead. "In truth, you would be doing me a kindness. Talk to Darcy about it."

"I will." She was touched by the suggestion, though she was certain that Darcy would wish to keep her family far from his noble connections.

As Lord Huntingdon was minded to look into the kennel possibility immediately, Elizabeth took this excuse to depart from the study as well. As he walked along beside her, the viscount said, "That was an excellent idea, Miss Bennet. The *ton* brings out the worst in Charles, and he lacks purpose. It was good of you to take the trouble; I know my father is not easy to approach."

"I hope it helps. I do feel somewhat responsible for his current ill humor."

He stopped and looked at her, his brows furrowed. "I cannot imagine how you could possibly think yourself responsible. You had nothing to do with all these misunderstandings."

She flushed and dropped her eyes. "Darcy did not tell you?"

"Tell me what?"

"That Lord Charles also made me an offer of marriage, and I refused him. That was what provoked his fight with Darcy. So you see, I am not without guilt."

"Did he really? Miss Bennet, you astonish me. Not because your charms are in any way deficient, but that my brother would have the good sense to recognize your value."

Elizabeth's face grew warm, and she tried to disguise her embarrassment with a laugh. "Apparently the secret to the heart of highly eligible young men of the *ton* is to laugh at them, be continually impudent, refuse to take them seriously, and never for a second consider the possibility that they might actually be falling in love. That was what made Mr. Darcy notice me as well."

"I am very glad you told me this. It helps me to understand better what it is that Charles needs. I will give this some consideration."

Elizabeth decided to take a risk. "You have a neighbor, Miss Holmes, whom Lord Charles seems to think well of, and she has a fondness for him."

"Miss Bennet, you are a fount of intriguing ideas. Are you certain you do not have a twin sister for Charles?"

As they approached the sitting room, she heard the sound of Darcy laughing, and then beheld an astonishing sight. Darcy, looking quite comfortable with his feet up on a footstool, was sitting with Lord Charles, apparently chatting quite amicably. Edward stopped short and looked at them quizzically. "Are we interrupting something?"

"Not at all," said Lord Charles cheerfully. "I was just telling Darcy what an insufferable prig he was during the summer he stayed with us, and he was informing me that I spent the entire summer whining and complaining."

Edward shook his head and looked down at Elizabeth with a smile. In a conspiratorial voice meant to be overheard, he said, "Both true. It took me weeks to convince Darcy to break even the smallest rule, and Charles thought that one domineering older brother was enough for him without borrowing a second for the summer."

"And in the meantime, you were all cruelly refusing to play with poor Eleanor," Elizabeth teased.

"Of course," said Edward, his eyes twinkling. "She was a *girl.*" Darcy and Lord Charles nodded in agreement, as if this were a perfectly reasonable explanation.

"I expect you were all perfectly despicable," she said.

Lord Charles shook his head. "And this from the young lady who put a snake in my bed."

Afterwards, Elizabeth asked Darcy, "How did you end up speaking to him? I thought there was nothing you agreed on."

Darcy leaned down and stole a quick kiss. "Actually, there *is* one thing we agree on. We mostly talked about you."

"About *me*?" It was the last answer she had expected.

"Yes. Whatever I might think of him otherwise, I cannot fault his taste in losing his heart to you. He, in turn, is perhaps the only person who finds nothing unusual about my desire to marry you."

"I cannot imagine what the two of you could say about me that would not lead to fisticuffs!"

He laughed. "In fact, I told him the entire story of our acquaintance, everything that you said to me at Hunsford, how infuriated I was with you afterwards, and then how I wanted to murder him when I saw you waltzing together. He found it quite entertaining, and added in a few choice remarks you had made about him as well."

She turned to stare at him. "I will never understand men, not if I had a thousand years to study them!"

Eleanor was feeling sufficiently improved that she had insisted on getting out of bed, although she agreed to allow Geoffrey to support her as she walked. Despite leaning on him heavily, even the intrepid Eleanor was ready to stop when she had travelled as far as the fainting couch in the private sitting room outside the bedroom. "It was worth it," she announced. "I might have lost my mind if I had to stare at those same walls for one more minute. They are very nice walls, admittedly, but four days of them is more than enough!"

Elizabeth set a pillow beside her friend, then turned to Paxton. "Do you think we could shift her so that her leg is on the pillow?"

"I can sit up perfectly well!" snapped Eleanor.

"You can lie down perfectly well, too," Paxton said firmly, "just as the apothecary said you should." Without further ado, he lifted her and set her down with her injured leg on the pillow.

"Will you always be so overbearing?" Eleanor asked, but without any sting in her voice.

He smiled. "Only when you do not listen to reason, dearest."

"I, however, am *always* overbearing." The Dowager Marchioness spoke from the doorway, then came to press a kiss on Eleanor's cheek. "But if *you* are not listening to reason, that must mean you are feeling better. I am glad to see Mr. Paxton is not without resources under the circumstances."

"Grandmama!" cried Eleanor indignantly. "You need not take his side quite so happily."

Elizabeth broke in tactfully. "I imagine you would enjoy visiting with your grandmother, so I will take myself downstairs and out of the way."

"Not so quickly, Miss Bennet," the dowager said. "You are the one I am here to see."

"Oh, dear," said Elizabeth with a laugh. "What have I done wrong now?"

"That remains to be seen. I understand that my son has expressed his desire to hold your wedding at Bentham Park."

"He did make that very kind offer, but you need not worry. I have no intention of accepting it."

Eleanor sat up straight. "Why not? I think it would be lovely."

"My thoughts exactly," said the dowager briskly. "More importantly, it would mend some bridges in our family."

Elizabeth shook her head with a smile. "I am sorry, but *my* family lives far from here, and I would not want to marry without them present. While you may be willing to make them welcome here, I cannot say that I advise it. My family is not the sort of company to which you are accustomed."

"They can stay here," offered Paxton. "My sensibilities are not easily disturbed."

"You have not met my family! You should ask Mr. Darcy about them before you make so cavalier an offer."

"Miss Bennet, I have some important advice for you," the dowager said. "When you pick your battles, my girl, do your best to select those you may actually have a chance of winning. This is *not* one of those. I have already written to your mother with an invitation for your entire family. We will send a carriage to fetch them."

Elizabeth stared at her in disbelief. Although she had seen sufficient evidence of the dowager's autocratic ways, she had not expected them to be applied to her in this way. How was she to argue when she knew full well that her mother would rather die than miss an opportunity to bring her daughters to Bentham Park, especially when Lord Bentham had an unmarried son in residence? "I do not think Mr. Darcy will be pleased with this," she said.

"What will not please me?" Darcy's voice came from behind her.

She turned quickly to smile at him. "I had not realized you had returned already."

"I accomplished my business in York swiftly, since there was a lovely lady I wished to rejoin as soon as possible." He came to stand next to her and squeezed her hand, but she knew that if the dowager had not been present, she would have received a much warmer greeting.

"I am glad you are here. The Dowager Marchioness has just informed me that we will be celebrating our wedding at Bentham Park regardless of our own wishes."

Darcy turned a quizzical look on the Dowager Marchioness, who gave a sharp laugh. "Although I did not say it quite that way, your intended has the gist of it."

"She has already sent an invitation to my mother! I tried to explain that my family is not what she might expect."

To her astonishment, Darcy burst out laughing. "Elizabeth, I do not think your family can compare to what we have observed among the Carlisles in the last week."

The Dowager Marchioness did not allow this potential weakness to pass. "So you agree to it, then?"

"That depends. Do you have a date in mind?"

"Miss Bennet's aunt and uncle are due to arrive here in three weeks, so that would be convenient, unless it is too soon for you."

Darcy smiled broadly. "For the chance to marry Elizabeth that quickly, I would be willing to have the ceremony in the Outer Hebrides."

"I thought that part might pique your interest," the Dowager Marchioness said. "You seem to be outnumbered, Miss Bennet."

Darcy said, "I hope you will permit us to speak privately for a few minutes." He took Elizabeth's hand and led her to the other side of the room. Speaking quietly, he asked, "Would you mind having the wedding here rather than at Longbourn? If you do, please tell me, and I will put a stop to these plans."

She shook her head. "I am content with this, as long as you are. Bentham Park was once like a home to me, and this will leave me with the happiest of memories of it. But is this what *you* truly want?"

His gaze grew warm. "What I truly want is you. The rest is details."

She drew in a sharp breath. "You do not object to my family coming here?"

"Not in the least. In fact, it might prove convenient, since if the wedding is here, it would make sense to invite Bingley. He is in Scarborough now, so it would be an easy journey for him, and I am certain he would be pleased to renew his acquaintance with your family." The smile he gave her was full of private warmth.

A burst of happiness rose in Elizabeth at his words. She had assumed that sooner or later there would be an opportunity to bring Jane and Bingley back together, but it gave her special pleasure to see Darcy planning for it. "Very well, but I must warn you that my mother will be making every effort to throw my dear Jane in Lord Charles's way!"

Darcy shrugged. "Charles could do much worse than your sister."

Elizabeth's eyes grew wide. "I was joking!"

He brushed his fingers against her cheek. "Stranger things have happened. But I am sorry this visit has been so difficult for you."

"How shall we decide what is difficult? When you became engaged to Eleanor, I thought my heart would break; but had that painful episode not happened, Eleanor would be marrying Lord Deyncourt rather than Mr. Paxton. Is not that outcome worth the suffering?"

He pressed his lips to the inside of her wrist, making her pulse race. "You and Edward have both become philosophers. Yesterday he told me he was glad to have spent four years among men who knew nothing of his titles or fortune. He claims he never before realized how much of the treatment he received was due only to his position, and now he knows his value as a man as well as a nobleman."

"He is wise, then." She put on an expression of mock seriousness. "However, I have failed to mention the most important reason to marry here, which is that I owe the Dowager Marchioness more than I can ever repay."

His eyebrows raised, Darcy asked, "And what do you owe her, my love?"

"Why, she is the one who began all this! It was she who ordered me to be taken to Eleanor's nursery when I accompanied my aunt on that fateful call. At the time, I thought she was annoyed because I was so restless; but in hindsight, I suspect she knew perfectly well that what Eleanor needed most was a lively playmate, the sort who would not be able to sit still through a dull condolence call. And if I had not met Eleanor and spent so much time here, I would have become a different person, one whom you never would have noticed – and we would not have had this opportunity to meet again and to work out our differences." She smiled up at him. "So, all in all, I would have to say that she has earned the right to choose when and where we marry."

"As long as it is *soon*." As they returned to the others, Darcy said to the dowager, "Very well, we have agreed your plan will suit us admirably."

"Of course it suits you admirably," the dowager replied. "All my plans work out admirably."

Paxton spoke up with an air of one making a great discovery. "Eleanor, my dear, I think I am coming to understand your grandmother."

The dowager gave him a sidelong look. "Somehow I doubt that."

He continued to address his words to Eleanor, but spoke loudly enough for all to hear. "In a few minutes, she is going to be struck by the marvelous idea that this could also be the solution to the problem of *our* wedding. Rather than the rushed and furtive wedding currently planned for us, what could be more natural for us than to desire to be united in a double ceremony with our dear friends? It would explain our indecent rush from engagement to the altar without reference to scandal." His eyes danced with laughter as he watched the older woman.

With her haughtiest look, the Dowager Marchioness examined him from head to foot. "I might yet decide you have some sense after all, young man, but you are not as clever as you think."

Paxton laughed. "Did I miss something, then?"

"Two things. One is the value of holding a major event here without Lady Bentham, so everyone will know we are not ashamed of putting her into retirement, and as for the other – " She paused and eyed Darcy assessingly. "It will give me the greatest pleasure to tell my idiot nephew Matlock that I not only managed to make Darcy see reason on the subject of marriage, but actually had him at the altar inside two months' time." Her expression reminded Elizabeth of a triumphant cat parading a dead mouse.

Darcy gave her a stern look. "You had nothing to do with my decision to marry."

"True, but that will not stop me from taking the credit."

Elizabeth covered her face with her hands. "And I used to think *my* family was troublesome!"

Darcy leaned down to speak softly in her ear, his warm breath tickling her tender skin. "I am sorry to disillusion you, my dear, but this *is* your family now."

Epilogue

Bentham Park, July 23

"YOU ARE SELLING your commission?" Darcy's shock was apparent.

"It is your fault, you know," said Richard Fitzwilliam.

"*My* fault? I never asked you to sell out!"

"No, but you refused to allow Lord Bentham to repay you for what you did for Edward, so he felt obliged to pour his largesse on me instead. I am now in possession of what was formerly one of the minor Bentham properties, a manor house near Nottingham with an income of a thousand pounds per annum."

Darcy blinked. "That is very generous of him."

"Do not give me that look, Darcy. Lord Bentham learned a lesson from his offer to repay you. He and Edward met with the solicitors and settled the estate on me before I had any inkling of his plans. The first I knew of it was when I received the deed from the solicitor."

"You are mistaken. I do not disapprove; I am just surprised. But I am delighted that you will not be returning to active duty."

"I will not argue that point!"

"How is Lord Bentham? Is he still furious over the entire matter?"

Richard furrowed his brows. "He is calmer, I think. He continues to blame himself for trusting his wife, but he is very glad to have Edward back. That has been the best medicine for him. It helps that Eleanor is ecstatically happy and thanks him constantly for allowing her to marry Paxton."

"And Charles?" Darcy was not sure he wished to know the answer.

"There has not been even a whiff of impropriety in his behavior toward your Elizabeth – and I assure you I have been watching closely. They have conversed several times, but always with others present. In fact...but I should let Elizabeth tell you that story. No need to fret; you will likely be pleased about it."

"I, pleased with Charles? That would be a first."

Richard chuckled. "Poor Charles. He always wanted you to like him, you know."

Darcy gave him an odd look. "No, I did not know. Usually he seemed to want to annoy me more than anything."

With a shrug, Richard said, "It comes down to the same thing. If you had any brothers of your own, you would understand."

"How did Charles take the news of your new estate?" Watching his father give property to a mere cousin when Charles himself was landless could not have been pleasant.

"Without a problem, since he is to have Newiston House now that Lady Bentham is in seclusion in Scotland and the Dowager Marchioness is in residence here. That will give him a home of his own, but nearby enough to visit frequently. Lord Bentham seems to believe he has many bridges to mend."

"He is correct in that," Darcy said darkly.

"Oh, come now, Darcy! He is an old man who trusted his beautiful young wife – not the first nor the last to do so."

And for his own father's sake, Darcy should have been keeping an eye on the old man all these years, rather than refusing to have anything to do with him. That was one of the realizations he had come to during his week at Pemberley. "I suppose so," he said grudgingly.

For at least the tenth time, Darcy glanced at the clock, the same one that had so infuriated him during his brief engagement to Eleanor. It still counted out the minutes ridiculously slowly. "How long does it take them to finish fitting one dress?" he asked impatiently.

Clapping him on the shoulder, Richard said, "You never used to be so impatient, cousin!"

"That was before I met Elizabeth!" Darcy had not been alone with her since before his departure to Pemberley. He had not been happy about leaving her for a week, but it had been the right thing to do. The official reason was that Elizabeth wanted some time alone with her family, who had just arrived. That was true enough, but the actual motivation had been that they were both finding it increasingly difficult to stop at kisses. After one occasion when they had succumbed enough to their longings to go somewhat beyond that, they had reluctantly decided a brief separation might be wise. After all, as Elizabeth had pointed out with amusement, there was no hope of hiding their shame if they fell into sin, owing to the Dowager Marchioness's astonishing ability to know everything that anyone at Bentham Park did, said or even thought.

None of that was important now. This evening Elizabeth would waltz in his arms in that same ballroom where he had discovered he still loved her, and this time she would be smiling at him - and tonight would be the last night they spent apart. Tomorrow morning, he would meet her at the altar, along with Paxton and Eleanor, and she would become his wife. "Is Paxton at Hillington? I have not seen him here."

"He is supervising the construction of his wedding gift to Eleanor. Tomorrow he will come to church via his new footbridge over the river."

Darcy laughed. "That is more of a gift to himself! He is worried Eleanor might try their stepping stones again someday. I must admit it seems more than likely that sooner or later she would."

A small hand slipped through his arm. "I do not think Eleanor has any desire to go near the stepping stones again," said Elizabeth. "She is tired of limping."

A rush of warmth filled him, and Darcy could not quite stop himself from leaning down to place a light kiss on her forehead. Although he could not imagine anyone objecting, he still glanced around to check if the Dowager Marchioness was watching.

Elizabeth was well able to comprehend his look. "You need not worry. She has taken Lydia and Kitty into town to do some final shopping."

"Oh, dear," said Richard, who had become acquainted with the Bennets during the last week. "That may prove interesting."

"Instructive for all concerned, I imagine," Elizabeth said. "The Dowager Marchioness seems to have taken on Kitty and Lydia as a personal challenge."

"My money is on her," Darcy said without hesitation.

"I agree," said Elizabeth. "After all, she managed to teach both Eleanor and me to behave properly, at least most of the time."

Since Darcy was particularly partial to those times when Elizabeth did *not* behave properly, it seemed wisest to keep his silence on the subject. "Richard tells me I should ask you about Charles."

Elizabeth laughed. "Ah, yes, that is an interesting tale! After Eleanor and I moved back to Bentham Park, I invited Miss Holmes to tea. When she arrived and discovered Lord Charles would be joining us, she refused to stay. Lord Charles asked her why, and discovered Miss Holmes' questionable reputation in the neighborhood was the result of her old friendship with him. He apologized profusely to her and left the three of us alone. The next day he called on her father and asked his permission to court her. I expect she will accompany him to the wedding tomorrow."

Darcy raised his eyebrows. "I am surprised. I thought his affection for you ran deeper than that."

"His affection was never so much for me as for a woman who would treat him as a friend rather than her potential marital property. I was simply the first he had met in some time, but Miss Holmes fits the description better and has the advantage of long years of friendship with him. I think she will be very good for him."

"Any woman who can distract Charles from you has my profound thanks! And I am glad you are finally done with your fitting. I missed you."

"You may yet decide it was worth the wait! The only reason it took so long is that we were trying out my hairstyle for tomorrow." She gave him a teasing smile, then stepped forward and turned slowly in a circle. "What do you think?"

The minx! She knew just what she was doing to him, he was sure of it. Her dark hair was gathered in a complex set of loops held together by no fewer than eight diamond hairpins, part of the set he had given her as a betrothal gift. A surge of pure desire ran through him.

Richard said, "Lovely! It will be perfect."

"Thank you. The poor maid had to try it three times before it worked. I told her there should be no little braids or weaving, and no pomades or feathers in it because I especially wanted my hairpins to show." Elizabeth looked back over her shoulder at Darcy with an air of innocence. "They are the only thing holding it up, you know."

Darcy cleared his throat, then took her by the hand. "I hope you will excuse us, Richard. I am in need of a private word with my future wife." Leading her toward the doors opening into the garden, he murmured in her ear, "*Very* private."

A Bonus Excerpt from

Mr. Darcy's Refuge

by Abigail Reynolds

Chapter 1

THE BREAK IN the rain seemed like a sign. It meant Darcy could ride to the parsonage and discover what was troubling Elizabeth. Her friend Mrs. Collins had said she was ill, but his cousin averred that he had seen her but a few hours ago, and she seemed well then. Darcy would have thought Elizabeth would stop at nothing to come to Rosings tonight, his last night in Kent, and her last chance to ensnare him. Instead she had remained at the parsonage, leaving her friend to make her excuses to his aunt, Lady Catherine.

She must be avoiding him. There could be no other reason for her absence. But why? She had every reason to wish to be in his presence, unless she had decided that winning his love was a hopeless cause. Perhaps that was it. Perhaps his failure to declare himself had left her believing that he was simply toying with her. Perhaps she thought it would be too painful to see him tonight, knowing it would be for the last time. Darcy's mouth curved a little with the thought. Dearest Elizabeth! How happy she would be to receive his assurances of love.

Just at that moment, the pounding of rain against the windowpanes finally began to slacken as the thunder faded off into the distance. His aunt's attention was focused on rendering unwanted advice to Mrs. Collins while Richard was attempted to engage Anne in conversation. He could slip away unnoticed. It was definitely a sign.

Once he had escaped the gloomy sitting room, he lost no time in making his way to the stables. In a clipped voice he asked a sleepy groom to ready his curricle.

The man squinted up at him. "I don't know if that be such a good idea, sir. With those wheels, 'twould be a moment's work to find yourself stuck, the road is that deep in mud after all this rain."

"Then I will ride," Darcy said firmly. He would not allow bad roads to keep him from Elizabeth's side, not tonight.

Yawning, the groom went off to saddle his horse. Darcy helped himself to a riding crop from a shelf, then tapped it impatiently against his leg until he heard the clopping of hooves. The air hung heavy on him, thick and full of moisture. Much more of this rain and the crops would rot in the fields before they even had a chance to sprout. He would have to speak to his aunt about relief for the tenant farmers, but now was not the time to think about such matters.

Soon he would be in Elizabeth's presence, where he would finally be the recipient of her dazzling smiles and hopefully even more. Elizabeth would not be *Miss-ish*, certainly. It was not in her character. Yes, he had every reason to assume she would allow him to taste those seductive lips that had been tempting him almost past the point of sanity. His body filled with fire at the mere thought. He would finally feel her warmth in his arms and hold that shapely form against him, her shining energy at last his, only his.

He could not afford these thoughts, not now, or he would be in no condition to be in Elizabeth's presence. He disciplined himself to think of something else, anything else – the weather, his aunt's latest rant, his horse. He swung himself into the saddle, ignoring the groom's proffered assistance.

The groom had been correct about the condition of the road. The horse's hooves squelched and spewed out droplets of mud. Darcy kept to a slow walk, since he did not want to be covered with mud when he paid his addresses to Elizabeth. The pace seemed interminable, leaving far too much time for thought and memories.

Memories of his father, telling him he must marry an heiress because Georgiana's dowry would cut into the Pemberley coffers. His mother, taking him aside so that his father would not hear, reminding him that he was an earl's grandson. She had married beneath her because it was the only way she could escape from the fate her brother had planned for her, but once she had hoped to catch a viscount at the very least. Her voice still echoed in his ears. "Pemberley does not want for money or land. You must find yourself a titled lady to bring honor to the family name."

Then there was his aunt, Lady Catherine, who was determined that he marry her daughter. Darcy snorted at the thought of Lady Catherine's insistence that it had been his mother's wish for him to marry Anne de Bourgh. His mother would not have thought her own niece good enough for her son and heir.

For all these years Darcy had been determined to choose a bride who would have pleased both his mother and his father, but he had yet to meet an aristocratic heiress he could tolerate for an evening, much less a lifetime, and here he was, about to completely defy his parents' wishes by proposing to a lady whose breeding was questionable and whose fortune was non-existent. The scandal of it might even hurt Georgiana's chances at a brilliant match. How could he do this, knowing he was failing in his duty to his entire family?

His decision to follow his heart and marry Elizabeth had been the hardest of his life, and even now he had his doubts. He was being a fool and he knew it, but for once in his life he was in the grip of a passion beyond his control. He could not help himself. At least that was his excuse, though he could just imagine his father's scorn and the curl of his mother's lip if he had ever dared to say such a thing to them.

For a moment he considered reining in his horse and returning to Rosings free of the encumbrance of a distasteful alliance, but the memory of Elizabeth's sparkling eyes and the way the corner of her lips twitched when she was amused spurred him on. He had to have her. There was nothing else to be done, at least not without dishonoring himself more than he already was by making this proposal. The wild young men at

White's would have some very different ideas about how he should slake his lust, caring nothing for who might pay the price as long as their own desires were fulfilled, but that was not for him. It was such things that made Darcy prefer Bingley's company over that of his peers. Bingley had been foolish to fall in love with Jane Bennet, but at least he had never considered dishonoring her. It had been marriage or nothing for Bingley, and it was the same for Darcy. But how would Bingley feel when he discovered that Darcy was marrying the sister of that same woman he had insisted was not good enough for his friend? He was a hypocrite as well as failing his parents' wishes, but Elizabeth would be his.

The sucking sound of the hooves in deep mud gave way to the thud of horseshoes striking wooden planks as he crossed the bridge. The flood waters rushed loudly beneath him, the usually peaceful, meandering river now a raging torrent after the last month of pounding rain. Even in the darkness he was certain that the water must be over the banks by now. The wind was picking up again, starting to lash against his coat.

A flash of lightning split the night sky, causing his horse to shy. Darcy automatically quieted him as the rolling rumble of thunder seemed to make the very air tremble. His skin was tingling, a certain sign that another storm was in the offing. Yes, it was far better to think about floods and rain than to hear voices from the past railing at him.

By good fortune he reached the parsonage at the top of the hill just as the skies opened. Dismounting hurriedly, Darcy led his horse into the slight shelter of the eaves and tied his reins to the waiting ring. Silently he made his apologies to the horse who deserved better than the drenching he was about to receive. Under normal circumstances he would never treat one of his mounts in such a shabby manner, but tonight was not normal, and the shelter of a stable was a quarter mile further along.

He thanked his lucky stars that the front entryway was covered. Already a cold trickle had found its way down the back of his neck, sending a shiver down his spine. He rang the bell loudly, hoping someone would come quickly. No one would be expecting callers, and it would be hard to hear anything over the drumming of the rain and the rolling thunder.

The door was opened, not soon enough for Darcy's taste, by a timid, half-kempt maidservant holding a single candle. Clearly she had not expected her services to be needed tonight. He set his hat and gloves on a small table and brushed the remaining drops of rain from his coat. His valet would have fits were he to see his normally immaculate master in such disarray, but there was nothing to be done for it. He had a mission, and he meant to accomplish it. "I wish to see Miss Bennet," he told the girl in a clipped voice.

He did not notice her reply, his entire being concentrated on the knowledge that in just a few minutes, Elizabeth would be officially his, putting an end to his months of torment imagining a lifetime in which he would only see her in his night-time fantasies. Half in a daze, he strode past the girl into the sitting room where Elizabeth stood, a pile of letters on the small painted table beside her. She was noticeably pale and did not smile at the sight of him. Perhaps she was in truth unwell?

Suddenly nervous, although he did not know why, he made a correct bow. "Miss Bennet, your cousin informed me that you were too ill to join us at Rosings. May I hope that you are feeling better?"

"It was nothing but a slight headache." Her tone was decidedly cool.

He took his usual seat, trying to make sense of her serious demeanor. Surely she must know why he was there? She should be delighted at his presence! Then it hit him. She must have been expecting his addresses these last several weeks, and his reticence had injured her sensibilities. It was only natural. What lady would not feel wounded when an eligible suitor seemed unable to make up his mind about her? In sudden generosity of spirit, he decided he must be completely open with her. He would tell her his dilemma and why he had delayed so long, and how his love for her had overcome all barriers. He would help her see that it was not a reflection on her charms or the depth of his feeling for her. On the contrary, the extent of his struggle showed the strength of his devotion. But how to begin? She seemed reluctant even to look at him.

303

His agitation of spirit could not be contained, so he left the chair to pace around the small room, searching for the words to express himself. He wanted nothing more than to pour his heart out at her feet, but first he must tend to the injury he had unwittingly inflicted upon her. What a fool he had been to wait so long to claim her as his intended!

He could not wait another minute. He approached her, coming as near as propriety would allow, and the words began tumbling forth. "In vain have I struggled. It will not do. My feelings will not be repressed. You must allow me to tell you how ardently I admire and love you."

What a relief it was to finally say the words! He had Elizabeth's complete attention now; she was almost staring at him, her cheeks becomingly flushed, apparently at a loss for words. Telling her was the right thing to do. With greater certainty, he continued, "I have admired you from almost the first moment we met, and it has been many months since I have known that my life would be incomplete without you in it. You may wonder why I have been silent until now, and question the strength of my devotion, but I can assure you it had nothing to do with the depth of my love. I had not known myself capable of a passion such as this. For the first time in my life, I have understood what it was that inspired the greatest poets to produce their masterpieces. Until I met you, I thought their words of love were but a form of artistic hyperbole, and I could not believe that any man would actually find himself so overcome with violent love. But in you I have discovered what it is to need another as I need the air to breathe."

He paused to collect his thoughts as thunder briefly drowned out his ability to speak. "Indeed, I should have made this offer to you long ago, had it not been for the disparity in our stations in life. My family has a long and distinguished history, with the expectation that I would marry a lady of rank and fortune, and you do not fall into either category. Your lack of dowry could perhaps be overlooked, but my parents would have been horrified at your low connections. Your father is a gentleman, although of a rank inferior to mine, but your mother's family must be seen as a degradation. I had no choice but to fight against my attraction to you with all the strength I could muster, my judgment warring with my inclination. I do not have the words to describe the battles I have fought with myself, but in the end, in spite of all my endeavors, I found it impossible to conquer my attachment to you. My sentiments have proved powerful enough to overcome all the expectations of family and friends. My devotion and ardent love have been fiercely tested and emerged triumphant. May I dare hope that my violent love for you will be rewarded by your acceptance of my hand in marriage?" He gazed into her bright eyes, awaiting her affirmative response.

Elizabeth, seeming at a loss for words, unfolded her hands, but at his eager look, she hastily refolded them. She inhaled deeply and said, "In such cases as this, it is, I believe, the established mode to express a sense of obligation for the sentiments avowed, however unequally they may be returned. It is natural that obligation should be felt, and if I could *feel* gratitude, I would..."

Loud pounding from the front of the house interrupted her words. Elizabeth's brows gathered as she looked over her shoulder towards the door of the parsonage.

A deep shout from without all but rattled the windows. "What ho, the house! For the love of God, let us in!"

Darcy frowned furiously in the direction of the racket. How dare anyone interrupt him at this tender moment and in such a manner? The voice betrayed low origins. Could there be footpads abroad on such a night as this? He could make out the sound of crying children now. Where was that maid? Just then a brilliant flash of lightning flooded the room with light, accompanied by an ear-splitting crack of thunder and a resounding crash. A child's scream pierced the night, and the pounding began anew.

Darcy strode to the window. Through the rain streaming down the window he could make out the shape of a fallen tree limb. The giant chestnut tree had been split down the middle, smoke rising from the ragged stump. A cluster of shapes huddled nearby.

Light footsteps behind him alerted him to Elizabeth's presence.

She stood just behind him, her hands covering her mouth. The whiteness of her face stirred him into action. He gripped her arm lightly, even in the crisis marveling at his right to do so, "There is nothing to fear. Lightning struck the tree outside, but we are perfectly safe. I will deal with this."

He walked purposely toward the front door, discovering the maid cowering in the entryway. Frowning at her, he threw open the door to reveal a roughly dressed old man, soaked to the skin, with perhaps two dozen others, mostly women, behind him.

The man said, "Please, sir, the water's rising somethin' fierce! It carried off Smither's cottage and his wife and children with it, and half the village is knee deep in water. We never seen the like of it, never! You have to help us, sir!"

For a moment Darcy wondered irritably if they thought he had the power to stop the river, then he realized the parsonage and church occupied the highest ground on this bank. They had fled to the safest spot they knew.

A high keening reached his ear as a woman appeared, tugging at the man's arm. "It's Miller's Jenny. She's trapped under the tree, and we can't lift it!"

Darcy swore under his breath, then turned to the maid. "Take the women and children to the kitchen and build up the fire." He frowned at the pouring rain. There was no help for it; he would have to go out.

The fallen chestnut was no more than a score of steps away, but cold rain was already trickling down Darcy's neck when he reached it, following the sound of a child's wails. He could barely make out shapes pulling at the fallen tree trunk. It was large enough that he would not have been able to wrap his arms around it. One of the figures slipped on the wet grass and fell hard, swearing in the shifting tones of a boy whose voice was starting to turn. Darcy's vision was beginning to adjust. It was nothing more than the old man and two lads trying to shift a limb far beyond their weight. Darcy crouched down by the small child whose legs were trapped, examining the position of the fallen limb.

"We'll need a lever," he said decisively. "You, boy – run to the house and tell them we need a crowbar or something like it, whatever they have." He pointed to the other boy. "You must find some other branches, big ones. Where are the other men?"

"In t' village still, tryin' to save what they can," the old man said. "Sent me with t' women, they did."

Darcy nodded, then turned to the little girl. "You must be very brave and listen carefully to what I say. We are going to find a way to move this, and when I give the word, you must pull yourself out from under it as quickly as may be. Do you understand?"

"Ye...Yes, sir," she whimpered. "Please, it hurts so much!"

"We'll have you out of there as soon as we can." And Elizabeth would be waiting for him, like the treasure at the end of a knight's quest. With a warm feeling inside despite the cold rain, Darcy pushed a lock of sodden hair out of his eyes, then broke a branch from the trunk and began wedging it under the fallen wood.

Elizabeth hurried upstairs to the closets so carefully arranged according to the direction of Lady Catherine de Bourgh. It was simple to find the blankets she was seeking, but there were not as many as she had hoped. She added the blanket from her own bed for good measure, then returned to the kitchen and began distributing them, encouraging the women with young children to wrap the blankets around them for warmth. The fire was as high as the maid had dared make it, but the soaked refugees still shivered.

An older women was standing alone, her chapped hands outstretched to the fire. Elizabeth approached her and said, "Can you tell me of the situation in the village?"

The woman shook her head. "You can't believe how high that water is, and the current strong enough to pull a man off his feet. There won't be much left by the time it goes down." Her voice trembled a little.

Elizabeth bit her lip. While Mr. Collins and his wife Charlotte were at Rosings Park, it was up to her to make arrangements for all these people. She had no idea what food stores were available or where they would sleep, but she could hardly send Mr. Collins's newly-homeless parishioners out into the storm with nowhere to go.

The kitchen door swung open to reveal Mr. Darcy, his dark curls sodden and dripping into his face, carrying a young girl in his arms. He called across the kitchen, "Miss Bennet, a word, if you please?"

She drew in a sharp breath. What was he still doing there? She had expected him to be long gone after she refused his startling offer of marriage. After that insulting proposal, she despised him more than ever, and as her rejected suitor, he must be furious with her. He had clearly expected her to accept him. What unlucky fate had forced them to be together, especially under these circumstances?

Still, she had no choice but to follow him into the hallway. The last thing she wanted to do was to meet his eyes, so instead she turned her gaze to the limp form in his arms. "Is she injured?" she asked.

"I believe her leg is broken. It is fortunate for her that she fainted when we tried to move her. What is the best place for her?" Mr. Darcy sounded remarkably calm under the circumstances. His tone carried none of the anger she had expected.

If he could be civil, she would as well. "Could you bring her upstairs? I will show you the way." The simplest thing would be to put the child in the room she shared with Maria, since the bed in the spare room was not made up.

He inclined his head. The gesture lost a great deal of its aristocratic air owing to the water dripping from his hair. Elizabeth barely controlled a smile as she fetched a candle from the sitting room and led him up the dark staircase to her room. She set the candle on the vanity and found a towel to spread across the bed.

The little girl moaned as Mr. Darcy set her on the bed, taking great care to move her as gently as possible. One of her legs was bent at an unnatural angle. Elizabeth tried to remove her shoe, but stopped as her action provoked another moan from the child. She only hoped the girl would remain unconscious long enough for her wet clothes to be removed.

Elizabeth dried her hands on a corner of the towel, then looked up to find Mr. Darcy's dark eyes fixed on her. She realized with a shock that, apart from the unconscious girl, she was alone in a dark bedroom with a man who claimed to be violently in love with her. To her utter astonishment, he smiled slightly.

"But you are quite wet, sir! Mr. Collins's rooms are just down the passage. I am sure he would not object to the use of some of his clothing. After all, he would be mortified if you were to take a chill while in his house," Elizabeth said, aware that she was babbling.

"An excellent idea," he said, but made no move to go.

"And I must find this child's mother. She will need comfort when she awakens." Elizabeth began backing out of the room, anxious to depart from his unnerving presence.

He picked up the candle and held it out to her. "Do not forget this. I would not want you to trip on the stairs."

His courtesy was unnerving, but she would not allow it to intimidate her. "I thank you, but I have been down the stairs many times, and you will need the light in Mr. Collins's room."

"I could not possibly..." Darcy paused, then his face lit up with a smile. "Perhaps a compromise is in order. I will see you downstairs with the candle; then, when you are safely ensconced there, I will return with it to Mr. Collins's room, if you will be so kind as to indicate where I might find it."

Was this a battle of wills to see who could show the most courtesy? "Very well, sir. An excellent idea."

He bowed and swept his free hand out, indicating the door. "Also, there would be no point to dry clothes before I find shelter for my horse. The shed in the garden – would it be large enough to accommodate him?"

Elizabeth nodded numbly. "Perhaps there will be a break in the rain soon and you will be able to return to Rosings." It could not happen soon enough for her.

He shook his head. "I cannot possibly leave you here alone under these circumstances. Besides, there will be no need for a break in the rain. No doubt Lady Catherine will order her carriage for Mr. and Mrs. Collins, and I will return in that conveyance."

"As you wish. Now, if you will excuse me, I must find out how many guests we must provide shelter for." Anything to give her an excuse to leave his company. She started down the stairs.

His voice continued from behind her. "However many there are here now, the number is likely to increase. Apparently some of them are still attempting to rescue their possessions, and they will most likely arrive later. I have already instructed the men outside to settle themselves in the church. Fortunately, it is not a cold night, so blankets and hot bricks should be enough to keep them warm until morning."

Trust Mr. Darcy to assume command of any situation, regardless of whether he had any rights in the matter! Elizabeth fumed, not least because she had not thought of that solution herself. She did not trust herself to answer him in a temperate manner, so she said nothing. She would not waste her energy on Mr. Darcy when there were so many others who needed her assistance.

Mr. Darcy's Refuge is now available
in paperback, e-book, and audiobook format
at all online bookstores

Acknowledgements

Many people assisted in the creation of this book. I'd like to thank Susan Mason-Milks, Rena Margulis, Colette Saucier, Pamala Knight, Elaine Sieff, Jennifer Redlarczyk and Maartje Verhoeckx for their feedback on the manuscript. It is a better book for their efforts. My fellow Austen Authors (www.austenauthors.net) provided support, knowledge, and general encouragement. As always, conversation with my readers helped shape the work in progress. I'm grateful to live in an age where I can connect so easily to readers and other writers.

A special shout-out goes to Angie Kroll, the developer of the free Austen Admirers smartphone app designed to bring together authors, bloggers and fans of Austen in one easy-to-use app. I'd like to thank the following readers and authors who contributed financially so that the app could be free for everyone to download: Melanie Schertz, Kara Louise (author of *Pirates and Prejudice*), Christina Boyd, Gayle Mills, Nancy Kelley (author of *Loving Miss Darcy*), Brenda Webb (author of *Mr. Darcy's Forbidden Love*), Ashley Renee Maxson, M. Yeager, Mary Lydon Simonsen (author of *The Perfect Bride for Mr. Darcy*), Erika Hoemke, Kari Holmes-Singh, Janet Taylor, Tobin Freid, Jeanna Ellsworth (author of *Mr. Darcy's Promise*) and Mary Linda Huggins.

About the Author

Abigail Reynolds is a great believer in taking detours. Originally from upstate New York, she studied Russian and theater at Bryn Mawr College and marine biology at the Marine Biological Laboratory in Woods Hole. After a stint in performing arts administration, she decided to attend medical school, and took up writing as a hobby during her years as a physician in private practice.

A life-long lover of Jane Austen's novels, Abigail began writing variations on PRIDE & PREJUDICE in 2001, then expanded her repertoire to include a series of novels set on her beloved Cape Cod. Her most recent releases are MR. DARCY'S REFUGE, MR. DARCY'S LETTER, A PEMBERLEY MEDLEY, and MORNING LIGHT, and she is currently working on a new Pemberley Variation and the next novel in her Cape Cod series. A lifetime member of JASNA and a founder of the popular Austen Authors group blog, she lives on Cape Cod with her husband, two children, and a menagerie of animals. Her hobbies do not include sleeping or cleaning her house.

www.pemberleyvariations.com
www.austenauthors.net

Join Abigail on
Facebook at www.facebook.com/abigail.reynolds1
Twitter @abigailreynolds

THE PEMBERLEY VARIATIONS
by Abigail Reynolds

WHAT WOULD MR. DARCY DO?

TO CONQUER MR. DARCY

BY FORCE OF INSTINCT

MR. DARCY'S UNDOING

MR. FITZWILLIAM DARCY: THE LAST MAN IN THE WORLD

MR. DARCY'S OBSESSION

A PEMBERLEY MEDLEY

MR. DARCY'S LETTER

MR. DARCY'S REFUGE

MR. DARCY'S NOBLE CONNECTIONS

Also by Abigail Reynolds:

THE MAN WHO LOVED PRIDE & PREJUDICE

MORNING LIGHT

Printed in Great Britain
by Amazon.co.uk, Ltd.,
Marston Gate.